MW00562185

Traces

TRACES

A Novel

PATRICIA L. HUDSON

FIRESIDE
INDUSTRIES

Published by Fireside Industries
An imprint of the University Press of Kentucky

Editorial and Sales Offices: The University Press of Kentucky
663 South Limestone Street, Lexington, Kentucky 40508-4008
www.kentuckypress.com

Library of Congress Cataloging-in-Publication Data

Names: Hudson, Patricia L., author.
Title: Traces : a novel / Patricia L. Hudson.
Description: Lexington, Kentucky : Fireside Industries, [2022]
Identifiers: LCCN 2022029669 | ISBN 9781950564286 (hardcover) | ISBN
    9781950564309 (pdf) | ISBN 9781950564293 (epub)
Subjects: LCSH: Boone, Daniel, 1734-1820—Family—Fiction. | Boone family—
    Fiction. | LCGFT: Western fiction. | Biographical fiction. | Novels.
Classification: LCC PS3608.U347 T73 2022 | DDC 813/.6—dc23/eng/20220628
LC record available at https://lccn.loc.gov/2022029669

To Sam, Elizabeth, and Erin—
for walking this long road with me.

And to my mother, Marjory, my father, Ed D.,
and my brother, Ed R.

I wish you were here to hold this book in your hands.

Women have constituted the most spectacular casualty of traditional history. . . . The forgotten man is nothing to the forgotten woman.

—Arthur M. Schlesinger Jr.

If our voices are essential aspects of our humanity, to be rendered voiceless is to be dehumanized. . . . The history of silence is central to women's history.

—Rebecca Solnit

Author's Note

When I open a history book, I hear whispers. Women call to me from between the lines; they perch among the footnotes and cling grimly to the margins. Their hold is tenuous—a careless shake of the book and I fear they'll tumble into the void, their stories forgotten entirely.

Rebecca, Susannah, and Jemima Boone are among those women whose words have been lost. There's only a trace of them in the tales told about the celebrated explorer Daniel Boone. Daniel became famous during his lifetime when a man named John Filson journeyed to Kentucky, collected the frontiersman's stories, and printed them in a book called *The Adventures of Colonel Daniel Boone*. Filson didn't bother to record any of the women's names.

The stories about the Boone women that have come down to us are largely rumors interwoven with a handful of glimpses from those who actually knew them. The most commonly repeated tale is that Daniel's younger brother fathered one of Rebecca's children, a story that impacted all three of the women's lives. Passed down through the years, the story often ends with this observation: "It might be true, or it might be a lie, but that baby's a Boone either way."

Other forgotten women appear in these pages as well, including an enslaved woman named Dolly, and Nonhelema, a Shawnee woman who was her tribe's peace chief. They are seen through the eyes of the Boone women, whose attitudes reflect the eighteenth-century mores of white culture, as well as the brutality of life on the frontier. On a few occasions, I've quoted historical documents that include language now considered insensitive. I've chosen to reproduce the language accurately rather than alter the historical record.

Despite being caught between warring cultures, when these women were given a chance to know each other, the record suggests some of them were able to see beyond the clash of cultures and recognize their shared humanity. For nearly three hundred years, all of these women have been little more than historical footnotes, defined by the words of others.

But once, they had words of their own.

PART ONE

1

A heavy pounding woke Rebecca from a deep sleep. She sat up among the blankets in the corner bedstead, still only half awake, and for a few seconds thought she'd dreamed the sound. But when she saw the shadow of her eleven-year-old nephew, Jesse, scrambling down the ladder from the loft, she realized it was not yet dawn and someone was on the porch, hammering their fists on the cabin door.

She reached for Daniel, then came fully awake as she remembered he'd been gone these past two weeks, serving as a scout for the Carolina militia, patrolling the mountains to the west amid rumors of Indian trouble. *Gone. Always gone.* Their closest neighbor lived more than a mile away; she and the children were alone.

She swung her feet over the edge of the bed, untangling the folds of her shift from around her legs. The winter air was icy. She pulled a blanket off the bed and tugged it around her shoulders as Jesse reached the bottom of the ladder, his linen nightshirt ghostly in the half-light. Nine-year-old Jonathan peered blearily down from the loft, but the two younger boys, James and Israel, remained asleep in the trundle bed pushed close to the fireplace; those two could have slept through the Second Coming.

By the time Rebecca stood up, Jesse had already slipped across the cold floor and pulled the rifle off the wall pegs. The gun was taller than he was, but Daniel had taught him how to use it.

"You'll need to be the man of the family while I'm away," Daniel had said.

Those words had made Rebecca's jaw clench. *That's your job,* she'd thought, *not his. He's just a boy.*

A metallic click echoed through the cabin as Jesse pulled the hammer back on the rifle and shook powder into the pan. Each night since Daniel's departure, he'd made sure the gun was loaded and ready. Rebecca gestured for him to follow her as she stepped toward the door.

A man's voice, muffled at first through the heavy oak door, grew louder, his tone desperate.

"Rebecca, open up!" She couldn't be sure the voice was Daniel's; it sounded too frantic, too full of fear, to be her husband. She hesitated a moment, then nodded at Jesse, and he steadied the rifle, leveling it at the door as she slid the crossbar away from the frame and stepped to the side of the casement. Clutching the bar like a club, she eased the door open a crack.

For a heartbeat she didn't recognize Daniel's face, shadowy in the moonlight. His eyes were wide, and he was breathing in great, shuddering gasps. She dropped the bar and flung the door open. Daniel took two steps into the cabin, then bent double, leaning on his rifle, sides heaving. She felt heat rising from him amid the bitter air that followed him inside.

"Jesse," she said, "close the door." She heard the scrape of wood as the boy obeyed, but her eyes remained on Daniel. She wanted him to speak, wanted him to look up so she could read his face. She was afraid to touch him. It seemed to her that even the weight of her hand might bring him to his knees.

Jesse lit a candle, and as the flame sputtered to life, Daniel straightened and the circle of light fell across his face, revealing a look of such love and relief that Rebecca gathered him in her arms.

"We've got to pack," he said. "We don't have much time." His eyes searched the room, seeking out first Jesse, who stood behind them with the rifle at his side, then Jonathan, coming down the ladder in bare feet, and finally the two tiny figures snuggled together in the trundle bed. "I've been running since nightfall. I was so afraid I'd find . . ." His voice broke, and he stopped to gather himself. "Get the children dressed, Becca. Indians, headed toward the Forks. We have to get out."

Part One

It was as if she were suddenly outside her body, watching everything from above. She heard herself ordering Jesse into the loft to pack whatever belongings he and Jonathan could carry and saw her hands wrapping last night's cornpone in linen cloth, but her hearing felt muted, and the scene faded and unreal. Her mind darted from one thought to another. Her grandmother's prized pewter platter—too heavy. The polished maple rocking chair her father had crafted as a wedding present—impossible to save. The rag rug beneath the rocker was her sister Martha's handiwork but hardly a necessity, no matter how much her heart ached to leave it behind. She focused on packing foodstuffs—bags of dried beans, a slab of salt-cured fatback, her best iron stewpot—even as her eyes continued to circle the room, saying a silent goodbye to possessions she'd thought would be lifelong companions.

The older boys scrambled around the loft gathering clothes and blankets, and she knew she needed to rouse the little ones and dress them warmly. She was stuffing jerky into a basket when Daniel returned from the barnyard, having tied the horse and cow to the porch and loosed the pigs and chickens to fend for themselves. He stopped alongside her for a quick, whispered account of what had led to his desperate run through the darkness. Her hands kept working as she listened.

"Not a soul left alive at a cabin twelve miles west of us," he said, glancing behind him to be sure the children weren't in earshot. "Must be several hundred warriors headed this way. The whole backcountry's on fire. Our only chance is to head north to the Virginia settlements."

He paused as Jesse leaned over the edge of the loft to toss down several bedrolls, hastily tied with leather thongs. When the boy withdrew into the shadows, Daniel added: "I pounded on every cabin door in my path and told them to meet up at your parents' place since it's on the north edge of the settlements, but I doubt most families west of us can move fast enough to get away."

Can we? Rebecca thought.

Gray light was just beginning to filter into the clearing when Rebecca pulled the cabin door closed. Just beyond the porch, the two older boys held the lead ropes of the horse and milk cow, both loaded with bedding, cook pots, and heavy bags of meal. Rebecca settled Israel onto her hip, then slid the handle of the basket of foodstuffs into the crook of her other arm.

"Where are we going?" two-year-old James whimpered, raising his arms to be picked up.

"To your grandma's house," she said. "And you need to talk quietly."

James's face reddened and he tugged hard on her gown, making the heavy basket sway and the handle bite into her arm.

"Stop it, honey. You'll spill the food." She forced herself to speak gently because James had a tender heart, and a harsh tone might result in sobs that could endanger them all.

Daniel had been circling the animals, checking the tie-downs on the pack frames, but when James began to fuss, he cinched the last line tight and hurried to the edge of the porch. He scooped the boy up and swung him across his broad back.

James erupted in giggles.

"Shush," Daniel said. "You get to ride as long as you're quiet."

James pressed his cheek against his father's heavy woolen hunting shirt and clung like a squirrel as Daniel hefted his rifle and headed toward the woods.

She looked up and saw that the cow had dragged Jonathan to the edge of the clearing and dropped her head to graze, ignoring the boy's insistent tugs. Jesse led the horse up from behind and smacked the cow's rump to get her moving. The boys fell in behind Daniel, who walked with his rifle poised and ready, his eyes scanning the underbrush. Rebecca brought up the rear, the basket bumping against her leg with every step. Baby Israel had never fully woken, even as she'd dressed him in several layers of clothing and swaddled him in a blanket. She'd tied the blanket over her shoulder so that it supported part of the baby's weight. She prayed he'd continue to sleep; if he woke she knew he'd cry to be nursed.

The woods loomed all around the clearing, and Rebecca felt as small and vulnerable as if she were a child herself, not at all like a twenty-one-year-old wife who'd believed all was right with the world when she'd tucked the children into bed just hours ago. She'd intended to grow old in this place.

When she and Daniel had moved to Sugartree Creek shortly after their wedding, she'd vowed she'd never move again, having lost, at thirteen, her first beloved home—the two-story farmhouse in the Shenandoah Valley that had belonged to her grandparents. That homestead, with its sturdy stone house and tidy green fields, was the last place she could recall feeling truly safe.

Most of her childhood memories centered around her Grandmother Bryan. Rebecca had learned at a young age that questions addressed to her mother, Aylee, would be answered curtly, or not at all, preoccupied as she was with the needs of an ever-growing brood. But Grandmother Bryan seemed to delight in providing answers. When her grandmother was thinking deeply about something, she would absently tap her finger against her lips, a sign that told Rebecca to wait—an answer was coming.

Her grandmother's kitchen garden had become a refuge of sorts. It was there that Rebecca had learned the names of green and growing things, and the thrill of sinking a spade into the dirt and turning up treasure—bright orange carrots in one row, lumpy brown potatoes in the next.

When Rebecca was five, her grandmother had caught her standing outside the barn on butchering day, her small hands covering her ears, horrified at the frantic squeals of the hogs as they were dragged from their pens. Rebecca felt the old woman's arms enfold her, and when she buried her face in her grandmother's apron, it smelled of apples and masked the smell of blood that hung over the barnyard. Rebecca never forgot the comfort of those arms, or her grandmother's words, said above her head that day like a prayer:

"You'd best learn early to toughen that heart of yours, child, for there's plenty of suffering in this world for both man and beast."

From that day forward Rebecca had done her best to wall off the tenderness she felt for the creatures of field and farmyard, knowing the men of her family would eventually harvest them for both food and profit. She'd learned that the long-legged fawn, whose gamboling delighted her in the spring, would one day be a pelt, stripped and stretched and hauled away to market.

She'd turned her attention instead to the songbirds who belonged to no one and the wildflowers that bloomed along the roadsides. She loved helping her grandmother gather flower seeds to plant outside the kitchen door of the stone house. At a young age, Rebecca had claimed these two things—birds and flowers—as her own, having discerned they weren't worth a man's time to shoot down or dig up.

Now, as they crossed the frost-covered pasture and entered the forest, Rebecca cast a hurried glance back at the cabin, sitting on its slope above the creek. It already looked lonely—its shutters clamped tight, all the life drained out of it. The seeds her grandmother had packed as a parting gift years before slumbered in the garden under a thick layer of frost, but the trout lily and fire pink would push through the dried leaves in the early days of spring, and the columbine planted along the fencerow would bob in the wind in early summer. Rebecca ached at the thought of not being here to see it.

She turned away from the clearing to follow her family into the woods. Daniel and the older boys were strung along the muddy trail with the dark woods all around. Jesse and Jonathan yanked on the lead ropes to force the animals into a shambling trot, trying to keep up with Daniel's long strides. Daniel's head turned continually from side to side, scanning the underbrush, his rifle ready. As Rebecca hurried to catch up, she shifted Israel just enough to ease the pressure off her shoulder, and his head bobbed against her breast. It made her breath catch in her throat to look down at his sleeping face, topped by a mop of thick blonde curls. It was up to her to be the rear guard, to spot any sign of pursuit early enough to sound the alarm. But would she even hear the whirr of an arrow if it flashed out of the darkness, destined for one of the children?

As the sky lightened from gray to pink, she searched the surrounding woods for movement in the shadows. Her arms ached with the effort of cradling Israel, and her feet felt weighted. She strained to detect any sound of pursuit behind them, but all she could hear was the scuffle of their own moccasins in the dried leaves that littered the trail. All around her, a heavy silence hung over the winter woods, as if even the birds had fled.

The cow's flanks were skimmed with sweat, and Rebecca's lungs were burning by the time she saw the large gray boulder alongside the trail that marked the turnoff to the Bryan homestead. Daniel motioned for them to wait while he slipped through the underbrush to the edge of the clearing where he called cautiously: "Halloo, the house."

When Rebecca heard her father's deep voice answer back, the tightness in her shoulders relaxed the tiniest bit.

The scene that greeted them as they stepped out of the woods was quiet chaos. The clearing around her parents' cabin swirled with Bryans, Boones, and neighboring families who'd hurried in from scattered homesteads. All of them were burdened with bundles filled with hastily gathered supplies. It was eerily quiet for so large a gathering; if a child cried or a dog barked, they were instantly hushed.

As Rebecca wove her way through the crowd, Israel woke and began to fuss. When she reached the cabin, she sat down on the edge of the porch, unpinned the front of her short gown, and loosened the drawstring on her shift so the baby could nurse. James, his blonde hair mussed, leaned heavily against her, snuggling close and looking out at the milling crowd with wide eyes. Rebecca's mother, small and dark haired, bustled in and out of the cabin, piling bundles on the porch. When she spotted Rebecca, Aylee paused just long enough to rest a hand on her daughter's shoulder and plant a kiss on James's head before hurrying off.

Across the barnyard, Rebecca caught a glimpse of Daniel's parents, Squire and Sarah. Her eyes searched the crowd for her sister, Martha, but saw no sign of her and felt a flicker of fear. *She'll be here,* she told herself, and turned her attention to Daniel and her father, who stood alongside the porch, conversing in low tones.

"Do you know what stirred them up?" her father asked.

"Word is some hot-headed settlers butchered a band of friendly Cherokee," Daniel said. "Thanks to those fools, every damn warrior on this side of the mountains is headed our way."

Her father nodded grimly, then stepped onto the porch and scanned the crowd. All eyes turned his direction as his deep voice carried across the barnyard. "We've waited as long as we can. Time to head out. Stay close together and move as fast as you can."

He motioned to Daniel, who hoisted his rifle and led the way down the path that would take them northward, out of the Carolina settlements and into long empty miles of wilderness. If they were lucky, they'd eventually find safety in the more settled colony of Virginia.

Israel had finished nursing and lay drowsily in Rebecca's arms. She straightened her clothes and hurried to stand. James clutched her skirts as she stood on tiptoe to scan the barnyard. Her mother and father had disappeared into the crush of bodies. *Surely they wouldn't leave without Martha.*

Rebecca picked up her basket, the boys clinging like burrs, and pushed her way into the crowd. She'd elbowed her way only a few yards when she felt a strong hand on her shoulder and turned to see her husband's blue-gray eyes just inches from her face. It took a moment for her to realize it wasn't Daniel but his younger brother, Ned.

"Thank God, Neddy," Rebecca said, spotting Martha right behind him. "I was afraid you two hadn't gotten word."

Rebecca handed Israel to Ned and gathered Martha in a hug. It was the first time she'd seen her sister since the day, just weeks before, when Martha and Ned had wed. The joy of that day now felt like a distant dream.

Though they shared the same dark hair and eyes as their mother, folks rarely thought she and Martha were sisters because Rebecca had taken after her father and was unfashionably tall for a woman, while Martha possessed their mother's dainty frame.

"They say there are hundreds of warriors just a dozen miles west," Martha whispered. "Do you think they'll follow us?"

"It's likely, but . . ."

Rebecca's words were cut short as the knot of people surrounding them began to move. Ned handed Israel back to Rebecca, and she nestled him back into his blanket. She was relieved to see Martha had picked James up, and she spotted the two older boys leading the horse and cow out of the barnyard as the crowd shuffled forward, jostling against one another until they reached the edge of the clearing, where they sorted themselves into an untidy line, following the trace into the woods.

As the forest closed around her, Rebecca felt her shoulders tighten again. She knew almost nothing about the vast, shadowy wilderness that stretched northward. Though she'd never stopped missing their Shenandoah homeplace, she'd done her best to make peace with Carolina and had settled into life as a married woman, surrounded by a community of family and friends. She knew she should feel something—deep grief perhaps—but for now, she just felt numb. Last night, she'd made plans to spend today repairing the fence rails around the garden plot where the old sow had knocked them down. Now everything had been left behind—cabin, garden, and sow.

The trace they followed was rugged, nearly impassable with wagons, and difficult even with pack animals. Much of the time they were forced to walk single file. Ned and Martha took turns carrying James, passing him back and forth, occasionally setting him down to walk to help warm him. There was little conversation, only a heavy silence with everyone scanning the woods constantly, those in the rear turning often to survey the forest behind them.

Daniel seemed to be everywhere, striding alongside the column, sometimes at its head, sometimes dropping to the rear, making constant adjustments to ensure the riflemen matched their strides to the slower pace of milk cows and young children. He was so preoccupied that he sometimes walked right past Rebecca without a word. She marveled at the way folks looked to him for guidance. He was only twenty-five, but men twice his age seemed certain he knew the safest path to take and the best way to position the guards around the caravan to protect them. With everything swirling out of control, his calm demeanor seemed to strengthen everyone. Even in the midst of her fear, Rebecca felt a ripple of pride.

Long before their marriage, Rebecca had heard folks talk admiringly about the Boone boy who could hold the heaviest rifle outstretched in one hand and still hit his target. They'd sworn he knew the woods better than anyone, that it wasn't unusual for him to return from a single day's hunt having shot thirty deer or more. Now, all of them were counting on Daniel's woodsmanship, his leadership, to keep them safe.

The February wind was bitter as they moved through the soggy tangle of leafless hardwoods and evergreen thickets. All Rebecca could see was the narrow ribbon of mud in front of her, churned up by hooves, wending its way through the woods. Her stomach growled. There'd been no time to eat, and there was little hope of stopping anytime soon.

"Martha—I don't have a free hand. Could you rummage in my basket for the pemmican? There should be enough for all of us."

Martha pulled a linen bag from the basket and offered a piece of pemmican to Ned, then James, who was riding on Ned's back, before serving herself. She bit off a chunk and popped the remainder into Rebecca's mouth. The greasy mixture of dried venison, chokeberries, and tallow was no substitute for a warm bowl of stew, but it would supply the energy they needed to keep moving.

"Jesse and Jonathan must be starved by now," Rebecca said. "Ned, I'd appreciate it if you and Martha could move up the line and take some to the boys. I bet they could use a hand with the livestock, too. That old cow's a handful for Jonathan."

"What about you?" Ned said.

"We'll be fine. James can walk for a bit."

She watched Ned and Martha pick their way through the crowd until they'd disappeared around a bend in the trail. They'd been out of sight only a few minutes when Israel began to whimper. She shifted him in his nest of blankets and touched his forehead. *Fever.* When she nestled him closer, she heard a faint hitch in his breathing. *Dear God, don't let it be croup.* She longed for the row of crocks that held her healing herbs, all of them lost to her now. With a growing sense of panic, she realized the only medicine she had was a small supply of willow bark tucked into the cloth bag that also held her sewing kit. Even that was useless until she could steep it into a tea.

She felt a nudge from behind, and turned to see an old man leaning on a walking stick. He pointed up the trail. "Move along, mistress."

Only then did she realize she'd stopped in the middle of the trace and was holding up the line. She settled Israel back on her hip, wrapped her woolen cloak more tightly around them both, and resumed picking her way along the rocky trail, keeping James in front of her to make sure he didn't wander off.

"My feet are cold," James said after he'd walked for a while.

She'd stuffed the family's moccasins with handfuls of deer hair at the first sign of cold weather, but she hadn't counted on them spending hours traversing frozen ground. She picked James up, squeezing him in between the basket on one side and Israel on the other, and carried him until her arms began to cramp. She set him back down and made him walk for a while until her arms had rested, then carried him again. She began to silently count her steps, carrying James for a thousand steps, making him walk for a thousand. Somehow the counting made the time go faster and kept her from dwelling on the possibility of pursuit.

The other women who were shepherding young children with no family to help had fallen to the rear of the column with her. Rebecca watched the woman just ahead of her, a widow with three young children, struggle to balance her youngest on her hip while keeping a hand on the large linen market wallet slung over her other shoulder. The cloth sack bulged—and likely contained everything the woman had left in the world.

Each time Rebecca glanced back, there were fewer people behind her, until only a handful separated her from the riflemen Daniel had assigned as the rear guard. Beyond them, there was nothing but forest.

She hadn't seen Daniel in quite some time, and in the midst of the fear that sat on her chest like a stone, there was a growing irritation that he hadn't bothered to check on her. If only he'd appear and carry James a mile or two, or at least relieve her anxiety by telling her the whereabouts of the older boys. But even as these thoughts filled her mind, she felt guilty, knowing the weight of responsibility he carried.

Time blurred and all she could feel was the weight of Israel on her hip and James like an anchor at the end of her arm. She was nearly sleepwalking when a shout rang out behind her. She froze like a rabbit beneath a hawk's shadow, then looked frantically about. The guards were scrambling off the trail and into the trees as an unearthly howl filled the air, echoing off the ridges around them. Off the trail to her left Rebecca saw movement, and for an instant glimpsed a man running through the brush toward her, tomahawk raised, his angry face painted black and red.

"Run!" one of the guards yelled.

She was swept up in a panicky mass of arms and legs as everyone surged forward. She heard one gunshot, then two. She scooped up James and dropped her basket, its contents spilling across the trail and rolling into the brush. The instant she felt the boy's arms tighten around her neck, she began to run. She glimpsed Daniel sprinting toward them, shouting to the riflemen: "Spread out! Take the high ground!" He veered into the brush before he reached her and disappeared from sight, crashing through the laurel at the side of the trail.

She fought the instinct to swerve into the brush and follow him, knowing that was madness since she and the boys would soon be lost and alone in the woods. Desperation kept her legs churning, even as her senses began to dim from both terror and exertion, turning everything around her gray and blurry, like a charcoal drawing smudged beyond recognition.

2

They ran, the sound of the guns growing fainter, until the forest was once more silent around them. The column slowed to a trot and then finally to a walk. Mud coated Rebecca's moccasins, weighting every step. The air was cold and her shift was clammy against her skin. She was too tired to think straight—all she could do was hold tightly to the boys and stagger along behind the worn, clay-stained shoes of the woman in front of her.

By the time the sun had fallen to the tree line, the column's pace was so slow it was hardly more than a crawl. At last, when Rebecca was sure she couldn't take another step, orders were passed down the straggling line, informing them the clearing ahead was where they'd camp for the night. The rag-tag company entered the clearing and spread out, searching for a likely place to bed down.

Rebecca found a spot under a large hickory and bent to set James down. As she straightened, she saw Daniel emerge from the trees on the far side of the clearing and felt a surge of relief. He waved and started in her direction, but before he'd gone three paces, a man caught his arm, asking for a word, and then another approached, wanting to speak to him as well. Rebecca sighed. She'd have to set up camp alone, when what she wanted to do was sink to the ground, pull off her moccasins, and rub her aching feet.

Jesse and Jonathan appeared amid the crowd, their faces dirt streaked, still leading the livestock. When they spotted her, their faces shone with such relief that she found herself smiling for the first time that day.

Jonathan dropped the cow's lead rope and threw his arms around her waist. She gave him a one-armed hug, still balancing Israel on her hip, while Jesse, ever responsible, collected the dropped rope, taking charge of both animals.

"Holding onto Ivy and the mare couldn't have been easy. I'm proud of you boys." Her praise made them stand a bit taller.

"Uncle Ned and Aunt Martha helped us," Jesse admitted.

Rebecca gave the boys a tired smile. "I need to get a fire going. After we unload the bedding, you'll need to water the animals and tether them for the night."

She bent to put Israel down, but he clung to her, his face flushed with fever. When she pried his fingers off her shoulder and set him on the cold ground he opened his mouth to wail, but all that came out was a feeble, wheezing sound.

Her half-frozen hands shook as she searched her pocket for her flint and steel, anxious to get a fire started to warm the boys. She knelt and made a nest of dried grass and leaves, then struck the flint, watching the sparks leap off the stone. They flickered out, again and again. As she worked, she took deep breaths to calm herself, glancing up every so often, praying she'd see Daniel coming toward them. She needed something—someone—to anchor her, adrift as they were in this ocean of trees.

When the tinder finally caught, James scooted near the flames to warm his hands.

"It's your job to keep the fire going, honey." She laid a tangled pile of hastily gathered twigs and branches alongside him.

He looked up and nodded, his tiny face solemn, no longer the giggly boy he'd been just hours ago. A spark of anger flared in her chest and lodged there. The sights and sounds of the day had stolen her little boy's innocence. Up to that moment she'd never harbored hatred toward the Indians, unlike many of their neighbors around the Forks who were openly hostile. The Indian villages lay much further west, on the slopes of the Blue Ridge, and though occasional tribesmen ventured into the Forks to trade their furs, Rebecca had rarely encountered them.

When there'd been rumors of Indian unrest in the past, she and Daniel had joined other families around the Forks in taking refuge within the sturdy, frontier stockade known as Fort Dobbs. Though she'd been fearful each time, the Indians had remained figures in the shadows of the tree line, glimpsed only at a distance, and she'd felt sure the fort's riflemen and the stockade's tall walls would keep them safe. But now, having seen the warrior's raised tomahawk and fierce face bearing down on her boys, the danger posed by the Indians had become shatteringly real.

She turned from the fire to wrestle their bedding, wrapped in a bearskin, off the packhorse while Jesse held the skittish animal steady. Jonathan helped her untie the leather thongs. The heavy skin plopped onto the frozen ground, and she spread it out to make a sleeping pallet, placing Israel in its furry depths. She covered him with quilts and stood over him, listening to his labored breathing, audible even amid the rustling sound of fallen leaves as the older boys led the livestock to the creek.

She had to force herself to focus on the countless chores that needed doing before nightfall—foremost, brewing some willow bark tea for Israel. Her hands were so swollen and stiff with cold that even the simplest actions took twice as long as usual, whether she was pouring water from their gourd canteen into the small brass cook pot or measuring dried willow bark out of the small linen bag that was stashed in one of the lumpy market wallets tied to the pack frame.

They were surrounded by others setting up camp, yet the woods remained quiet, as if the forest itself was holding its breath. All she could hear was the murmur of nearby voices and the occasional crackle and pop of kindling laid on a fire. As the comforting smell of wood smoke began to fill the clearing, she did her best to convince herself they were safe. She knew the men would take turns standing watch through the night, but despite their vigilance and her own weariness, she knew she wouldn't sleep; she'd be listening for every hitch and rattle in Israel's breathing, as well as every sound of leaf-stir in the gathering darkness.

Jesse and Jonathan had led the horse and cow to the nearby creek, then retraced their steps and tethered the animals a safe distance from the fire. Their chores done, they edged close to the flames. She studied them as they sat, huddled together, hands stretched toward the fire. They shared the same dark hair and stocky build, but Jesse, the elder, was half a head taller and often wore an endearing, lopsided smile. Solemn-faced Jonathan was his older brother's shadow, and it was rare to hear him speak. Rebecca counted it a major accomplishment to even draw a smile from the boy. As the oldest girl in her birth family, she'd tended children as far back as she could remember, but she'd never known a child quite so withdrawn. Though the boys were her nephews by marriage, she'd grown to love them as if she'd borne them herself.

She stooped to rummage among their bags of provisions and pulled out a linen-wrapped cornpone, breaking some off for the boys to share. They took the bread and stuffed it into their mouths, crumbs dribbling down their shirt fronts. They chewed methodically, nearly asleep even before they'd burrowed into the bearskin and snugged in tight beside the two younger boys.

Rebecca took the last bite of pone. It tasted like sand in her mouth. Had it only been yesterday that she'd baked it in the coals on her hearth? They'd fled with few supplies, and though it was nearly winter's end, these were the leanest months of the year even at the best of times. The loss of her market basket meant some of their foodstuffs were gone. She stared down at the children with a growing sense of dread. She had no idea how she'd keep everyone fed.

The last rays of light were fading, and the woods had dimmed to black. She didn't dare leave the boys long enough to search for Martha or her parents among the fires that flickered around her. It was an odd feeling to be alone in the midst of so many others. More than anything, she wanted to look up and see Daniel emerge from the darkness.

A woman at a nearby fire stood, backlit by the flames, then headed toward Rebecca's campfire. As she drew closer, Rebecca realized it was Daniel's mother, Sarah. A thin, dignified Quakeress, Sarah still spoke the old-fashioned plain speech; listening to her always put Rebecca in mind of hearing the Bible read aloud. Even Sarah's mundane remarks took on an air of importance because they were cloaked in the language of the Good Book.

"Rebecca," Sarah said, stepping into the flickering light of the fire, "I came to see if thou canst use this forcemeat." She held out a small clay porringer. "Did I hear one of the boys coughing?"

"Israel," Rebecca said. "He's asleep for the moment. I'm brewing willow bark."

Sarah frowned. "Should I send Hannah to help thee till Daniel returns?"

Hannah, at fourteen, was the youngest of Daniel's siblings; she and Rebecca had forged a special bond, but tonight, Rebecca doubted she had the strength to follow the swoops and swirls of Hannah's thoughts.

As if reading Rebecca's mind, Sarah smiled and said: "If thou's too tired to welcome company, Hannah can happily carry on both sides of the conversation."

The women shared a weary smile that vanished as the crack of a branch breaking underfoot somewhere in the shadows made them jump and swing round.

"It's me," Daniel said, stepping into the firelight.

With a sweet smile and a nod for her son, Sarah retreated to her own campfire while Daniel moved across the clearing and gathered Rebecca in his arms. They remained, unmoving, for a long while, soaking in each other's warmth, content to stand and watch the sleeping boys. Though Rebecca had often wished for her sister's dainty frame, Daniel had never seemed to mind having a wife who was nearly as tall as he was. Whenever he enfolded her in a hug, they stood eye to eye. Rebecca opened her mouth to tell him about Israel's fever, and how she and James had seen the warrior, and how short they were on foodstuffs, but Daniel spoke first.

"I can't stay," he said. "I just wanted to be sure you and the children were settled. I'm taking first watch."

"And second and third."

He nodded. "We haven't suffered a single casualty, and the rear guard tells me most of the warriors have turned back. Only a handful are still on our trail."

A handful is more than enough, Rebecca thought. She shivered, imagining watchful eyes in the darkness. Daniel hugged her tighter. "They could have overrun us, Becca, or picked us off a few at a time; it's pretty clear they just want to keep us moving." He gave her a reassuring squeeze. "I'm scouting back down the trail to be certain."

As he started to step away she tightened her grip, anchoring him beside her.

"I'll be careful. Don't worry."

But of course she'd worry. For her, the wilderness was a fearsome place; for Daniel, it was where he felt most at home. As hard as she tried, that was a part of her husband she couldn't understand.

Daniel studied her face. "You're exhausted. You need to get some rest."

She nodded. Disarmed by the tenderness in his voice, she swallowed the words that had drummed in her mind all afternoon. *The children and I need you. I can't keep the boys safe by myself.*

Daniel took a last lingering look at the boys, tangled together in the nest of blankets, squeezed Rebecca's hand, then picked up his rifle and slipped into the blackness. She watched him go, then sank onto the edge of the pallet and slid her legs beneath the blankets, doing her best not to jostle the boys. Israel's breathing was ragged, and every so often he coughed in his sleep.

She pulled the hood of her cloak up and leaned back against the broad trunk of the hickory tree, resigned to a long, watchful night. The stars flickered coldly through the bare limbs above her, and her thoughts flitted hither and yon, like a flock of birds unable to land. She listened to the rasp and rattle of Israel's breathing and whispered a silent prayer for him, and also for Daniel, out there in the darkness keeping watch over their ragged caravan of souls.

When she felt herself getting drowsy, she pushed her back into the tree's rough bark and willed her mind to focus on something—anything—to keep herself awake and on guard.

She was fifteen, helping her mother and the other women in the kitchen, filling trenchers with slabs of ham and piles of corn dodgers, as everyone from around the Forks had gathered at Squire Boone's tavern to celebrate a wedding. Her hair was tucked under a white linen cap, but stray strands clung damply to her neck and sweat rolled down her back and collected beneath her tightly laced stays, a piece of finery she'd have gladly forgone if not for her mother's insistence that it was high time she presented herself as a lady at public gatherings.

When the heat of the kitchen grew unbearable, she slipped outside in search of cooler air, her ears ringing with kitchen gossip. Her leather shoes, worn only for special occasions, pinched her feet and made her long for her everyday moccasins. Turning the corner at the rear of the tavern, she heard the rhythmic bark of dogs and a child yelling amid the cluster of cabins that formed the Boone homestead. As the barking continued, she followed the sound uphill and spied two little boys, arms and legs flailing, trying to block the path of two baying coonhounds that had cornered something beneath a cabin porch. The older boy hollered as he kicked, while the younger fought silently, his face streaked with tears.

The dogs lunged and danced back from the youngsters' blows and didn't hear her coming. She grabbed a stick off the ground and brought it down hard across the closest dog's hindquarters. He yelped, scrambled sideways, and fled with the second dog on his heels.

The boys sank into the dust, breathing hard.

"Are you all right?" The sound of her voice sent the younger one scooting around so his back was turned, hiding his tear-stained face. The older one, who looked to be about seven, said: "Those dogs ran Jonathan's kitten up under there."

She gathered her skirts and squatted down to peer under the porch but saw only darkness. The crawl space smelled dank and musty. She turned to the oldest boy. "What's your name?"

"Jesse Boone, ma'am."

"Well, Jesse, if your brother will run to the kitchen and ask for a scrap of meat, we'll have his kitten out in no time."

Still not looking at her, Jonathan scrambled to his feet and trotted down the hill. She watched him bend a path through the tall grass, which stood more than waist high on his tiny frame. "Is your brother always so quiet?"

"Yes'm, least ways since Mama died."

"I'm so sorry. When was that, honey?"

"Two months ago."

"So which of the Boone boys is your father?"

"Israel." His face clouded. "He's took bad with consumption, too, just like Mama was. Grandma expects he'll pass soon. I ain't supposed to know, but I overheard her talking to Grandpa. Don't let on about it to Jonathan," he added hurriedly as his brother emerged from the kitchen.

She nodded to show she understood, all the while wishing she could gather both these solemn boys into her lap and hug them until she'd forced a smile out of them.

Jonathan arrived at the top of the hill, out of breath. "They gave me a chicken gizzard," he said, keeping his eyes downcast as he held it out to her.

After a few seconds of waving the greasy scrap of meat alongside the porch, they heard a faint mewing from the darkness. All three of them were down on their hands and knees, coaxing the kitten out of the gloom, when Rebecca spied a moccasined foot next to her hand and sat back abruptly, catching her shoe in her petticoat hem. She sat down hard, which sent the kitten scuttling back into the shadows.

She felt a hand on her shoulder, and when she looked up, Daniel was standing over her. He must have moved quiet as an owl on the wing for her not to have heard him.

"I'm used to women falling hard for me," he said, breaking the silence, "but not quite this way."

She couldn't abide pridefulness, but there wasn't a hint of arrogance on his face; his expression was one of gentle good humor, as if he were laughing at himself and inviting her to join him. A sharp retort died on her tongue, but she ignored his outstretched hand as she untangled her skirts and got to her feet without his help.

She'd seen Daniel from time to time at community gatherings over the years, but because he was nearly five years older, they'd never so much as spoken to each other. All she knew about him was that folks said he was a crack shot who understood the ways of the woods better than most men, and that he'd recently returned from fighting the French and Indians in far-off Pennsylvania.

"Nubbin won't come out, Uncle Daniel," Jesse said.

"Move over, son; let me have a look."

Daniel stepped around Rebecca and in one smooth movement, pulled off his broad-brimmed hat, dropped to his belly, and crawled under the porch until only the tip of his moccasins showed. When he backed out, he was clutching the squirming kitten. His fringed hunter's shirt was begrimed, and cobwebs clung to his thick, reddish-brown hair.

"Easy now," he said, cradling the kitten against his chest before passing him to Jonathan.

Rebecca couldn't honestly say she fell in love with Daniel in those few moments, but she remembered feeling drawn to the gentle way he'd held that tiny scrap of fur in his hands, as well as the tenderness in his eyes as he'd looked at his nephews. She'd been struck, too, by the breadth of his shoulders, and it flashed through her mind just how nice it would feel to have him reach out and gather her into his arms. The thought left her as flushed as if she'd just danced a full set of reels.

It was Jesse, standing at his uncle's shoulder, who spoke first.

"Uncle Daniel? Shouldn't we take Nubbin home? If Jonathan puts her down she'll likely run off again."

Daniel smiled at Jesse, then reached down with one hand and swung Jonathan onto his back, making the youngster grin for the first time that evening. Daniel touched his hat good night to Rebecca as the trio started down the hill.

Looking back, it was easy for Rebecca to see that this chance encounter was the hinge on which the rest of her life would hang. From that day forward, she was never again free from the restless energy that surrounded Daniel, bringing adventure and heartbreak in equal measure. Early on, she'd recognized there were deep differences between them. For starters, she harbored a girlish yearning to see the civilized east—especially the city of Williamsburg. All her life she'd heard tales of gilded carriages, servants in livery, and shops set shoulder to shoulder for an entire mile along Williamsburg's main street that ran between the College of William and Mary and a brand-new capitol building made entirely of fine brick. Folks said the houses had real glass windows that spilled candlelight into the streets at night so that passersby walked from light to shadow and back again.

She hungered to hear the music she'd been told filtered out of the open doorways of the city's many taverns. Rich folks, with the coins to buy food and drink, could sit inside and listen to their hearts' content, but poor folks could find places in the shadows of the outbuildings and listen for free.

But more than anything, she wanted to see the tidy flower gardens that folks said graced most of the town lots. Her flowers grew largely untamed, but she'd heard that town folks confined their flowers to well-weeded beds with pathways where they could stroll among the blooms. Instead of rough cedar railings, Williamsburg gardens had white picket fencing. She couldn't imagine someone having enough time left in their day to paint a garden fence just to make it pretty, but folks swore it was true.

Unlike her, Daniel made no secret of his fascination with the wilderness that lay to the west. His conversation was filled with images of giant trees, waterfalls, towering mountains, and the abundance of wild creatures. It was clear his gaze was turned west while hers was turned eastward, but Rebecca reasoned that all married couples had a few such differences, and she'd told herself that surely love could overcome them.

One thing she and Daniel had agreed on from the beginning was that Jesse and Jonathan should become a permanent part of their newlywed household. Those solemn-faced boys had begun to work their way into her heart from the moment she'd laid eyes on them; it seemed the most natural thing in the world to welcome them into their home when, after long months of suffering, Daniel's brother, Israel, died of consumption as his wife had before him.

When her firstborn, James, arrived nine months after the wedding, the older boys became his willing caretakers, freeing Rebecca to step out of the cabin for a bucket of water, or down to the kitchen garden to gather produce. Their vigilance spared her the dilemma most new mothers faced—the necessity of tending to endless household chores while keeping a baby away from the cook fire that burned night and day on the hearth.

"It's like having two sheepdogs standing guard over one little lamb," she told Daniel.

Every chance she got, she told the boys she couldn't manage without them. She knew they needed to hear it, heartbroken as they were, and still not fully trusting that they were truly wanted.

The night her second child arrived, twenty months after James's birth, Rebecca held the newborn up in the firelight, all red and squalling, for Jesse and Jonathan to see.

"His name's Israel," she told them.

Their faces kindled, then shone as if she'd lit candles in the depths of their eyes.

"Pa'd be powerful proud," Jesse said. He bent over the quilt and stroked the baby's clenched fingers. "Howdy, Israel," he said softly.

Rebecca spent the remainder of that sleepless night with her back pressed against the hickory, tensing at every rustle of leaf and limb. It was sobering to realize that she was responsible for four boys, ages one to eleven, and they were all now homeless. The woods seemed to have swallowed Daniel. Please, she prayed over and over, let him return. When a thin gray light began to filter through the trees and the camp began to stir, Rebecca felt weak-limbed with relief that they'd survived the night.

Israel had slept restlessly, coughing in his sleep. She'd dosed him with tea several times during the night, but his forehead still felt hot under her hand. There was no time to brew a new batch of tea; she'd have to make do with the dregs from last night's pot. No doubt he'd fight swallowing the bitter liquid now that it was stone cold.

"Boys," she called, "time to get up. Jesse, help me roll up the bedding. Jonathan, go ask around to see if anyone's seen your uncle this morning."

They were nearly packed when Jonathan trotted back to report that he'd found Daniel on the far side of the camp giving orders to the forward group of riflemen. It was fortifying news and despite her sleepless night, she felt ready to face the day as she joined the ragged line and resumed their trek northward. When Daniel finally appeared, pausing long enough to give her a hasty hug before hurrying off again, she offered up a weary thanks to whatever guardian angel had the burdensome task of watching over him.

But as the day wore on, her sense of relief dissipated until she was once again strung tight as a bowstring. It was a strain to keep track of all four boys. She feared one of them might stray away from the caravan; just wandering into the bushes to relieve oneself was dangerous since the riflemen were ready to shoot anything that moved. Even with Ned and Martha's help, she wished for three pairs of eyes and eight arms in order to keep the boys safe. That day and the next blurred together into an endless slog of mud and cold and weariness, every moment punctuated by Israel's hacking cough.

It wasn't until the third day that Israel's fever finally broke, which heartened her considerably, and then, shortly afterwards, Daniel returned from scouting to report that the handful of warriors who'd continued to harass the rear guard had finally abandoned the chase. For the first time in three days, Rebecca felt she could draw a full breath.

"The Indians were content just to run us out of Carolina," Daniel told her. "I expect the ones that trailed us were itching to turn back and join their friends in helping themselves to what we left behind."

With the realization that her family was no longer in immediate danger, Rebecca leaned her head on Daniel's shoulder, shut her eyes, and allowed herself to mourn the many things they'd lost. They'd abandoned a crib bulging with corn from last year's harvest, and half a dozen hams that hung in the smokehouse. Their pantry and root cellar had been packed with crocks and bins filled with the foodstuffs she'd put up during the summer and fall. She wondered if the warriors would carry her provisions into the mountains to keep their own children fed over the winter. She imagined an Indian child running his hand around the rim of one of her crocks and licking wild plum preserves off his fingers.

She found the image strangely comforting. *Far better someone enjoy it than leaving it all to rot.*

The thought of dried pumpkin, turnips, and shuck beans made her mouth water; their fare on the trail would be little more than johnnycakes day after day, and any game the men shot was sure to be stringy and tough after months of sparse winter forage.

She sighed, and Daniel hugged her tighter, his breath warm in her hair. "We'll have some lean months, Becca, but we'll manage."

But she didn't see how. She could barely see beyond the next day, nor begin to imagine where this muddy, endless road was leading them.

Daniel and his parents had their sights set on Culpeper County, Virginia, where Squire and Sarah had friends they were sure would offer Daniel and Ned's families sanctuary. Squire and Sarah planned to continue on to Georgetown to stay with relatives.

Rebecca's parents and siblings intended to take a different path, heading northwest, back to the familiar territory of the Shenandoah Valley. Rebecca yearned to go with the Bryan clan, back to the fields of her childhood. Though she knew her grandmother was gone, buried years back in the tiny cemetery that sat on the hill behind the stone house, she would have welcomed the chance to stand alongside the grave and run her fingers across the letters etched into the rock. It would have been a balm, an anchor point, when the rest of her world was spinning wildly. She knew, however, if she voiced this desire, everyone, including her parents, would say it was her duty to go wherever her husband chose to take her. She wondered, not for the first time, why it was that men could marry and carry on as themselves, but women were expected to set aside large parts of themselves the moment they became wives.

Their pace had slowed after the panic of the first few days on the trail, taking into account the exhaustion of both children and livestock. Daniel calculated that by the ninth day they'd reach the cut-off point where the Boone and Bryan parties would split up.

"And how much further to Culpeper after that?" Rebecca asked.

Daniel rubbed a hand across the stubble on his chin. "At a hunter's pace, a handful of days, but at this rate, the better part of a week."

During the days they journeyed together, Rebecca spent as much time with her mother as possible. She'd been Aylee's right-hand helper throughout her childhood, and though she'd sometimes resented the way her mother depended upon her, she'd also taken pride in the role. Now, knowing they'd soon be parted, Rebecca was eager to learn whatever her mother might still be able to teach her.

When the path widened enough for them to walk two abreast, Rebecca took the opportunity to fall in alongside her mother so they could talk. Aylee seemed old to her, a woman in her forties grown heavy through the waist and hips. Rebecca remembered how pretty her mother had been in the years before hard work and bearing ten babies had plowed deep furrows into her face.

One afternoon, as they picked their way along a rocky stretch of trail, her mother said, "I'm sick to death of journey cake. I'd give anything for a slice of hot pigeon pie for dinner."

"My pigeon pies have never been as tasty as yours," Rebecca said, balancing Israel on her hip and holding James's hand to steady him as they skirted a moss-covered boulder that jutted into the path.

"After you clean the bird, are you remembering to put a pat of fresh butter in its belly?" Aylee asked. "The bird will be dry if you don't. And how much salt are you using—one pinch or two?" She glanced over her shoulder and caught Rebecca's eye. "I hear that in towns like Charleston, women write out their recipes, but a woman shouldn't need such things if she has kinfolk to teach her."

Kinfolk—that word echoed in Rebecca's head the rest of the day. It was the presence of kinfolk that kept her sane during those long miles when Israel was fussing and tugging at her bodice, weak but improving, wanting to be nursed; or at nightfall when the tinder was damp and she couldn't get the fire lit, and Daniel and the older boys were complaining of hunger after a long day on the trail. On those days, her mother was her anchor. They divided their chores instinctively, drawing on years of working side by side. By the time Rebecca unbagged the meal, her mother had a kettle of water ready to hang over the fire, and when her mother was busy adding wood to the flames, Rebecca stirred the mush so it didn't burn. It was a ragged sort of dance, but they were good partners and rarely trod on each other's toes.

At the end of each weary day of walking, Rebecca settled the boys down to sleep on the bearskin pallet cushioned with hemlock boughs. When she and Daniel finally joined them, they eased under the blankets, and each cradled one of the younger boys to warm them. Most nights they were too tired to talk.

Of all the folks in the caravan, only Martha and Ned seemed oblivious to the hardships of the trail. Flush with the newness of young love, they walked side by side no matter how narrow the path, Ned's arm protectively around Martha's shoulders, shielding her from the wind. The newlywed joy that radiated between them sometimes lifted Rebecca's spirits, and other times made her feel even more raggedy and worn.

The day Rebecca dreaded finally arrived when they reached the trailhead that would lead the Bryan party away from her, across the Blue Ridge and back to the upper reaches of the Shenandoah. She'd never been separated from her parents by more than a dozen miles; the prospect made her feel childishly anxious, as though she were about to be orphaned. Her only consolation was that Martha would continue the journey alongside her, being a Boone now herself.

Rebecca, Martha, and Aylee broke camp together for the last time, sorting out the pots and pans, wash rags and meal bags that they'd shared over the previous weeks. A soft rain began to fall, dampening their clothes and adding to the melancholy of the morning.

"Goodbye, Mama," Rebecca said, bending to give her a hug. She clung to her, breathing in her familiar scent, and all the tears she hadn't allowed herself to shed in front of others since the moment they were uprooted rose to the surface and spilled down her cheeks as her mother slipped from her embrace and turned to hug Martha goodbye. Only God knew when, if ever, they'd see each other again.

James and Israel stared up at Rebecca with frightened eyes, having rarely seen their mother cry, while Jesse and Jonathan looked away, as though witnessing something shameful. She had no explanation to give the older boys, nor comfort to offer the little ones. She felt as if she'd been walking shaky ground on a cliff's edge these past days and the earth had finally given way.

As the Bryan caravan moved away from her along the trail, the horses and cattle splashed through muddy puddles that pockmarked the path, and her mother stared resolutely ahead, pulling the hood of her cloak over her hair in the misty rain, the scarlet material a bright spot of color amid the dripping gray tunnel of trees.

Rebecca knew every thread in that vivid piece of cloth, every knot, every flaw. The year before her marriage, she and her mother had spent many winter evenings tediously threading their loom to weave that material, laughing when, more than once, Rebecca had risen up beneath the crossbar and bumped her head on the solid oak beam.

"This isn't a job for a tall woman," Rebecca had said, rubbing her head.

"What you're saying is it's a job for me or Martha," her mother had replied. "Go ahead and get those long legs of yours out of there. I'll fit just fine."

During long winter nights spent weaving in the firelight, there'd been time for stories and laughter, their voices raised to be heard over the thump of the treadles as the scarlet material had come to life, inch by inch, across the loom's face.

Rebecca's eyes clung to the cloak as if her gaze could reach across the distance, pluck one of those brilliant red threads, and tug her mother back to her side. She thought for a moment that Aylee would disappear around the bend without a backward glance, but at the last instant, she turned and waved. Rebecca raised her hand so her mother could spot her in the crowd. She imagined Aylee was smiling at her and knew exactly how her eyes would crinkle at the corners.

Martha had turned away to rejoin Ned even before Aylee was out of sight. As Rebecca stood waving, she could hear Martha and Ned behind her, conversing in low tones. Martha giggled at something Ned said as they worked to sort and repack the remaining supplies. Rebecca felt sure Martha would miss their mother, but unlike herself, Martha wouldn't dwell on it, nor would she regret all the things left unsaid or undone.

Long after Aylee had passed from sight, Rebecca stood in the rain, staring at the empty tunnel of trees, wishing with all her might for an accepting heart, a heart more like Martha's.

3

One morning, not long after their arrival in Culpeper, Rebecca woke before sunrise with her stomach churning. She slipped off the pallet, pulled on her cloak, and felt her way outside the cabin, then ran her hand along the rough log wall that led to the necessary. She sat in the dark confines, retching and shivering.

By the time she made her way back to the cabin, the sun was just breaking over the horizon, bathing the bare limbs of the apple trees that marched in rows across the hillside in pink-hued light. She climbed the rickety porch steps and leaned on the railing to catch her breath. The Boone family friends who had taken them in had offered them the use of this tenant cabin, but despite the aura of friendship that surrounded the arrangement, it was clear they were expected to work the surrounding fields just as any other tenant would.

The one-room cabin was sparsely furnished; their worn traveling pallets had to suffice for beds, and Rebecca served their meals on several rough boards laid across two upturned logs. Daniel had hurriedly fashioned two crude benches so at least they didn't have to sit on the floor.

"How long are we gonna stay here, Uncle Daniel?" the normally silent Jonathan had said when they'd first seen the tiny cabin that would be their new home. The boy's nose had wrinkled at the musty smell that wafted through the wide gaps between the logs where the chinking was missing. Their chicken coop in Carolina had been cozier.

Daniel's only response to Jonathan's question had been a helpless shrug.

Rebecca turned her back on the first rays of light that shone above the orchard, crossed the porch, and eased open the cabin door, hoping the rusty hinges wouldn't squeak. The interior of the cabin was beginning to grow lighter. When she lay back down beside Daniel, chilled to the bone, he opened his eyes and looked at her quizzically.

"I'm expecting," she said.

"When?"

The look on his face told her this was unwelcome news.

"Late October—maybe early November." She tugged on the blanket and turned her back to him to hide the tears that pricked her eyelids. The first two times she'd told him she was pregnant, his response had been to lift her in his arms and whirl her joyfully around the room. Now, she lay stiffly in the dark, her mind racing.

The small crock of ginger that had kept her nausea at bay during her previous pregnancies had been left behind on her worktable in Carolina; she had no idea where to get more in this unfamiliar place. Would her ankles swell as badly as they had with Israel? Had she even packed the oversized shift she used when her belly grew big? She'd need to wean Israel now that another baby was on the way, and she dreaded that struggle. Couldn't Daniel see that the prospect of caring for their family in this cramped, unsettled space, all the while growing bigger and more ungainly, was even more daunting to her than it was to him? It certainly wasn't something she'd have chosen, given a chance to choose differently.

After a bit, Daniel slid across the pallet and spooned his body against her back, draping his arm over her side so he could rest a hand on her stomach. He let out a long sigh. "You know I love young'uns, Becca. But another mouth to feed . . ." His voice trailed off.

And that was all he said.

As Daniel began to breathe deeply, his arm heavy on her side, she lay awake, listening to the rustle of the boys as they shifted in their blankets. Since their arrival in Culpeper, Rebecca had felt Daniel growing more distant from her with each day that passed. Their abrupt uprooting had changed him, and though she wanted to unburden her heart to him, she no longer knew how to start.

It had been a shock for all of them to go from being in charge of one's own homestead to scraping by as hired help, farming someone else's land. Culpeper County was a good deal more civilized than the Forks, and here they were viewed as refugees from the backcountry. *Which is exactly what we are,* Rebecca thought.

Being suddenly uprooted had been hard on everyone, but Daniel had taken it hardest. Ned and Martha had settled into a second tenant cabin on the other side of the orchard. While Ned seemed perfectly content to farm, Daniel had never intended to be a farmer. He'd managed to find occasional work as a wagoner hauling tobacco to market in Fredericksburg, but tenant farming was really the only way to keep the family fed.

At home in Carolina, Daniel had plowed and planted just enough ground each spring to feed the family and livestock for the year, and even that was more grubbing in the dirt than he wanted to do. He'd always made a living with his gun and traps, and the rhythm of their family life had centered around the steady accumulation of hides and furs. But in this settled land, large-scale hunting was impossible.

Rebecca watched a shaft of light trace a slow course across the cabin wall, and a girlhood memory came to mind—the time her brothers had found a crow with a damaged wing. She'd watched as they fashioned a cage and carved a splint, then helped them scour the barnyard for worms to feed the glossy bird. The injury healed nicely, yet one morning they'd found him lying stiff and glassy-eyed.

"Wild things can't be caged," her father had told them.

Rebecca shifted uneasily as she realized the expression she'd seen on her husband's face in the thin morning light was the look of a wild thing desperate to make his escape.

"Time to get moving, big brother; we've got corn to hoe." Ned's voice floated in through the open front door, just after sunrise.

Rebecca stepped onto the porch and saw Ned leaning on his hoe at the edge of the road. Rebecca waved and ducked back inside just as Daniel pushed the bench back from the breakfast table, crumbs clinging to his shirtfront.

Rebecca crossed paths with him, brushed off the crumbs, and leaned forward to give him a quick kiss. She was six months along now and her belly had grown so large that she waddled rather than walked. The baby seemed never to be still, shifting and turning like a fish swimming in dark water. This one, she'd warned Daniel, would arrive running.

"Jesse and Jonathan finished picking the beans in the kitchen garden for me yesterday. They're hoping to work with you today," she said, stepping back so her belly didn't block his path to the door.

Daniel shook his head as he squeezed past her. "I'll never understand those boys, wanting to do field work. Guess they got their love of farming from Ned—they surely didn't get it from me."

As if summoned by his name, Ned appeared, silhouetted in the doorway. "I'll consider that last remark a compliment, big brother, though I doubt you meant it that way."

Rebecca smiled at her brother-in-law as he stepped inside. Ned's resemblance to Daniel had only increased during these past months. They shared the same blue-gray eyes, thick brown hair with reddish highlights, and muscular build. Ned was the same age as Rebecca, five years younger than Daniel, but the two men now looked so much alike that from a distance, she couldn't tell them apart. Each day, when she stood on the porch and looked out at the fields, what she saw were broad-shouldered twins toiling side by side.

She heard a thud on the porch as Jesse and Jonathan set the heavy milk pail down on the rough plank floor.

Ned looked out the door. "Go grab the hoes from the barn, boys, and we'll get started."

The boys clattered down the porch steps, not bothering to bring the bucket inside. Rebecca knew they were avoiding her, afraid she'd set them to work toting water or hauling wood. They relished days when they escaped the chores of women and children and worked alongside the men.

Ned turned to Daniel. "We got word last night the militia's forming along the Carolina border. They intend to run the Cherokee back toward the mountains. There's even talk of marching all the way to the Middle Towns and leveling them."

Daniel's eyes suddenly looked alive. "Who's leading the militia?"

"Most likely, Major Waddell."

The men stepped outside, still talking, though Rebecca could no longer hear their words. She walked to the doorway and leaned against the frame, watching their figures grow smaller as they headed to the fields. Jesse and Jonathan trailed behind like ducklings, their hoes over their shoulders. She was dismayed to see a purposefulness in Daniel's step that hadn't been there since their arrival in Virginia. He looked like a man who was more than ready to walk back to Carolina.

The baby arrived that fall, shortly after harvest. Daniel's parents had headed north to Maryland months earlier, so there was no one to tend to Rebecca but Martha, who was seven months pregnant with her first child and had little experience birthing babies. As Rebecca's labor lengthened, Martha hovered above the bed, worry etched across her face.

Daniel's footsteps echoed on the porch planks as he paced back and forth. Between contractions, Rebecca watched the sunlight glow golden through the open doorway, then slowly dim as the sun sank below the apple trees. As her pains grew even fiercer, she saw fear in Martha's eyes.

"Jesse," Martha said, "Take the young'uns to my cabin and tell Ned they'll need to stay there tonight."

Rebecca heard Martha and Daniel have a whispered exchange on the porch, followed moments later by the sound of hoofbeats disappearing down the road.

Martha leaned over the bed and laid a damp rag on Rebecca's forehead. "Daniel's gone to get the midwife."

"We didn't think we'd need a midwife, given this is my third."

"Maybe you wouldn't have if you had a sister who knew what she was doing."

Rebecca gave Martha's hand a quick squeeze, then grabbed a fold of the quilt as her entire body tightened. She longed to hear her mother's soothing voice above her, calm and confident, keeping her safe as it had during her previous labors.

By the time the midwife hurried into the cabin, throwing off her cloak and rolling up her sleeves, Rebecca's contractions were so strong she was barely able to keep from crying out. Daniel stepped to the side of the bed and rested a hand on her damp forehead. "Ada's here to help." He started to say something else, but the midwife bustled up and shooed him away.

Ada's hands were cool as they moved across Rebecca's rounded belly, assessing the baby's position. Rebecca felt herself relax just a little under the midwife's gentle touch, until, without warning, Ada pressed down forcefully. Rebecca gasped and felt a surge of pain that left her vision blurry and her hearing muffled. Only when the pain receded a bit did she realize that Ada's hands were once again moving lightly across her belly.

The midwife nodded, satisfied. "The babe had a shoulder caught, but it won't be long now."

Rebecca took a deep breath as another contraction began to build. She felt as if she and the baby were cut off from the rest of the world, alone and encased in a chrysalis of pain as they labored together toward the moment when one would at last become two.

Less than an hour later, Ada placed the child, naked and crying, into Rebecca's outstretched arms. "It's a girl," she said.

Giddy with relief, Rebecca counted the baby's fingers and toes, marveling at how delicate this child was. Her first daughter was so much smaller than the boys had been as newborns. As the baby's cries grew louder, Rebecca gathered the blanket around her. "Hush, little one," she said. But the baby continued to cry, her breath coming in ragged gasps, as Ada stepped back and let Daniel move alongside the bed.

He was smiling, apparently pleased at the addition of a daughter to their household of boys.

"I'd like to name her Susannah," Rebecca said, raising her voice to be heard over the baby's insistent cries.

Daniel nodded and bent to examine the child. Unlike her brothers, who were fair headed, Susannah had a downy head of darker hair that held a hint of red.

"Looks like she may have my Daddy's coloring," Daniel said. He folded the blanket back to study the soft fuzz. "Daddy's been wanting another redhead in the family. I swear, the way Miss Susannah is carrying on, my folks will be able to hear her all the way up in Maryland."

Three days after Susannah's birth, Rebecca was seated on a low stool by the hearth, brushing coals off the lid of the Dutch oven so she could check the cornbread. It was her first day out of childbed, and she was shaky from lack of sleep and tending to the swirling needs of all five children. She'd just hugged a teary Israel for the dozenth time that day, reassuring him that he was still her baby, too, when Daniel stepped through the door and cleared his throat.

"It's time I went back to Carolina, Becca. I aim to join up with Major Waddell and help run the Indians over the mountains. That's the only way to make the Forks safe for you and the children. I plan to head out in the morning."

She stared hard at him until he finally looked down, shuffling his feet like a little boy caught in a lie. There was nothing to lose now; she was determined to have her say.

"You're going," she said through gritted teeth, "because you can't stand to farm, and you hate being cooped up in this poor-excuse-for-a-cabin with me and the young'uns and barely enough room to turn around. Running the Indians away from the Forks is an afterthought."

He was honest enough not to deny it. "You knew when you married me I wasn't a farmer, Becca."

"That's true—but I didn't reckon on being left with a cabin full of children to care for, nursing a newborn, living on acres that aren't our own, and you traipsing off to fight a war. I'll spend months not knowing where you are—whether you're alive or dead. Don't ask me to live like that. We need you here." She hated the needy, begging tone of her voice, but was helpless to control it.

"I'll be back by planting time in the spring." He spoke as if he hadn't heard her; already there was a distant look in his eyes.

She forced angry words to the back of her throat and swallowed them. His heart had already headed south, and she could tell from his expression there was no use saying more. Only later did she realize that this point in their lives had offered them two paths, and they both chose ones that led them astray. She should have spoken up more forcefully. He should have stayed home.

When Daniel shouldered his gun the next morning, she held her tongue and walked stiffly to the door to see him off. Standing together on the porch in first light, he held her tight and said into her hair, "I love you, Rebecca."

She knew he meant it, but she couldn't help but wonder—if love wasn't enough to keep him with her, how could she trust it would bring him back?

All that autumn she could feel Daniel walking further away from her, each footfall a weight on her chest. She tried hard not to think about the growing distance between them, choosing to picture instead his arrival at Sugartree and his relief when he found their home intact. She refused to consider the opposite image: Daniel picking through the charred ruins of their homeplace, though she knew this was the likelier scenario.

Daniel's plan was to check on the farm, then meet up with Waddell's militia and be part of whatever action was undertaken against the Cherokee. She could follow him to Sugartree in her mind, but after that, he disappeared completely, as if he'd walked out of sight into a dark, impenetrable fog. It was one thing to have him leave the family in an effort to reclaim their home; it was something else entirely for him to pursue the Indians into the furthest reaches of the mountains, intent on revenge.

With each day that passed, Rebecca's longing to return to their home on Sugartree Creek grew deeper. In Carolina there had been seasonal rhythms she could count on. Each spring and summer of their married life, Daniel had stuck close to home to hunt because deer, which were plentiful around the Forks, were his main quarry during the warm months. He'd arrive home from a two-day trip with a load of deerskins in need of dressing, and then she and the boys would take a break from their regular chores and work alongside him.

It was a smelly, dirty job, scraping and stretching the hides, but they'd had the satisfaction of watching the stack of skins grow higher and higher as summer wore on. She and the children took turns naming all the wonderful things Daniel would trade for them: store-bought cloth, bullet lead, a sugar loaf for a year's worth of baking.

Rebecca had always felt sad at summer's end, because she knew that when the air grew crisp, Daniel would grow restless. He'd take his traps down from the barn walls where they'd hung since early spring, oil them, and load them onto pack frames, preparing for the long hunts that filled his fall and winter months.

He'd set out each October, and they wouldn't see him for weeks, or maybe months, and when he did return, it would be only for brief visits to pick up supplies and drop off the beaver, mink, and otter pelts he'd accumulated. Each winter he'd roamed the woods of western Carolina, following the hidden forest trails, the twists and bends of the mountain streams. Not until the first breath of spring crept across the land would he settle in with them again.

That had been their yearly pattern, and though she and the boys had missed Daniel when he was away from the Forks, they'd been held securely in a web of kinship during his absence because their Sugartree cabin was situated midway between the Bryan settlement, where her parents and younger siblings lived, and the Boone family's homestead where her in-laws and many of Daniel's brothers and sisters had put down roots. She'd thought their lives would spin out that way forever—not perfect, but familiar. She'd envisioned rocking on her front porch at Sugartree, an old woman with grandchildren playing at her feet.

During daylight hours, Rebecca set her hands to the endless household tasks. The baby's soiled clouts piled up daily. None of the children were strong enough to heft the heavy wash kettle, and only Jesse could lift the wooden bucket once it was filled with water, so she spent each washday toting water from the creek, bringing it to a boil in the wash kettle in the cabin yard, beating the clothes with a paddle on the wash bench, then rinsing and draping the soggy material over the fence rails, where it froze stiff overnight.

The repetition of daily chores left her with little to do but think, and she did her best to recall happier times, scenes from the early days of her marriage, such as the evening when she was standing at the hearth roasting venison and saw Daniel pull a book out of the buckskin bag filled with the sundries he carried when he went hunting.

She'd stared, nearly as startled as if he'd plucked out a silver tea set. She'd had no idea Daniel could read; in the six months they'd courted and the handful of weeks they'd been wed, the topic had never come up.

"What's that?" she asked.

He looked at her blankly, and she pointed to the book.

"*Gulliver's Travels*," he said. "Have you read it?"

"I don't know how to read." Most of the women she knew couldn't read—for that matter, neither could many of the men—yet somehow she felt ashamed.

Daniel patted the bench. She gave the spit a final turn, wiped her hands on her apron, and sat down beside him, unable to meet his eyes.

"I wasn't much for schooling," Daniel began, running his fingers across the book's worn leather cover, "but I love to read. I always carry a book when I go hunting so I can read by the fire at the end of the day."

She watched him trace the letters on the book's cover with his fingers, a caress that was almost reverent.

"My father taught my brothers to read," she said, eyes downcast. "But when I asked him to teach me, he said, 'If you learn to read and marry a man who can't, it will just cause trouble. A man doesn't want a wife knowing more than he does.'"

Daniel shifted on the bench and cupped her chin in his hand, turning her to look at him. There was a tenderness in his eyes that made her heart turn over. "Well, I'm pretty sure your father can't object if your husband teaches you."

How fiercely she'd loved him at that moment. He'd offered her the key to a secret world previously denied her. In the weeks that followed, she sat beside him in the firelight and worked hard to learn her letters, lessons squeezed into odd moments, punctuated by frequent interruptions from Jesse and Jonathan and the endless flow of household duties. Still, she'd made steady progress until, just nine months after their wedding, James had arrived. The constant demands of a newborn had left little time for anything but necessities, and the lessons had dwindled, then ceased all together.

She hadn't had time to mourn that loss until now, stranded in Culpeper with little adult company. She hungered for the companionship that Daniel seemed to find in the printed word, but when she opened the worn Bible that sat gathering dust on the mantel, she recognized only a few letters here or there. No matter how hard she stared, the type stubbornly refused to form into words.

As winter settled in, there were days when Rebecca cracked the door open, hoping to spot chimney smoke rising above the orchard from Ned and Martha's cabin, just to reassure herself that she and the children weren't the last beings on earth. With the door pulled tight and the shutters closed, the children's voices filled the tiny cabin, most often containing a request or demand that required her attention. She yearned for actual conversation.

In her trips back and forth to the creek with the water bucket, she discovered a sort of solace in standing on the bank, listening to the ripple and flow of the water. After dipping her bucket into the current, she'd set it down on the frosty ground and pause, breathing deeply and listening to the creek's cheerful voice. While it didn't flow as swiftly as their Carolina creek, it still seemed to talk to her, and for those few minutes each day she felt less alone.

Day after day the rhythm of her life was centered on the same chores she'd done when they lived at the Forks, but she had no sense of them adding up to anything. She and the children were marking time in Culpeper, waiting for Daniel, waiting to return to Carolina, waiting for life to resume.

Once, when she was a girl, she and one of her older brothers had taken a canoe into the middle of the Yadkin and attempted to hold the boat stationary in the midst of a strong current just to see if they could do it. They'd discovered it took a lot of hard paddling to stay in the same place, and they were soon exhausted from the effort. That's what living in Culpeper without Daniel felt like; it took all her strength to go nowhere.

In the past, when Daniel had been away on his winter hunts, Martha or her mother had been in and out of their cabin, spending a night every so often, helping with the heaviest chores, keeping the children's needs from overwhelming her. But for most of the winter of 1760–61, she and the children were alone, and the days crawled by. She had occasional help from Ned, but after Martha delivered their first child, Charity, just two months after Susannah's arrival, Ned was busy caring for his own growing family.

Rebecca thanked God daily for Jesse, who had just turned twelve and was a sturdy, dependable soul. He did his best to keep Jonathan, who was quiet but stubborn, in line. Three-year-old James was in awe of his older cousins and followed them everywhere, while Israel, now two, still clung to his mother, sometimes fascinated, but often infuriated, by his infant sister.

One midwinter night, James, who sometimes teased Israel about being a baby, surprised Rebecca by crawling onto her lap, something he hadn't done in months. She shifted Susannah into the crook of her arm to make room for him, marveling at how long her firstborn's legs had become. She glanced around to see where Israel was, anticipating a jealous outburst, but he was watching Jesse and Jonathan crack hickory nuts on the hearthstones, opening his mouth like a baby bird so the older boys could feed him tiny pieces.

James leaned against her and she smelled the sharp scent of wood smoke in his fair hair and the tang of the bayberry soap she'd made him wash with before dinner. When he looked up at her, his gray eyes were just like Daniel's.

"When will Daddy come home?" he asked.

The activity in the room ceased as all the boys turned to hear the answer.

"Most likely in the spring, around planting time," she said.

"How long's that?"

"March, April, May—three more months."

"That's too long. I want Daddy home now."

"I know, sweetheart, but he . . ."

"He can't come home because the Indians got him," James said softly. His shoulders sagged as if the weight of the words were too much for him to carry. "The scary man with the paint on his face found Daddy in the woods."

Her heart jumped, but she did her best to keep her voice calm. "Why do you say that, honey?"

James ducked his head and pressed his face into her gown as if seeking a place to hide. "I saw it," he said, his voice muffled. "I saw it when I was sleeping. The scary man chased me, too, and I ran . . ."

His whole body shivered and he burrowed deeper into her shoulder.

The other boys remained frozen, eyes wide. Israel's lips begin to quiver.

"It's only a dream," she told them. "I'm sure we'll hear from your father soon. The militia's made up of volunteers, so men are always traveling home to check on their families. Any day now, I bet someone will knock on our door and bring us word of your father."

But February melted into March, then March into April, and when May finally arrived, there was still no word from Daniel.

4

Rebecca could hear Ned singing down at the barn as he unhitched the horse from the plow. He'd spent the day on the south side of the cabin preparing the kitchen garden for planting; the rich smell of fresh-turned earth hung in the air, accompanying Rebecca as she went about her chores. It was early May, and for the first time in months, she'd let the cookfire burn down to coals because the cabin was uncomfortably warm. To escape the heat, she'd pulled the heavy cradle out on the porch and settled onto a bench to mend a tear in Jonathan's breeches, using her foot to rock the cradle as Susannah drifted to sleep.

It was a rare moment of peace, occasioned by all four boys having gone to the creek to search the banks for spring greens. After a winter of meat and meal, they all hungered for the taste of something freshly picked. She'd intended to keep Israel home, but he'd been so distraught at seeing the older boys start off without him, Jesse had doubled back, taken him by the hand, and promised to watch him.

At this time of year, their yard in Carolina would be filled with blossoms. She shut her eyes and pictured it in her mind—the vibrant yellow blooms on the cluster of spicebushes beside the porch, the mass of bluets that graced the path to the springhouse, the shoulder-high stand of false indigo that grew along the sunniest wall of the barn. She had worked hard to add new plants each year, gathering them from the meadows and surrounding woods. Here, when she opened her eyes, all she saw was a yard of bare red clay, pockmarked with hoof prints. She was grateful that at least the apple trees across the road would soon be covered with fragrant blossoms.

Ned came around the corner of the cabin, still singing, but stopped abruptly when he spied the cradle, trying to muffle the jangling metal buckles on the harness that was slung over his shoulder.

"Don't worry," Rebecca said, "once she's out, all four boys hollering at once won't wake her."

"Good thing," Ned said with a grin, slapping his dusty hat against his leg, "otherwise she'd never sleep at all. At our house, Martha has me tiptoeing around whenever Charity's napping."

"Well, that's what you do with your firstborn; it'll change when another one arrives."

Ned laid the harness on the porch floor and sat down on the bench beside her. Rebecca didn't feel the need to speak. She'd grown comfortable around Ned during their year in Culpeper. He shared Daniel's easygoing ways but, unlike Daniel, possessed a settled soul. It was nice to just sit beside him and not feel the need to fill the silence with words.

Ned watched as she stitched a patch onto a pair of Jonathan's well-worn breeches, then turned the newly mended cloth right side out and smoothed the material across her lap. She figured the patch would hold until Jonathan outgrew them, and they might still be serviceable enough to hand down to James.

Seeing that her sewing was done, Ned shifted, opened his mouth to say something, then shut it again, running his fingers restlessly around the brim of his hat that sat perched on his knee.

"What is it, Neddy?"

When he looked up, his eyes were worried, and she felt the peace of the morning slipping away.

"I've got your garden plot plowed," Ned said. "Next week I'll begin planting corn in the tenant fields. I know you intended to plant your kitchen plot when Daniel got home, but . . ." He paused and took a deep breath, the way a body does when they're about to jump into an ice-cold creek. "I think we need to go ahead and get your kitchen seed in the ground."

Her stomach knotted. Ned was giving voice to thoughts that had trod heavily through her mind these past weeks. "You think he's dead."

"Rebecca, it's been seven months. The militia hasn't disbanded, so that may be why he hasn't come back, but he should at least have sent you word." He paused and cleared his throat. "All I know for certain is you can't hold off planting; the children have to eat. Martha and I think—"

She interrupted. "You've been discussing what's to be done with me because you think I'm a widow?"

"We're just concerned . . ." His voice trailed off as she turned away. The certainty of Daniel's return at planting time had anchored her life through the winter, giving her a point on the horizon she could walk toward. Now, with these words, Ned had stripped that away.

"Rebecca," Ned said, but she shook her head, unwilling to listen and unable to speak.

After a long moment's silence, she heard the scrape of the bench as he stood up and the jangle of harness as he walked away.

"I know it's silly," Rebecca told Martha several days later, "but allowing Ned to do the work Daniel said he'd be home to do makes me feel like I've given up on him." She was standing on Martha's front porch, swaying back and forth, trying to pacify a squirming Susannah who wanted down because she could hear the boys squealing with laughter as they chased each other through the orchard.

Charity was asleep in Martha's arms. She was a placid baby, content to play quietly on a quilt whenever her mother set her down. Rebecca took in the serene picture before her with a sigh. Her Suzy was about as content as a bag full of cats. It was a battle to keep the child safe now that she could crawl. More than once it had occurred to Rebecca that Susannah's restlessness might be a reflection of her family's unsettled life in the months she'd carried her. Or maybe she simply took after her father.

"Ned and I will feel better knowing your garden is in," Martha was saying. Martha managed to look every bit as tidy as she had prior to motherhood. Her apron was clean, and every hair was in place.

Rebecca looked down at her own grease-splattered apron. She'd put off doing the laundry, dreading the heavy work of hauling water from the creek and filling the wash kettles when there were so many other chores left undone as well.

As Susannah arched her back and renewed her efforts to escape, Martha eyed her niece with a bemused expression. Rebecca bit her lip to keep from saying: *Don't be too smug. Your next one may be exactly like her.* But even as the thought came to her, she knew she wasn't being fair. None of her unsettled feelings were Martha's fault. It pained Rebecca to admit that she was jealous—jealous of her sister's well-behaved child, of her ordered household, and most of all for possessing a husband who was content to be home.

Rebecca sat down on the porch steps and cradled Susannah, settling her to nurse, hoping that would calm her. When she looked up at Martha, her sister met her gaze with the same sweet expression she'd worn since they were children together in the Shenandoah Valley. It made Rebecca ache for those familiar green fields. She felt abandoned in this place, as if she'd washed up on some foreign shore.

Rebecca shut her eyes, drifting as Suzy nursed, traveling back to the days when she and Martha had been in perfect harmony, sitting safe and snug on their grandfather Bryan's lap, where they'd listened to tales of the Old World, of lost Irish lands and of their family's journey across the Atlantic that had been prompted by equal parts hope and desperation. Martha would sometimes nod off to sleep, nestled against Grandfather's rough woolen waistcoat, but Rebecca had hung on every word, imagining the steeples of Belfast, the rock walls that lined the fields like jagged ribs, and the scent of peat smoke that hung over the whitewashed cottages. Grandfather's stories had clung to her as tightly as the beggar's lice that dotted her skirts on summer evenings when she fetched the cows home.

Most marvelous of all were Grandfather's word-pictures of the ocean. Over and over Rebecca had made him tell about the endless reaches of blue-green water that swelled in and out like a person drawing breath. As hard as she'd tried, she couldn't conceive of an expanse of water so vast a fast ship took six weeks or more to cross from one side to the other.

The spring she was ten, after an afternoon of such stories, she'd sat behind her grandparents' house in a meadow grown tall with wild bluebells and sunk down so low that all she could see were waves of blue as the breeze tossed the blossoms. She'd squinted, turned her face to the wind, and imagined herself on the deck of a sailing ship with the ocean rolling beneath her.

When Martha had found her there in the midst of her imaginings, she'd laughed and said, "Why do you care so much about those old stories, Becca? What's wrong with where we are right now?"

It had been this childhood moment that had made Rebecca recognize, for the first time, that she and Martha didn't see the world in exactly the same way. That realization had made her feel as if the earth had suddenly tilted. Even now, Martha remained largely indifferent to the past, while Rebecca was always drawn backward, doomed to mull over the happenings of her life, rearranging them in her mind, wishing more often than not that she could change things.

As they sat on Martha's porch with their babies on their laps, Rebecca prayed for the strength to rejoice in her sister's good fortune and the willpower to rid herself of the jealousy that had crept into her heart and threatened to lodge there permanently.

Less than a week later, Rebecca and Ned met alongside her cabin in the dim light of dawn to plant her kitchen garden. Rebecca had worked this same ground with Daniel the previous spring, and as she and Ned moved up and down the freshly turned rows, she felt as if she'd conjured her husband's ghost.

When Ned looked up and caught her watching him, he grinned, and Rebecca's heart froze in mid-beat because it was Daniel's face—the same wide mouth and laughter-filled eyes—staring back at her. She felt her body begin to tingle, as if someone had poured liquid fire into her veins, and she ducked her head to hide her flushed face. *This is Ned, not Daniel.* She repeated those words to herself, but her body had other ideas. She bit her lip and kept her eyes on the ground, afraid to even glance at Ned as they worked their way down the rows, their hoes clinking against rocks as they broke up the clods of dirt left behind by the plow.

This morning she'd set the older boys to work mucking out the barn, but now she wished they were working alongside her; their chatter might keep her disordered feelings at bay. She didn't dare look up, knowing if she did she'd see the same broad shoulders that had made her weak-kneed the first day she and Daniel had met. *This is Ned. Daniel's gone. This is Ned.*

By midmorning her back ached and she was dirt streaked and sweaty. When a baby's cry echoed across the field, she looked up to see Martha rounding the corner of the cabin carrying a red-faced Susannah. Rebecca laid her hoe and the leather bag of seeds down in a furrow to mark her spot, then walked stiffly toward the edge of the plowed ground to meet them.

Martha raised her voice to be heard over Susannah's forceful cries. "Sorry, Becca—I stalled her as long as I could, but this little girl has a mind of her own."

Rebecca held out her hands and Suzy reached for her, snuggling into her arms and nuzzling her breast. "Patience, little one," she said. "Let me sit down first."

She watched Martha hurry back toward the house to tend the rest of the children, pausing at the edge of the field to exchange a few words and a quick hug with Ned. His dusty shirt left a streak of dirt across Martha's forehead, and when Ned tried to brush it off, his hand left an even bigger smear. Their laughter floated across the field.

Rebecca sat down in the shade of the fencerow and loosened the drawstring on her shift, sliding the material off her shoulder and settling Susannah to nurse. Across the field, Ned picked up his hoe and moved slowly along the furrows, dropping seeds and tamping the dirt in place.

From the moment Daniel had departed, Ned had stepped in to care for her and the children. Early on, when she'd tried to thank him, he'd shrugged and said, "I promised Daniel," as if that were reason enough. She and the children were beholden to him in so many ways. Everywhere she looked she saw evidence of his work: the new cedar shakes he'd riven to patch a hole in their roof; the fence he'd repaired when their milk cow broke through the rails; the venison he'd left hanging on the porch when they'd run out of meat.

She rarely saw anyone other than Ned and Martha, except on the rare occasion when someone stopped to chat as they passed by on their way to or from the mill that sat a few miles downstream. Slowly, without her realizing it, the sight of Ned crossing the footbridge over the creek, headed toward her cabin, had become the happiest moment of her day.

Beyond the plowed field where Ned was working, the orchard marched in rows that followed the curve of the land. Today, the ground beneath the trees was white with fallen apple blossoms, though here and there a few still clung to the branches. She didn't know how she'd maintain their tenant fields through the summer or pay her share of the rent when fall arrived. Jesse was a big help, but he was still a child, and though she knew she was capable of shouldering a man's load in the fields, she couldn't leave the children all day to work alongside the boy. Her thoughts skittered here and there like water droplets on a hot griddle. Providing for a family of six was no small matter, and she couldn't rely on Ned forever.

"How could you leave us like this," she muttered, feeling foolish for talking to herself but needing to say the words aloud as if Daniel was there to hear them. "Staying home and being a father takes as much courage, day in and day out, as marching off looking for a fight." She was bone weary, too tired to continue to pretend that her husband was ever coming home.

The summer was dusty and hot and seemed to drag on forever. Rebecca tended the house and the barnyard chores, while Ned, in addition to working his own acreage, shouldered the fieldwork on the parcel that would pay her share of the rent. The children, sunburned and grumpy, chafed at the tedium of constant chores. The days when Rebecca and Martha found an excuse to work side by side offered the only break in the monotony. On one such day, after spending several sweaty hours rendering tallow over an outdoor fire for a new batch of soap, the sisters gathered the children for an afternoon picnic alongside the creek.

"The air is so much cooler down here," Martha said, lifting damp strands of hair off her neck. She scooted over, offering Rebecca a place beside her on the blanket that she'd spread in the shade of a willow tree. Before Rebecca could sit down, James raced past and tapped his mother's arm.

"Tag," he called over his shoulder, hardly breaking stride.

Rebecca handed Susannah to Martha, then lifted her skirts and took off after him. James squealed when he looked back and saw she was gaining on him. Her long legs carried her along the leaf-littered creek bank, her bare feet sending up puffs of dust as James led her on, darting and dodging, moving from sunshine to shadow beneath the low-hanging trees. He ducked around the trunk of a large sycamore and surprised her by reversing course, heading back upstream. As he shot past her, Rebecca reached out to tag him and caught nothing but air. She slowed to a walk and laughed as she lifted her apron to wipe her face.

"You win," she called.

He grinned at her over his shoulder and slowed, jogging past Martha to rejoin the other boys who'd moved further up the creek and were splashing in the shallows. Their laughter carried along the water in joyful bursts.

Rebecca plopped down next to Susannah, who was lying on her tummy, her pudgy hands pulling up fistfuls of grass at the blanket's edge.

"You're pretty fast for an old married lady," Martha said.

"Most days I feel a lot older than twenty-two." Rebecca tilted her head back to watch dust motes dancing in the streaks of sunlight that sifted through the willow's fronds. She breathed in the creek's moist air, reveling in the rich smell of leaf mold and moss. "Let's put blankets out on the hill tonight and look at the stars with the children. We haven't done that since we left Carolina."

Martha raised an eyebrow. "That's because we're wrestling young'uns into bed the moment the sun goes down. Keep them up on purpose? Lord, Becca—think what you're saying." She shook her head in mock disgust, but her smile gave her away.

Rebecca smiled back. She wanted to reach up and stop the sun, to pin it in place on that velvet blue sky so this lovely day would never end.

When harvest time arrived, Jesse and Jonathan went to the fields with Ned. Rebecca's heart ached to see the youngsters struggling to do a man's work, dragging home at twilight so worn out they could barely walk.

One night, Ned and the boys came in from the fields even later than normal. Jesse and Jonathan trudged onto the porch to take turns at the washbasin, while Ned waved and continued down the road as usual.

"I've got supper on the table," Rebecca called to Ned from the porch. "Come join us."

Ned hesitated, a shadow in the gathering dusk. "Thanks, Rebecca." He climbed the porch steps. "I'm about done in. Martha'll have supper waiting, but I'd welcome a drink and a chance to sit a minute."

Inside, Jesse and Jonathan slumped onto their bench and sat in exhausted silence while Ned sank into Daniel's place at the head of the table. Rebecca set two steaming trenchers filled with greens and corn pone in front of the boys. Ned waved a third trencher away, but accepted a mug of cider with a murmured, "Thanks."

The younger children had eaten earlier; they were wrestling and rolling on the floor beside the table and sometimes beneath it. Rebecca shot the little ones a stern look and shooed them away. She sat down next to Ned without speaking, sensing the tired trio had no desire to engage in conversation.

Jesse put his head down on the table and shut his eyes with his trencher still half-full. Jonathan spooned greens into his mouth even as his head drooped.

Rebecca turned her attention to her own meal and was using a piece of pone to sop up the juice from the greens, when she felt Ned's hand on her shoulder. She looked up and was surprised to see his eyes lit with laughter. He nodded toward Jonathan who was now sound asleep, face down in his trencher, a smear of greens across one cheek and crumbs in his hair.

The table vibrated with Ned's silent laughter, and Rebecca began to chuckle. The more they both tried to stay quiet, the harder they both laughed, until they were whooping out loud as the little boys romped around them and the big boys slept on. Each time one of them gained control they caught the other's eye and were off again, laughing until they were red-faced and breathless.

When their laughter was finally spent, she and Ned sat grinning at each other, and she thoughtlessly reached up and rested her hand on his cheek, as she would have with Daniel.

Ned's eyes widened in surprise, and she snatched her hand away as if scalded, standing so abruptly she tipped the bench over with a clatter.

"Jesse—Jonathan," she said, her voice shrill. "Wake up. We've got milking to do."

The boys roused and stretched. She couldn't bring herself to look at Ned. She heard the scrape of a bench, then his footsteps heading toward the door.

"Good night," was all he said as he shut the door behind him.

Rebecca avoided Ned in the weeks that followed, frightened by what she'd read on his face in that unguarded moment, unsure what he might have seen in hers. Whether she was churning or baking or playing with the children, she kept turning that evening over in her mind, trying to make sense of it. Was she mistaking a moment of simple shared intimacy for something deeper? She tried to comfort herself with the thought that such feelings were only natural, seeing that Ned was the image of Daniel. She'd grown comfortable in Ned's presence, and her feelings for him had deepened because of the care and concern he'd shown for her and the children.

Ned had taken time to teach her boys the things a father would: how to bait a hook, the best way to sharpen a scythe, the wisdom of apologizing to their mother when they'd tracked dirt across a newly swept floor. Most of all, if she was honest with herself, what drew her to Ned was that he talked of land and fences and other homelike things. Unlike Daniel, Ned was content to settle down and sink roots.

But how could she let herself have feelings for him? Her sister's husband. Not once in all these months had Martha complained about the time Ned spent helping her and the boys. Likely it had never occurred to Martha to worry, because what sort of woman betrayed her own sister? It was unthinkable, and yet . . .

As a girl, she'd heard a preacher tell the story of the prodigal son, the one who left his responsibilities on his brother's shoulders and went off to live however he chose. Though she was very young when she first heard that story, she still recalled siding with the brother who stayed home and did his duty. Now, no matter how much her mind warned her not to think such things, she couldn't help imagining what her life might have been like if Ned had been the brother who'd first caught her eye.

After dark one evening, when the children had fallen into an exhausted sleep and she sat nodding over her mending, she was startled by a soft tap at the door. She rarely had visitors of any sort, and never this late in the day. She ran a hand through her hair, knowing the once-neat coil had loosened during the day's work and that her apron and shift were stained with grease.

Three figures stood in the gloom of the porch: Martha, with Charity asleep in her arms, Ned, and a stocky, heavily bearded stranger in a worn hunter's shirt. The stranger's beard caught her attention because most men went clean shaven unless they'd been journeying in the wilderness for a length of time. Before her mind had completed the thought, her heart began to pound.

"Becca," Martha said. "This is Mister Bishop. He's just arrived from Carolina."

She froze. In the absence of voices, she heard the rattling sound of the wind blowing through the dried shocks of corn stacked in the barnyard. "I take it you have news of my husband?" She could hear the quaver in her voice.

The man nodded, but before he could speak, Martha stepped forward and put a hand on Rebecca's arm. "Perhaps we should go inside first; the wind's chilly tonight." Her voice was gentle, but firm.

Rebecca had no interest in playing hostess. She wanted to seize the man by the shirtfront and shake the news from him, but instead she led everyone inside, offered them seats, and got down mugs for the men. Her hands trembled so badly she couldn't pull the plug out of the cider keg, and after a couple of futile tugs, Ned stepped in and steered her to a seat, his hand warm on her elbow, before pouring the cider himself.

Bishop took several long swallows, wiped his lips with the back of his hand, and began: "I served with your husband in the militia, ma'am. Didn't know him well, mind you, just enough to match a name to his face." He nodded toward Ned. "When I ran into Mister Boone at the mill today, I thought he was Daniel."

Martha broke in, sensing Rebecca's impatience. "Mister Bishop is headed home to his farm on the Rappahannock. He tells us the militia's disbanded."

Bishop nodded. "The Cherokee signed a treaty at Fort Robinson on the Holston about a month ago." He looked at Rebecca, then added: "Your husband was with us a couple months back, ma'am, acting as a scout as we marched along the headwaters of a river they call the Little Tennessee. We had orders to destroy the Cherokee villages all up and down that river—what folks call the Middle Towns." His eyes grew hard and there was an ugly light in them. "We burned more than a half-dozen villages and shot anything that moved, man, woman or child."

Rebecca felt her stomach lurch at the thought of the militia shooting children. She couldn't imagine Daniel having a child in his sights and pulling the trigger. *Surely he couldn't, he wouldn't have—*

Bishop's voice broke into her thoughts. "Whenever we leveled a town, we set fire to the crops." For the first time, regret crept into his eyes. "That last village had as pretty a stand of corn as I've ever seen; it was hard to put a torch to it . . ." He sat quiet for a moment, then shrugged. "Anything left alive in those mountains will have precious little to eat this winter." He looked squarely at Rebecca. "As for your husband, Miz Boone, all I can tell you for sure is that he marched in with us the day we leveled that first village, and that's the last we saw of him. When the fighting was over, he was gone."

Rebecca felt Martha's eyes on her, and she turned to see a look of motherly concern on her sister's face. It dawned on Rebecca that not only had Martha already heard Mr. Bishop's story, but most likely she'd believed for some time that Daniel was dead, though she hadn't been willing to say so aloud.

Rebecca sat dry-eyed, listening to the pop and snap of the hickory logs in the fireplace. The forest had swallowed her husband, leaving her no last words, no explanations, not even a gravesite to mourn over. She'd cried for Daniel since May, many nights stuffing a corner of the straw tick into her mouth to keep the children from hearing her, but now no tears came.

What she felt instead was a sweeping anger as she thought of the children and how they'd longed for their father these many months, how the older ones would spend the rest of their lives missing him, while the younger ones would be left with no memories of him at all. Daniel had been alive this spring and yet sent no word to them, despite having promised to be home for planting. Whatever his fate had been—killed by an Indian tomahawk or felled by an arrow—he'd apparently turned his back on them months before his final day with the militia.

Rebecca's anger grew hotter until it burned like a live coal buried deep in her chest.

Martha rose from her chair, cradling Charity in one arm, and laid the other across Rebecca's shoulders, drawing her close.

"Ned," Martha said, "pour her some cider. She's in shock, poor lamb."

Rebecca couldn't raise her hand to take the mug Ned held out to her. She was afraid that if she did she'd hurl it across the room. She wanted to smash something, to shake off Martha's arm, turn the table over, break every piece of crockery she owned into tiny pieces. There was no way she could explain that what she was struggling with was not simply grief, but the futility of being furious at a dead man.

She carried on as usual throughout the next day, needing time to absorb the news before she told the children. Daniel had been gone from their lives for more than a year; the few memories Israel possessed of his father would soon fade, while Jesse and Jonathan were already well acquainted with grief, having lost both parents at a young age. Though it would be a hard blow for all of them, it was James she feared for most. He was still plagued by nightmares of Indians; every few months he woke up sobbing, reliving their flight from the Forks.

That night, after she'd nursed Susannah to sleep and laid her in the corner bedstead, Rebecca gathered the boys in front of the fire. Israel climbed into her lap and snuggled close, anticipating a story, while James settled cross-legged by the hearth and leaned his cheek against her skirts, staring into the flames. Jesse stood nearby with the poker, watching the sparks dance upward as Jonathan threw a fresh hickory log onto the coals.

"I have some news about your father," she began.

James looked up at her with joyful eyes. "Daddy's coming home!"

"No, baby, he's not," she said.

James chattered on. "He told me he'd teach me how to make a hickory whistle as soon as he—"

She reached down and placed a hand on James's shoulder. "I'm sure he planned to do that, honey. But in a war, not all the soldiers get to come home. Your father . . ." Her voice broke as a look of slow-dawning horror spread across James's face.

"No!" he shouted. He shook her hand from his shoulder and jumped up, fists clenched. "Daddy's coming back. He's coming back . . ." He pushed past her and darted up the ladder into the loft.

"Let him go," she said to the older boys as Jesse started toward the ladder. After a moment, they began to ask questions, and she told them everything she knew, which was precious little. Mostly she just let the boys talk, letting them air their sorrow and disbelief.

The fire had burned to coals when Jesse finally carried a drowsy Israel up the ladder. Rebecca slipped beneath the quilts in the corner bedstead alongside the sleeping Susannah, but her thoughts continued to swoop and dive like swallows in a twilit sky.

She wasn't surprised when James appeared, shivering, at her bedside in the middle of the night, his nightshirt ghostly in the dark. She lifted the bedcovers, and he slid in beside her. She held him, his hair soft against her throat, as he cried himself to sleep.

5

It was shortly after New Year's Day 1762 when James spotted a distant figure at the edge of the orchard making his way across the icy log that served as a footbridge over the creek. Rebecca and the three oldest boys were taking advantage of a sunny winter's day to restock the woodpile on the front porch, ferrying logs from the stack of hickory and oak that sat curing beneath the eaves of the barn.

"Uncle Ned's coming," James announced as he dropped an armful of logs atop the untidy pile on the porch.

Rebecca straightened from stacking the wood and squinted into the sun, puzzled, since she and Ned continued to avoid each other. Ned still came to help with chores now and then, but he always brought Martha with him. The sight of him walking her way unaccompanied made Rebecca's heart beat faster.

As Ned made his way beneath the bare-limbed apple trees, ducking here and there under low hanging branches, Rebecca kept stacking logs, glancing up every so often to mark his progress. He was still fifty yards away when he called out: "So what's a fellow got to do to get a proper welcome around here?"

Rebecca's hands froze as the voice echoed in her ears. She swung round as James, quicker than she, darted past her down the porch steps. Across the barnyard, Jesse and Jonathan were already pelting downhill.

It wasn't until James reached Daniel and was swept up in a bear hug that Rebecca was sure he was real, and that's when she began to run, too, her feet moving of their own accord. By the time she drew close, he was submerged beneath the boys, a laughing, wriggling pile of arms and legs.

"Mercy, young'uns," Daniel said, his voice muffled. "I didn't come all this way to drown on my own doorstep."

His head emerged, hat askew, eyes sparkling.

Rebecca choked back a sob as she reached for him. "You're home," she said, and then began to cry in earnest. Daniel disentangled himself from the boys and pulled her close. His worn buckskin coat felt icy against her cheek, and he smelled of wind and rain. "We thought you were dead," she said, and he hugged her tighter, rocking her gently as if she were a child.

"Daddy," James said, tugging at his sleeve. "Look how tall I've gotten. I'm as high as your belt."

Daniel continued to hold her, resting his chin on her bowed head as he addressed James. "Looks to me like you've grown near a foot since I saw you last. Or maybe you're the exact same height you've always been, and it's just that your legs have stretched downward."

That sent James into a gale of laughter and made the older boys grin.

Daniel stepped back to look at her. "Boys, I think we need to get your mama up to the cabin. She looks like she's seen a ghost."

She had a thousand questions, but no time to ask them since the boys raced across the orchard and soon returned with Ned, with Martha following close behind, Charity on her hip. The cabin overflowed with greetings and tears and everyone talking at once.

"I'm famished, Becca," Daniel announced. "The thought of a home-cooked meal is all that's kept me upright these last miles."

She and Martha set to work cooking a celebratory meal while Daniel and Ned settled down at the table and were soon deep in conversation, occasionally raising their voices to be heard over the children who chattered and romped around them. Rebecca moved from hearth to table, setting out the mugs and pouring drinks. Once, as she passed by, Daniel caught her hand and gave it a squeeze. It was a gesture they'd shared countless times in the past, but this time, to her surprise, she felt herself tense, as though she'd been touched by a stranger. She ducked her head in confusion, but Daniel continued his conversation with Ned as though he'd sensed nothing out of the ordinary.

Rebecca retreated to the hearth and stirred the soup beans. The long-handled spoon was warm to the touch, and she leaned into the steam. The shock of Daniel's return had begun to wear off, and with it, the unreserved joy she'd felt on first seeing him. What she felt now was confusion, laced with anger. *Where the devil had he been all this time?*

Ned's laughter suddenly filled the cabin, and its warm familiarity made her breath catch in her throat. Though she and Ned had grown cautious around each other these past months, he'd remained her anchor, the person she continued to lean on to help her family scrape by. Only yesterday, she and Ned and Martha had sat at this very table and discussed what should be done about the dwindling supply of meat in her smokehouse. It was odd and disconcerting to realize that when she looked at the two men side by side, it was her husband who felt unfamiliar.

Martha had put a rabbit on to roast, and Rebecca bent to turn the spit while straining to follow the men's conversation.

"I signed up as a scout for the militia," Daniel was saying, "and served the better part of a year, but when our orders shifted from fighting warriors to burning villages, I left. I wanted no part of butchering women and children. Little wonder the Indians hate us. Our troops went through those villages intent on killing anything that moved. I saw them bayonet a woman that . . ."

Ned cleared his throat and tilted his head toward the boys, who'd stopped tussling and were listening intently.

"At any rate," Daniel said, turning to the boys, "the Indians didn't burn the cabins around the Forks. After I left the militia, I went back to check on things and most of the settlement's still there. There's lots of repairs to be done, but we won't be starting from scratch."

The boys cheered, and Rebecca's pulse quickened at this piece of news; she'd long ago convinced herself that their home in Carolina had been reduced to ashes. To hear that it was still standing, and that Daniel was contemplating their return there, was welcome news indeed.

"So you've been to the Forks," Ned said. "Why didn't you send Rebecca word? We were sure you were dead."

Rebecca let go of the spit handle and wiped her hands on her apron as she turned to listen.

Daniel's face was puzzled. "I did send word."

Ned shook his head. "Today's the first we've heard of you in fifteen months."

"But I sent a letter to Becca last spring, and my wages along with it." Daniel scooted his chair back and addressed her directly. "Didn't you get the money? A fellow who'd served out his time and was headed home to Fredericksburg promised to bring it to you and let you know I wouldn't be home as soon as I'd hoped . . ."

Ned snorted. "I expect your money got spent at every tavern this side of the Blue Ridge. Becca didn't get word or money. She and the children have had a devil of a time making ends meet."

Rebecca felt warmed by Ned's words. Even now he was her ally, making sure Daniel knew what his absence had cost her without her having to utter a single word of reproach.

Daniel's eyes sought hers. "Becca, surely you didn't believe I'd leave you and the children unprovided for?"

She cleared her throat. "I assumed you were dead since we hadn't heard from you. Ned and Martha paid our rent. Without them, the children and I wouldn't have a roof over our heads."

Daniel stared into his tankard. When he finally looked up, he was looking at Ned, not her. "I'm much obliged, Ned," he said. "I'll settle up with you as soon as I can."

Ned looked thoughtful. "Seems to me, big brother, Becca's the one you need to settle things with."

Throughout the first evening of Daniel's homecoming, Rebecca did her best to tamp down the resentment that had woven its way into her heart over the past year and a half. She was determined to count her blessings and revel in the children's deep joy at their father's return. Later that night, with the children tucked into bed, her body proved it had a mind of its own, responding to Daniel as if she'd never once harbored a doubt about the rightness of their union. After months of deep loneliness, it was wonderful to be held again, and when she woke the next morning, she felt like a plot of parched ground, nourished at last by life-giving rain.

Yet in the days that followed, she was caught in a web of conflicting emotions: tenderness warred with bitterness; relief was mixed with anger. She kept telling herself there was no need to rehash the past. Daniel hadn't abandoned them; his letter had simply gone astray. Only a shrewish wife would blame her husband for a miscarried letter, and she resolved to look forward rather than back.

Then one morning, not long after Daniel's homecoming, she pushed open the door to the barn, milk pail in hand, and discovered her husband seated on the milking stool with the traps that had hung undisturbed on the barn walls since their arrival in Culpeper scattered in the straw around his feet. He was whistling, rubbing grease into the iron joints, and didn't hear her enter.

"You've no use for those traps around here," she said, "what with this country so settled."

Daniel looked up. "True enough. But I don't intend to use them here." His voice was quiet, but something about the set of his shoulders told her he was as tense as she was, both of them knowing a storm was about to break.

"So where, exactly, do you intend to use them?"

He sighed and let the chain slide to the floor. "Western Carolina—it's practically empty now, what with the Indians pushed over the mountains and most of the whites not back to the settlements yet. There's an abundance of game for the taking, Becca. I've already missed half of the trapping season, but if I hurry, we can still turn a good profit."

His words sparked her pent-up anger.

"You're not leaving us again."

"Becca—"

"No," she said through gritted teeth. "I don't care what you say. I don't care if we have to sell every blessed thing we own to pay this year's rent. You've only been home two weeks; we need you here."

"Even if we scrape together enough to pay rent for this year, how do you expect me to repay Ned for last year? My militia wages are gone."

She stared at him, eyes narrowed. He knew she hated debt, so this was his trump card, but even that wasn't enough to sway her. "We'll think of a way."

"It doesn't make sense for me to sit here the rest of the winter when a good trap line could help get us back on our feet. And when fur season's over, I mean to go back to the Forks and put in a crop so we'll have something ready to harvest when we go home. We have a lot of ground to make up."

She felt her face flush. "You have ground to make up with me and the children." She hated the bitter edge in her voice but was powerless to hide it. "You should have stayed home instead of marching off to play soldier."

Anger sparked in Daniel's eyes, and she was glad to see it. Anything was better than feeling her own insides boil with rage while Daniel sat there, outwardly calm.

"Do you even care that your brother's been more of a father to our children than you have? Doesn't it bother you that Susannah screams whenever you pick her up? You may look like Ned, but you're a stranger to her."

Her words hung in the air between them like a living thing drawing breath for the first time. She saw deep hurt in his eyes, but she was beyond caring. "If you were half the man your brother is—"

Daniel stood abruptly, fists clenched. His stool tipped into the straw with a muffled thump. It flashed through her mind that if she'd been a man, he'd have swung at her. He took a deep shuddering breath and turned silently back to his traps.

That dismissive gesture was more than she could bear. "If you go," she said, "don't bother coming back."

Daniel left the next day despite the boys' pleading faces and Rebecca's sullen silence. They spoke barely a word to each other as Daniel moved around the cabin in the early morning light, gathering his things, filling linen bags with some of the foodstuffs she and the children had worked hard to lay-by for the winter. She clung to her anger as she stood on the porch, her cloak wrapped tight around her, watching him lead two of their horses out of the barn, their pack frames laden with traps. Susannah stood unsteadily beside her, a pudgy hand clinging to her skirts, while the boys circled around Daniel in the barnyard, asking questions and doing their best to help by tucking oilcloth around the frames and tightening the cordage that held it in place.

One by one Daniel hugged the boys goodbye, then paused at the edge of the porch and reached up to hug Susannah, but she backed away and hid her face in her mother's skirts. When he looked up at Rebecca, his eyes were forlorn, but she wasn't about to give him her blessing or offer him words of comfort.

They stayed frozen that way for a long moment, him staring up, her looking down. Finally he pulled his hat low over his eyes, clucked to the horses, and walked away without a word. The breath of both man and beast hung suspended in front of her for the briefest of moments, marking their passage, until all that remained was empty air.

* * *

A month later, in the coldest, darkest part of winter, their milk cow, Ivy, took sick. She was off her feed one morning, and by evening her udder felt hot to the touch. The cow shifted uncomfortably as Rebecca milked her and there were streaks of blood in the pail.

Rebecca had counted on having milk for the children through the winter so that when the shuck beans and other produce they'd preserved ran out, she'd have something to feed them besides cornmeal. Even the Good Book said that man could not live by bread alone. Rebecca had been six or so when she'd heard a preacher intone those words, and they'd stuck in her head because even at that young age, she'd known families who ate little but water-cooked mush all winter long. By spring, their eyes were sunken and their gums were bleeding.

The thought of her own children in that condition set her to scouring her memory for remedies her father used for sick livestock. She had a vague recollection of him treating a cow with such symptoms by milking her every few hours, then massaging her udder with some sort of salve. Rebecca had no earthly idea what the salve contained, but since comfrey was healing for people, she hoped it might work for Ivy.

On the third day of Ivy's illness, the cow stood in her stall, head down, breathing heavily. She was too lethargic to walk down to the creek for water, so Rebecca lugged buckets of water up to the barn. By this time, Rebecca was nearly as exhausted as Ivy. For days she'd been in denial of what her own body was telling her: morning nausea, afternoon lethargy. The signs that another child was on the way were undeniable.

All day, Rebecca moved between the cabin and the barn, checking on the children, tending the cow. At nightfall, she cooked a hurried supper, nursed Susannah to sleep, and tucked the boys into bed, letting them sleep on pallets in front of the fire so they could all snug in together. She leaned across the thick bearskin robe to give each of them a good-night kiss.

"Jesse," she said, tightening her cloak around her, "I expect I'll be at the barn all night again . . ."

The February wind was bitter as she made her way across the barn-yard, a bedroll of blankets slung over her shoulder. The candle's flame in her lantern danced and wavered with every step, reflecting brightly off the frost-covered ground.

She was shivering by the time she pulled the barn door open, but once inside, the warmth of the animals made the small space almost cozy.

Bess, their plow horse, whickered as she walked past; her breath hung in the air like a plume.

For what felt like the thousandth time, she milked Ivy and tossed the pink-tinged liquid out the door, shutting it quickly to block the wind that whipped inside. She rubbed the comfrey balm on Ivy's udder and checked to be sure there was water in her bucket. When she'd made the cow as comfortable as possible, Rebecca wrapped the blankets around herself and settled into the straw at the back of the stall, prepared for a long, watchful night.

She was drowsing in the dark, her candle having guttered out, when she heard the door hinges creak. The warm light of a lantern lit the aisle behind the stalls and stretched long, flickering shadows across the barn wall.

"Rebecca?" Ned's voice floated softly out of the darkness. "I've come to help with Ivy. Martha told me she was ailing." His voice, so unexpected and so full of concern, brought tears to Rebecca's eyes. She ducked her head in an effort to hide them as Ned moved into the stall, preceded by a halo of light.

"Rebecca?" he said again, his voice uncertain.

She still didn't look up, needing a moment to collect herself. Straw rustled underfoot as Ned hung the lantern on a peg. He hesitated, then knelt beside her. His fingers brushed her cheek, gently pushing her hair back from her face. With no hope of hiding her tears, she lifted her head to look at him.

His eyes softened. "You're working yourself to death."

She felt as if she were choking on unshed tears. "What choice do I have?" She looked down at her roughened hands. "When Daniel left, I told him not to come back." She hadn't confessed this to anyone, and when she looked up she expected to see either shock or disapproval on Ned's face. Instead, his gray eyes—Daniel's eyes—looked at her with loving concern.

She began to sob, and Ned gathered her to him. She sank against him like an exhausted child. It felt familiar, like holding her husband— the same broad shoulders under her hands, the same reddish-brown hair glinting in the lantern light. The same, yet not entirely. Ned's shirt held the dusty scent of hay and shelled corn, while Daniel smelled of wind and rain and the hemlock needles he loved to chew. This flashed through her mind in an instant, and made her cry all the harder.

Ned held her as she wept for Daniel, for her orphaned children, for the child yet to come, and for the sorrow she felt at having married a roaming man who hadn't loved her enough to stay home. When she'd cried herself out, she shifted in Ned's arms, the straw rustling beneath them, and began to mumble apologies.

Ned shushed her. "Daniel will come back. You'll see." He gathered her closer and kissed the top of her head. "It will work out, I promise."

Drowsy and exhausted, she relaxed into Ned's embrace and she must have dozed, because the next thing she remembered was a man's voice echoing through the barn like a clap of thunder.

"Good God Almighty," the voice boomed.

She and Ned jerked apart and scrambled to rise, the straw slipping and shifting beneath their feet.

Their landlord, Mr. Slaughter, stood just inside the barn door, lantern held high. The light danced across the log walls, illuminating her rumpled skirts and the straw that clung to her hair and Ned's breeches. A second man, a neighbor named Dryer, peered over Slaughter's shoulder. She watched a sly, knowing look spread slowly across Dryer's face.

Slaughter's nostrils flared. "I'd never have thought this of either of you."

Ned stepped forward: "You've misunderstood, sir."

"I know what I saw," Slaughter snapped. "Dryer and I were headed home from the publick house and saw a light in the barn. We feared Miz Boone might need help." He sniffed. "Clearly you're providing all the assistance she requires."

6

The sun had just broken over the horizon when Rebecca hurried across the orchard and up the hill to Martha's cabin. She'd tended Ivy alone, distracted and sleepless, after Ned followed the men out of the barn, doing his best to convince them they were mistaken. As he left, his eyes never once met hers, as if even looking at her had become an adulterous act.

She found Martha alone in the chicken yard, tossing handfuls of cracked corn to the noisy flock that circled around her. When she saw Rebecca, she shook the chaff out of her apron and crossed her arms over her chest. "Ned tells me there's going to be some ugly gossip."

Rebecca took a deep breath. Martha's face was stone, offering no clue to her thoughts. "What did Ned tell you . . . ?" Rebecca began, but stopped when Martha's eyes flashed a warning.

"That doesn't matter—I want to hear what you have to say."

Rebecca bit her lip. *Where to start?* Last night had been the culmination of months of frustration and unspoken yearning. There was no way to help Martha understand without explaining so many other things. Haltingly, with the hens scratching and clucking around their feet, Rebecca confessed everything: her fractured marriage; the despair that had haunted her since their arrival in Culpeper; the jealousy she harbored at Martha's good fortune in possessing a husband with a settled heart.

Martha stood silent through it all, lips pursed.

"When I broke down last night," Rebecca said, "Ned tried to comfort me. I know it looked bad. I can't blame Slaughter for thinking the worst."

Martha uncrossed her arms. Her eyes searched Rebecca's face. "But in all this time—not just last night—nothing's happened between you and Ned?"

"Nothing," Rebecca replied.

And that was the truth, as far as it went. But what she didn't dare admit to Martha, and could barely admit to herself, was how often she'd wanted something to happen. She'd come close to confessing her desire to Ned in that darkened stall, but something had stopped her. Now, in the light of day, it was clear to her that what had held her back weren't her frayed feelings for Daniel, but her love for her sister.

She reached for Martha's hand. "I was exhausted last night and terrified about the future." She paused, her next confession sticking on her tongue. "You might as well know that when Daniel left, I told him not to come back."

Martha's eyes widened.

"Even if he does return, I'm not sure I'll be able to forgive him for leaving when I begged him not to. To make matters worse, he left me something to remember him by." She rested a hand on her stomach.

Martha reached out to take Rebecca's hand, her expression softening. "Oh, honey. That's the last thing you need."

Word of her supposed indiscretion with Ned raced through the county like water down a mill flume. Though Rebecca had rarely left the farm since her arrival in Culpeper, people who'd never laid eyes on her suddenly had nothing better to do than discuss her marriage and her supposed inability to keep her hands off her sister's husband. In the weeks that followed, when it became apparent that Rebecca was with child, the tongues wagged even harder.

"Has to be Ned's," the gossips said.

A handful of people had seen Daniel during his brief visit home, but their voices were drowned out by those who preferred a tale of betrayal. How fitting, folks said, that Rebecca should pay for her sin by bearing a bastard child.

For much of that spring, Jesse returned home from the grist mill with bruised knuckles and a tear-stained face, doing his best to defend Rebecca's honor among the boys who gathered there weekly to grind their families' corn.

"I keep telling them Uncle Daniel was home this winter, but they don't believe me," Jesse said as Rebecca dabbed at the blood from yet another cut, this one above his eye. "They say awful things about you, Aunt Becca."

She tilted his head back to get a better look. "Ignore them, Jesse. We don't owe them an explanation."

But it was hard to stay silent as the gossip continued unabated. Rebecca watched Martha's face cloud whenever Ned so much as acknowledged her presence. And as the weeks dragged by, and Rebecca's belly grew bigger, she was forced to accept that even Martha couldn't dismiss the rumors entirely. Perhaps more damning than the stories about a single night were the things Martha had observed with her own eyes: that Rebecca was deeply fond of Ned, that she enjoyed his company, and that she depended on him in much the way a wife would.

There was nothing Rebecca could do to set her sister's mind at ease or change the way the community viewed her because no matter how vehemently both she and Ned denied the rumors, they were the only ones who knew, beyond a shadow of a doubt, what had passed between them.

Rebecca endured that spring and summer with no news of Daniel, all the while growing slower and more ungainly. By late summer she'd made up her mind that as soon as the child was born, she'd join her parents in the Shenandoah Valley. If she had to be dependent on others, far better her Bryan kin than Ned and Martha.

The only bright spot during those months was the return of Daniel's parents, along with his sister, Hannah, from Maryland. They settled into Ned's cabin, and Hannah, now sixteen, crossed the orchard daily to help Rebecca with the children. Her cheerful presence was a balm, and Hannah's stories of the time they'd spent with Squire Junior in the city of Georgetown proved a welcome distraction. Their friendship, forged in the years when Rebecca had first entered the Boone family, blossomed now, adult to adult. Hannah listened patiently as Rebecca mourned the end of her marriage and her lost reputation.

"I told Daniel not to come back," Rebecca confessed, "but I'm still not sure if I meant it."

Hannah's dark eyes were gentle. "Seems to me my brother comes and goes as he pleases, Becca; I doubt your words will keep him away if he has a mind to be here. As for all these ugly rumors—I believe you're telling the truth, and Mama believes you." She paused. "Martha wants to believe you—she just needs some time. I think she hopes the rumors will die down if she and Ned keep their distance."

One evening Rebecca sat at the table staring at the supper remains long after the children had excused themselves. She felt heavy and slow and too tired to move. Outside, a blustery autumn wind whistled around the cabin's log walls, but inside it was cozy, with everyone crowded together. Hannah began to clear the table, balancing the heavy trenchers and stepping carefully over and around the children, who played like puppies on the rough plank floor.

"You take that big belly of yours over to the fire and sit down," Hannah said. She gave Rebecca a gentle nudge with her elbow while she balanced the dishes with both hands. "Rest while you can. You'll have plenty of sleepless nights once the baby arrives."

Rebecca gave Hannah a tired smile, hoisted herself off the bench, walked a few steps, then sank heavily into the sturdy maple rocking chair that Ned had crafted for her before the rumors began. Despite their estrangement, sitting in it made her feel comforted and cared for.

The door swung open with a thump, and Ned appeared as if Rebecca's thoughts had summoned him. His arms were loaded with firewood, so Hannah hurried over to shut the door behind him. Ned's visits to Rebecca's cabin were rare, and when he did appear, he barely looked at her and always made sure he was accompanied by Hannah or his mother, Sarah, so there'd be no new occasion for gossip. He cast a quick glance in Rebecca's direction, then busied himself stacking the wood alongside the hearth.

The floor creaked as Rebecca rocked back and forth, listening to the welcome hum of adult voices and the rustle of Hannah's cornhusk scrub brush scouring the dinner dishes. She picked up her knitting and shifted in the rocker so the firelight fell across her lap. With winter edging closer, the sight of the children's bare feet had goaded her into spending most of her evenings knitting a supply of woolen stockings. Every so often, when a particularly strong gust of wind swirled down the chimney, a loose shutter slammed against the wall outside with a thud, and she made a mental note to ask Jesse or Jonathan to fix it in the morning. Once her labor started, it would be maddening to listen to that muffled thumping, hour after hour.

The boys trooped in, having taken turns at the washbasin on the porch. They called their goodnights as they climbed the ladder into the loft. Israel, now three, had to stand on tiptoe to reach the first step; his toes curved around the rungs as he climbed.

"Bedtime for you, too, little miss," Hannah said, scooping Susannah off the floor and carrying her to the corner bedstead. It was rare for Susannah to go to bed willingly, but on this night she snuggled into the bedclothes and was soon breathing deeply, her auburn hair trailing across the blankets. Susannah's delicate features were angelic in repose, but of all Rebecca's children, she was the least biddable. Hardly a day went by without Susannah butting heads with her mother or one of her siblings. Rebecca prayed that the child she carried now possessed a more accommodating nature; she felt sure a second Susannah would be more than one family could handle.

Hannah finished rinsing the trenchers, then hefted the wash bucket on her hip and stepped outside to toss the dirty water off the porch as Ned added a log to the fire, sending up a shower of sparks.

A muffled cry came from the porch and Rebecca started up from her chair, leaving it rocking drunkenly. Ned, poker in hand, had almost reached the door when it swung open and Hannah hurried inside, eyes wide. A man stepped through the doorway behind her, his shadow looming large across the wall.

"Daniel," Rebecca breathed. Her heart jumped, then began to race.

He smiled and was about to speak when his gaze dropped to her belly and his face froze. After a long moment, he said: "For the last twenty miles folks have been eager to tell me how well Ned's taken care of you . . ." The words were threaded with ice.

Dark patches swirled across Rebecca's vision and she swayed, suddenly lightheaded. She felt herself stagger and heard both men shout her name. The last thing she remembered, before the blackness engulfed her, was the feel of strong arms around her.

She came to, groggy and disoriented, amid the sound of angry voices. She clung to the darkness, unwilling to open her eyes as words that she couldn't quite make out swirled around her. She sensed she was in the corner bedstead with Susannah asleep beside her; she could feel her daughter's warm breath against her cheek.

"Quiet!"

Her mother-in-law's voice, sharp as a knife, sliced through the room and penetrated the fog in Rebecca's brain. The silence was immediate. She struggled to open her eyes, but when she did, the rafters overhead spun dizzily and she quickly shut them again. Clearly Sarah had been summoned and had taken charge. A log popped on the hearth, and the wind whistled through a gap in the chinking above the bed.

"Sit down, Daniel." It was Sarah's voice again. Rebecca felt the older woman's hand on her forehead. "Her breathing's normal. I expect she'll come around soon." Sarah's voice grew less distinct as she turned away from the bed. "Daniel—as glad as I am to see thee, I could happily take a belt to thee the way thy father used to. How dare thee accuse thy wife and brother of such a thing—and with Becca in her condition."

"Her condition," Daniel said bitterly. "I first heard rumors of her condition days down the trail, but I laughed it off. Then I met Dick Dryer on the road this evening, and he relished telling me how he'd seen Becca and Ned rolling in the straw together and that everyone knew she was carrying his child."

"It's a lie," Rebecca cried, struggling to sit up. The room spun into view—Sarah standing alongside the bed, Daniel seated at the table, face anguished. Ned stood nearby, fists clenched. "The baby's yours," Rebecca said, focusing on Daniel. "Ned and I never . . ."

Daniel stood abruptly, eyes furious. "And yet, when I arrive home you're together, and you're at least eight months gone . . ."

"That's enough," Sarah hissed. She laid a gentle hand on Rebecca's shoulder and eased her back on the bed, tucking a pillow beneath her head. Rebecca could hear Hannah crying in the shadows, and she felt her own eyes filling with tears so that the rafters overhead grew blurry.

"Give thy wife a chance to speak before accusing her," Sarah said, turning back to Daniel, "and thy brother an opportunity to explain before judging him. There's blame enough to go around, but I expect thee to put thy anger aside and do what's best for the child, whatever thou chooses to believe. As for thee and thy brother, if thou insist on bristling at each other like tom turkeys, take it outside and settle it out of thy wife's hearing. She's been through enough for one night."

Rebecca's hands moved to her belly as the baby shifted, poking her under the ribs with a foot or a fist. Despite the forceful movements within her and the voices that surrounded her, she'd never in her life felt more alone.

7

In the days that followed, they barely spoke to each other. Daniel slept each night on a bedroll in front of the fire, avoiding the corner bedstead even when the autumn winds grew blustery and the temperature dropped. He'd intended to pack up the family as soon as he arrived and head back to the Forks.

"There's a wagonload of work to do in Carolina and precious few weeks before winter sets in." He gestured at Rebecca's belly. "I hadn't counted on this sort of delay."

"I didn't get this way by myself."

"So I hear," he said.

Anger exploded in her chest, but she managed to keep her voice low. "If you'd been home for more than a heartbeat those whispers would never have started."

"Sometimes whispers are true," he said.

They quit speaking entirely after that.

In the final weeks of her pregnancy, Rebecca clung to her anger like a shield. *How dare you,* she thought. *How dare you blame me.* Her fury made her estrangement from Daniel bearable; what she found harder to bear was the growing divide between herself and Martha. Daniel's return had unleashed a new round of gossip, and Rebecca watched helplessly as Martha wilted under the weight of half-truths and lies.

One dreary gray morning in November, Rebecca bent over the fire to hoist one of the heavy cook pots off the coals and felt a familiar tightening in her belly. She kept working, but sent Jesse across the orchard to warn Martha that she'd be needed before the end of the day.

By late afternoon, she sent Jesse again, this time to tell Martha to come right away. She made her way to the corner bedstead and lay down, breathing deeply into the pain. When she finally heard footsteps on the porch, it was Sarah who appeared, throwing off her cloak as she hurried to the bedside.

"Martha wouldn't come?" Rebecca asked, searching her mother-in-law's face.

Sarah rested a cool hand on Rebecca's sweaty cheek, her eyes kind. "Hush now," she said. "Save thy strength."

Sarah placed the newborn, with her downy head of dark hair, in Daniel's arms. Weeks earlier, Rebecca had chosen the name, Jemima, if they had a girl, and Daniel hadn't objected. She watched him now as he held the baby up in the firelight and studied her face, as if he hoped to read the truth in her tiny features. After a few minutes, he laid the baby in the cradle and walked out without a word.

Within days, Rebecca marshaled the energy to begin packing up the household. Since all the Boones were making preparations to return to the Forks, Rebecca held out hope that she and Martha could work together, sorting through items and deciding what needed to be packed and what could be left behind, but Martha continued to keep her distance.

Daniel frowned when Rebecca directed Jonathan to carry her maple rocker out to the porch and set it amid the things to be packed.

"It's unwieldy," he said.

"It's going. Ned made it for me." She knew she was goading him, but she didn't care.

Daniel shot her a sour look, but on the day of their departure, the rocker was carefully nested among several bags of meal on Ivy's pack frame. Rebecca rode one of the packhorses, Jemima in her arms, while the two youngest children, Susannah and Israel, rode as well, nestled into panniers padded with bedding and other supplies.

Rebecca found the long hours on the trail even more tedious than usual with Ned avoiding her entirely and Martha having little to say, even when they were forced to work alongside each other. Though Sarah and Hannah did their best to be kind, they clearly didn't want to take sides, so they, too, were subdued in her presence.

She had no desire to talk to Daniel, but even if she'd been willing, there was little opportunity because he was usually surrounded by a half-dozen young adventurers from Culpeper who'd heard him praise the land around the Forks and wanted to see it for themselves. Clearly the men had heard other things as well. More than once she was subjected to sideways glances and whispered conversations that were cut short when she came within hearing distance. Daniel spent most of his time in the midst of the men, relaxed and smiling as he swapped stories and jokes, but if he happened to spot her watching him, his smile faded, and his face grew guarded.

Among the traveling party was a fair-haired eighteen-year-old named John Stewart. After several nights on the trail, Rebecca heard Daniel invite Stewart and the other young men to share their family's fire and enjoy a "woman-cooked meal," having seen the skimpy fare the bachelors subsisted on.

After milking Ivy, Hannah moved among the men with her bucket, offering them a drink. Several of the men looked her up and down and winked as she passed by, but Rebecca noticed that John watched Hannah's slow progress around the circle in respectful silence. By the time Hannah stopped in front of him, she was flustered, having sensed the stir she was causing. When she tilted the heavy wooden bucket to pour John some milk, she missed his cup and soaked his shirtfront.

"I'm so sorry, sir," she stammered.

Even in the dim light of the fire, Rebecca could see that Hannah was blushing; it made her seem even younger than her sixteen years.

John met her apology with a smile so wondrously sweet it stopped Rebecca in her tracks; she could only imagine the effect it had on Hannah. If Hannah had dumped the entire bucket of milk over that man's head Rebecca bet he'd have come up smiling.

For the rest of the journey, Rebecca watched John and Hannah stare longingly at each other across the flames each night. Long ago, she and Daniel had looked at each other that same way, but as far as Rebecca could tell, those feelings were dead in both of them.

Rebecca stood on the cabin porch with Jemima asleep in her arms and looked across the clearing toward Sugartree Creek. She'd yearned for this place every day since their abrupt departure almost three years ago, and though it was a relief to be back at the Forks, it was a shock to see how much their homestead had changed.

The yard was overgrown. Waist-high broom sedge covered the paths that led to the barn and the springhouse, while Virginia creeper laced the porch railings, spilling across the porch in a cascade of frost-bitten green. Rebecca settled Jemima in the crook of one arm and used her free hand to yank some of the vines away. She tossed them off the porch and wiped her hand on her apron. Clearing off the vines would be a good job to give four-year-old Israel; Susannah, not yet three, would insist on helping him, which would keep the pair blessedly busy and out of mischief for at least a bit.

Daniel and the children had disappeared with the animals through the waist-high grass and into the log barn. Their voices drifted up to her, and she hoped their excited chatter meant they'd discovered the barn loft still held some hay, or by some miracle, that the heavy wooden grain bin hadn't been emptied, either by Indians, backwoods travelers, or rats, who, given enough time, could chew through even the thickest wood.

Everywhere she looked, nature had done its best to reclaim their homestead. There were several abandoned wren nests in the eaves of the porch, and from somewhere in the surrounding trees, she could hear the scolding of a mockingbird and the sweet trilling notes of a song sparrow. The birds would have to learn to share this space with humans again.

Sections of the spilt-rail fence that had once surrounded the garden plot had been knocked down. The hardiest garden plants had come up as volunteers, spreading far beyond their once-neat rows. The pumpkin vines that rambled everywhere were now brown and shriveled, victims of a November frost. As best she could tell from the porch, very few of the pumpkins were salvageable, having rotted or been broken open by foraging animals.

She was anxious to wade into the weeds along the fencerow, hoping to see the withered remains that would tell her her grandmother's flowers had continued to come up. But before she did anything else, she needed to face what years of absence had done to their cabin.

Rebecca took a deep breath and pulled the latchstring. The door creaked open, and when she stepped over the threshold, there was a skittering sound beneath the cabin's puncheon floor. *Mice,* she thought, *or maybe a possum. God forbid, a skunk.* As she surveyed the room, her heart sank. It was nearly empty except for their sturdy plank table, several benches, and the bed frame in the corner. For nearly three years, anyone who'd lifted the latchstring had been free to carry away whatever their conscience would bear: the iron poker by the fire, the smooth-handled churn that had stood in the corner by her worktable, the heavy pewter serving platter she'd proudly displayed on the mantel. *Nearly everything's gone. We're starting over.*

James and Israel burst through the open door and ran past her, Susannah following a little ways behind like the tail of a kite. The children's bare feet raised a cloud of dust that hung above the plank floor. Rebecca's nose wrinkled, and she stifled a sneeze. *Dust everywhere.*

The boys scurried up the ladder into the loft, but Susannah stopped at the bottom, momentarily unsure. Then, with a look of dogged determination, she grasped the first rung and began to climb.

Rebecca stepped to the side of the ladder, Jemima still asleep in her arms. "Susannah—wait until Jesse or Jonathan get here so they can go up the ladder with you."

Susannah cast a stormy glance over her shoulder and continued upward. She had to stretch her arms as high as she could just to reach the next rung.

James's voice floated down from above. "There's a squirrel's nest in the corner!"

"And a pile of hickory nuts!" Israel shouted.

Rebecca held her breath as Susannah pulled herself up to the top rung, then crawled safely into the loft.

"Watch your sister," Rebecca called up to the boys.

She turned back to the table, ignoring the scuffling above her head. The dust was thick on the tabletop, and she traced a wobbly "R" on the worn surface with her finger. Once, she'd known how to shape a half-dozen letters, but even though she could still see those letters in her mind, she could no longer get her fingers to make the proper movements. She tried to remember what letter came next in her name, but before she could conjure the shape, Jemima woke up and nuzzled her breast. Blowing the dust off one of the benches, she sat down and pulled Jemima close.

That night around the fire, the worst of the dust having been swept out the door, Rebecca set the boys to work carving a new supply of wooden tableware: spoons, trenchers, and noggins.

"Like this," Jonathan said, showing five-year-old James how to angle his knife to shave thin pieces off a slab of buckeye destined to be Rebecca's new dough bowl. James sat beside the older boys, chewing his lip in concentration as he struggled to copy their movements.

Israel and Susannah scooped up the colorful shavings of poplar and buckeye that dropped from the boys' knives and draped the curling pieces across their shoulders, giggling and daring each other to blow them off.

Daniel sat to one side, his hands lit by the flames, his face in the shadows, cutting cloth patches to store in the patch box on the butt of his rifle. Whenever he bent toward the fire and the light played across his face, his expression was always the same, calm but distant. Rebecca had no idea what he was thinking.

A week after their arrival home, Daniel and the boys clattered up the porch steps after a day of hunting. They were in high spirits, excited about having shot a black bear that hadn't yet denned. They'd dressed their kill in the field—skinning off the pelt and cutting up the choice pieces of meat—then loaded it onto the packhorse and brought it home. It took all three boys—Jesse, Jonathan, and James—to carry the heavy pelt up the steps and dump it inside the cabin door.

Rebecca wrinkled her nose. A fresh pelt was never a pretty sight—bloody and grease-stained, with shards of fat clinging thickly to the underside—but worst of all was the smell. This one reeked of blood, bear dung, and whatever else that old bear had wallowed in during its final days. She prided herself on keeping a fresh smelling cabin; when the air became heavy with odors, she'd bring a pot of water to boil and dump in a bundle of sweet herbs to mask the greasy smell of tallow candles, dirty laundry, and the odor of muddy wet moccasins drying on the hearth. One whiff of that bear pelt was more than enough.

"Boys, take that smelly old thing to the barn."

They looked at her in surprise, but turned to obey.

Daniel stepped through the door. "Leave it, boys. We need to do more fleshing on it."

Rebecca faced Daniel, hands on her hips. "You can work on it tomorrow, somewhere outside. Tonight, it goes to the barn."

"I've always cleaned pelts in front of the fire."

"Yes, you have, and I've never liked it—I just bit my tongue and put up with it. Now, I won't."

"But we've always done it this way."

"And now we're not," she said, turning her back to him to stir the corn mush. "The sooner you get that thing to the barn, the sooner we'll eat."

She stood, eyes on the bubbling pot, listening for his response. After a long moment, she heard the sound of retreating footsteps and a thump as the door closed behind them.

Each day Rebecca expected Daniel to pack up his traps and head out for his winter of trapping. Normally he departed sometime in October, so he was already much later than usual. Only gradually did it occur to her that he was remaining at home to court the children, slowly repairing the rifts his long absence had created. Daniel and the older boys worked side by side in the woodlot nearly every day, cutting firewood for the winter. Their voices carried across the barnyard, punctuated by occasional laughter. When they all sat around the fire at night, Daniel rarely addressed Rebecca, but he engaged the boys in discussions on everything from foxhounds to hunting knives to seed corn.

Among the children, only Susannah resisted Daniel's overtures. He'd been absent during her first two years, and though she tolerated his presence, she fussed and pushed him away whenever he tried to pick her up. Children were normally drawn to him, but Susannah resolutely resisted his overtures, and it was clear her rejection stung. One day Daniel arrived home with a kitten tucked in the folds of his hunting shirt, which made the child dance with excitement, but even that hadn't won her affection.

One night, Rebecca came into the cabin after her evening chores and found Daniel down on his knees on the plank floor, the boys clustered around him. A stormy-faced Susannah watched from the corner bedstead.

"Shoot it like this," Daniel said.

Rebecca stepped closer to see over the boys' shoulders. They each were armed with a clay marble and were aiming at a cluster of marbles.

James's blonde hair shone in the firelight as he turned his face upward to look at her. He held up a marble. "Want to try, Mama?"

"No thank you, sweetheart. This is your chance to practice with your father."

"Susannah kept picking up the marbles," Israel reported, "so Daddy says she has to stay on the bed till they're all put away."

Rebecca collected the pouting Susannah from the bed and retreated to the rocker where the child could view the game at a safe distance. A quick glance told her Jemima was asleep in the cradle.

Suzy squirmed, pushing hard against her mother with arms and feet. "Sorry, little one," Rebecca said, holding tight and nuzzling her daughter's auburn curls. "You'll have to settle for watching."

The room was warm with so many bodies crowded together, and the marbles bumped loudly across the puncheon floor. Caught up in the game, Daniel's face was relaxed and smiling in the shifting firelight, and Rebecca took the opportunity to study him. He looked almost boyish, and to her surprise, she felt the icy indifference that had encased her heart for months melt ever so slightly.

Rebecca stood alongside Sugartree Creek and listened to the chatter of the water as it ran across the rocks. Though the sound was soothing, it was a poor substitute for the companionship of working alongside other women. Sarah, Hannah, and Martha had returned to the Boone homestead ten miles southward, where Rebecca envisioned them sharing stories and laughter as they tended their chores.

She comforted herself with the thought that any day her parents would return to their farm in the Bryan settlement, little more than a mile away, but for now, their cabin remained shuttered. She had no one but the children to talk to, which made the continued silence between Daniel and herself harder and harder to bear.

In the three months since they'd been reunited, he hadn't once reached for her. It was understandable at first, what with her just out of childbed, but as the weeks went by, she'd expected he'd insist that they share a bed for something other than sleeping.

At first, she'd counted his inattention a blessing, but the longer it continued, the more it unsettled her. How could he wrap himself up in his blanket night after night and act as if she wasn't there? At random times when she least expected it—scouring crocks or pitching soiled straw out of the cow stall—she imagined Daniel's hands on her body or his face buried in her hair. Sometimes these thoughts invaded her dreams, and she'd wake, sweaty and disoriented. At other times she woke from even more disturbing dreams of Ned.

By daylight, she shook all such images of both men from her mind. She reminded herself what a fool she'd be to seek out her husband's attentions since sooner or later he'd disappear into the wilderness and she'd likely be left with little more than an extra mouth to feed. Culpeper had taught her the dangers of being dependent on anyone. It wouldn't happen again.

8

While she cooked and scrubbed and did her usual chores, Rebecca made mental notes of the skills she needed to master before Daniel lit out for the woods again. She didn't want to simply survive when he was absent; she intended to thrive.

The family's most pressing need would be a supply of fresh meat. She'd known how to load and fire a gun from the time she was a youngster, but that was a far cry from bringing down a deer and keeping the family in meat over the winter. Her first challenge was acquiring a gun of her own since Daniel's rifle was his constant companion and the family's only other rifle was shared among the boys, who took turns accompanying their father on short hunts so he could teach them the ways of the woods.

She recalled that, years ago, her father had buried a few supplies beneath the floor of their smokehouse in the event of a house fire or other disaster. She prayed the cache was still there. Even if there wasn't a firearm, there might be something of value she could trade for one.

Rebecca thrust her shovel into the dusty soil of her parents' smokehouse, and the scent of hickory smoke and salt wafted into the empty rafters. Her mouth watered at the rich smell, which was all that remained of the dozens of hams that had hung there. Such abundance seemed part of another life. Her parents' cabin sat shuttered and forlorn nearby, with weeds grown stalky and tall around the rock foundation.

Her shovel clinked against something hard, and she felt a surge of hope. Laying the shovel aside, she used her hands to scrape the dirt away from a package wrapped tightly in oilcloth. Several hard tugs freed the heavy bundle from the soil. She knelt to unwrap it, and when a gun barrel appeared, she breathed a silent thank-you.

Triumph turned to dismay as the metal barrel rolled out of the cloth, unattached to the other metal pieces that clattered against each other. She spread them out on the oilcloth and studied them. Though the parts were old and worn, they looked serviceable. Mixed in among the rifle parts were leather pouches of seeds, a powder horn, a supply of rifle balls, an ax-head, and a small bag of coins.

As she hefted the barrel, smooth and cold beneath her fingers, she dismissed the thought of asking Daniel for help putting the gun back together. Now that the militia had forced the Indians to the other side of the Blue Ridge, folks were trickling back to the settlement, and she'd heard Daniel mention the return of a man named Russell who was putting his smithy in order. She felt sure he could assemble the rifle, and thanks to her father's foresight, she had the means to pay him. Slipping the bag of coins into her skirt pocket, she rewrapped the oilcloth, collected her shovel, and headed southward.

The deep ring of a hammer on iron greeted her as she stepped out of the woods at the Russell home site. Like most of the farms around the Forks, the cabin spoke of years of neglect. Weeds grew up through the porch planks, and ironweed, dry and stalky this time of year, had taken over the garden plot. A thin plume of smoke above the smithy was the only sign of life.

She balanced the heavy bundle in one arm and used the shovel to push through the waist-high weeds. "Hello," she called loudly.

The metallic pounding faltered, then stopped. Russell's broad, bearded face poked out of the smithy doorway.

"Why, welcome, Miz Boone," he said, wiping his hands on his leather apron as he stepped outside. "What brings you here?"

"I'm in need of help assembling a gun." She laid the oilcloth on the grass outside the smithy and unwrapped its contents. The metal parts gleamed blue-black in the sunshine.

Russell squatted to examine the parts, sorting through them, occasionally picking one up to examine it. "Putting this together will take some time." He paused. "But all the metal parts are here, and I have an old gunstock that should work, though it isn't much to look at."

"I don't care what it looks like as long as it shoots."

He straightened up to face her. "I'm sure your husband could put this in working order."

"My husband's busy elsewhere. What will it cost to have you do it?"

Russell ran a hand through his beard. "Well," he said slowly. "I reckon we could work out a trade." He paused and cleared his throat. "My family's still in Virginia, and . . . well, a fella gets lonely." His eyes dropped to her bodice.

Before the words were out of his mouth, she'd taken a step back, tightened her grip on the shovel and raised it, ready to swing. "How dare you," she hissed. Her heart pounded so hard she was sure he could hear it.

"Now, now," he said, "no need for that. I'm not a man who'd force a woman. It's just that from what I'd been told, I didn't think force would be necessary."

"You've heard wrong, sir." Her voice sounded steely, but her insides felt weak as water. "I'll send Jesse to collect the rifle in two weeks." She tossed three coins at his feet, unwilling to step close enough to hand them to him. "This should be sufficient to pay you for your trouble."

Russell flushed. "I meant no disrespect, Miz Boone. But I'd heard . . ."

He stuttered to a halt as she turned on her heel, still clutching the shovel. She forced herself to walk, straight-backed and proud, feeling his eyes on her as she crossed the clearing. With each step she thought: *I will not cry. I will not cry.*

She walked out of the sunlit clearing and followed the narrow path into the cool shelter of the surrounding woods. When the clanging sound of the smithy had grown faint, she sank down beside a moss-covered log and buried her head in her hands. She winced as her palm brushed against her mouth, tasted blood, and realized she'd bitten her lip. She stared at the rust-colored smear on her palm, then clenched her hand into a fist and brought it down hard on the log—once, twice, then over and over, as if each blow could beat down the ugly things people were saying about her.

They're wrong about me, she thought with each blow. *They're wrong.*

When her hand began to throb, she swiveled around and rested her back against the log. The woods were silent except for a lone blue jay flitting through the treetops, fussing as it hopped from branch to branch. Normally she welcomed the company of birds, but today the jay's raspy calls seemed to mock her: *I'll say what I want. I'll say what I want—you can't stop me.*

Rebecca pushed herself to her feet, then bent to pick up the shovel. The jay was right. She was helpless to silence him and just as helpless to squelch the rumors that had followed her here from Virginia.

They'll say what they want, she thought. *I can't stop them.*

In the weeks that followed, she quietly observed Daniel as he moved from chore to chore: molding bullets, cleaning his flintlock, sharpening his axe. She'd seen the men in her life do these things countless times, but now she watched with an eye toward storing away the finer points. Exactly how did you hold an axe against the whetstone to get the sharpest edge? How much lead should you melt at one time when making bullets?

She'd sent Jesse to collect the rifle from Russell, and when the boy placed it in her hands, she felt her shoulders relax for the first time in weeks. The stock was battered, and the lock plate was chipped and scarred, but to her it was beautiful. She made no effort to hide the gun, propping it up by the hearth where Daniel spotted it immediately.

"Where'd that come from?" he said.

"It's mine—from my parents' cabin." She didn't mention the bag of coins or the supply of rifle balls that now lay secreted at the bottom of her sewing basket.

"It isn't much to look at," he said, hoisting the rifle to his shoulder and sighting down the barrel.

"It'll do."

Daniel studied her face. "I reckon it's a good idea for you to have a rifle here at home when the boys and I are out hunting. You never know what sort of varmints might be lurking about."

She nodded and bent her head to her sewing.

One cold morning Daniel set the boys to work around the barnyard, then gathered supplies for a day of hunting. Rebecca watched him disappear into the forest alone, headed west. She hurriedly finished the breakfast dishes, nursed Jemima until she was drowsy, and left Jesse in charge of the children. Taking her rifle and shot pouch down from their pegs, she headed east.

A half-mile away from the cabin, she stopped in a large clearing with a broad oak tree at the edge of the woods. Pacing off thirty yards, she turned, loaded and primed the rifle. Over the past weeks, she'd managed to slip away to practice only once, using a knot on the trunk of the giant tree as her target.

The sound of the gun echoed against the ridge and sent a flock of crows wheeling into the sky, cawing raucously. When she walked up to the tree, she was disappointed to see she hadn't come close to the spot she'd been aiming for. She'd chosen a broad target on purpose so she could dig the bullets out of the wood and recast them. Lead was hard to come by; she couldn't afford to waste it.

After a dozen shots, she'd managed to hit the target only twice and her shot pouch was nearly empty. She steadied the rifle for a final try. As she sighted down the barrel, she sensed someone behind her and jerked around but was stopped by a strong hand clamping the rifle barrel tightly. Her heart leapt into her throat.

"Careful with that thing."

She relaxed only slightly when she recognized Daniel's voice. He was standing so close his breath was on her cheek.

"How long have you been watching me?"

"Long enough to know the only safe place to be when you're shooting that thing is behind you."

There was enough truth in what he said that her temper flared. "You could have hallooed and let me know you were here instead of sneaking up on me. It'd served you right if I *had* shot you."

She struggled to back up, but his hand tightened on the gun. She thought he would answer her with angry words of his own, but instead he stepped closer, using the rifle like a lever to force her around until her back was to him and she was once again facing the target.

"You're missing high and to the left," he said. "Every gun's different. You have to adjust."

As he spoke, he guided her hand, helping her raise the rifle to her shoulder. His chest was pressed against her back; she was shocked at the heat he radiated.

"Lean into the stock—like this." His hair brushed her cheek as he tilted his head, showing her how to sight along the barrel. He smelled of gunpowder, wood smoke, and the tangy scent of hemlock needles. The combination of odors was so uniquely Daniel she was suddenly awash in memories: the warmth of his lips on a cold winter night, the summer afternoon they'd stood in the shallows of Sugartree Creek, laughing as they'd flung water at each other.

She stepped away from him, letting go of the rifle entirely. The barrel dipped sharply downward, almost touching the frost-covered grass. As he struggled to steady it, she swung around to face him.

"You—were—gone," she yelled, hammering her fists against his chest with each word. She took a shuddering breath, tasted salt on her lips, and realized she was crying. "I waited for you—I waited and there was no word. Nothing happened between Ned and me . . ." She ground to a halt.

He stared at her, eyes unyielding as granite.

She stumbled on then, trying to find words to make him understand. "That night in the barn—I felt so alone—Ned tried to comfort me. But Jemima's yours—she's yours, and no one believes me." By now she was sobbing.

The cold wariness in his eyes had given way to a thoughtful look, as if he were replaying her words in his mind, trying to see what he could fashion from them. She stood looking at him through her tears, breathing heavily, shivering in the frigid air.

"Here," he said, pulling a flask from inside his hunting shirt and holding it out to her.

She pulled the stopper, and the sharp odor of whiskey swam in her head. She took a sip and savored its burning descent down her throat.

"Let's get out of the wind," he said, steering her toward a large outcropping of rock near the forest's edge.

She sat down on a hollowed shelf of stone and gathered her wool cloak around her, sniffing quietly and trying to compose herself. Daniel sat down beside her, facing outward, so that they looked toward the meadow rather than each other.

He took a sip from the flask and handed it back to her.

"Did I ever tell you the story," he said slowly, "of the chestnut mare I had as a boy?"

She shook her head, puzzled.

"I got her cheap from a farmer who told me she couldn't be broken. I was about fourteen at the time."

She took another sip of whiskey and felt the tension ebb from her shoulders. Daniel's voice was soothing; she'd forgotten how much she loved to hear him talk like this, the gentle rise and fall of his voice as he told her a story or read to her by firelight.

"At first this mare was so skittish she wouldn't let me anywhere near her, but every day I went to the pasture and sat, just watching her. Each day she came a bit nearer, began to trust me a little more. Somehow I sensed the only way things would ever work between us was if I waited until she was ready to accept me. I learned a lot about patience that summer."

Her skin began to tingle all up and down her body. She looked squarely at him: "Are you saying I'm like that mare?"

He considered a moment, then shook his head. "Now if it had been a mule . . ."

As they sat on the rock, laughing together, she felt a spark of hope. "So all these months you've been ignoring me, partly because you were angry, but mostly because you were waiting to see how I felt about you?"

He nodded. "I thought you needed time to decide what you want."

"What I want," she said firmly, "is to not be an afterthought in your life. But most of all . . ." She leaned forward as if to kiss him and felt a glint of triumph at the surprised look on his face when she didn't, reaching past him instead to grasp the rifle that leaned against the rock. "Most of all," she said, looking directly into his eyes, "I want you to teach me how to shoot this blasted rifle!"

That night, after she nursed Jemima to sleep, she laid her in the cradle at the foot of the bed and slipped under the blankets where Daniel was waiting. They lay face to face for a moment, just looking, and when he finally reached for her, he was what she wanted.

PART TWO

Rebecca
Susannah
Jemima

"It was on the first day of May, in the year 1769, that I resigned my domestic happiness for a time, and left my family and peaceable habitation on the Yadkin River in North Carolina, to wander through the wilderness of America in quest of the country of Kentucke in company with John Finley . . ."
—Daniel Boone, as told to John Filson in
The Adventures of Colonel Daniel Boone

"She is by nature a quiet soul, and of few words. . . . She told me of her trouble, and of the frequent distress and fear in her heart."
—Journal entry by Moravian missionary
during his visit to the Boone cabin in 1771

9

Rebecca
(1769)

Rebecca wasn't sure if it was God or the devil that brought John Finley to their cabin door. A long hunter and adventurer, Finley was the first person who uttered the word "Kentucky" to Daniel.

She'd been happy in the half-dozen years before Finley appeared because she and Daniel had reached an understanding. He'd agreed to keep her and the children, who now numbered six, provided for by being a diligent farmer each spring and summer. For her part, she'd accepted his need to roam and trap on the far side of the mountains during the winter months. She'd even agreed to leave the Forks and move westward to the headwaters of the Yadkin River on the mountains' eastern slopes so Daniel could be closer to fresh hunting grounds. Although she missed her parents and siblings, she'd also hoped the change of location would distance them from the rumors that had continued to circulate whenever folks gathered at the Forks.

"I'll move west," she'd told Daniel, "on three conditions."

He'd looked at her quizzically.

"First of all, I pick the house site; I want the sound of a free-running creek nearby and a pretty view to rest my eyes on when I'm sitting on the porch."

He nodded.

"Secondly, I won't move unless Hannah and John come, too. Being newlyweds, they'll need to find land of their own, and I need another woman for company."

"I'll talk to them," he said. "And the third thing?"

"No more wandering off into the wilderness for long hunts alone. I'm sure John will be glad to accompany you, or maybe Squire will take time out from his smithy at the Forks to hunt with you. I need you to promise me you'll take two or three other men with you on your long hunts."

He frowned. "I can take care of myself in the woods."

"Maybe so, but I want someone who can bring me word if something happens. Not knowing just about killed me in Culpeper."

After their move to the western edge of Carolina, she'd taken charge of the farm and the children with a newfound confidence. She was no longer overwhelmed by Daniel's winter absences the way she'd once been. She'd become a pretty good shot, and she could handle an axe as well as most men. It helped a great deal that during the months he was home, Daniel took his farm work seriously, focusing on it with a vigor he'd never shown in the past. It had proven a workable arrangement.

But Finley's arrival changed everything.

Jemima was the first one to see the stranger riding along the trace, headed toward the ford on Beaver Creek. The six-year-old had been impatient all winter for the world to warm enough so she could wade in the creek's shallows. The March air was still brisk, but the sun was shining, and she'd spent the morning begging to go down to the water. Jemima was as drawn to water as her mother was, so much so that the family had taken to calling her "Duck." Rebecca longed to join her, but her youngest, Becky, was fretting with teething, three-year-old Levina was tugging at her skirts, and she'd hardly given a thought to what she'd make for dinner.

From the doorway, she watched Jemima trot toward a shagbark hickory and gather an armful of the bark strips that littered the ground, knowing the child would carry them down to the creek and launch them into the swirling water, tiny boats headed on a watery journey to far-off places. Jemima was a quiet child who spent a great deal of time alone; Rebecca often worried if the rumors that encircled the family might prove too heavy a burden for such a gentle soul to carry. She'd hoped moving to the furthest reaches of western Carolina would put an end to the whispers that portrayed her as an adulteress, but it had soon become clear that she remained a topic of conversation in even this sparsely settled land. Most upsetting of all, the rumors were leaving a mark on Jemima as well.

James had taken it upon himself to be Jemima's protector, shielding his little sister from the worst of the gossip and comforting her when a stray remark, which Jemima was still too young to fully understand, made her tearful. Whenever Rebecca saw the two together, James's fair head bent protectively over Jemima's dark curls, her heart swelled to bursting.

Jemima had been playing in the creek for nearly an hour when she spotted the rider urging his horse into the water from the far bank; she flew up the hill and burst into the cabin to announce the rare appearance of someone unknown to her.

Cool air swept through the doorway in Jemima's wake, startling little Becky, who was playing on a pallet at Rebecca's feet while she chopped dried herbs for the evening stew. Becky's tiny mouth puckered in surprise, then crumpled, and she began to cry. Rebecca scooped her up, settled her on her hip, and stepped through the door into the thin, bleached light of a late winter afternoon. Jemima and Susannah followed a step behind, peering around the doorjamb, while Levina clung to her mother's skirts.

By then, the approaching figure had crested the hill and was near enough that Rebecca could see he was middle-aged with a road-weary face and a stubbly beard. She smoothed her hair with her free hand, then wiped a smudge off Becky's nose. The baby squirmed and turned her face away but stopped fussing as the rider pulled his horse to a halt alongside the porch. His fringed hunting shirt was spotted with clay flung up from his passage through the ford, and muddy water dripped from the horse's belly.

"Good day to you, ma'am." His voice was deep and raspy, as if he went long stretches without using it. He cleared his throat. "Fellow a couple ridges over said this's the Boone place. My name's John Finley—served with your husband under General Braddock fighting the French and Indians up in Pennsylvania more than ten years back."

She bid Finley welcome and offered him a mug of fresh spring water while Jemima raced off to the fields to get her father. Daniel had arrived home with a final load of winter pelts just days earlier and, in deference to their ongoing agreement, had immediately set to work clearing new ground for spring planting.

Finley settled onto the log bench on the front porch, mug in hand; leaned his head against the cabin wall; and closed his eyes. Relieved she didn't have to make small talk, Rebecca slipped into the cabin, tugged off her greasy workday apron, and pulled her best linen one from the shelf above her worktable, shaking it to get the wrinkles out. This man had known Daniel in the years before their marriage. They'd soldiered together in far-off Pennsylvania and had likely shared confidences she knew nothing about. She felt a prickle of anxiety, recognizing that Finley's life as a trader meant he remained free to wander as he chose, and she knew it wouldn't take much to stir those feelings up in her husband. She found herself wishing that when the man had ridden up and asked if this was the Boone cabin, she'd denied it. *Too late for that now,* she thought, as she tied her apron, then ran a hand through her hair to tidy it.

When she returned to the porch, Daniel had just rounded the corner of the cabin, his face and arms streaked with dirt. He broke into a wide grin when he spotted Finley.

"Why, you old river rat."

Finley opened his eyes and jumped to his feet. The men met at the top step and exchanged a bear hug. After a moment, Daniel stepped back and looked Finley up and down.

"I heard, years back, that you'd gone west."

"You heard right. I floated the Ohio River into the heart of Shawnee country. Got plenty of stories to tell you." Finley spat over the porch rail. "As for you, it's clear what you've been up to since the last time I saw you." He nodded toward Rebecca and the children who'd gathered at the porch's edge. "From the look of you and them young'uns, I'd say your lady can cook. You've put some meat on that frame of yours—not sure I could outwrestle you anymore."

Daniel took off his hat and raked a hand through his damp hair. "I was hardly more than a boy in '55. As for Rebecca's cooking—stay with us a spell and judge for yourself."

The moment Daniel voiced the invitation Rebecca ducked back into the cabin, thinking about what dinner fixings would stretch to satisfy an extra mouth. Their supplies were always lean this time of year, and she hadn't counted on company. If she scraped the bottom of the meal barrel, there might be enough for a second corn pone, but that meant no mush for breakfast unless she sent one of the boys to the mill to grind the last of their corn. In her mind, she was already saddling the mare by the time she heard Finley accept Daniel's invitation.

* * *

Once the stew pot was scraped clean and the benches pushed against the wall, Finley began to talk about Kentucky. The children had begged to stay up. Susannah was playing a finger game to entertain Becky and Levina on the trundle pulled out from beneath the corner bedstead. The boys sat on the floor, forming a half-circle around their father and Finley, who were tilted back in the family's two best chairs, their faces lit by the fire.

Rebecca prized those chairs almost as much as she did her maple rocker. They were walnut, with woven husk bottoms. If one of the boys had reared back like that, they'd have gotten the sharp side of her tongue, but she wasn't about to shame Daniel in front of a guest. He was listening to Finley's stories of adventure as intently as if their guest were Gulliver himself. James shot his mother a mischievous look, and Rebecca knew he'd remind her of this occasion the next time she told him to sit his chair flat.

"Kentucky," Finley was saying, "is a hunter's paradise. Why, there's otters sunning themselves on every creek bank and beaver lodges so thick you can use 'em like steppin' stones to cross a pond dry footed. There's great shaggy beasts called buffalo, big as oxen. Nothing like 'em on this side of the mountains, leastways not anymore." He took a deep draw on his pipe, making the white clay bowl glow pink in the gathering shadows.

"Are they dangerous?" ten-year-old Israel asked, his voice high and tight with excitement.

Finley's eyes dropped to the boy, and he nodded. "They've two big horns coming out of their head, like this." He pressed his fingers to his own head, careful to keep the smoldering pipe away from his hair. "I've seen 'em run a man through like a chicken on a spit, then toss him into the air with no more effort than it'd take for you to throw your sister's doll." He gestured toward the rag doll clutched in Becky's hand.

"What would the pelt from such a beast be worth?" Daniel asked.

Something in Daniel's tone made Rebecca look up. She'd settled onto a low stool at the fire's edge with Jemima nestled against her, the child's head in her lap. She'd been running her hand through Jemima's hair, absently checking for lice, letting the soft strands slide through her fingers. She didn't hear Finley's answer because all her attention was suddenly focused on Daniel. He was leaning forward, listening intently, his chair legs flat on the floor for the first time that evening.

She didn't realize she'd gone perfectly still until she felt Jemima's hand grasp her own and slide it gently through her hair. "More, Mama," she said sleepily.

Rebecca resumed trailing her hand through her daughter's dark hair, and Jemima settled down with a contented sigh, but Rebecca sat mute the rest of the evening. She listened to the men talk of Kentucky and felt her family's hard-won contentment slipping away as surely as the smoke swirling up the chimney and into the night sky.

Rebecca watched with a growing sense of dread as Daniel spent most of his time over the next few weeks gathering supplies, preparing to join Finley for an expedition into the Kentucky territory. When she pointed out he was neglecting the fieldwork, his cheerful response was: "The corn crop's in the ground, Becca, and the plowing for the kitchen garden's finished. The boys can handle things from now through harvest. Going to Kentucky with Finley is the chance of a lifetime."

She'd seen that faraway look in his eyes before and knew there was nothing more she could say to change his mind—he was already gone.

Rebecca watched James grow more and more withdrawn, dreading his father's departure nearly as much as she did. Fair-haired and gentle, James, though nearly twelve, still harbored strong memories of their escape from the Indians when he was not quite three. Whenever Daniel ventured into the wilderness, James slept restlessly, unsettled by his father's absence. Though James no longer spoke of it, Rebecca suspected his dreams were filled with that long-ago glimpse of the warrior's painted face.

Daniel had taught both James and Israel to read and write a good farmer's hand, but James particularly enjoyed his studies and often volunteered to read a chapter or two aloud to the family in the evenings from the handful of books Daniel kept on the mantel. Rebecca envisioned James growing up to be a minister or a teacher, but Daniel was intent on shaping their son into a woodsman.

"The boy has the makings of a good hunter, but he's jumpy in the woods, always looking over his shoulder," Daniel told her. "If he were a couple years older, I'd take him along to Kentucky. A few months in the wilderness would settle him down. It'd be the adventure of a lifetime for the boy."

Or the death of him, Rebecca thought.

10

Susannah

"Susannah, I swear you were born angry."

Susannah tossed her head and glared at her father. "How would you know? I doubt you were around."

Daniel's face froze in surprise, and eight-year-old Susannah held her breath; after a moment her father began to chuckle, and the knot in her stomach unraveled. Her mother was always telling her to think before she spoke, but thoughts spilled out of her like water streaming from a cracked cup. She'd been told often enough that it was wrong to lie, but it dawned on her now that speaking the truth could be just as troublesome.

She knew she shouldn't voice how much she hated the daily round of household chores that tied her to her mother's side—and both of them to the hearth, the garden, the springhouse. Being stuck in the cabin was unbearable on the mornings when her father took her brothers hunting. On those days, she'd stand on the porch as the barnyard swirled with guns and dogs and boys and bite her lip till it bled, wanting so badly to go with them.

When she'd been very young, her brother, Israel, who was less than two years older, had stayed behind, too. They'd been shirttail kids together, set to the same household duties, making a game of everything: searching the woods and fields around the cabin for eggs the hens had tried to hide from them or sweeping ashes from the hearth and carrying them to the hopper, where their mother would turn them into soap. But one day, when Israel was five and she was almost four, the gown-like shirt he'd always worn, just as she had, was replaced by his first pair of breeches like the big boys'.

"When will I get breeches, Mama?" Susannah had asked. The room had exploded in laughter, and she'd frozen, as startled as if a gun had gone off in their midst. The entire family was laughing at her, but she hadn't a clue why. She'd stood wide-eyed, as laughter rolled around the room.

After a moment, her mother had set baby Jemima down and pulled Susannah close. Susannah had buried her face in her mother's apron, breathing in the dusty scent of the cracked corn she poured into its folds each morning to carry to the chickens.

"Girls don't wear breeches, Suzy," her mother had said.

"Not ever?"

Her mother had shaken her head. "Sometime soon I'll make you a gown to go over your shift, and then you'll dress like me."

"But I want breeches, like Israel."

Another explosion of laughter had rocked the room, and Susannah had clutched her mother harder.

After that day, Israel went to the fields with the men, and Jemima had taken his place around the house, trailing after Susannah on determined legs, more an annoyance than a companion. Susannah's anger had simmered each time her mother called on her to stir the stewpot that bubbled endlessly on the hearth, or asked her to rinse out the baby's dirty clouts. She'd hold her nose with one hand and rinse the soiled linens up and down in the pail, making sure her loathing of housework was wordlessly clear to everyone.

"If you don't curb that one's spirit, Rebecca, she'll come to no good end."

Susannah couldn't remember which aunt had said it, but she remembered spending a great deal of time afterwards wondering how far away Nogoodend was, this place she was expected to journey to.

Susannah noticed her mother's lips were often set in a tight line in the weeks before her father left for Kentucky, as if she were afraid to let loose the words that buzzed in her mouth like angry bees. On several evenings Susannah heard her parents' voices late in the night—rising and falling, sometimes angry, sometimes pleading.

For as long as she could remember, her father had spent winters away from them, but this trip would be different. He meant to travel to the top of that looming blue wall, drop over the other side, and keep on going. *Kin-tuck-ee.* Susannah sounded the word over and over in her mind. She decided it was magical because the men who visited her father spoke it constantly, as if bewitched by it. Only a few shook their heads and declared the expedition a fool's errand.

A fool's errand. On more than one occasion, Susannah had heard her mother argue that point with her father after Finley had put the notion of Kentucky in his head.

"West of the mountains is Indian land," her mother had said.

"According to King George," her father had replied.

"Well, it seems to me the King's Proclamation Line is a perfect solution. Everything west of the Line is for the Indians, and whites stay east of the mountains. If that keeps the peace, I'm for it. I'm for anything that allows my children to grow up safe."

"I'm thinking of the children, too, Becca. The fur trade's the only business I know. I have to follow the game. Besides, nearly all the Indians I've met are friendly. They're a generous people. It's only when they see someone take more than their share that they grow angry. I'm careful to cache my furs in different places so they never see a whole season's haul at once."

"So you admire them, yet you trespass onto their land and deceive them about why you're there?"

Her father's brow had furrowed. "I suppose that's true. But I have to do it to keep you and the children fed."

Her mother had shaken her head. "We've got more than enough land right here to keep us all fed." She let those words hang in the air between them. When no response came, she added, "I expect the Indians and I agree on one thing—all of us would be better off if you'd take that Proclamation Line seriously."

For days afterward Susannah had tried to imagine what the Proclamation Line looked like. She finally decided it was some sort of ribbon that the King's surveyors had laid down along the crest of the mountains, something you had to step over—one side for whites, the other for Indians. She knew her father ignored the line. He'd made winter excursions down the western slopes into Indian lands for years. Befriended by Cherokee hunters, he'd spent time learning their language and often spoke admiringly of their woodsmanship. One winter he'd traded one of his powder horns for a colorful cloth belt woven by one of the Cherokee women.

"Your father's turning into an Indian," her mother said. "I believe he'd like nothing better than to disappear over those mountains and settle in with them." Though her tone was light, the look in her eyes told Susannah she wasn't at all amused.

One night Susannah woke to the sound of her mother's voice, hardly more than a whisper in the darkness. "But we agreed. You promised you'd spend summers with us—you said you'd never again leave us the way you did in Culpeper." And then Susannah heard muffled sobs coming from the big corner bedstead.

The cornhusks in her bed tick rustled as she sat up, startled, and the room was suddenly silent, so that all she heard was the soft murmur of a spring rain on the roof's cedar shingles. She lay back beside Jemima, who hadn't stirred, and pulled the quilt to her chin. Just days ago, her mother had aired the blankets over the garden fence, and the quilt still held a hint of sun and wind amid its folds. She took a deep breath, closed her eyes, and pictured the layers of blue-green mountains that loomed above their cabin. She felt her bare feet sinking into the leaf-softened slopes, moving from shadow to light through the trees as she clambered upwards toward the mountain's crest, determined to see what lay beyond.

When the day of her father's leave-taking arrived, a half-dozen men, including Mister Finley and two of her uncles, John and Squire, gathered at the Boone homestead. Uncle John usually greeted Susannah by scooping her up and whirling her around till she was dizzy with laughter. But on this day, he hurried past without noticing her.

Susannah stood to one side, tracing a line in the dust with her toe, as she watched the men lug the heavy packs out of the barn and settle them, one by one, onto the horses' backs. They had been loading the packs for weeks, filling them with slabs of salt pork, cloth bags of cornmeal, and small river-cane containers filled with her mama's dried herbs. They divided the heavy items like traps and skillets and cook pots so that no single animal carried too much iron.

Susannah felt a hand on her shoulder and looked up into Uncle John's smiling face.

"Why so glum, Suzy?"

"I wanna go." She ducked her head, determined not to cry. "I'll never get to see what's over those mountains."

Uncle John squatted down in front of her, his eyes kind. "Never is a very long time, young'un. There's no telling where life will take you. And I promise to come home with so many stories you'll get sick of hearing them." He smiled. "In the meantime, I'm counting on you to help care for your Aunt Hannah."

Susannah nodded.

"Now give me a hug. I've got to get back to work or the fellas will say I'm not pulling my weight."

All that morning the men continued to shift items, laboring to get the loads balanced, even after the packs were placed on the horses' backs. The horses stamped and sometimes shied, showing a white-rimmed eye to the men and dogs that moved among them. Susannah stood to one side, feeling sad and invisible until Israel came and stood alongside her. She was startled to see that his eyes were red.

"Israel?"

He swiped his sleeve across his face. "Daddy says he's taking Blue," he said, not looking at her.

She stiffened, and Israel added: "I told him he could."

"Why?" Of their three dogs, the gangly, lop-eared hound was Israel's favorite; he'd raised him from a pup, and she'd rarely seen one without the other.

"Jake and Brandy are both too old to go so far. Besides, Blue's got the best nose."

He said it proudly, though his voice wavered.

"But, Israel, you—"

"Hush up. I ain't gonna carry on like no girl about it." He planted his feet solidly and crossed his arms across his chest.

Susannah opened her mouth to remind him that not all girls were crybabies but swallowed the words when she saw that his jaw was clamped tight in an effort to hold back tears.

The rest of the day was blurred in her mind, the way things look on a fog-bound river in the early morning, figures appearing from the mist for an instant, then fading from sight. She remembered her father gathering her up for a goodbye hug—the scratch of his hunting shirt against her cheek and the way his blue eyes danced with excitement. She remembered the womenfolk calling goodbyes to their men as the string of horses began to move—the creak of leather, the yapping of the hounds, the long line of men and animals snaking across the pasture, disappearing one by one into the deep shadows of the tree line.

But one image from that day would remain in her mind as sharp and clear as if every detail was etched in glass: the sight of a towheaded boy standing stiffly, his eyes following the loping form of a speckled hound that hesitated once it reached the trees, ready to turn back, until a whistle summoned him into the darkness.

11

Susannah

"Don't expect to hear from us till next spring," her father had told them. "We'll spend the summer exploring and the winter trapping." *A whole year.* It made Susannah's heart hurt to think about it. The countryside felt achingly empty, and the distances between the scattered home sites seemed to grow longer now that they were a community of women and children.

A few weeks after the men left, her aunts gathered at her mother's cabin to card the wool shorn from their small flock. Susannah hadn't realized how silent the cabin had been until it was suddenly filled with the swirl of greetings and the chatter of her cousins. James suggested going down to the creek to search for crayfish, an offer that was greeted enthusiastically by the other children and won him a grateful smile from the women. The children followed James out the door, their bare feet thudding across the porch.

Susannah hung back, pretending to rummage for a tin cup they sometimes used for catching crayfish and minnows. She could barely believe her luck when the women ignored her. *For once I don't have to babysit.* She knew that when the women's hands were busy, their tongues would be, too, and this unexpected reprieve from shepherding children offered her a perfect opportunity to hear what interesting things women talked about when they thought no children were around to hear them. As her mother pulled chairs from around the table to move to the porch, Susannah slipped out the door and hid behind the wood box. She sat scrunched against the box, knees to chin, so she could peep through a small crack in the tall stack of logs.

She knew she'd be in for a tongue-lashing if she was caught eavesdropping, but she was accustomed to being reprimanded, unlike Jemima, who never wanted to do the least thing to make their mother mad. It seemed to Susannah there were a thousand ways for a girl to get into trouble, while boys were given leeway to explore and fight and have all sorts of adventures. Susannah loved her mother, but she didn't want to grow up to be like her, forever stuck on a farm with her husband away, tied to the same old chores day after day. Susannah vowed that if she were ever silly enough to get married, her life would be very different.

Susannah scrunched down as low as she could when Aunt Jane came through the doorway, carrying a chair. She set it down on the porch beside the large woven basket piled high with washed fleeces. Her blonde hair, braided and coiled on her head, shone like a crown. Susannah loved this newest aunt who was a kindred spirit, unafraid to speak her mind. She'd married Uncle Squire a few years earlier, and the couple and their two young sons had recently taken up land several miles away.

Aunt Jane was tugging at a stray burr caught in the fleece that was laid across her lap when Aunt Hannah and her mother appeared in the doorway, already deep in conversation.

"Your fourth child, my seventh," Susannah heard her mother say.

Susannah squeezed her lips tight to stifle a groan. *More babies to tend.* She watched her mother and Hannah embrace, leaning against each other as if the very weight of those words made them weary.

"At least Squire didn't leave me in *that* condition," Aunt Jane said, her fingers sunk in the fleece, working to disentangle a burr. "My two run me ragged."

Out of the corner of her eye, Susannah saw Jemima skipping up the hill from the creek. She paused when she spotted Susannah, then headed straight for her sister's hiding place.

Susannah shook her head. *Go away,* she mouthed. Jemima stopped, confused, but when Susannah continued to glare at her, Jemima ducked her head and walked past without speaking. Susannah let her breath out slowly and shifted her attention back to the women's conversation.

"How in heaven's name did all three of us wind up marrying men with restless streaks?" Aunt Jane was saying. "Becca and I both married

Boones—but you, Hannah—you had the wide world to choose from. How'd you manage to pick a man as restless as your brothers?"

"John Stewart had the sweetest smile I'd ever seen," Aunt Hannah said. "I guess I didn't think much beyond that or I'd have noticed he was cut from the same cloth as Daniel and Squire. Course, not all my brothers are wanderers—Ned's content to farm . . ."

Hannah's voice trailed off, and Susannah saw her aunts exchange a nervous glance.

Her mother had been focused on the tufts of wool in her lap, but she looked up as the silence lengthened.

"It's alright," she said, "you can talk about Ned around me." She shrugged. "I've given up hoping those stories will disappear. I can't blame Martha and Ned for keeping their distance."

Aunt Jane's face registered her relief. "Well, all I can say is I wish Squire was more like Ned. We'd barely been married a month when he left me to go off on a long hunt. I went crying to my mother, thinking I must be an awful wife." Her tone was so indignant that Susannah stifled a giggle.

"I thought moving way out here would help keep John home," Aunt Hannah admitted, "but it hasn't made a whit of difference. I don't expect he'll ever settle down."

"Knowing what we know now, do you think we'd marry them again?" her mother asked.

Susannah leaned forward expectantly, but all she heard was silence.

By the time winter arrived and the cold deepened, her mother and Aunt Hannah had grown so heavy that they didn't have the energy to traipse back and forth between the homesteads. Aunt Jane wasn't slowed by pregnancy, but she was nearly as worn out from tending her farm alone with only two little boys for company.

Jesse checked on both aunts from time to time, making sure their cabins were well stocked with firewood and other necessities, but when their mother asked how the aunts were feeling, she got a blank stare.

"Feeling?" Jesse said. "I don't know. They didn't say."

"But how did they seem? Lonely? Tired?"

He shrugged helplessly.

Their mother shook her head and began sending Susannah along with him, knowing that way she'd get a full accounting.

"Aunt Hannah's ankles are swollen something fierce," Susannah reported. Or: "Aunt Jane got all teary when she asked me how you were doing."

When the air sweeping down off the mountains grew bitter and snow filled, visits between the cabins became infrequent. The dreary winter darkness wrapped itself around their cabin, and Susannah felt as if they were the last human beings anywhere on earth. As the nights lengthened, she lay in the bed beneath a heavy fur pelt and snuggled close to Jemima's back. Jemima was warm, but the air surrounding them was so cold Susannah could see her breath hanging in the air. She touched a finger to the tip of her ice-cold nose and shivered, thinking of her aunts in their isolated cabins and her father and uncles wandering through a snow-covered wilderness to the west with no way to let anyone know how they fared.

On a sun-drenched May morning, nearly a year to the day after the men had first set out for Kentucky, Susannah settled the newest addition to the family, four-month-old Daniel Morgan, onto a quilt in the shade of the garden fence. Her mother was hanging laundry on the other side of the split rail fence, humming as she draped the wet clothes over the top rail.

Susannah bent over the baby, rubbing his back and watching the gentle rise and fall of his chest as his breathing deepened. When his eyelids finally fluttered shut, she eased herself off the quilt and stood, stretching to ease the kink from her back. She looked toward the creek and froze; Uncle Squire was climbing the hill toward the cabin. *Where's Daddy*, she thought, and felt her body go numb. She heard her mother gasp and turned to see her standing motionless, a wet shirt clutched in her hands.

As Squire drew close enough to see their faces, he called out: "He's alive, Becca."

Her mother raised the damp cloth to her forehead and whispered, "Thank God."

Squire reached the fence and rested a calloused hand on the top rail. "But, Becca . . ."

Her mother lowered the shirt.

"John's gone."

"What do you mean, gone?"

Susannah felt as if her heart had stopped, then began to beat double time.

"Daniel and John were hunting along opposite sides of a creek when a hard rain made the water rise. When the water went down, Daniel crossed over, but all he found was an abandoned campsite and John's initials carved on a tree."

"Then he might be alive," her mother said quickly.

Susannah felt a leap of hope. It simply wasn't possible that she'd never see her warm, wonderful uncle again. His words to her on the day he'd departed echoed in her ears: "Never is a very long time."

Squire shook his head. "That was back in January. If John were alive, we'd have seen sign of him by now." Squire's voice was gentle, as if he were speaking to a child. "Daniel's still searching, only now he's looking for John's body. He said he couldn't face Hannah until he could tell her how John died. I came home alone with our furs, but as soon as I resupply, I'm headed back to Kentucky."

"You came home alone?" her mother said. "Even if Daniel couldn't come, why didn't he send someone with you?"

"Finley and the rest of the men got spooked by the Indians. They lit out for Virginia months ago." Squire looked up at the ridgeline behind the house, as if he was afraid to meet her mother's eyes.

"Indians?" her mother said faintly. "The other men left? Then who's with Daniel?"

Squire shifted his rifle uneasily, settling it in the crook of his arm. "He's alone."

"Oh, God."

Susannah opened her mouth to say, *Daddy isn't alone—he has Blue.* But the minute she thought it, she realized if the wilderness could swallow Uncle John, there was no telling what might have happened to Blue.

Her mother leaned on the railing to steady herself as Squire continued, his tone apologetic. "Daniel wouldn't leave, Becca. We were nearly out of powder and lead. I had to come east for supplies."

Her mother straightened and drew a deep breath. "Let's go inside, Squire. I need to sit down, and you need to start at the beginning."

Sunlight filtered through the trees, dappling the trail with shadows, as Squire and her mother set out for the Stewart homestead to break the news of Uncle John's disappearance. When Susannah insisted on going along, her mother reluctantly agreed, then, at the last minute, beckoned for James and Israel to come as well.

They walked in silence under the late afternoon sun. Despite the heat, Susannah was relieved to be out in the fresh air; all morning their cabin had been filled with a sadness so heavy the very air felt weighted. She wanted to believe Uncle Squire was wrong—wrong about Uncle John and wrong about Blue. Susannah bit her lip at the memory of Israel's face when Uncle Squire told him the dog had been put down after being severely clawed by a bear.

"He didn't suffer long, son," Uncle Squire said.

Israel had nodded, his face solemn, but a few moments later he'd slipped out of the cabin. Susannah had followed him, and watched as he went around the end of the barn. As she drew closer, she heard Israel's choked sobs. She hesitated, wanting to turn the corner and comfort him but knowing he wouldn't want her to see his tears. After a moment, she turned back to the cabin, leaving him to grieve alone.

Now, as they walked silently toward Aunt Hannah's, Susannah could hear cattle lowing in the distance and the drone of insects in the trees around them. She thought how odd it was that Uncle John had been dead for months, and yet, a few miles ahead of them, Aunt Hannah was going about her normal chores, still unaware. Susannah wished they could walk more slowly because once their news was told, Uncle John would die all over again, this time for good. She wondered if maybe a person wasn't totally dead as long as there was someone in the world who still believed they were alive.

She thought her mother would want to be the one to tell Aunt Hannah, but when they walked into the clearing, she motioned Squire ahead of her, forcing him to take the lead.

Aunt Hannah spotted them through the open doorway and stepped outside, wiping her hands on her apron, her face excited and smiling. Susannah and the boys stopped several paces behind the grownups, so she didn't hear what Squire said, but moments later Aunt Hannah backed away from him, eyes wide. Susannah covered her ears as her aunt's screams echoed through the clearing. It was the first time Susannah had heard the sort of scream that claws its way out of a person's throat from the depths of their being, like a wild thing freed from a dark place.

Her brothers stood stiffly beside her, but as Aunt Hannah's screams turned to sobs, James's face crumpled, and he tried to turn away. Her mother grasped James by the shoulder and forced him to look, saying in a low, fierce voice: "Remember this. This is the other side of all that roaming men do. Remember, and maybe someday you'll have the sense to spare the women in your life this sort of pain . . ."

Both boys nodded, their eyes glistening with tears. Through tears of her own, Susannah watched the hard edges around her mother's mouth soften as she stepped around Squire and gathered Hannah in her arms.

Susannah stayed with her Aunt Hannah for much of that summer, helping care for the children. The eldest, Sarah, was not yet five, closely followed by Mary and then Rachel. Hannah's youngest, Betsy, was just five months old, a beautiful baby, with big blue eyes and a toothless smile that made Susannah laugh. But looking at Betsy also made Susannah's heart ache because the child would never, in this life, lay eyes on her daddy.

Hannah seemed lost during that endless summer. Normally a spotless housekeeper, she let the dishes pile up on the oak table and the girls' hair go uncombed for days at a time. Sometimes she would start a task, like picking up the water bucket as though she intended to go to the spring, only to walk a few steps and stand, frozen, as if she no longer remembered where she was headed. Susannah wasn't surprised when Hannah decided to return to her parents' home at the Forks, unwilling to face another winter alone on her isolated homestead.

Susannah pitied her aunt and hated to see her in such pain, but there were times, as she helped her pack, that she also wanted to take Hannah by the shoulders and shake her—because hardly a day went by that she didn't wish aloud that Betsy had been a boy.

"If only I'd borne John a son," she'd say. "Then at least his name would have lived on."

Each time her aunt said it, Susannah looked at Betsy and felt a smoldering anger at a world where a girl-child, even one as lovely as this, was counted a disappointment.

12

Jemima

Jemima couldn't begin to count the number of times someone had looked at her, then at Susannah, and said: "Well, you don't look like sisters."

Susannah's hair was a rich, dark auburn that Jemima envied with an intensity that only grew as the years passed. Her own hair was plain old black. And though Susannah was two years older, Jemima couldn't recall a time when her sister had been taller. Suzy was dainty, like their Aunt Martha, while folks told Jemima she looked just like her mother—"tall," they'd say, and some would add, "willowy" to be kind if they noticed her crestfallen face. When Jemima thought of Susannah, she thought of a cardinal, a colorful bird that was rarely still and glistened in the light as it flew; one's eyes were inevitably drawn Susannah's direction. As for herself, she felt sure she was a sparrow—dark and drab and utterly common.

As far back as she could remember, she'd felt people's eyes on her and sensed she was "different." When she was very young, and they were still living at the Forks, she'd passed a cluster of adults and heard someone say: "Whatever the truth of those stories, she's a Boone either way." And everyone had laughed.

She'd puzzled over those strange words, then sought out her big brother James to ask what it meant. He'd leaned his hoe against the fence and picked her up, setting her on the top rail so they could look each other in the eye.

"First of all, Jemima—don't listen to gossip." He paused, as if gathering his thoughts. "You know, don't you, that Jesse and Jonathan aren't really our brothers?"

"They are, too!"

He smiled. "They're our cousins, not our brothers." He let that sink in, then said, "That doesn't change how you feel about them, does it?"

She shook her head.

"That's what you need to remember. It doesn't really matter who their Daddy was, or who our Daddy is—we're all family."

He lifted her off the fence and gave her a gentle swat on the rear. "Now don't give this another thought."

And she tried not to, no matter what else she overheard. James's words made her hope that the whispers were wrong, that she really wasn't different. She adored James, her gentle brother who looked out for her in so many ways. He'd patiently taught her to swim in the creek's cool waters, and, unlike Susannah, never seemed to mind when she tagged after him. It was James who filled the space in her heart that the whispers, and Susannah's indifference, left empty.

Several weeks after Uncle Squire had departed to rejoin her father in Kentucky, Susannah ran up to Jemima as she toted a bucket of water back from the springhouse.

"Come on," Susannah said, her eyes wide with excitement, "there's a missionary up at the house, talking to Mama."

"What's a missionary?" Jemima said, setting the heavy bucket down and pushing a strand of hair out of her eyes.

Susannah didn't answer and didn't offer to help with the bucket; she was already hurrying up the path toward the cabin. Jemima followed as fast as she could, the heavy bucket banging against her legs.

The missionary was a round-faced man named George Soelle who rode a mule and carried a Bible wrapped up in his bedroll. He complimented Rebecca on her cooking and bounced the baby on his knee. Jemima thought it odd that this stranger was holding little Daniel Morgan when her father hadn't yet laid eyes on the child.

"So Brother Soelle, what news can you tell us?" her mother asked.

"The people in Boston have grown even more restive since the redcoats massacred a group of citizens there last year," Soelle said. "Even here in Carolina, there's been bloodshed over the unfair way we're taxed. Heaven only knows where it will end." He shook his head. "But the Lord is our refuge. I see you have a Bible on the mantel. Would you care to read us some verses, Miz Boone?"

"I'm afraid I read very poorly, Brother Soelle. Hardly at all, in fact."

The flicker of embarrassment in her mother's eyes goaded Jemima into saying: "Mama doesn't have to read—she tells us the stories by heart."

Her siblings turned to stare at her, as surprised as if she'd suddenly grown two heads. It was a grievous breach of etiquette for a child to address a guest before being spoken to, something only Susannah might have dared. Indeed, all eyes had first turned Susannah's direction. Jemima shrank down on the bench and felt her face flush as Brother Soelle's eyes traveled down the table and found her.

"That was well said, child," he said. "I only wish more parents in these western lands followed your mother's example."

Her mother offered her a ghost of a smile, and Jemima breathed a sigh of relief.

Rebecca turned back to their guest. "My husband started to teach me to read shortly after we married, but as soon as the babies started coming, I found little time to practice. Early on, I discovered that telling the children stories, rather than reading them, left my eyes and hands free for other tasks. Now," she said, "my son, James, usually reads to us."

Brother Soelle turned to James. "Will you do us the honor, young man?"

James scooted off the bench and retrieved the battered Bible. "What verses would you like me to read, sir?"

"Whatever your mother most likes to hear."

Without hesitation, James opened the book and began: "Blessed are the poor in spirit: for theirs is the kingdom of heaven. Blessed are they that mourn: for they shall be comforted . . ."

For several days, Brother Soelle visited with other families along the Yadkin but rode back to the Boone homestead each evening before dusk. While he waited for supper, he sat at the table with his quill and inkpot writing in his journal. After the evening meal, he held devotions, then sat up talking with her mother and the oldest boys. Jemima found it odd to drop off to sleep to the sound of adult voices droning away in conversation late into the evening; it was almost as if her father were home again.

They hadn't seen him in nearly two years, and Jemima struggled to conjure the sound of his voice in her head. Lying in bed next to Susannah each night, she squeezed her eyes shut and did her best to recall her father's voice as he sat by the fire reading aloud to the family. She found it harder and harder to remember, which left her uneasy and felt oddly like a betrayal. When she said as much to Susannah, her sister replied: "Why should *you* feel guilty? *He's* the one who left."

Susannah was always sure of everything. Jemima had discovered at an early age that if you dared disagree with her, she'd hammer you with a cascade of words that left you so befuddled you were no longer sure what you thought. It was easier just to let Susannah have her way.

On the third morning of Brother Soelle's visit, Jemima and Susannah were clearing the breakfast dishes when Susannah said: "What do you think he writes in that journal?"

James and Israel were the only other ones in the cabin; Brother Soelle had mounted his horse and headed downriver for the day, their mother had taken the younger children and gone to Aunt Jane's, and Jesse and Jonathan were clearing a stretch of bottomland.

James glanced at the worn, leather-bound book and shrugged. "He probably writes church stuff—like how many souls he's saved."

Susannah swept the table crumbs into her palm and tossed them in the fire. "I bet he writes about us."

"Bet he doesn't," James and Israel said, nearly in unison.

"I dare you to check," Susannah said.

Israel shot her a quizzical look. "Why do you want to know what's in his journal?"

"I caught him staring at Mama last night," Susannah said, "like maybe he's finally noticed she's something more than just a good cook. After he'd watched her a while, he scribbled something in that book."

"But he's a minister." James wrinkled his nose at the thought of a man of the cloth having unseemly thoughts.

"And besides, Mama's more than thirty," Israel added, as if that piece of information should end any discussion along those lines.

James stared at the book uncertainly, then pulled it toward him. He flipped it open and searched through the pages for the most recent entries. He read silently a moment, until Susannah pointedly cleared her throat.

"Oh, all right," he said, running his finger across the spidery dark lines covering the page. "Let's see—he's writing about the women that live here in the backcountry . . ."

"See," Susannah interrupted, "what did I tell you?"

"About how hard their lives are."

"Oh," Susannah said, deflated.

James ran his finger down the page. "Right here he says, *How do these women survive? If a woman is ill, has a high fever—where is the nurse, medicine, proper food? The wife of the nearest neighbor lives, perhaps, several miles away, and she has children of her own, her cattle, her own household to care for, and can give only a couple of hours, or at most one day or night.*"

James stopped, suddenly reluctant to continue.

"James?" Susannah prodded.

His mouth tightened, and when he began to read again, his voice was hardly more than a whisper: *"Miz Boone cannot read or write. She is by nature a quiet soul, and of few words, but she told me of her trouble and the frequent distress and fear in her heart."*

James closed the book abruptly, slid it back to its former spot, then stood up and walked out the door without looking at anyone.

Jemima ducked her head. It was as if they'd all peeked through a window and seen Mama naked. From that moment on, all four of them knew that despite their mother's confident pronouncements that their father was safe, she was as frightened as they were that he might never come home.

The moon sat just above the treetops as the clearing filled with more people than Jemima had seen in one place since they'd left the Forks. Folks from all across the Upper Yadkin Valley had gathered to help build a cabin for a newly arrived family, and though cabin raisings were usually well attended out of a sense of neighborliness, when word got out that a fiddler would be present, the crowd had swelled considerably.

Though the days were warm, the May evenings were still cool, and campfires burned around the edges of the clearing, weaving a pattern of light across the tree branches. When the fiddle struck up, Jemima danced in the shadows with the other girls who were too young to have partners, and when she grew tired, she studied the older couples' movements, storing them away in her mind so one day she'd know the steps.

Her mother was sitting off to the side, nursing Daniel Morgan. Jemima went to stand next to her, but as the rich voice of the fiddle continued to echo through the clearing, she found it hard to stay still. She bounced in place, tapping her feet in time to the music.

Her mother smiled. "So, who do you think's the best dancer?"

Jemima considered a moment. "Not her," she said softly, after a matronly woman swirled past them, her face puckered in concentration as she did her best to keep up with her partner. Jemima stepped in front of her mother, her back to the dancers, and puckered her own mouth in a perfect imitation, making her mother laugh out loud.

"How do you always capture people so well?"

"I just watch them."

Watching people had become second nature to her. She supposed it began because people so often seemed to be watching her; it seemed only fair that she watch them in return, trying to read the meaning behind a raised eyebrow or a curled lip.

Jemima could still recall the first time she'd made her mother laugh by mimicking a visitor after they'd departed. Having seen her mother's delight that day, Jemima had made a game of noticing the expressions or movements that were unique to someone, then recreating them to entertain either her mother or James. The one time she'd attempted to make Susannah laugh in this manner, her sister had looked at her as if she was crazy, and she'd never dared try it around her again.

Jesse glided past them, flushed and smiling, with a pretty young woman on his arm. For the first time, it struck Jemima that Jesse and Jonathan might soon leave to start families of their own; the thought made her feel hollow inside. She wondered if her cousins felt trapped, unable to get on with their lives in the face of their uncle's continued absence. Her father had been gone this time for more than two years, and though Jemima knew her mother had doubts he'd return, no one in the family dared speak that thought aloud.

Her mother got up to dance, having nursed Daniel Morgan to sleep. She squeezed Jemima's shoulder in silent thanks as she handed her the baby. Jemima leaned against a tree, cradling Daniel Morgan just outside the circle of firelight, and watched her mother join the dance. She wove her way through the steps, following the caller's instructions—"All join hands. Now two hand turn." She was taller than the other women—and many of the men as well—so it was easy to keep track of her. Jemima thought she looked like a queen with the firelight shining off her dark hair and her head held high as she swept round and round.

Daniel Morgan breathed deeply on Jemima's shoulder, his breath milky against her cheek. She swayed back and forth to the music, doing her best not to wake him so her mother could keep dancing.

When she felt a hand on her arm, she turned to see a man in the shadows with a bushy beard and a hat pulled low over his eyes.

"Yes, sir?" she said.

He tilted his head back so the light flickered across his face.

"Daddy," she breathed, though even as she said the word, she felt a familiar undercurrent of uncertainty.

He raised a finger to his lips, then rested a weathered hand on the baby's downy head and smiled. As the song ended and the laughing couples broke apart, her mother wound her way toward them through the crowd, and her father stepped back, tugging his hat lower.

By the time her mother reached them, the fiddler had launched into another tune; its buoyant tones filled the clearing, accompanied by the thud of dancing feet. Her mother's face was aglow as she held out her arms to take Daniel Morgan from Jemima, but her father stepped between them and swept off his hat.

Her mother shrieked so loud the fiddle stopped in mid-note and the dancers froze. An instant later, her mother was in her father's arms while the baby screamed on Jemima's shoulder. The neighbors crowded round, slapping her father on the back and greeting Uncle Squire, who emerged from the trees, laughing and hollering for Aunt Jane to come get a hug of her own.

Her father spent a good part of that evening dancing with her mother, then afterwards, sitting by one of the fires, recounting his adventures to anyone who cared to listen. Her mother sat beside him, quietly taking it all in. As the evening wore on, Jemima saw her mother's jaw tighten as she watched her husband sell Kentucky to his audience as smoothly as a peddler touting the benefits of a homemade elixir. Clearly, he meant to go back across the mountains, and he didn't intend to go alone.

13

Rebecca

The morning after Daniel's return from Kentucky, Rebecca looked up from the hearth and noticed her battered rifle, which normally hung on pegs near the door, was missing. She'd learned its idiosyncrasies and had grown protective of that old gun. The boys knew not to carry it off without asking her, so she felt sure her husband was the culprit.

She hurried outside, spotted the bent grass that marked his path, and caught up with him at the edge of the tree line. Her rifle was cradled in the crook of his arm.

"So where's your rifle?" she said. "I know you've never thought much of mine."

"Truth is, Becca, the Shawnee robbed Squire and me on our way home. Remember how I told you the thing that angers Indians the most is someone taking more than their share? Well, that's what they caught us doing, so they took everything: our horses, our furs, even our rifles. I figured they'd kill us, but they let us go with just a warning, telling us to never come back. Two years of hard work, and we've come home with nothing."

As bad as that was, she could see from his face that wasn't everything.

"And . . ." she prompted.

"There's a warrant out for my arrest back at the Forks; I'm overdue paying Colonel Henderson money I borrowed to finance the Kentucky expedition."

"I see," she said, and crossed her arms.

Daniel cleared his throat. "When Squire brought supplies back to Kentucky, he told me about the warrant, and it seemed like a good idea to keep the mountains between me and the law until I had enough furs to pay Henderson back." He gave her a lopsided smile. "If we hadn't gotten robbed, I could have cleared our debts easily, but now . . ."

"I thought the reason you stayed so long in Kentucky was to search for John."

Daniel's smile faded. "It pains me that I didn't find out what happened to him. But while I was searching for John, I was scouting, too. There's not a white man on earth who knows that country better than I do. People like Colonel Henderson are anxious to invest in western lands. Kentucky's gonna make us rich."

"That may be," she said, "but before we get rich, we have to keep you out of jail, get out of debt, and scrape together enough provisions to feed our family this winter. I reckon you'd better study on how to do all that while you're out hunting."

He nodded glumly and hoisted the rifle to his shoulder.

"And Daniel," she said.

He turned to look at her.

"The *first* thing you need to do is figure out how to get yourself another rifle. That one," she pointed, "is mine."

Rebecca took a deep breath and counted to ten when Daniel announced that his plan for getting out of debt was to take James and Israel into the backcountry for a winter of trapping. He hoped the three of them working together could earn enough to pay back what he owed and save enough to move the family to Kentucky. Rebecca didn't say anything about his Kentucky idea, figuring she'd fight that fight when she had to, but she wasn't about to let Daniel take her sons into the wilderness on his own.

"So where's the safest place you can set up your trap lines and make a profit?" she said.

Daniel thought a moment. "I reckon we could still get a good return along the Watauga. The King considers it Indian territory, but white folks are beginning to move there. It's safer than Kentucky because the Cherokee are leasing land to some of the settlers."

"Fine," she said, "that's where we'll go."

"We?"

She nodded. "We'll go as a family. If the girls and I work as camp keepers, it will leave you and the boys free to hunt."

She had her doubts about how safe they'd really be, but at least it would keep Daniel from traipsing off alone with the boys. *Lord only knows where they'd wind up.*

Rebecca kept her misgivings about the trip to herself, not wanting to infect the children with her worries. Their reactions varied widely. Jesse and Jonathan, now in their early twenties, had been agreeable to Daniel's plan that they stay east of the mountains to tend the farm in the family's absence. James, almost fifteen, and Jemima, nine, accepted Daniel's decision without comment, though Rebecca could tell James harbored unspoken fears about setting foot in Indian territory. Thirteen-year-old Israel, a happy-go-lucky soul, was always ready to go adventuring, but of all the children, eleven-year-old Susannah was the most excited about the prospect of a winter in the wilderness. In the days before their departure, she whistled as she went about her chores and no longer responded in anger at being asked to help around the house. More than once as summer faded into fall, Rebecca saw her daughter look up at that looming blue wall and smile.

Rebecca had to admit, as they journeyed west, that the land was beautiful. The rolling hills along the headwaters of the Yadkin soon gave way to steeper, tree-covered slopes that were smoky gray in the morning mist, then turned a rich blue-green in the midday sun. The trees on the higher slopes were already laced with the reds and golds of early autumn. They followed trails through virgin forest that were often little more than faint deer paths. Daniel said the wild things knew the best ways through the mountains, and it was a wise man who followed their lead. Some of the chestnut and oak trees were so large that even when their entire family held hands and stretched as far as they could, their arms weren't long enough to encircle the trunks.

To help pass the tedious hours of walking, Rebecca made up games for the children. She'd call out the names of a half-dozen trees—*chestnut, sycamore, beech, oak, hickory*—making sure the final item was a bit harder to spot, like a sassafras grove or a silverbell tree. It helped the younger children learn the tree names and kept the older children occupied, hoping to be first to spot them all. When the children grew tired of using their eyes, Rebecca changed the game and had them listen and see how many birds they could identify by their songs.

Daniel joined in the fun by pointing out animal tracks, teaching the children how to distinguish the tracks of a beaver from an otter along the muddy bank of a mountain stream or the way a black bear had left claw marks and tufts of hair on the roughened bark of a white pine. Rebecca marveled at how he seemed to notice everything, as if the mountains were a book he'd read over and over and could now recite by heart.

Now that he was back in the woods, the worry lines lifted from Daniel's face, as if the debt that was driving them over the mountains had already been erased; in truth their debt had grown because they'd been forced to purchase supplies and a trio of sturdy horses to carry their hoped-for furs back to the settlements. For now, the horses' burdens were light enough that the youngest children could ride, packed safely into panniers that hung from the pack frames. Rebecca, Daniel, and the older children walked, taking turns leading the horses. The beasts were large and slow and frustratingly stubborn. Rebecca's hands burned from hours of tugging a lead rope, urging her balky charge along the trail.

"Horse steaks," she muttered, yanking the rope. The animal's ears flicked forward at the sound of her voice. "That's how you'll wind up if you don't move along."

One afternoon as they approached a grove of large oaks, Rebecca spotted a flash of orange flitting in the branches above them. "Look, children," she said softly, not wanting to scare the bird. "It's a parakeet."

They all stood, looking up, trying to track the bird's orange head and iridescent green body amid the oak leaves. But when Israel suddenly sneezed, the entire crown of the tree exploded with wings as hundreds of the bright-feathered birds flew upward, calling loudly. They all stood, transfixed, as the orange-and-green flock wheeled above them, and then, with a whoosh of wings, disappeared from sight.

"There were hundreds of them," Jemima said, her eyes wide. "I've only ever seen one or two back home."

"One of the older trappers told me there used to be huge flocks of them all along the Yadkin," Daniel said, "but parakeets like virgin timber, so when settlers move in, the birds move out."

Having traipsed up and over the mountains' crest and down into the great valley of the Tennessee, they finally reached the Watauga territory and set up a rough hunter's camp, complete with several three-sided lean-tos, near a place called Sycamore Shoals. Daniel said the Cherokee called the place Wata'gi, which meant "broken waters." Just being near that rocky stretch of river soothed Rebecca, and she slipped away to the shoals whenever she could, though finding time to tarry there was rare since most days were filled with work from dawn to dusk.

Rebecca, Susannah, and Jemima worked as camp keepers, stretching, scraping, and preparing pelts, while Daniel, James, and Israel hunted and tended the trap lines. Susannah chafed at being stuck in camp instead of traipsing the woods like her brothers, but it was clear her mother needed her. Even five-year-old Levina was put to work in camp, keeping an eye on her two younger siblings so the older girls could spend their time working with the furs. As the stack of pelts piled higher and higher, they envisioned the family's debt growing smaller and smaller. At any given time, they'd have fresh pelts stacked in piles waiting to be worked, skins stretched up on frames to be scraped, and finished furs ready to be tied into bundles.

Rebecca and the girls were hard at work on a bitterly cold day when two Indians, the first they'd seen, walked out of the woods. The two men leaned their rifles against a tree at the edge of the clearing, then stepped up to the fire and silently held their hands over the flames.

Weeks earlier, Rebecca had questioned Daniel about the likelihood of encountering Indians in this place.

"You can bet they'll know we're here," he'd said, "but I expect they'll stay out of sight."

Rebecca hadn't found this particularly comforting since the image that came to mind was of unseen eyes watching her family from the depths of the forest.

"But if they do appear?" she said. "What do I do?"

"You need to make them welcome—offer them something to eat. The Cherokee are a hospitable people. It's a grave insult not to welcome a guest warmly."

Now Daniel's advice echoed in her head. She forced a smile and motioned for the pair to have a seat on two upturned logs near the fire. As she bent over the stew pot to ladle meat and broth into two wooden bowls, she saw that her hands were trembling. *I need to stay calm.* She took a deep breath and tried to quiet the butterflies in her stomach. *I can't let the children see I'm afraid.* She straightened up, a bowl in each hand, and walked around the fire to serve the men.

The shorter of the two had a friendly countenance. He smiled and nodded his thanks as Rebecca handed him the stew. The taller man took his bowl in sullen silence. He had an odd-shaped face with high cheekbones and a sharply pointed chin. Both men were dressed entirely in buckskin except for red-and-black trade blankets draped across their shoulders. Rebecca felt her stomach turn over as she spotted the toma-hawks tucked into the men's belts. The iron blades gleamed dark against the red blankets, and it took all of her willpower to keep her fear under control at the thought of what might befall her family if the men decided to wield them.

When she turned back to the fire, she realized all the children were standing stock still, staring with wide eyes at their guests. *Would Indians think that was as rude as whites would? Or would going about one's usual chores be even more offensive?* She had no idea. *Dear God, help me choose the right thing to do.*

She motioned for the older girls to sit down and take up their knit-ting, and she shooed the younger children into one of the log shelters, silently warning them, with a finger to her lips, to be quiet. By the time she was back to the fire, the men's bowls were empty.

She ladled refills, and the men ate more slowly this time, glancing around the camp as if studying its contents. The shorter man's eyes fol-lowed the motion of Jemima's knitting needles, and when he glanced over and caught Rebecca watching him, he smiled, set down his bowl, and tapped his fingers against each other, mimicking the needles' movements. He looked questioningly at her.

"Knitting," Rebecca said.

He nodded, his expression thoughtful.

She pulled her brown knitted scarf from around her neck and held it out to him.

He took it, clearly surprised at the way his fingers sank into the soft cloth, a very different texture from his buckskin shirt or the stiff woolen trade blanket wrapped around his shoulders.

Rebecca pantomimed having him put the scarf around his own neck. He grinned broadly, and when he did as she suggested, she found herself smiling back at him. But seconds later, her smile faded and her heart began to pound as the taller man stood up and walked around the fire toward the girls.

Rebecca stooped and picked up the iron poker, making a show of raking the coals under the stew pot. She knew she'd only have one chance to strike the man from behind before all hell broke loose, but if he laid a hand on one of the girls, she wouldn't hesitate. Her eyes cut to the men's rifles, and she knew she couldn't move fast enough to reach them. Her only hope was to hold them off with the poker long enough for the children to run. It all flashed through her mind in an instant, and she braced herself as the tall man stopped in front of Susannah and eyed the stack of pelts that were piled up alongside her.

He spoke a few words in Cherokee, his tone angry, and gestured toward the furs. Susannah froze, her needles hovering in mid-air, but when the man reached up and pulled the top pelt off the pile, Susannah's eyes sparked in anger and her fingers tightened around her knitting needles.

"Stay still, Suzy."

The voice came from the edge of the clearing and Rebecca turned to see James, his rifle cradled casually in his arms. Though he was nearly as tall as his father, his frame was still more boy than man. His cheeks were flushed, and Rebecca had no doubt his heart was racing as fast as her own.

James spoke a few halting words in Cherokee: "Siyo, Scolocutta."

The shorter man responded, his tone friendly, then stood, his hands out with palms up, as if offering an apology. He gestured for the big man to follow him, then turned to Rebecca and tapped a finger against the brown scarf, bowing his head in silent thanks. With a final pointed glance at his companion, he picked up his rifle and disappeared into the forest.

Rebecca held her breath, poker still in hand, as the tall man turned from Susannah and walked toward James. He stopped in front of the boy, bent to look him in the eye, then raised the pelt and shook it in the boy's face.

"The English call me Big Jim. These furs belong to the Cherokee. Tell Boone he's a thief." With a final furious glance around the camp, the big man turned on his heel, still clutching the pelt, and strode into the woods without looking back.

14

Jemima

Sometimes Jemima wondered if the fact that her family's hard work along the Watauga had gotten her father out of debt was actually a good thing because as soon as his creditors were paid, his thoughts turned west again, this time all the way to Kentucky.

Her mother flatly refused to move so far into the wilderness unless a large party of folks came with them. Her father grumbled about the delay, imagining all manner of people flooding into Kentucky ahead of them and staking out the best lands. But as far as Jemima could tell, folks weren't lining up to make the journey; most of them were afraid, pure and simple, and after her experience at Sycamore Shoals, she figured they had good reason.

Whenever Jemima recalled the hatred she'd seen in Big Jim's eyes, she couldn't suppress a shiver. James confessed to her that since that encounter his childhood nightmare of running from the Indians had returned, startling him awake, night after night.

"But you were so brave," Jemima told him.

"I was terrified." He gave her a lopsided grin. "Anyway, don't tell Mama I'm having those dreams again. She's got enough to worry about."

Jemima nodded, proud her big brother trusted her with this glimpse into his heart. James was always looking out for everybody. She ached for him, knowing how the dreams bedeviled him. But despite his fears and their mother's resistance, she never doubted their father's obsession with Kentucky would one day lead their family deeper into the wilderness. As for herself, their encounter with the Cherokee men had shown her that Indians were just people, same as white folks. Big Jim was scary, but the shorter Indian had looked at her with kind eyes. It made things easier somehow to have seen them for herself.

If going west would please her father, then she was willing to do it. In truth, she'd have done a great deal more than brave a few angry Indians to secure a place in her father's heart. Though he'd always claimed her publicly as his own, Jemima couldn't escape the feeling that he didn't love her as deeply as her siblings—*How could he?*—since she was a constant reminder of the darkest stain on their family's story.

She'd been eight years old when the nagging feeling that she was different from her brothers and sisters welled up inside her so strongly she couldn't keep silent. Her family had spent the day at a cornhusking, and on the way home, she'd lagged behind the rest of the them, scuffling her bare feet in the dried leaves that covered the trail, pondering the moment earlier that day when a group of adults had burst into laughter after she'd walked past. That sort of thing had happened at other gatherings over the years, and on those occasions she'd sought out James for reassurance. Somehow, this time, she felt sure his kind words wouldn't be enough.

That evening, when the supper dishes had been cleared away, she tugged on her mother's sleeve.

"Mama, why do people whisper things and laugh when I'm around? I hate it."

A moment earlier the cabin had been filled with voices, but now it grew quiet. Her father shifted in his seat and stared into the fire, avoiding Jemima's eyes, but her mother took her hand and said: "I need some fresh air. Let's go down to the creek."

As they walked along the creek bank in the twilight, they were accompanied by the soothing sound of water swirling across the rocks. Jemima took deep breaths, savoring the moist air, and felt the knot in her stomach loosen the tiniest bit.

After a while, her mother sat down on the mossy bank and patted the ground next to her. "This is one of my favorite spots. I come here when I have things I need to think through."

Jemima sat down and leaned against her mother's shoulder. She reached for her mother's hand and cradled it in both of hers. She almost never had her all to herself. Whatever unsettled feelings she had about her place in the family or her father's feelings toward her, she'd never once doubted her mother's love.

The creek was so clear Jemima could see fish, tiny darting shadows, amid the small stones that covered the bottom. The water seemed to whisper to her, and unlike the human voices that often left her anxious, the creek spoke of comfort and grace and belonging.

She looked up at her mother. "Sometimes I hear voices in the water."

Her mother smiled down at her. "So do I."

As the shadows slowly gathered around them, her mother spoke of the rumors that had begun even before Jemima's birth and the misunderstanding that had brought them about.

"Folks love to gossip, sweetheart, so you and I will just have to do our best to ignore them. The main thing I want you to know is that none of it's your fault. Your Daddy claims you. It doesn't matter what anyone else says."

Jemima nodded and snuggled closer. But in her heart, she believed it did matter, perhaps to her father, most of all.

After their family's return from Sycamore Shoals, her father spent a year going from cabin to cabin up and down the Yadkin, talking about Kentucky to anyone who'd listen. It was a hard sell. Jemima overheard one neighbor say: "You might be right that I'll be sorry if I don't go, Daniel, but at least I'll be alive to have regrets." Such talk didn't deter her father. He never wavered, even on the night when Jesse and Jonathan, who by this time were courting young women whose families lived along the Yadkin, announced they intended to stay behind in Carolina. Jemima's heart sank as she watched her mother's eyes fill with tears.

"Don't cry, Aunt Becca," Jesse said, reaching across the table and taking her hand.

"You've found yourselves good women," her mother said. Her voice broke and she paused to gather herself. "You treat them proper, you hear. I don't want folks saying I didn't raise you right."

"Why, I'm always telling folks how proper our family is," Jesse said, straight faced. "Just the other day I told my future in-laws that my Mama and Daddy got married when I was seven years old."

Her mother's eyes widened in surprise, then she started to laugh and wagged a finger at Jesse.

Despite her father's impatience to leave for Kentucky, her mother had unfinished business that couldn't be hurried. On May 23, 1773, she bore her eighth child. Susannah, at twelve, was deemed old enough to help the midwife, while Jemima was still banished to the porch with her father and brothers. When the family finally trooped in to see the newborn, her mother pulled the blanket back in the flickering firelight to show them the baby's face.

"His name's Jesse Bryan Boone," she said.

Jemima watched as Big Jesse's eyes flew to her mother's face, and she sensed a shared remembering pass between them. Wiping a hand across his cheek, Jesse bent over the newborn and said softly: "Howdy, Jesse Bryan."

Her father was in high spirits and her mother was subdued on the day they departed for Kentucky. He'd managed to gather five families from Carolina, including Uncle Squire and Aunt Jane, as well as a party of forty Virginians, led by William Russell, a man of substantial property whose home at Castlewoods in southern Virginia would be the rendezvous point before the company headed down the trace toward Cumberland Gap.

Jemima thought the Gap must be a magical place because it drew her father the way a lodestone attracted iron filings. When she was very small, she'd imagined there was literally a door at the Gap that one had to open and pass through to arrive in Kentucky. Even when James had corrected this childish misperception, she'd continued to visualize it that way. A door in the side of a mountain. A magical place, indeed.

Jemima was surprised to learn that Captain Russell, along with his oldest son, Henry, intended to journey with them. Plenty of rich men were eager to acquire land in Kentucky, but few actually wanted to face the dangers that lurked there. She was surprised, too, that her father didn't seem to mind that folks were calling the company "the Russell expedition." The Virginians referred to her father as "the guide," as if he were no more than the hired help, but her father shrugged it off; all he cared about was getting to Kentucky ahead of the crowds he was certain would soon pour into the territory.

The autumn air was crisp, and the mountains were bathed in shades of red and gold as they set out, leading heavily laden pack animals and driving cattle and hogs down the trace toward the Gap. Some of the livestock were belled so they could be found if they wandered off the trail. What with the clanging of bells, the barking of hounds, and the high-pitched cries of the children, there was no hope of hiding their progress through the woods.

As darkness fell one evening, Jemima asked, "Aren't we in Indian territory now? Shouldn't we try to be quieter?" Her father studied her a moment, as if judging whether, at eleven, she was old enough to handle the truth.

"It's hard for a half-dozen woodsmen to move through Indian lands unnoticed, Jemima. But with a crowd like this . . ." He swept his hand through the air, indicating the dozens of people around them whose forms were lit by the flames of scattered campfires. The flickering light elongated their shadows, stretching them high into the branches of the trees. "Our best bet is to stay vigilant and move as quickly as we can through the Gap and on to the place along the Kentucky River that I've picked out for us. Once we're there, we'll be in a position to defend ourselves."

"How long will that take?"

He frowned. "We're moving slower than I'd hoped; at this rate we'll be out of supplies before we get to the Gap. I'm sending some men back to Castlewoods in the morning to get more cornmeal and cattle." His expression lightened and he gave Jemima a reassuring smile. "We'll be fine. Just wait till you see where we're going to settle. There's a salt spring where the buffalo gather in herds so large you could walk across their backs for a quarter mile and never set foot on the ground. It's beautiful land."

Later that evening, after Jemima spread out her bedroll, she tugged open the drawstring bag that held her most valuable possessions: a small polished stone from the creek back home; her only piece of jewelry—a tiny locket that contained a strand of James's hair she'd secreted away one day after her mother had given him a haircut; her knitting needles and a skein of yarn her mother had dyed pink using sumac berries. Holding each one in turn made her feel as if her world was still solid even though everything around her seemed off balance and unfamiliar. She felt around the bottom of the bag, searching for the final item, a strip of blue velvet that she wore in her hair on special occasions. Her fingers pressed into the bag's soft corners, slowly at first, then frantically. It wasn't there.

She closed her eyes, trying to think when she'd last seen it, then felt her stomach lurch as she remembered draping it over a branch at their campsite several nights earlier because it had gotten damp. *Lost.* She slid under the blankets and turned her face away from the fire, doing her best to muffle the sobs that welled up in her throat. After a moment she felt a hand on her shoulder.

"Jemima?"

Jemima sniffed and looked up. James's blonde hair shone white against the dark trees that arched above their heads. "What's wrong?" he whispered.

The story of the forgotten ribbon spilled out of her. She knew James wouldn't laugh or tell her it was just a piece of cloth and not worth fretting about. When she'd finished, James leaned over and kissed her forehead. The newly sprouted stubble on his chin was scratchy, and his breath was warm on her cheek.

"Go to sleep, little sister," he said, "things'll look better in the morning."

When she woke at daybreak, it was so foggy that the people moving around her looked like ghosts flitting in and out of clouds that had fallen to the ground. Shivering, she slipped out of her blankets, unwrapped a piece of cold pone, and ate quickly. Wiping the crumbs from her fingers, she began to pack the panniers with the cooking utensils. Her mother had given her the task of making sure nothing was left behind when they broke camp each morning. Given her failure with her hair ribbon, Jemima vowed to scour the campsite, not once, but twice each morning for the remainder of the journey. A few steps away, Susannah was busy with her own chores, using a curled slab of hickory bark to scrape dirt over the smoldering remains of their campfire to ensure no embers remained.

"Have you seen James?" Jemima asked.

Suzy straightened and brushed a strand of hair back into her white linen cap, leaving a sooty smear on her forehead. "He left this morning," she said. "He volunteered to go with the men who're backtracking to Castlewoods to get more supplies. He said he needed to look for something."

All that morning, despite the chill in the air, Jemima felt warm all over. With any luck, her ribbon would soon be hers again, and while that was wonderful enough, what warmed her even more was knowing James had volunteered to retrace all those long miles on her behalf.

Several days later, Jemima woke to the sound of hoofbeats at dawn. By the time she sat up, the sentries were shouting a warning, the dogs were barking, and everyone was tossing aside their blankets and scrambling to their feet. A disheveled man on horseback burst through the tree line at the edge of the camp and was greeted by a host of rifles.

"Indians," he yelled, and the men swarmed around him, blocking Jemima's view. Only the mounted man's head and shoulders remained visible, silhouetted against the red and gold of the trees. She saw him gesturing wildly, but she was too far away to hear his words. She exchanged a frightened glance with Susannah, who stood nearby with baby Jesse on her hip; he whimpered as Susannah hugged him closer.

After a moment, Jemima saw her mother emerge from the crowd. Her face was drained of all color, and her eyes looked glassy. Jemima felt a chill run through her body.

"Mama?"

Her mother passed her without speaking and headed straight to one of their tall, woven panniers. Bending deep into the basket, she surfaced clutching her best linen sheet.

Several men, including Uncle Squire, had mounted their horses, reining them in next to her father, who was looking up at Squire with a dazed expression. The milling horses raised a swirl of dust, and Jemima ducked her head. When she looked up again, her mother was handing the tightly folded sheet to her uncle.

"For James," her mother said.

Uncle Squire nodded, his face grim, and tucked the sheet inside his shirt. As the riders wheeled their mounts and spurred them down the trail, Jemima began to shake. *It's James. The sheets are for bandages.*

But when her mother turned around, Jemima saw the truth on her face: James was dead, and her mother's finest sheet would be his burial shroud.

15

Rebecca

Rebecca set the bucket on the creek bank and stared down at the slow-moving water. She'd come here each morning since their retreat to the Clinch settlements, praying to find the solace that water had given her in the past, but in the weeks since James's death, the creek spoke of nothing but sorrow. She sat down on the grass and let her bare feet sink into the sluggish current, too weary to contemplate the trudge back up the hill to the tiny cabin that friends had offered them as a refuge while Daniel decided what they should do next. She scooted forward so that her feet were ankle deep, then realized the hem of her gown had trailed into the water. She let it be. Nothing mattered, least of all a muddy hem, when a body couldn't sleep, could barely eat, and had no tears left to cry.

She could recall only flashes of the events immediately following James's murder. She had a vague memory of the men arguing about whether to go on to Kentucky or turn back to the settlements in southwest Virginia. She remembered Daniel walking beside her horse, his hand resting on the mare's shoulder, grasping her elbow if she wavered, a sturdy presence that kept her upright in the saddle. She couldn't recall how the company had dispersed, or if she'd said goodbye to the women who'd been her traveling companions. She had only a hazy memory of hugging Jane on the day she and Squire had departed to head back over the mountains to Carolina.

But two images remained clear in her mind: the shattering sorrow on Daniel's face when the horseman had delivered the news of James's murder and the mound of raw earth that marked their son's grave, a lonely spot alongside the trace that led them back to Castlewoods. She remembered putting her hand on the mound of bare soil, still unbelieving, certain there'd been a mistake and that James would come whistling out of the woods to tell her the story of his escape.

She shifted on the bank and looked over her shoulder at their borrowed cabin where Susannah and Jemima would be cooking breakfast for the rest of the family. The girls had stepped in to take care of so many things because she couldn't summon the energy to care about meals or dishes or laundry. She spent most of each day searching for glimpses of James.

She might see him when Jemima tilted her head a certain way. Or it might be Israel's voice floating down from the loft, sounding so like his brother that she felt a momentary leap of joy before the pain of remembrance washed over her. The crisp air that met her when she stepped out of the cabin each morning was a mockery, reminding her of James's childish delight at the turning of the leaves each fall. How could the ridgelines turn gold and crimson as they always had when he was no longer there to see it?

The days were hard, but the nights were worse. She tossed and turned for hours, and even when she finally slept, she was plagued by vivid dreams; often James was a little boy again, and she was comforting him after one of his nightmares. Even after she woke, she could still hear his voice calling her.

Weeks had passed before Rebecca learned that Adam, a slave owned by Captain Russell, had been part of James's party and had somehow escaped the slaughter. He'd staggered into the settlements, ragged and starving, eleven days after the massacre. Daily she found herself looking in the direction of the slave cabins that sat along the creek bottom at the rear of the Russell property. On one occasion she saw Adam from a distance and discerned which cabin was his, but for weeks, she made no move in his direction. She felt torn between wanting to know the truth about that night and fearing the truth would be more than she could bear.

She knew few details. All Squire had said, when he'd returned from burying the bodies, was that James and Captain Russell's son, as well as two other young men and a slave, had been killed where they'd slept. She clung to the hope that their end had been quick, that perhaps the boys hadn't even wakened. But slowly, as her initial shock wore off, she realized she'd go mad if she spent the rest of her life imagining what James had endured that night. She needed to know.

One evening, when the moon offered just enough light so she could make her way across the field without carrying a lantern, she slipped out of the cabin and headed downhill toward the creek. She stepped into the shadows of the tree line, looked over her shoulder to be sure no one was watching, then moved silently through the trees toward the row of slave cabins. Daniel had refused to answer her questions, and she felt sure the only way she'd get a full recounting of what had happened to James was to confront Adam when no one else was around. The soft glow of hearth fires flickered between the cracks of the poorly chinked structures; as she moved down the slave row, she heard a woman's voice, beautiful and weary, singing softly in the darkness.

The rough plank door of Adam's cabin was slightly ajar. At her soft knock, it swung open, revealing a man who looked to be in his twenties. Adam's rough-woven shirt was stained with grease, his breeches were tattered, and his feet were bare. Though he was only slightly taller than she was, his broad shoulders made him seem massive. Facing him alone might have frightened her if it hadn't been for the moonlit sorrow she saw in the young man's face. Here was a soul as wounded as she was.

Adam glanced hurriedly about. "Miz Boone, it ain't seemly for you to be here."

Seemly. It had been years since she'd been "seemly" in most folk's eyes. If this gave them one more thing to talk about, so be it. She was past caring.

"I made sure no one saw me, Adam. I'm not leaving until you tell me what happened to my son."

"Miz Boone, this ain't safe for either of us." His voice was threaded with fear.

She didn't move. Her determination must have shown on her face because after a slight hesitation, Adam stepped back to let her inside.

The cabin's one room was tiny, with a dirt floor that was bare except for a blanket spread across a pile of straw in one corner, a rough stool by the fire, and a battered cook pot on the hearth. A heavy homespun jacket hung on a peg by the door. Adam motioned her toward the stool, and after she was seated, he sank to the floor, sitting cross-legged in the dirt alongside the fire so that his face was lit by the flames.

"Do you live here by yourself?" she asked. There'd been few slaves at the Forks, so her experience with the institution was limited; she'd assumed privacy was a rarity.

"My wife and child were sold out of here two months ago when Master Russell decided to take me to Kentucky. My father, Charles, lived here, too, until . . ." Adam's voice trailed off.

A slave named Charles had been among the dead in James's party. It dawned on Rebecca that while the loss of a single precious soul had left her reeling, Adam had lost his entire family in a matter of months. "I'm so sorry, Adam."

He'd been sitting stiffly, as if he expected harsh words from her, questions, perhaps, about why he'd survived while James had perished. As her words of condolence hung in the air, Adam raised his chin and looked straight at her for the first time.

"Master James was a good boy," Adam said. "He was kind to me." His eyes softened. "And I know he loved his Mama."

Her heart lurched heavily in her chest. "What makes you say that?"

"Because he was calling for you when he died."

She swallowed the sob that welled up in her throat but let her tears fall where they would, not bothering to wipe them away as Adam continued.

"We were hurrying to catch up with your party, but twilight overtook us along the trace. When it was too dark to go on, we camped alongside a creek. Wolves howled all around us, and the Mendinhall boys were scared witless. Your James pulled a book out of his pack and read aloud to calm them down. It was so dark he had to lean close to the fire to make out the words. He was still reading when I went to sleep."

Adam shifted uneasily. "Along about daybreak, the Indians fired into the camp, then rushed out of the woods, screaming so loud I thought there was a hundred of them." He grimaced as if the sound still echoed in his ears. "The Mendinhall brothers died right away from the gunshots. Your boy and Master Russell's son, Henry, were hit bad and couldn't get off their blankets, but they were still alive. I was sleeping furthest from the fire, so I was able to slide out of my bedroll and down the creek bank without being seen. There was a big snag of logs caught up against the bank, and I hid behind them. I saw everything from there."

His voice had grown increasingly harsh as the memories rolled over him until his words cracked, and he began to cry. "I couldn't save my father; I couldn't save nobody."

She nodded, unable to speak, her own face wet with tears.

The slave's eyes darkened with anger. "There was a tall Indian who was the leader; he was a devil. He cut . . ." Adam stopped.

"I need to know what you saw, Adam."

"Don't make me speak it, Miz Boone. It won't change nothing—your boy'll still be dead."

"Squire wouldn't tell me anything, Adam, wouldn't even look at me when he got back from burying the boys. Nothing could be worse than not knowing."

"Not knowing's a blessing," he said.

But little by little she coaxed the rest of the story out of him until he was reliving that night so completely it was as if he were alone, speaking aloud to himself.

"The big Indian came up to the boys and stood over them with his knife, like he was going to finish them off, but then your boy called him by name, said to him, 'Big Jim, it's me, James Boone.'"

She gasped, instantly seeing the pointed face of the Indian who'd come to their campsite on the Watauga.

"Big Jim lowered his knife," Adam continued. "For a minute I thought he might put a stop to the killing, but then he started to laugh. He began to taunt them boys, thrusting his knife toward their chests, then moving it up to their heads. They used their hands to block the blade, and pretty soon their arms was sliced all to pieces and covered with blood. Master James was hollering at him the whole time, asking if his family was alive—begging Big Jim to spare the rest of you—but that Indian just kept laughing. Wouldn't tell him nuthin'. That's when your boy began calling for you."

She moaned, unable to bear any more. She sank onto the hearth and retched a mouthful of bile onto the stones; her throat burned as the sour smell filled the room.

Behind her, Adam's voice grew soft again. "One of the other Indians finally came up and finished them off, tomahawking them in the head. It was a mercy."

She remained on her knees, doubled over, while Adam sat quietly beside her.

Dear God, how could You let my gentle boy die like that? I'll never forgive You. I'll never forgive myself. He was calling for me . . .

When she finally straightened up, Adam stood and helped her to her feet. She swayed unsteadily on the hard clay floor, her face swollen and her insides hollowed out and empty.

She didn't know how long they stood that way. For a time, she wasn't aware that she was clutching Adam's arm, but even after she realized it, she couldn't let go; his solid presence was all that anchored her body to the world.

"Miz Boone," Adam said. His voice sounded muffled, as if she were listening to him underwater. "Please—if they find you here . . ."

She knew he was right. She knew, too, that once she stepped outside, she and Adam would never speak freely again. If they chanced to meet, they would act as if nothing had ever passed between them, but she knew she'd always remember him. She'd been with James when his life began; Adam was there when it ended.

16

Susannah

Susannah slipped out of the cabin and took a deep breath. *Fresh air.* Their borrowed cabin was so cramped that just moving from hearth to table was like dancing—someone else had to move whenever she took a step. She sank into the grass and looked up at the tree limbs above her head, fanning herself with her apron. At fourteen, she knew she was capable of handling every household chore, but it didn't mean she enjoyed it. Her shift was soaked with sweat from hours of bending over the hearth, and the lingering smell of burnt cornpone clung to her clothes and hair.

These days she felt as if someone was standing on her chest, making it hard to draw a breath. She was a castaway—like the character called Gulliver in her father's favorite book—washed ashore here in Castlewoods amid the wreckage of her father's plans. Each day she struggled to tamp down feelings of rage—rage at her brother's killers, rage at God and his angels for allowing it to happen, rage that gentle James, of all people, had been taken so cruelly. She was angry, too, at the men in the company who'd insisted on turning back after the massacre. For her, every eastward step felt like a defeat, like an act of cowardice. It meant that James had died for nothing. In a single night, she'd lost a brother and also her best chance—perhaps her only chance—to explore those wild lands she'd spent her childhood dreaming about.

In the weeks since James's death, there'd been an increasing number of Indian raids all across the backcountry, and now no one, no matter where they were, was safe. Every able-bodied man had been called to serve in the militia in what folks were calling "Lord Dunmore's War" after Virginia's royal governor. Her father had been awarded the rank of lieutenant and ordered to range the countryside with a dozen men, keeping track of the Indians' movements between the Clinch settlements and Cumberland Gap.

Susannah rubbed her aching feet. She rarely had a minute to herself or even a chance to sit down. How she envied her father, free to roam while she was stuck shouldering many of the duties that normally fell to her mother. Since James's death, her mother had spent long days sitting listlessly, nursing baby Jesse, or just staring into space. While the baby was thriving, her mother's cheeks had grown so thin that her dark eyes dominated her face. It unnerved Susannah to realize her mother wasn't invincible. Always before, her mother had carried on no matter what, but losing James had broken her.

As badly as her mother was affected, Susannah sometimes thought Jemima was suffering as much or more. Her sister's response to the trag-edy had been to stay in constant motion—tending the younger children, chopping vegetables for the stew pot, hauling firewood—but while she rarely stood still, she almost never spoke. It was like having a ghost flitting through the cabin. At night, Susannah often heard Jemima's muffled sobs in the bed beside her. Susannah wanted to comfort her, but since they'd never shared sisterly confidences in the past, she didn't know how to begin; she'd always left such things to James.

One steamy morning in late June, Susannah had just finished feeding the younger children breakfast when her father entered the cabin, hung his hat on a peg, and announced he'd been chosen to go to Kentucky to warn several surveying parties that they needed to retreat to the settlements due to the Indian unrest.

Susannah watched as her mother slowly turned to look at him.

"How can you agree to go?" her mother said, shifting Jesse Bryan onto her hip. Her voice was low, but the cords in her neck were tight as fiddle strings, as if she were using every muscle in her body to keep her voice under control.

Susannah felt a surge of joy. There was a flicker of life in her mother's eyes for the first time in months.

"I have to follow orders, Becca," her father said.

"So if they ordered you to stand in front of a cannon and catch the ball, you'd do it? I can't see a heap of difference between that and sending you off to Kentucky with the Indians in an uproar."

"We're in a war, Becca," he said in the same patient tone he used when four-year-old Daniel Morgan didn't understand something.

Susannah looked over at her mother just in time to see her eyes spark, then blaze up like flint struck next to dry tinder; before her father had finished speaking, her mother had handed Jesse Bryan to Jemima and headed around the table, ready to stand toe-to-toe.

"So what are the children and I supposed to do while you run all over Kentucky looking for those surveyors?"

"You'll have to fort up," her father said.

That was the final straw. Her mother, who almost never raised her voice, was yelling: "So you expect us to stay in Virginia without you, penned up like hogs alongside a bunch of strangers for God knows how long while you run off to Kentucky and get yourself scalped? We just lost James! How come wherever you are is never where you want to be? How come the children and I are never enough?"

Susannah took Becky and Daniel Morgan by the hand. Israel shooed Levina outside ahead of him, and Jemima followed with the baby, shutting the door behind them. The shouting carried through the door and accompanied them as they walked away. Jemima was frowning and Israel looked worried, but their parents' angry words sounded like music to Susannah. Since James's death she'd been afraid her mother might never again care about anything in this world enough to fight for it.

Her father went to Kentucky, and her mother was right: living in Fort Moore was like living in a hog pen. When she first saw the nasty conditions, her mother said under her breath, "Lie down with dogs, arise with fleas."

After a few days in the fort, Susannah figured fleas were the least of it. Living cheek by jowl with all manner of folks meant that soon they all had lice, and their food stores were overrun with vermin. Israel hung their bags of cornmeal from the rafters of their ramshackle cabin, but the mice still managed to nibble holes in the sacking and pilfer the contents. Each morning, Susannah and Jemima pulled the families' bed ticks into the open air so the chickens could peck all manner of bugs from the coarse linen folds.

As the summer dragged on, the Indians ranged up and down the backcountry, burning isolated cabins and scalping unwary settlers. Susannah lay in bed at night, scratching first one bite, then another, feeling as if she was watching a dark storm roll toward her with no clue when or where the lightning would strike. It was a strange sensation to spend each day bored to tears one moment, anxious the next.

Most of the fort's inhabitants were men, many of them single. They gathered at the rear of the stockade each evening, and it wasn't long before Susannah was slipping off to join them. She listened as the men swapped stories of faraway places: Williamsburg and Philadelphia to the north, Charleston and Savannah to the south. She marveled at the freedom they took for granted, the ability to pack up and move whenever they took the notion. The more she heard their stories, the more she chafed at her own shrunken world.

When Israel discovered her there one evening, he pulled her aside. "Suzy, you need to be careful. You know what folks say about Mama; they'll be twice as quick to judge you because of that. Mama'd skin you alive if she caught you here."

She knew he was right, yet each night, after the supper dishes were done, she felt pulled in that direction, as if by an invisible thread. Women of any age were in short supply in the backcountry, and though she was only fourteen, the men greeted her enthusiastically. For the first time in her life, she sensed a newfound power as she watched the men jockey for position, each doing their best to catch her eye.

For the first few weeks, they were on their best behavior, but then one young man, hardly older than herself, leaned in and stole a kiss. It was her first, and it was so anticlimactic after years of girlhood imaginings that she burst into tears. The boy blushed and became stutteringly apologetic, but after that boundary had been crossed, more than one of the men managed to coax a kiss or two from her. Each time she hoped it would make her heart pound fast, the way she'd heard older girls describe, but while most of the kisses weren't unpleasant, they left her wondering what all the fuss was about.

One night, having left the gathering to walk home, someone reached out from the darkness of the stable and pulled her roughly into the shadows. The next moment she was pressed against the stable wall, with a hand groping her bodice and the other covering her mouth so she couldn't scream. She bit down hard, sinking her teeth into the man's palm. He yelped and backed away.

"Bitch," he spat. "You'll pay for that."

She pushed past him and ran, lifting her skirts as she escaped the shadows. She didn't slow down until she reached home, where she leaned against the outer wall of the cabin to catch her breath. *No one needs to know,* she thought.

That was the end of her evening excursions, but her assailant got his revenge by starting ugly rumors that spread like plantain across a newly plowed field; soon folks were saying Suzy Boone had done a great deal more than just kiss a few men in the shadows of Fort Moore.

Will Hays rode into the fort toward the end of the summer, tall, dark, and clad in a frock coat with silver buttons. Susannah watched as he reined in his horse and folks clustered around him, eager for news of the outside world.

The handsome newcomer was the topic of fierce debate among the women who gathered at the creek to do laundry the next morning.

"I hear he attended the College of William and Mary," one said.

"Pshaw," said another. "My husband said he's nothing more than a weaver's apprentice who grew tired of the trade and came west to seek his fortune."

"Well, I saw him reading a book on the steps of his cabin last night," the first replied. "Clearly he's an educated man."

A few days later, Susannah was carrying a bucket of water back from the well, picking her way through the manure that littered the dusty ground inside the stockade, when Will stepped into her path.

"Mistress Boone," he said, sweeping off his hat. "Would you do me the honor of walking with me for a bit?"

Without waiting for an answer, he took the heavy bucket out of her hand, and as he reached for it, a spicy scent wafted from his clothes, an exotic smell that spoke of fancy dress balls and parlors and other such places she'd dreamed about but never seen.

They were both silent as Will carried the bucket to the cabin and set it down on the bench outside, but as they continued walking, they began to make small talk, weaving their way among the fort's residents, stacks of firewood, piles of dung, and the chickens, cows, and dogs that wandered through the stockade.

"Tell me about your family," Will said.

"My father's in Kentucky, but we're praying he'll return soon."

"I hear he's quite a woodsman."

She nodded. "He knows Kentucky better than anyone. He talks about it like it's Eden. I can't wait to see it."

"So your family intends to move there?"

"If my father can talk my mother into it."

Will frowned. "I should think it's a wife's duty to obey her husband's wishes."

It was Susannah's turn to frown. Seeing her face, Will quickly added: "Though of course your mother's wishes should be considered as well."

Shortly after nightfall she and Will wound up in the shadows of the blacksmith shop, and when he kissed her, she felt as if warm honey flowed through his mouth into every muscle in her body. It was so different from the furtive kisses she'd experienced earlier in the summer that, as Will walked her back to her cabin that night, she felt sure she'd found true love and the man she'd marry. It took her months to realize she was only half right.

17

Jemima

Fort Moore was the nastiest place Jemima had ever laid eyes on. The moment she walked through the gate, she began counting the days till she could walk out again, which she knew couldn't happen until her father returned from his mission of warning the surveyors in Kentucky. All manner of fetid odors wafted across the stockade. She covered her nose with the hem of her apron as she followed her mother and Susannah toward the tiny cabin they'd been assigned.

James would have laughed at their miserable surroundings and made up games to help pass the time—challenging her to sing as many verses of "Black Jack Davey" as she could in the time it took to draw a bucket of water from the well or having her count how many cow patties she passed when running an entire loop around the stockade. The world felt so empty without him. Night after night, she was startled awake by the fleeting belief that she'd dreamed his death and that if she turned on her pallet in the crowded cabin, she'd see his fair hair peeking out of a bedroll nearby. *How can he be gone forever? How can it be that I'll never see him again?* Her grief felt bottomless, and it was mixed with a sense of guilt so profound that she couldn't speak of it to anyone, even her mother. Deep in her heart, Jemima felt certain that if she hadn't told James about her lost ribbon, he wouldn't have volunteered to backtrack down the trace, and he would still be alive.

Just days after the massacre, her father had handed her the length of blue velvet.

"Squire found this tucked inside James's shirt," he'd said, his eyes hollow with grief.

She'd stood, frozen in place, clutching the ribbon as if it were her lost brother's hand. Later, as she rolled it up to store in her cloth bag, she discovered a dark stain on the underside. *Blood.* Her hands shook as she tucked the ribbon away. After that, she could barely bring herself to touch it, though she'd have fought tooth and nail if anyone had threatened to take it from her.

She couldn't share these feelings with anyone. She felt certain Susannah would only remind her there was nothing she could do to change things. Her father was gone, as usual, not that she'd ever felt comfortable confiding in him anyway. Most disconcerting of all, her mother was not herself. That, more than anything, left Jemima feeling utterly untethered.

As the weeks dragged on, her grief slowly changed into anger; anger at herself for her part in causing James's death; anger at James for leaving her, however unwillingly; anger at her mother who seemed unable to notice that others were suffering too. The more Jemima thought about it all, the angrier she got, until she was slamming doors and snapping at the younger children.

"Jemima, you need to tell Levina you're sorry for fussing at her like that," Susannah said one night as they were readying the table for dinner. "You know she didn't mean to spill the mush."

"Mind your own business, Susannah."

All the children turned to look at Jemima, as astonished as if she'd suddenly grown horns. Normally she was the sister everyone turned to when they needed a kind word, and none of them, except Israel, dared talk back to Susannah.

Susannah stared hard at Jemima, waiting for her to back down, but Jemima continued to stare back defiantly.

Susannah was the first to look away. "Well, what do you know," she said, bending over the hearth to stir the stew. "The kitten's grown claws."

When no Indians were spotted in the vicinity of Fort Moore for several weeks, the men assigned to guard the fort grew increasingly complacent. Her mother fretted daily about their lack of vigilance.

"If your father was here, things would change in a hurry," she said at supper one evening.

"Do you want me to talk to them, Mama?" Israel asked. His tone made it clear he dreaded the prospect. With James dead and their father away, Israel was the oldest male in the family, but at barely fifteen, he wasn't privy to the councils held by the men. Once so full of fun, Israel had grown solemn since James's murder.

"Don't fret, son," her mother said. "It's not your place to talk reason to empty-headed men twice your age. I just pray we don't all pay for their foolishness."

A few days later, Jemima heard her mother express her concerns to several of the other women, asking if they'd speak to their husbands about the need to tighten the fort's defenses.

"I'd be happy to talk to them with you," her mother said.

"You stay away from my husband," one of them snapped. "I've heard all about you."

Talk back to her, Jemima thought. *Stand up for yourself. Stand up for me. You've always said to ignore what folks say, but I'm sick of it. They call you an adulteress. They believe I'm a bastard. They say Susannah's loose. I hate the way they talk about our family, and you never do anything about it.*

A few days later, when Jemima was helping her mother drag the bed ticks into the sun, she overheard a woman say: "It must run in the family—that oldest daughter has turned out just like her."

Jemima bit her lip, holding back words of denial that blistered her tongue, praying her mother would speak up. As usual, her mother acted as if she hadn't heard, but as she bent to fluff the tick, Jemima saw tears in her eyes.

Her mother's patience ran out on a sweltering afternoon in July when the air was so thick it was a struggle to walk through it. The day started out like so many others, with Jemima following her mother out of the cabin to fill their buckets at the spring outside the fort, preferring that water's fresh taste to the silt-filled water from the fort's well. Before venturing beyond the safety of the walls, they paused the way her father had taught them, surveying the tree line that edged the cleared area around the fort. He'd trained everyone in the family to watch—not so much for human figures in the shadows of the trees—but for the glint of a gun barrel sticking up above fallen tree trunks or from the midst of heavy underbrush. He'd explained that the untrained eye might mistake

Indian guns for tree branches, but an observant person could spot them if they knew what to look for.

What they saw on this particular day made her mother suck in her breath and stand rigid with anger. A half-dozen soldiers had ventured beyond the walls and laid down their weapons to play a spirited game of ball using a hog's bladder they'd inflated and tied off with a leather whang. Several other militiamen were sitting lazily by the large pond at the bottom of the hill a hundred yards distant from the fort; two of them had fishing poles, and another was stretched out on his back, asleep. You'd have thought they were spending a quiet Sunday somewhere back east instead of at a western fort with raiding Indians roaming the countryside.

Her mother turned abruptly and strode back through the fort gate with Jemima hurrying to keep up. Once inside their cabin, her mother slammed her bucket down and snatched her rifle off its pegs.

Jemima looked around the empty cabin. "Where are the children?"

"Israel took them to watch the blacksmith shoe his mare." Her mother slung her powder horn over her shoulder. "Jemima, I need you to find Susannah and tell her to borrow Will's rifle, then both of you meet me by the back gate."

Jemima bristled at being ordered about but swallowed a sharp retort when she saw the determined look on her mother's face.

By the time Jemima had found Susannah, her mother had gathered several other women at the back gate and was talking earnestly. Jemima saw in a glance that the women who'd made disparaging remarks about her mother weren't among them. "Remember," her mother was saying, "act as if you're just going about your chores, but when you hear our guns, close the front gate as fast as you can."

Jemima saw her mother had collected three borrowed rifles, in addition to her own and Israel's. Susannah had Will's rifle as well, for a total of six. Her mother's mouth was set in a determined line as she divvied out the rifles so that each of them carried two.

The three of them ducked through the unguarded back gate and slipped along the stockade wall, pausing a moment with their backs against the rough log palings before hurrying across the open space behind the fort and ducking into the nearest grove of trees.

Her mother passed her powder horn to Susannah. "Use half a charge of powder, and don't put a ball in."

At those instructions, Jemima looked up and met Susannah's eye. Anyone who'd spent time in the backcountry knew the Indians' habit of loading their guns light in order to conserve powder. It was easy to tell the echoing report of an Indian gun from that of a white man's just by the sound.

Jemima's heart hammered as they readied the guns. It was hot, even in the shade of the trees, and she slapped a mosquito that buzzed near her ear. Her mother looked composed as she put the stopper back in the powder horn and slung it across her shoulder.

"Ready?" she asked.

Jemima nodded.

"I'll fire first. Suzy, then you fire, and then Jemima. As soon as we've switched rifles, we'll all shoot the second round together and then run as fast as we can for the back gate. Don't forget to grab both your rifles."

After her mother's first shot shattered the midday silence, everything happened fast. Jemima was enveloped by the smell of gun smoke. There was a succession of deafening roars, and then she felt the brittle grass crunching under her feet as they raced back to the fort. By the time they were inside and the rear gate had slammed shut behind them, there were already whoops of female laughter coming from the corner blockhouse overlooking the front gate. The three of them hurriedly climbed the ladder to view the scene outside the walls.

"You should have seen them panic as soon as the guns went off," one woman said. "The men came hightailing it back to the fort so fast they left their rifles lying in the grass."

A second woman, still chuckling, added: "When they realized the gates were shut, they scattered like a flock of frightened chickens. A few of them even dove into the pond to hide."

As she spoke, several bedraggled figures emerged from the cattails at the pond's edge. Their soggy appearance caused a new wave of laughter among the women.

"Come on back, boys," one woman yelled. "You've protected us enough."

Jemima scrambled down the ladder after her mother and joined the other women who'd gathered at the front gate, which was now wide open. They watched the soldiers filter out of their hiding places. A few of the men looked sheepish, but most were furious. Several of the women whose husbands had been humiliated were as red-faced with anger as the men and cast enraged looks toward her mother.

As the men approached the gate, their lieutenant, his hunting shirt muddied and his face crimson with anger, bellowed: "Who's behind this?"

Jemima held her breath as her mother stepped forward.

The lieutenant's hands curled into fists, and for a moment Jemima thought he was going to strike her. "I'll see you horsewhipped for this."

There was a rumble among the other men and several of the women that signaled their agreement.

Her mother responded: "Captain Russell might have a mind to do some horsewhipping of his own when he hears the entire garrison was caught outside the fort without their weapons near to hand."

Jemima felt a rush of pride. Her mother might choose to ignore the gossip, but she could still be fierce when it came to protecting the family. While it didn't make up for everything, Jemima found herself smiling for the first time in a very long while.

The men shifted, casting glances among themselves and muttering. After a moment, they began to disperse, their wives following behind. When the lieutenant saw he'd been left to face the women alone, he turned on his heel and stalked off, his soggy moccasins leaving wet spots on the dusty ground.

Several of the women crowded around her mother, offering their thanks and taking turns hugging her. Jemima watched her mother's stoic expression soften, registering first surprise, then relief at this sign of acceptance. She'd once said things would change in a hurry "if Daniel was here," but it seemed to Jemima that her mother had done a pretty good job of changing things without him.

"Maybe now the men will take their duties seriously," one woman crowed.

"If nothing else, Rebecca finally got some of them to take a bath," said another.

At that, her mother laughed along with the others, a sweet, welcome sound that Jemima hadn't heard since the day James died. Soon, she was laughing, too.

18

Susannah

On the day Will asked for Susannah's hand, her mother studied the two of them for a moment, then said: "It appears you two have made up your minds, but you need to wait until Daniel returns and get his blessing."

"Certainly, Miz Boone," Will said, though impatience flickered in his eyes.

It was clear to Susannah that her mother had reservations about Will and undoubtedly believed that, at not yet fifteen, she was too young to marry. If anything, that made Susannah even more determined to have her way, and after she discovered Will shared her own desire to escape the settlements and see faraway places, the angel Gabriel couldn't have kept her from him.

"We'll go to Kentucky together," Will told her during one of their stolen moments in the shadows of the stockade. Those words alone were enough to convince Susannah they were meant for each other.

By the time her father made it back to Fort Moore, Will was already a fixture at their cabin, and he wasted no time in doing his best to win her father's approval.

When her father sat down to pen a militia report to Captain Russell, he dipped his quill in the inkpot, stared into space, then laboriously formed a few letters.

"May I be of service, sir?" Will asked.

Her father looked up from the parchment. "Can you write, Will?"

"Certainly, sir. Perhaps you'd prefer to dictate and let me handle the pen?"

"I'd be most appreciative. Writing has never come easy to me."

Susannah and Jemima were working side by side at the hearth, and as the two men began to confer, Jemima leaned over and whispered: "So who's Will courting? You, or Daddy?"

"Shhh," Susannah hissed. "What would you know about courting?"

"Folks say Will's been asking around the fort about Daddy," Jemima said softly. "He seems to think our family stands to make a fortune on Kentucky land." Jemima's eyes were worried. "And folks say he drinks too much."

Susannah glared at her. "You of all people should know that gossip isn't always true."

Jemima jerked backward as if Susannah had slapped her. There were tears in her eyes as she turned away, and Susannah spent the rest of that evening cursing her inability to think before she spoke, wishing she could return to the moment she'd uttered those hurtful words and pluck them from the air before they reached her sister's ears.

As soon as Susannah heard her father had been hired to mark out a trace to Kentucky, she was determined to go along, and doubly so when she discovered Will had signed on as part of the crew.

"I aim to be the first white woman to set foot in Kentucky," she told him. She knew her mother would be against her going, so she thought long and hard about the best way to convince her father to include her in the company.

"I can cook for the men," she told him. "They'll work better if they're well fed."

"Cooking on the trail is hard work, Suzy."

"I can do it," she said. When his expression told her he was actually considering it, she played her next card: "Course, it wouldn't be good for an unmarried woman to traipse into the wilderness with a bunch of men."

And that's how she wound up not only being hired as the camp cook, but also getting her father's permission to marry Will. The wedding was a hurried affair, but she didn't care; it was enough to be Will's wife and know that she could finally go exploring. At every opportunity, she gloated about her part in the impending journey to Israel.

"Who'd have thought I'd get to see Kentucky before you," she said, arching an eyebrow at him. "It's a pity you're stranded here with Mama and the children while Daddy and I go cut the road."

Israel stuck his tongue out, then grinned and reached over to ruffle her hair the way he had since they were children. "You may be an old married lady now, Suzy, but you're still my little sister. Tell Will to take good care of you, or he'll answer to me."

The road-building company was under the employ of Colonel Richard Henderson, an old acquaintance of her father's from Carolina. Henderson had negotiated a private land purchase with the Cherokee nation, acquiring an enormous tract of Kentucky wilderness in exchange for six wagons loaded with woolen garments, blankets, jugs of liquor, and firearms.

Susannah marveled that Colonel Henderson had never laid eyes on his just-purchased land; he was relying on her father to pick a spot, plant a settlement, and lay out a trace so settlers could make their way to Kentucky. In return, he'd promised her father two thousand acres of prime property.

The whole enterprise struck Susannah as odd. "Even if Colonel Henderson bought the land from the Cherokee, surely he knows the Shawnee claim it as well? Seems to me all the Colonel's done is pay for a chance to fight with the Shawnee."

Her father laughed. "The Colonel knows he'll have trouble with the Shawnee, Suzy, but buying the land from the Cherokee should give his claim legitimacy with the royal governor in Williamsburg."

Susannah shook her head, marveling at how their family's future was now entwined with a business deal that resembled a high-stakes card game; nobody knew who held the winning hand—not her father or Colonel Henderson or the Shawnee or even the King himself.

Her father gathered his company of road builders at the Long Island of the Holston River. Susannah thought their rendezvous point, on the banks of the Holston in the Tennessee Valley, was one of the prettiest sites she'd ever seen. A tall mountain rose abruptly and came to a sharp point at a bend in the river, like the prow of a giant ship docked at the water's edge. A small outpost of scattered homesteads and a trading post stood beside the Holston where it split into two channels separated by a narrow island that was several miles in length. Her father told her the island was a traditional gathering place for the Cherokee, who regarded it as sacred ground. Susannah asked Will to borrow a canoe so they could paddle to the island and explore, but he dismissed the idea, saying: "In a few days, you'll have your fill of exploring."

One of the road builders was a man named Colonel Richard Callaway. Tall, with an angular face and a heavy shock of salt-and-pepper hair that flowed to his shoulders, he was a man of some property and a great deal of self-importance. Since Henderson had chosen her father, now a captain in the militia, to lead the expedition, Colonel Callaway had no choice but to take orders from a lesser officer, though he clearly resented the arrangement.

One afternoon, Callaway sought her father out to inform him that one of the Callaway family's slaves would be accompanying him on the trail to attend to his meals and laundry.

"Dolly's a dependable wench," Callaway said. "I guarantee the men will eat well if you put her in charge of the cook pot." He glanced at Susannah. "I'd have thought your daughter a bit young to, um . . . provision so many men."

Susannah felt herself blush.

Her father stood abruptly, fists clenched. Susannah placed a hand on his arm, and said softly, "It's not worth it."

A muscle twitched in her father's jaw. "Let me remind you, Colonel," he said coldly, "Suzy's newly married, and her husband will be quick to defend his wife's . . . *cooking* . . . if anyone's foolish enough to call it into question. As for your slave woman, I have no objection if she's fit for hard travel."

The company of road builders—two dozen men, plus Susannah and Dolly—set off for Kentucky on a cold day in March 1775. Susannah sat her horse proudly, feeling like a queen headed off to battle. Israel had ridden down from Castlewoods to deliver some final supplies and to see the company off. Susannah blew a kiss to her brother as she rode past. Israel laughed and pantomimed catching it in midair, then kissed his fist and pretended to toss it back to her.

Her father rode in the lead, with Will and herself riding just behind. She knew cutting a path through the wilderness would be dangerous, but she didn't feel daunted, knowing the two of them were with her. She'd yearned to explore like this since she was a child, to see new sights each day, and now, thanks to Will, her wish had come true. He rode straight backed and proud beside her, her own dark-headed knight, like Lancelot in the tales she'd heard as a child. It pleased her immensely to realize Colonel Callaway was riding somewhere to their rear.

She didn't see Callaway's slave woman until her father called a halt late that day. Susannah had butterflies in her stomach as she unpacked the kettles to cook the company's first meal. She'd never been in charge of cooking for so many people. When Dolly appeared alongside her and silently set to work, Susannah studied her out of the corner of her eye, noting that they were about the same height but that the slave woman was at least twice her age.

There had been very few slaves around the Forks or along the Yadkin, and Susannah wasn't sure how to act around the woman. It felt rude not to acknowledge her, but she had no clue how to begin a conversation. They moved awkwardly around each other as they mixed batter for the Dutch ovens and chopped meat for the spits. Dolly worked with downcast eyes, measuring meal, going to the nearby creek for water, seeming to anticipate each need before Susannah thought to ask for it. She tried a time or two to catch Dolly's eye, but without success. She knew, as a white woman, she was free to order Dolly about, but the confidence she'd felt about keeping so many hungry men fed had long since evaporated, and she was silently grateful for Dolly's presence.

On the second day, the terrain grew more difficult, and they were reduced to leading their horses for long stretches. The weedy undergrowth caught at Susannah's skirts and snagged her woolen stockings. She longed for a pair of sturdy leather leggings like the men wore. Will and the other axmen hacked their way, step by step, through dense underbrush, shoving logs off the path and blazing trees at regular intervals to mark the trace.

Late that afternoon, when it was time to set up camp, the exhausted men wrapped themselves in their blankets against the late winter chill and dozed while she and Dolly gathered wood, started the cookfire, hauled water, and prepared the evening meal. Though they worked side by side, Susannah still hadn't heard the woman speak beyond an occasional: "Yes, Miz Hays." The first time Dolly said it, it took Susannah a minute to realize the woman was addressing her, unaccustomed as she was to her new name. Mistress Hays—she liked the sound of it.

After the men were fed, the two of them still had to wash the iron pots, skillets, wooden bowls, and tin cups for the entire company. By the time they were finally able to lie down, most of the men had been snoring for quite some time.

By the third day, Susannah was sure she'd never been so tired in her life. She was also uncomfortably sore from riding for long hours each day, then bending over a cookfire or washtub for hours afterwards. Everything ached. The air was frosty, and as the last pot was scrubbed and packed away, ready for an early morning departure, Susannah was looking forward to slipping under the blankets next to her sleeping husband and spooning her body against his back to warm herself.

"Good night," Susannah said to Dolly as she turned to find Will among the sleeping figures.

"Night Miz Hays," Dolly answered, but something in her tone made Susannah stop and look back.

Colonel Callaway had appeared in front of Dolly holding a pair of muddy riding boots. He dropped them in the dirt at her feet and said, "Have these clean by morning," before turning on his heel and disappearing into the dark.

"Yes, Master Callaway," Dolly said, her voice weary.

As Susannah watched Dolly pick up the boots and head toward the creek, she felt a flare of anger. *That man's insufferable. He should clean his own damn boots.* She walked over to the picket line where the horses were tethered and rummaged in Will's saddlebags. She pulled out two brushes they used to curry mud off the horses, picked up a lantern, lit the candle inside it from the cookfire's coals, and headed to the creek.

Dolly was kneeling, rubbing one of the tall leather boots across the grass, trying to knock the dried mud off, but it was so dark it was impossible to see if she was making any progress.

"Here," Susannah said, handing her one of the brushes and setting the lantern down between them. "You do one and I'll do the other."

Dolly sat frozen for a moment, then managed a quick glance upward as she took the brush. "Thank you kindly, Miz Hays."

They worked side by side as they had these past days, but now the silence felt companionable. When they were done, having wiped the boots down with creek water and dried them with twists of grass, Susannah sat back on her heels, held up her boot, and said: "I would dearly love to stuff a chestnut burr in the toe of this thing."

Dolly didn't reply, but Susannah could feel the woman's shoulders shaking with silent laughter.

After that, she and Dolly began to talk as they cooked and cleaned, most often in whispers so as not to disturb the men who worked or slumbered around them. At first they talked of basic things—recipes or places they'd lived. Then, one evening, Dolly told Susannah about the five babies she'd borne—tenderly listing each of them by name—before confessing that one by one they'd been sold away from her so that now she was alone in the world. Susannah couldn't begin to fathom the grief contained in those few words; it left her breathless.

One day, as they broke camp, kicking dirt on the ashes and scouring the pots for what felt like the thousandth time, Dolly shook her head and said, "Lordy, Miz Hays, I can't believe you came on this trek of your own free will. If I'd had a choice, I'd have stayed east for sure."

"But I wanted to be free . . ." Susannah said, then stopped, embarrassed.

Dolly looked at her with kind eyes. "You think 'cause you're white and your man's brought you to this godforsaken place, that makes you free? Far as I can tell, ain't no woman in this world truly free." She snorted and turned back to the dishes, shaking her head.

One evening Susannah and Dolly left the men sitting around the camp-fires and moved back up the trail searching for a thick stand of brush. It had become their habit to serve as lookouts for each other when either had to answer a call of nature. Dolly had just stepped off the trail and was out of sight when Susannah heard footsteps behind her and swung around to discover Will had followed them. He swayed drunkenly in front of her for a moment before reaching out with rough hands and pulling her against him.

"Will," she said, smelling the whiskey on his breath. Knowing what he had in mind, she said hurriedly: "Dolly's here."

"So . . . she's just a slave," he said, his words slurred. "It's not like she's a lady."

She pushed him angrily away, then felt her head explode as a blow to her cheek knocked her backward against the boulder. She gasped for breath as Will lurched toward her, pushed up her skirts, and forced himself on her. The rock pressed painfully into her back, and her head throbbed from the blow, but when she shifted her weight, trying to escape the pain, he hit her again, splitting her lip.

"Hold still, woman."

She did, despite the rock's sharp edges. She couldn't breathe; the weight of him kept her arms pinned so she couldn't fight back, and she couldn't draw enough breath to scream. But in those few moments, it flashed through her mind that she wouldn't call for help even if she could because she didn't want her father to know what Will was capable of in this drunken state.

She remained silent, despite the pain, and when Will finally stumbled away, buttoning his breeches, Dolly slid around the edge of the boulder and gathered Susannah in her arms. Her shift smelled of wood smoke and warm bread, and as Susannah pressed her face into the rough material, she was overcome by a wave of longing for her mother. She began to cry as Dolly cradled her.

19

Susannah

The next morning Susannah moved gingerly around the camp, her body aching and her mind numb with disbelief. As she loaded pots onto a pack frame, her father paused alongside her.

"Morning, Suzy."

She watched his smile fade as he cupped her chin in his hand, tilting her head so the morning light shone across her cheek.

"That's a nasty bruise. And your lip . . . What happened?"

"I fell," she said quickly. She cleared her throat, trying to steady her voice. "When Dolly and I went back up the trail last night I—I fell against a boulder."

She couldn't look at her father, afraid he'd see the truth in her eyes. She focused, instead, on a point over his shoulder and felt her heart clench as Will stepped into her line of vision, his jaw tense.

Her father gave her arm a sympathetic squeeze and turned away, believing her, and Will's face relaxed. That morning was the beginning of her lying, not just to her father, but also to herself. She vowed never to speak the truth to anyone, too prideful to admit that what her relatives had predicted long ago had come to pass; she'd found the road to Nogoodend.

A few days later, near daybreak, Susannah and Dolly were feeding kindling onto the coals of the fire they'd carefully banked the evening before. The men had begun to rouse from their blankets, stretching and yawning, when one of them yelled, and Susannah swung toward the voice just as blasts of rifle fire shattered the morning stillness.

She stood frozen in horror as a slave named Sam, a big strapping fellow who served as Captain Twitty's manservant, pitched headfirst into the coals at her feet, a dark stain blossoming across the back of his coarse linen shirt. A few paces in front of her, Captain Twitty lay on his bedroll, writhing in pain, his bulldog barking loudly beside him. Disjointed thoughts flashed through her mind—the urge to pull Sam out of the fire, the desire to go to Captain Twitty's aid, but most of all an overwhelming impulse to run. She froze as a figure burst from the woods and ran straight toward her, tomahawk raised. The Indian was steps away when Captain Twitty's dog launched himself into the air, hitting the man square in the chest and tumbling them both to the ground. The Indian screamed as the dog's teeth sank into his neck, and Susannah screamed, too, as someone grabbed her arm.

"Run!" her father's voice hissed in her ear. His hand was on her back, pushing her toward the woods. They crashed through the tangled under-brush in the faint morning light, but when they'd gone a few hundred yards, her father grabbed her shoulder and motioned for her to duck behind the dark bulk of an uprooted tree.

"Keep your head down," he said, then squatted beside her and hurriedly primed his rifle. She looked up and saw her father's moccasins, which he tied to his gun barrel each night when he went to bed, swinging, ghostlike, in the air above her head.

In the distance she heard shouting, the dog yelping, and then nothing but silence. Her thoughts skittered around like a water bug on a pond, and when they landed on Dolly, her stomach turned over. Susannah sat with her back pressed against the log, breathing its moldering scent and staring stupidly at a rip in her skirt. *Will.* Until that moment she hadn't given him a single thought. *Is he alive or dead?* She shivered as she realized she wasn't sure which she hoped for.

She and her father stayed where they were until the rising sun pushed the shadows from the woods and the trees around them were bathed in gold light. Only then did they move cautiously back toward camp.

Captain Twitty and his slave lay where they'd fallen. Sam was dead, lying facedown in the dying embers of the fire. The stench of burned skin made Susannah retch as she helped her father roll the man's body off the coals. The captain's labored breathing filled the clearing, and he moaned as her father turned him over. Bullets had ripped open both his knees, exposing splinters of bone that looked like jagged teeth set in the midst of bloody gums. Nearby, the captain's bulldog lay dead, his head crushed.

"Hit by a war club," her father said, nodding toward the dog, "but he saved Twitty's scalp."

Susannah knelt by Twitty and felt bile rise in her throat. She'd never seen wounds this severe. She looked up at her father, and he shook his head, his face grim.

Over the next hour, the rest of the men trickled back to camp. Susannah was bent over Twitty, wiping the man's face with a damp rag when she looked up and saw Will enter the clearing; his thin face was smeared with dirt, and his eyes were haunted. She was surprised to feel a surge of relief, and when Will spotted her across the clearing, his face came alive, registering such joy that she found herself standing and hurrying toward him. As she settled into his arms, she wondered if perhaps there was hope for their marriage after all.

It was midmorning when Dolly walked into the clearing behind Colonel Callaway. Dolly's dark face shone with sweat, but her features were set in the same expressionless mask she always wore whenever Callaway was around. When she saw Susannah, her eyes flashed with feeling, but Susannah knew better than to approach her. Sharing their relief with one another would have to wait.

Susannah spent the rest of the day sitting alongside the dying man. Her father had helped her bind his wounds and staunch the flow of blood, but there was little else they could do. Twitty remained mercifully unconscious, his breathing shallow. She had no idea what to do to comfort him, or if he was even aware of her presence, but it felt wrong to leave him alone. She held his hand, giving it a squeeze every so often, to let him know someone was with him. When he took his last shuddering breath, she wondered if his spirit might remain for a while, hovering above them, confused by such an abrupt ending to his earthly story.

By afternoon, the buzz of voices in the clearing had grown louder and angrier as the men argued about what to do next. Some announced their intention of turning back to Virginia.

"It's safer for everyone if we stick together," her father said.

But when he saw he couldn't change their minds, he asked them to carry a note back down the trace to Colonel Henderson. He wrote slowly, balancing the paper on his knee, pausing every so often to stare into space and tap his quill against his chin. When Will offered to help, her father shook his head, though when he was done he called Will and Susannah over and read the letter aloud to them.

Dear Colonel,

After my compliments to you, I shall acquaint you of our misfortune. A party of Indians fired on my company about half an hour before day—killed Mr. Twitty and his Negro, and wounded others. My advice to you, Sir, is to come or send as soon as possible. Your company is desired greatly, for the people are very uneasy, but are willing to stay and venture their lives with you, and now is the time to flusterate the Indians' intentions, and keep the country whilst we are in it. If we give way to them now, it will ever be the case.

I am sir, your most obedient,

Daniel Boone

"I don't believe 'flusterate' is really a word, sir," Will said.

Her father looked up. "But is my meaning clear?"

Will nodded.

"Then I expect it will do, real word or not."

When they finally reached the place along the Kentucky River that her father had chosen for Henderson's settlement, they dismounted on Hackberry Ridge to survey the plain below. Susannah had listened to her father's stories of buffalo from the time she was a girl, but it took her breath away to see the river bottom covered with hundreds of the beasts. They wheeled when they sensed the men's presence, then snorted and began to trot, then run, their hooves shaking the ground. The thunder of their passing entered her body through the soles of her feet and continued for minutes after the last beast disappeared into the woods.

Susannah marveled at the beauty of the place as they rode down off the ridge and into the meadow. The buffalo had cleared off the brush and all but the largest trees along a wide stretch of river bottom thanks to the presence of a salt lick in a nearby hollow. The beasts had gouged out the ground around the lick, which was ringed by immense sycamores. After many long miles of deep woods and creeks lined with nearly impenetrable cane breaks, it was delicious to look up and see a broad expanse of sky overhead and view a stretch of river not obscured by tall cane. Susannah dismounted and stood on the riverbank, relishing the cool, fresh-smelling air that rose off the water. She could see why her father had chosen to settle here.

The men immediately set to work pitching tents and felling saplings to construct rough, three-sided shelters that would serve the company until cabins could be built. An argument broke out about exactly where to locate a blockhouse, the first log structure that would provide both a dry space for supplies as well as some protection from the Indians. Susannah did her best to ignore the men's raised voices while she and Dolly unpacked the pots and kettles for the final time, setting up a fire pit that would function as their open-air cooking space until a log kitchen could be built. Susannah felt a sweeping sense of relief that they'd made it to their destination. Most of all, she was thrilled that she wouldn't have to spend the next day, or the day after that, jouncing along on the back of a horse.

In the first weeks after their arrival, the men killed buffalo by the score, despite her father's strenuous objections. They carved off only the choicest pieces of meat—the humps and tongues—and left the remainder of the beasts to rot in the sun. Soon, fly-covered carcasses littered the woods and fields. Within little more than a month, the men assigned to hunt for the community had to go more than fifteen miles from the settlement to find a trace of the animals.

Her father fumed to Susannah: "There's nothing we could do that would anger the Indians more. They kill only what's necessary as a rule, and then use every part of the beast. Not only are these idiots making it harder for us to find game easily, the entire Shawnee nation will be ready to march against us when they hear about this slaughter."

Colonel Henderson arrived at their campsite on the banks of the Kentucky River three weeks behind the road builders, bringing with him an additional four dozen men. Though the arrival of reinforcements made Susannah feel somewhat safer, she and Dolly remained the only women at the settlement, and all these additional mouths to feed made their workload even heavier than before.

Most of the men were still living in tents or lean-tos because much of their time was spent hunting and scouting out acreage they wanted to file claims on. Her father had managed to get enough work out of them to build a sturdy blockhouse that would form one corner of a future stockade; as soon as Henderson arrived, he claimed the solitary log structure as his residence.

Henderson's reinforcements meant a fresh supply of liquor. Susannah's heart sank at the eager look on Will's face as the men pulled the first heavy jug from a pannier and passed it around. Toasts were drunk to Colonel Henderson, to her father, to the King, and then, in a nod to those with opposite sensibilities, to the Continental Congress as well. She felt a growing sense of dread as the banter grew louder and rowdier.

The further they'd journeyed into the wilderness, the angrier Will had become. He viewed himself as a cut above most of the men who surrounded him, disdainful of their inability to read or write. They, in turn, viewed Will's lack of skill with a rifle as reason enough for endless teasing that wounded his pride and fueled his already short temper. On the nights he'd been drinking, he often used his fists on her, though after the first incident, he'd made sure the bruises he left were easy to conceal. He was always apologetic when he sobered up, but she'd grown weary of his tears and promises to do better. She now spent her days avoiding him while dreading what evening might bring.

On the night of Henderson's arrival, when Will staggered to bed, thumping and bumping his way through the brush to their campsite, he'd drunk so much that all he did was look blearily at her, ease himself down on their bedroll, and pass out cold.

Susannah smiled. Apparently a great deal of liquor could keep her nearly as safe as no liquor at all.

Henderson didn't bother to hide his displeasure when he discovered the men had dubbed the fledgling settlement "Boonesborough." Every so often during those early weeks, Henderson suggested a "more suitable" name, but the men ignored him, and eventually, to Susannah's secret amusement, Henderson grudgingly conceded. Having lost the battle to name the infant community, he was adamant that the vast acreage surrounding it should be called "Transylvania," a grand-sounding name for what he hoped would one day be Britain's fourteenth colony.

Late that summer, when her father announced he was heading back to the Clinch settlements to collect her mother and the rest of the family, Susannah felt a prickle of fear. Not only would their fledgling community be in less competent hands during his absence, but even though she'd never told her father about Will's abuse, knowing someone from the family was nearby had given her some small sense of safety.

The night before her father's departure, the men gathered to bid him goodbye. Some of them handed him letters to deliver to loved ones in the Clinch settlements or to be passed on to other hands for delivery to far-flung parts of Virginia and Carolina.

"I reckon my folks back home have about given up on me," one man said as he handed her father a scrap of paper. Her father grinned as he read the entire message aloud: "I'm fine. Corn in. Home to get you after har-vast."

The man nodded solemnly. "I want my people to know we're standing our ground and that I expect to get a bumper crop."

The conversation and whiskey flowed freely among the men all through the afternoon and well into the evening; they reminisced about loved ones left behind, passed on rumors of Indian sightings, and spoke hopefully of the harvest to come. By the time the sun had set, there was an air of drunken jocularity around the encampment.

"Hey, Will," one grizzled woodsman bellowed across the campfire, "maybe you could finally get yourself a buffalo if you stabbed him with that quill pen of yours."

All the men laughed heartily. Will's face reddened, and he drained his mug, then went in search of a refill. As the evening wore on, Susannah did her best to steer clear of him. The moon had risen over the treetops when Will shot a scowling look her way. Her heart sank like a stone tossed into a millpond. He was drunk, but not drunk enough.

Her father had already retired for the evening, and only a few men were left around the fire when Will stood and brusquely motioned for her to follow him to bed. She hesitated, and Dolly, who'd been moving quietly in and out of the firelight gathering dishes and piling them into a washtub, said loudly: "Excuse me, Miz Hays—Captain Boone wondered if you could patch this for him tonight." She held a worn leather moccasin up in the half-light and stuck her finger through a large hole in the heel. "Said he hates to bother you so late, but since he's leaving in the morning . . ."

Will turned unsteadily to stare at the two of them. As the meaning of Dolly's words registered, he shrugged, gave Susannah a dismissive wave of his hand, and stumbled alone into the darkness.

Susannah stepped around the fire and took the moccasin from Dolly, turning it over in her hand. "This isn't . . ." she began.

"Shhh," Dolly hissed, putting a hand on Susannah's arm and turning her away from the men who lingered around the fire. "It's mine," she whispered, raising her skirts slightly to show Susannah a bare foot. "I wasn't about to let you go off with that man, given the mood he's in. You wait until you're sure he's asleep before you follow him, you hear?"

Susannah grasped Dolly's hand.

"'Tain't nuthin, Miz Hays." Dolly's voice took on a teasing tone. "I just figured if I played my cards right, I'd have that hole in my moccasin fixed by morning." She gave Susannah's hand a squeeze, then picked up the tub of dishes, adding: "You ain't gonna outfight that man, so you best start thinking about how to outsmart him. If you figure out the things that matter most to him, likely there's a way you can bargain with him."

"Is outsmarting men a specialty of yours?" Susannah said it lightly, but her smile faded as Dolly's face grew stern.

"Lord, child, you have no idea the things a woman like me has to learn to stay alive in this world. I just never thought I'd need to teach them to a white woman."

20

Rebecca

Rebecca stared out the window at the tiny grave on the hill above the cabin. Daniel had arrived in the Clinch settlements, intending to lead the remainder of their family to Kentucky, only to discover Rebecca near to term and unable to travel, a delay that had left him so anxious that he'd paced the cabin floor for hours at a time. When Baby William had arrived, pitifully thin and unable to nurse, Rebecca had cradled him every moment of his short life. She'd named him in honor of her new son-in-law, but the babe had lived less than three days. When he'd drawn his final breath, she'd tearfully commended his soul into James's care; it comforted her to think of them together.

Willie was her ninth child and the only one she'd lost as an infant; to her mind, he was as much a casualty of the massacre in Powell Valley as James had been. She'd had no appetite during this pregnancy and had actually resented the child growing within whenever well-meaning folks suggested a new baby would replace the son she'd lost.

They were a melancholy group as they left the Clinch settlements and headed down the trace toward Kentucky. They were all grieving, and Rebecca still felt shaky and weak. It was the thought of Suzy in that isolated settlement that drew her toward Kentucky despite the discomfort of lurching along on a horse from dawn to dusk so soon after childbirth. Having lost James, and then Willie, what she wanted more than anything was to gather her remaining children together. That goal helped her endure long days on the trail when she felt so unsteady that the trees blurred around her and she feared she might tumble from her horse.

"Tell me about Suzy," she said to Daniel one night as they sat alone by the campfire after everyone else had retired to their bedrolls. "I still can't think of her as a married woman."

"Suzy has a lot of grit," Daniel said. "She and Dolly work as hard as the men and complain a good bit less than most."

"And Will?"

Daniel frowned. "Will has more of a taste for liquor than I'd like, but to be fair, journeying along this trace makes most men crave a drink." He smiled. "He and Suzy may not be a perfect match, Becca, but I expect they'll settle in."

He turned away to rummage in his haversack and pulled out a powder horn. "I've been waiting for the right time to show you this— guess this is as good as any."

He handed her the horn, and she leaned forward, holding it near the flames. She fingered the letters carved into the smooth surface and tried to sound them out in her head. Slowly they shaped themselves into a word.

"It says Stewart," she said. She felt her face flush. "It's John's?"

Daniel nodded. "We found this and his skeleton in a hollow syca-more along the Rockcastle River while we were building the road. John's shoulder was shattered. My guess is he hid in the tree after Indians shot him, and he bled to death there."

As Daniel spoke, she envisioned John and his sweet smile, then heard the echo of Hannah's screams when Squire told her John had vanished. She closed her eyes, suddenly awash in memories: John's face as he stared across the fire at Hannah when they first met; the gentle sound of James's voice, which she missed every minute of every day; the tiny face of baby William, whom she'd never have the chance to get to know. *So many losses.*

Daniel reached over and took her hand. "We should be grateful John wasn't carried off to one of the Indian towns; he was a free man to the last. We gave him a proper burial, and now Hannah will have the comfort of knowing what happened to him. Really, it's a miracle we found him."

They sat in silence for a moment, hand in hand, until Daniel said: "It's been five years since John died, Becca, but Lord, I still miss him."

The tiny settlement known as Martin's Station was the final outpost of civilization on the road to Kentucky. They lingered there for several days, resting the horses, molding bullets, and bargaining for the final supplies that would have to last until they reached Boonesborough, more than a hundred and fifty miles distant.

At twilight, Rebecca walked among the cluster of cabins, soaking in the low thrum of voices that spilled out of doorways amid the flicker of firelight. The forested ridgeline that loomed darkly above the station looked ominous against the fading sky, and when she stared up at it, she couldn't suppress a shiver. Cumberland Gap was still a hard day's travel westward from here, offering a gateway through that towering ridgeline, into territory the Shawnee claimed as their own. She'd heard tales of the Gap since the night John Finley first uttered the word "Kentucky" in their Carolina cabin, and in the years since then she'd prayed, more than once, that she'd never lay eyes on it.

A burst of laughter spilled from one of the cabins, and she froze at the bell-like innocence of her children's voices. *What have we done, bringing them here?* The wilderness that surrounded them offered neither welcome nor warmth, and from this point onward there'd be no cabins, no company, no one to turn to if disaster struck.

It was a long day's travel from Martin's Station to Cumberland Gap, and they arrived near nightfall. Daniel led them to a clearing some distance from the foot of the mountain, where they set up camp. After supper, with cicadas buzzing in the trees around them, he gathered the company together and announced they'd break camp later than usual the next morning.

"I want it to be full light when we go through the Gap," he said.

He didn't need to explain; it was apparent to everyone that the Gap was a perfect place for an ambush.

The next morning, as they toiled upwards, the mountains rose steeply on both sides, and Daniel grew visibly uneasy. His eyes darted here and there, scouting the terrain on either side of the trail. Rebecca's rifle was primed, and she rode with it across her lap, having reined her horse into line behind the children, positioning herself so she could be sure no one strayed off the path or straggled behind.

Daniel led the column, accompanied by a half-dozen riflemen. Israel followed closely, leading a horse loaded down with panniers that carried bedding as well as the two youngest children, Daniel Morgan, who was five, and two-year-old Jesse Bryan. Next came Jemima, riding double with

Levina, who was nine. Rebecca and seven-year-old Becky came last; her daughter's skinny arms encircled Rebecca's waist, loosening and tightening as their horse picked its way slowly up the rutted trail. Close behind them rode two other families, followed by an assortment of livestock driven by a dozen or so armed men who brought up the rear.

Halfway up the mountainside, a narrow stream cascaded down the slope, spilling across the trail and forcing their mounts to splash through it. As they stepped into the cool water, the horses and cattle tried to lower their heads and drink, but Daniel hollered to keep them moving.

Rebecca scanned the tree line, searching the green depths around them for a flash of sunlight off polished metal or the gliding movement of human forms in the shadows. Adding to her nervousness was a growing sensation that their little party wasn't alone. She could almost hear the tramp of hundreds of feet all around her, as if every soul that had ever funneled through that narrow portal was still present. As she rode upward, their voices—Indian and white—crowded around her, whispering tales of hope and fear, triumph and discouragement. Her neck prickled with the sense that they were accompanied by a host of others. For her, the Gap was a haunted place.

Once they'd descended and were standing on Kentucky soil, Daniel let them pause at last to catch their breath. When Rebecca looked back at the mountain, standing tall against the sky, she had the odd sensation that the door to the civilized world had just slammed shut behind them.

"It's the first time I've seen the river this high in late summer," Daniel said as they gathered on the banks of the swift-flowing Cumberland. Rebecca could tell from his voice that he was worried. He pointed to a boulder in the middle of the river. "That rock marks the best crossing point. If the top of it's underwater, it isn't safe to cross. With the water this high, there'll be a stretch toward the middle where the horses have to swim."

Several of the men exchanged nervous glances before turning to the task of tightening girths and tying down items on the pack frames. Rebecca rearranged their meal bags, tucking the oilcloth around the top of the frame and cinching the cordage tight, praying their foodstuffs would stay dry.

When the column splashed into the water, Jemima was near the front, riding double with a little girl from one of the other families. The child had taken a shine to Jemima, following her around camp each night like a chick trailing a hen. As their horse splashed into the river, Rebecca heard Jemima say soothingly: "I love the water, don't you? My big brother James used to call me 'Duck' because Mama couldn't keep me out of the creek."

Jemima's mount had just splashed past the stone that marked the deepest part of the crossing when the gelding stumbled and went under, pitching both girls into the swirling current. Weighted down by her heavy skirts, Jemima struggled to keep her head above water. She reached for the child, who'd surfaced nearby, arms flailing, but the current quickly separated them.

The child wailed, her dress billowing around her. One of the men riding just behind managed to grasp her skirts as she swept past him, but the swift current carried Jemima away from the riders.

"Daniel!" Rebecca screamed, unable to abandon her horse with Becky astride behind her. There were frantic shouts from the men on both banks as the water closed over Jemima's head, once, then twice. Rebecca saw Daniel reach the far bank, leap from his horse, and sprint downstream, dodging through the brush and stripping off his hat, shot bag, and powder horn as he ran, trying to keep pace with Jemima's bobbing head. He scrambled up a rock that jutted into the river and was poised to jump when Jemima broke free of the river's current and began swimming toward shore.

Rebecca's limbs went weak with relief as she watched Jemima drag herself up the muddy bank and into her father's waiting arms. In that moment, she sent up a prayer of gratitude to James for the childhood hours he'd spent teaching Jemima to swim. She could almost feel his spirit hovering over the river.

After Rebecca's horse carried her safely across, she slid from her saddle and gathered Jemima in her arms. Her sodden clothes were cold to the touch, but when Jemima stepped back from her embrace, Rebecca was amazed to see, not fear, but laughter in her daughter's eyes. It was one of those unexpected moments when she saw one of her children fresh, as if meeting them for the first time. Rebecca was startled to realize how tall Jemima had grown; her features were now those of a young woman, not a child.

"I'm all right, Mama. Better a dunking than an arrow."

Rebecca felt humbled in the face of her daughter's courage; her own mind continued to quiver with the horror of what might have been. There was a steadiness to Jemima that hadn't been there just months ago. She'd risen from deep grief at the loss of her brother and now faced the world with a calm determination that reminded Rebecca of Daniel. *Surely the Lord has a sense of humor,* she thought, *because of all our children, the daughter who folks doubt is Daniel's has grown to be the most like him.*

The day Rebecca first laid eyes on Boonesborough, she was sure Daniel was playing one of his practical jokes. "Where's the stockade?" she said, reining in her horse. She turned to look at him as he pulled his mount up beside her. They'd crested Hackberry Ridge, and their party was stretched out behind them on the trail, a scraggly procession of three dozen settlers, horses, pack animals, cattle, and dogs. From this wooded height, a rolling grassland stretched beneath them, bordered on the far side by the Kentucky River. As Daniel had promised, it was a beautiful place, but the only signs of a settlement were a half-dozen scattered cabins, several large stands of late-planted corn ripening in the warm September air, a handful of ragged tents, and a solitary two-story blockhouse. There were no fences around any of the structures—nothing that spoke of a community ready to defend itself.

"They should have made more progress by now," Daniel said, tight-lipped.

Rebecca's breath caught in her throat. She couldn't believe the children would be living on that open plain with only a hastily constructed cabin for protection. *Why in God's name hadn't they built a stockade?* She'd trusted Daniel's judgment when he'd allowed their son to backtrack down the trail for supplies, and it had cost James his life. Now another of Daniel's decisions had brought them here, and as she looked off the ridge at the motley settlement below, she felt sure it would be a miracle if any of them left that grassy plain alive.

Before she could voice any of this to Daniel, there was a welcoming shout from the river bottom as one of the men caught sight of them. She saw Susannah duck out of a rough cabin nestled in a grove of sycamores near the river and shade her eyes to look up at the ridge. When she spotted them, she began to run through the tall grass, her auburn hair shining in the sun. Rebecca urged her mount down the grassy slope, and when she reached Susannah, she slid off her horse and they clung to each other, swaying back and forth.

That night, Susannah outdid herself, setting out a hot dinner of roasted buffalo hump, freshly dug turnips, and snap beans. She even buried a dozen sweet potatoes to cook amid the coals, knowing they were her father's favorite, a piece of thoughtfulness that earned her an appreciative wink from Daniel. It warmed Rebecca to see how the hardships they'd shared while cutting the road had brought those two closer together.

Her own contribution to the feast was a block of tea, a luxury she'd hoarded for just this occasion. The dumping of tea in Boston Harbor eighteen months earlier had been the prelude to a general boycott of tea by colonial patriots. Merchants who dared offer tea for sale were sometimes subjected to mob violence, so it had become a rare commodity.

When Rebecca pulled the dark fragrant square from the depths of her pocket, Susannah's face brightened. She shaved curlings from the block, guarding every precious flake, and held her face over the first steaming cup to savor its delicate aroma before handing it across the fire to her father.

"You're not to speak of us having tea," Rebecca warned the younger children. "Folks will say we're Tories, and that's not a safe thing to be called these days."

They nodded, wide-eyed, before burying their faces in their cups.

The truth was, neither she nor Daniel had strong feelings about the growing animosity between England and the Colonies. Her father was a Loyalist who favored remaining under British rule, but Daniel had done his best to steer clear of taking sides. *Perhaps,* she thought, *such things won't matter so much out here.*

As she sipped her tea, Rebecca studied Suzy's face in the firelight. They'd been apart for less than a year, but Suzy looked so much older now. Not only was she thinner, but whenever their eyes met, her daughter's seemed full of shadows, as if the dark things she'd witnessed these past months had gathered behind her eyes. Most unsettling of all, she was no longer quick to speak her mind. Will did most of the talking, while Suzy moved silently around the fire and spoke only when spoken to.

Rebecca was surprised to realize that she missed her eldest daughter's sharp-tongued remarks, something that had been part of their family banter from the time Suzy could first string a sentence together. She reminded herself that most folks would think it only proper that Suzy defer to her husband. But to Rebecca, Susannah seemed like a church bell whose strong, clear tones had been inexplicably muffled.

21

Rebecca

Having lived at Fort Moore, Rebecca thought she was prepared for life in a wilderness garrison full of men, but the conditions at Boonesborough were crude, even by backcountry standards. Everything in the settlement—from skillets to hairpins—had to be carried along the trace and through the Gap on packhorses; she was forced to do without things she'd always viewed as necessities. It was months before there was a spinning wheel in the settlement, and a loom was beyond even dreaming about. Rebecca patched and repatched the family's clothes until finally there was nothing she could do but let everyone go about threadbare.

Thanks to Suzy and Will's diligent tending of a garden plot prior to her arrival, their family had a decent amount of corn put by for the winter, but without a gristmill, converting corn into meal was a laborious task that took up huge portions of each day. Lacking any sort of grinding stones, Rebecca and the girls resorted to the Indian method, hollowing out the upper third of an upended oak log to form a crude bowl, then using a heavy wooden pestle to pound the corn into meal.

It took all Rebecca's strength to balance the pestle over the log, then slam it downward against the dried corn. Each blow made the heavy oak block vibrate, and within minutes her arms were sore and tingling. After a few days of this, Daniel rigged up a rope to a flexible pole, fashioned from a sapling, to act as a spring that helped raise the pestle up between blows. Even so, Rebecca was breathing hard long before she'd ground enough corn to satisfy the family for even a single meal.

Israel, now a gangly sixteen-year-old, always appeared at the point when she felt sure she couldn't lift the pestle one more time. In the previous months, he'd shot up so quickly that he was nearly as tall as Daniel, with a head of unruly blonde hair and his father's gentle smile.

"I'll take a turn, Mama," he'd say, taking the pestle out of her hands. "You rest a bit."

"How do you know when I'm about to give out?"

"I listen to the sound. It changes when you're tired."

There were several of these crude mills, what folks called hominy blocks, scattered around the settlement, and someone was nearly always grinding corn. Their rhythmic beat accompanied Rebecca's every waking hour, making her feel as if she were living in the middle of a giant drum.

All day, every day, she was aware they were well beyond the reach of civilization, a pitifully small cluster of folks plunked down in the midst of a hostile land. She began to imagine Boonesborough as a solitary ship adrift in an ocean of trees, an image sparked by the long-ago stories her Grandfather Bryan had told her of his voyage across the Atlantic, of the fear he'd felt when he first realized the sheer size of the ocean and of the fragility of the ship on which his life depended.

One day's ride southwest of them, two tiny garrisons—Harrod's fort and Logan's Station—had sprung up near each other and were struggling to put down roots as well. All three settlements were so small they could offer only limited aid to one another, but the fact that these other islands of white folks existed in this sea of trees was a comfort of sorts. Men from the settlements sometimes encountered each other while out hunting and passed along reports of Indian sightings as well as any news from back east that had managed to trickle through the Gap.

During Rebecca's first months in Kentucky, the Indians remained silent shadows in the forest. Daniel explained that the Shawnee had moved all their villages out of Kentucky and now lived across the Ohio River to their north. "Only the tribe's hunters frequent these parts," he said, "but they prize this land as a hunting ground, and they'll surely fight to keep it."

Things remained peaceful just long enough for Rebecca to drop her guard. Then one of the men sent out to hunt game for the community went missing, and another man was scalped while working in his cornfield. After that, she had no doubt the Indians were watching them even though they couldn't see them, and she moved through her days accompanied by a constant, gnawing fear, unnerved by an enemy that seemed to be both everywhere and nowhere.

"We need solid cabins and a fort with proper walls," she said bluntly to Colonel Henderson when he joined her family for dinner one night.

"I quite agree, Miz Boone, but most of the men seem content to throw together ramshackle huts and plant just enough corn to give them a legal claim to the land. No one shows up when I ask for a community work crew." He stared morosely into his mug. "Unless the Shawnee start scalping a man every week or so, I wager we'll never get a fort built."

For most of the fall of 1775, Rebecca, her girls, and Dolly were the only women at Boonesborough because the families that had accompanied them through the Gap had chosen to settle at Harrod's fort. But at year's end, Colonel Callaway returned from Virginia with his wife and children, and Rebecca was delighted to discover that two of Callaway's daughters were close to Jemima's age.

The oldest Callaway daughter, Betsy, was sixteen and as dark-headed as Jemima. A motherly soul, she was both protective and proud of her younger sister, Fanny, a bubbly blonde who was fourteen, like Jemima, but—unlike Jemima—was rarely quiet. Betsy quickly won Rebecca's affection by showing Jemima the sort of sisterly attention Susannah rarely had, soliciting Jemima's opinion on everything from knitting patterns to recipes. Rebecca watched with quiet satisfaction as her naturally reserved daughter blossomed amid these new friendships. On many nights, as winter deepened, the Boone cabin overflowed with the three girls' infectious laughter.

It surprised Rebecca to see that Israel, who was normally outgoing, became hopelessly tongue-tied whenever Betsy appeared. For her part, Betsy treated Israel with the easy familiarity of a sibling. Rebecca was secretly relieved she didn't return Israel's interest since Colonel Callaway would never have thought a Boone boy good enough to court one of his daughters. In truth, Betsy could have her pick of any bachelor in the settlement. Even Jemima and Fanny had men of all ages flirting shamelessly with them.

"Don't rush into marriage," Susannah counseled Jemima when she saw the attention her sister was attracting. "I wish I . . ." Her voice trailed off.

"You wish what, Suzy?" Rebecca said.

For an instant, Suzy looked at her mother like the defiant Suzy of old, ready to speak her mind, but then her eyes clouded and she looked away.

"Nothing," she said.

Boonesborough's church services were held under the spreading branches of an enormous elm that stood at the edge of the settlement. It amused Rebecca to watch Daniel reluctantly don his only pair of knee breeches each Sunday, trading them for the breechclout and leggings that he often wore on weekdays. She knew he did it solely to keep peace with Mrs. Callaway, who had told the men in no uncertain terms that Indian attire was an abomination when Christian folk gathered for prayer. Daniel had always been a grudging churchgoer, but now, as one of the leaders of the fledgling community, he dutifully attended services. "Better under a tree than stuck in a meeting house," he said.

When they were newlyweds, Rebecca had asked him about his religious beliefs. She knew he'd been brought up in a Quaker household, but he didn't use plain speech like his parents, and he'd rarely attended Meeting. He'd thought a moment before answering, then said: "My beliefs are pretty simple, Becca: love and fear God, believe in Jesus Christ, do all the good I can to my neighbor and myself, and cause as little harm as possible. As for the rest, I'll just have to trust on God's mercy." After a moment, he added: "Most church folks seem so concerned with heaven and hell, they're blind to this world. It doesn't make sense to me that the Lord would put us in such a wondrous place and intend for us to spend all our time thinking about the next world."

One Sunday morning in mid-July 1776, Daniel came home from service and stretched out on the bed to take a nap. The air inside the cabin was so sweltering that Rebecca didn't have the energy to complain when she saw his discarded shoes and stockings in a pile beside the bed. She stepped over them to hang her best bonnet on a peg and smoothed a hand through her damp hair. A fly buzzed lazily past her ear, and even that sound seemed slow and drawn out. She squatted by the hearth and began to bank the fire, covering the coals with ashes to cool the cabin's stuffy air. On days like this, she missed the summer kitchen she'd had in Carolina, a separate outbuilding that had kept their living quarters bearable during the summer months.

"Mama," Jemima said, stepping inside the doorway, "I'm going down to the river with Betsy and Fanny so I can soak my foot."

Rebecca turned from the fire. "Let me see it."

Jemima balanced against the edge of the table and held her foot up. Two days earlier she'd stepped on a cane stob in one of the newly cleared fields, driving it deeply into her heel. The wound still oozed blood, but Rebecca was relieved that the surrounding skin remained cool to the touch with no sign of infection.

"It aches pretty bad," Jemima admitted, setting it gingerly on the dirt floor.

"If you girls gather some green onions while you're down at the river, I'll make a poultice," Rebecca said, watching Jemima pull extra pins from her gown pocket and tidy her waist-length hair, gathering the stray strands and pinning them into a neat bun. "If you find a stand of willows, peel me some bark. A nice willow tea will help dull the pain. Here, take my penknife with you."

Jemima gave her hair a final pat, took the penknife and slipped it into her pocket, then gave her mother a peck on the cheek. "I'll be back in time to help with supper," she said.

She hobbled toward the doorway, moving carefully around her younger siblings and tousling Jesse Bryan's hair as she passed. Before she stepped outside, Daniel's voice drifted drowsily from the corner bedstead.

"If you take the canoe out, Jemima, be sure to stay on this side of the river."

Several hours later Rebecca heard shouting in the distance, then the sound of feet pounding past their cabin. She stepped outside and saw several men running to meet Caleb Callaway, who'd crested the top of the riverbank, his legs pumping furiously.

"Indians," he yelled.

As that word carried clearly across the meadow, Daniel exploded off the bed, grabbed his rifle, and swept past Rebecca. It took him only a dozen strides to reach the knot of men already gathered around Caleb. The young man had staggered to a halt near the blockhouse and was bent over, sides heaving. When he finally looked up, he searched the circle of faces until his eyes settled on Daniel.

"Cap'n Boone," he said in a choked voice, "the Indians have the girls."

22

Jemima

Jemima could hear Fanny's ragged breathing somewhere behind her as she scrambled up the steep hillside. She struggled to maintain her balance, trying to keep up with Betsy, who was climbing just in front of her. Hindered by her aching heel, Jemima had fallen twice already. The first time she'd lost her footing, she'd grabbed hold of a spicebush and pulled it up by the roots, tumbling backwards and crashing into the tall Indian behind her, who wore a silver nose ring and smelled strongly of sweat and bear grease. He grunted as she slammed into him, then shoved her forward and shook his war club to let her know what would happen if she didn't keep moving.

For the first few miles after their capture, Betsy had dug the heels of her Sunday shoes into the moist ground at every creek crossing or buffalo wallow, but when one of the Indians had noticed, he'd brought the column to a halt and gestured for her to remove her shoes. Reluctantly, she'd kicked them off, and a stocky Indian had knocked the stubby heels off with his tomahawk before handing them back to her. After that, their captors had grown more watchful and moved them to the ridgelines so that now Jemima feared there were long stretches where even her father wouldn't find a trace of their passage.

Since leaving the river, the Indians had set a blistering pace, avoiding the moist, well-watered places in an effort to leave as little trail as possible. Using her foot as an excuse, Jemima took every opportunity to mark their path. She grasped at trailside underbrush, breaking twigs and limbs, and used her stumbling gait to disturb the soil as much as possible, hoping her father could pick up their trail.

All that afternoon she told herself a rescue party would be right behind them—that surely someone had heard their screams and sounded the alarm. But as the hours ticked by, another part of her whispered that she was fooling herself, that perhaps it was only now, as twilight drew near, that they'd been missed; if that were the case, how could a rescue party ever overtake them? She'd learned from her father that tracking was a slow, painstaking process—doubly so if one's quarry was smart enough to cover their tracks.

It's our own fault, Jemima thought. They'd fully intended to heed her father's warning to stay away from the river's northern shore, but a moment's inattention had spelled disaster.

When they'd set out from the settlement, Fanny and Betsy had offered to paddle the dugout canoe so that Jemima could trail her foot over the side and soak it in the cool water. They'd floated easily downriver to an island, where they'd put ashore to gather onions. It was shady and cool in the shadow of the trees. They'd used her mother's penknife to peel some willow bark, then spent time in the shallows, skipping rocks and splashing each other, thankful for a respite from the fierce summer heat.

When they'd finally clambered back into the canoe and pushed off, a strong eddy caught them and swept them toward the river's far bank. Jemima had leaned over the side and was using her hands to help paddle when an Indian, hardly older than themselves, slipped out of the cane and splashed toward them through waist-deep water.

They froze in disbelief as he caught hold of the tug line on the front of the canoe and pulled them toward the far bank. Fanny, who was in front, screamed and began pounding him with her paddle. Rough hands grabbed Jemima from behind, and the dugout tipped, spilling them into the water. All three of them were screaming, fighting back as best they could, when several more Indians appeared and dragged them onto the riverbank.

The tallest Indian drew his knife and pantomimed slashing Betsy's throat, making it clear what would happen if they didn't hush. The silence was so immediate that Jemima suddenly heard the riffle of water running over the rocks at her feet and the pop and snap of brush as the Indians pushed Betsy into the canebrake along the bank.

The river's cool waters were hours behind them now. Jemima's petticoats and shift had dried stiffly to her body after her dunking, only to slowly soak through with sweat as their captors hurried them up and down the dips and swells of the ridgelines. Under her breath, Jemima began to chant pleas to the Deity, matching the rhythm of her words to her steps as a way to distract herself from the burning pain in her heel. At first she prayed for their safe return to the settlement, but as the light began to fade and her legs grew more and more wooden, she prayed simply for the chance to stop and rest.

She marveled at how well Betsy and Fanny were holding up. Colonel Callaway owned a fair number of slaves, so his daughters had been spared much of the everyday drudgery Jemima took for granted. On more than a few mornings, she'd walked past the Callaway cabin, headed to the fields for a long, hot day of hoeing, and seen the girls sitting in the shade breaking beans or husking corn. She'd taken those occasions to tease them about being pampered Virginia ladies, but at this moment, she was the one struggling to keep up.

As best Jemima could tell, there were five or six Indians in the party, though she'd been unable to make a careful count. She knew there were two in front of Betsy and one behind Fanny and herself, but she was pretty sure there were others in the woods to their rear, watching the trail for pursuers. It was clear the Indians intended to put as much distance as possible between themselves and the river before nightfall, but beyond that she had no idea what their plans might be. None of the men she'd seen were wearing paint, which at least meant it wasn't a war party, and that might work in their favor.

She'd had few chances to study their captors in any detail, other than to note that they all had shaved heads except for a scalp lock at the crown, and were bare-chested in the summer heat. The rest of their dress consisted of breechclouts, buckskin leggings, and moccasins. Several wore silver armbands that occasionally caught the light as they walked. She wished she could understand their words. She knew a few phrases in Cherokee, but on the rare occasions when the men spoke to each other, it seemed to be in a different tongue, which she suspected was Shawnee.

Jemima did her best to recall everything her father had told her about Indian customs, searching for any scrap of information that might help keep them alive. She knew from listening to the men at the settlement that the Shawnee commonly took their captives north, back to their villages across the Ohio River. Once there, prisoners were sometimes adopted into the tribe but might also be killed.

During the season they'd lived on the Watauga, she'd seen her father's easy manner with the Indians who stopped by the family's camp. The Cherokee, she knew, had dubbed her father "Wide-Mouth" because he always greeted them with a smile and seemed comfortable in their midst. The way to win an Indian's respect, her father had told her, was to appear unafraid, even if you were terrified on the inside. She worried that feigning fearlessness would require a good deal more courage than she possessed.

When the light had faded to the point that Betsy's light blue gown, which Jemima had followed like a beacon all afternoon, turned a ghostly gray, the Indians halted in a sheltered upland hollow set between two ridges. Jemima's mouth was so dry she could hardly swallow, and it was a bitter disappointment to see their captors had chosen a campsite that lacked a stream or spring. The Indians also made no move to light a fire to cook supper. They were apparently unconcerned about nourishment of any sort, not only for their captors, but themselves.

The stocky Indian motioned for all three girls to sit down at the base of a hickory tree. After sinking stiffly to the ground, Jemima was finally able to look directly at Fanny and Betsy for the first time since their capture. They stared intently back at her, their eyes full of questions, undoubtedly the same ones that were running through her own mind: *Where are they taking us? What should we do? Why hasn't someone come after us?*

As she sat there, she heard her father's voice in her ear, as clearly as if he were sitting next to her. *Stay calm. Study your surroundings.* She shifted slightly to observe their captors, trying to size them up in the rapidly waning light. There were five of them, and the man who appeared to be the leader was older than her father, with muscular arms, though a bit paunchy around the middle. He was talking animatedly to the stocky Indian, as well as to the slender youth whose lanky build reminded her of Israel.

Her observations stopped abruptly as the men quit talking and headed their direction. She noted that the youngest one carried several strips of leather. He stopped in front of Betsy and gestured for her to stand. She slowly pushed herself to her feet and said, under her breath, "They're going to rape us."

As soon as Betsy uttered those words, Jemima recalled a scrap of conversation she'd overheard between her mother and father years earlier. *Indian men don't violate women, Becca. The Indians say the fact that white men treat womenfolk that way proves it's the whites, not the Indians, who are the savages.*

Betsy was on her feet now, standing quietly, eyes wary. The young man motioned for her to put her hands behind her back, then wrapped the leather binding around her wrists and tied it tightly. He then moved to Fanny and repeated the process.

When it was Jemima's turn, she struggled to her feet, wincing as her heel dug into the dirt. When the young Indian finished tying her hands, their eyes met. He was standing so close that even in the dim light she could see the stubble on his shaved head and smell the sweet scent of sassafras on his breath. She expected to see hatred in his face, but his dark eyes held only curiosity. Most likely they were the first white women he'd ever seen up close.

Uncomfortable with his continued closeness, Jemima looked over his shoulder and stiffened as the older Indian pulled his knife from its sheath. Out of the corner of her eye, she saw Fanny bury her head on Betsy's shoulder.

When the knife-wielding Indian stopped in front of her, Jemima wanted to look away like Fanny had, but heard her father's voice saying, *Be brave.* She forced herself to stare straight ahead and struggled to keep her face impassive, even as she braced for the bite of the blade across her scalp.

When the Indian unexpectedly thrust the knife downward, slitting her skirts just below her knees, she gasped and tried to step back, but was held firmly in place by the younger one. She expected any minute to feel the knife slice into her legs, but instead, the sound of tearing material was accompanied only by a steady tugging at her skirts and a sudden swirl of cool air against her legs.

She held her entire body rigid, ready to kick as hard as she could. *Betsy must have been right after all.* Even after the Indian stood up and calmly began ripping the shorn material into long strips, she remained frozen in confusion. That's when she saw the man's features clearly for the first time and felt a buzzing shock of recognition. He was the Cherokee warrior who'd come to their camp on the Watauga with Big Jim, her brother's killer.

She felt the blood rush to her face, and she strained at the leather whang that bound her hands. For nearly three years, she'd fantasized about confronting James's killer, and though she had no way of knowing if this man had actually been there the night her brother was murdered, it was damning enough that he was acquainted with Big Jim. From somewhere deep in her memory she dredged up the Cherokee name she'd heard James call him: "Scolacutta."

The man's hands froze and his eyes flickered upward.

Betsy and Fanny looked at Jemima with wide eyes.

"Scolacutta," she said again, louder this time, following it with his English name—"Hanging Maw."

To her astonishment, the man answered her, not in Cherokee, but English.

"How do you know me?"

She swallowed hard, suspecting their lives might hinge on what she said. Her mind raced through the possibilities before settling on the truth.

"You know my father—Daniel Boone."

Hanging Maw's dark eyes widened. He pointed to Betsy and Fanny. "Your sisters?"

She hesitated a split second, then nodded, deciding it was best they were all judged alike, whether for good or ill.

Hanging Maw's broad face split into a satisfied grin. "Ahhh—we have done pretty well for old Boone this time."

"Where are you taking us?" she asked.

He continued to smile but didn't answer right away. Instead, he passed the knife to the young man and motioned for him to cut off the lower half of the other girls' skirts. Then he knelt in front of Jemima and began wrapping her bare legs with the cloth strips.

"Long skirts will slow you down. The cloth will keep the brush from cutting your legs." He looked up at her. "We're taking you north, across the Ohio to Chillicothe."

"But you're Cherokee," she said.

"*They* are Shawnee," he said, nodding toward his companions. "I travel north with them. Our tribes talk of many things these days."

"Where's Big Jim?" she blurted out. It wasn't at all the question she'd meant to ask, and she swallowed hard as Hanging Maw's smile faded.

He looked at her for a long time, and when he finally spoke, his voice was soft, almost gentle: "When Big Jim killed your brother, our people were at peace with each other. For that, our chiefs condemned Big Jim to death, along with two others of our tribe who were with him. The other warriors in that party were not our people."

"Big Jim's dead?"

Hanging Maw shook his head. "Two were put to death, but Big Jim escaped; if he ever returns to our tribe, the sentence will be carried out. My people believe in justice."

"If you believe in justice, then let us go," she challenged.

"If you believe in justice, stop stealing our land," he snapped.

Jemima's jaw tightened. Beside her, Betsy made shushing noises under her breath.

"Your people *sold* this land to Colonel Henderson," Jemima said.

Hanging Maw gestured toward himself and his companions. "*We* did not sell this land. So tell me—if your neighbor sells your land, are you obliged to hand it over?"

He took a step forward and bent slightly so he could look Jemima in the eye. "We have no choice but to protect our land from thieves." He held her gaze for a moment before straightening up. "Here, in our own land, my people are hunted like wolves. Your chiefs on the other side of the mountains pay five pounds for each Indian scalp—man, woman, or child. Do not speak to me of justice."

Before the Indians retired, they double-checked the girls' bonds to be sure they were tight, then tied the end of their leather bindings around the hickory trunk, leaving just enough slack so they could scrunch down at the base of the tree and lie on their sides. None of them slept that night. Fanny cried quietly, Betsy murmured encouragement to her sister, and Jemima spent the night straining to work her hands loose, hoping to reach her mother's penknife buried deep in the pocket of her gown so she could cut them free. Despite hours of effort, by the time the sky began to lighten and the Indians started to stir, all she'd managed to do was break three fingernails and rub the skin raw on both of her wrists.

23

Jemima

The next day passed much like the first, though they were finally led to a spring and allowed to drink their fill. Not having eaten since noon the day before, Jemima's stomach was rumbling, and she felt as if she were looking at everything through a gathering fog. Surely their captors were hungry, too, though they gave no sign of it; apparently their sole concern was reaching the safety of the Ohio River.

As the day wore on she hobbled more and more, until finally Hanging Maw halted the column and took her foot in his hand, gently probing the wound. Even though his touch was light, she bit her lip to keep from crying out. One of the men went into the woods, and in a bit he returned with some sort of sap, which Hanging Maw packed into the wound. It felt cool at first, then burned for several minutes, but after that she was able to walk more comfortably.

By the afternoon of the second day, Jemima felt so weak from lack of food and sleep that she stumbled over roots and rocks, barely able to stay on her feet. The woods had become nothing but a continuous green blur when, unexpectedly, one of the scouts appeared, leading a bony gray horse that he'd found abandoned in the woods. The poor horse looked nearly as starved as Jemima felt.

Hoping to increase their pace, the Indians boosted Jemima up on the gray's bony back. It felt wonderful to be off her aching foot, but it took her only a few minutes to realize that they were now moving faster, which was the last thing she wanted. When she was certain no one was watching, she clapped her good heel into the horse's ribs, and the startled creature skittered sideways. She tumbled off and hit the ground with a thud.

The Indians were amused. The youngest helped her to her feet, his lips twitching in silent laughter at her inability to sit such a docile animal. He laced his hands to give her a leg back up, and she scrambled clumsily astride, then dug her knee into the horse's knobby back so that he bucked again, sending her headfirst over the other side.

This time the men roared with laughter while Jemima sat in the leaves, feigning more discomfort than she actually felt. One of the Indians took hold of the horse's woven lead rope and vaulted gracefully astride. He urged the creature into a shambling trot and circled around the clearing before leaping smoothly off beside Jemima amid a second round of laughter.

Rubbing her shoulder, she stood up and motioned that she was willing to try again. She was fully prepared to fall off that horse a thousand times if it delayed their progress northward. But as Jemima moved toward the horse, Hanging Maw shook his head and pointed to Betsy.

"She rides now."

Having seen Jemima ride some of Boonesborough's most unruly horses, Betsy knew her falls weren't due to a lack of horsemanship and had apparently discerned her motive; no sooner had the group set out with Betsy astride, than the horse suddenly danced sideways and threw her off, too. Betsy slowly got to her feet and grasped the horse's mane, preparing to mount again, but the old horse, thoroughly provoked by this time, swung his head around and sank his teeth into the girl's upper arm. She screamed and the horse jerked back with a startled snort, leaving a crimson stain on Betsy's sleeve.

The Indians had seen enough. Impatient with the delay, they waved their arms and spooked the horse so that it went crashing off into the brush. Jemima could hear Betsy choking back sobs as Hanging Maw ripped her sleeve open to examine the wound.

"This will scar," he noted, before binding it tightly.

Despite Betsy's injury, they immediately set off again at a pace that was so rapid the girls had to trot to keep up. At one point, they were forced to wade down the middle of a creek for a quarter mile. Their captors also divided the party into two groups, sending Fanny and Betsy one direction with two of the men, while the rest led Jemima the opposite direction, only to have both parties merge an hour or so later. By nightfall, their captors had pushed the girls to the brink of exhaustion, and Jemima figured even a woodsman as skilled as her father would need a miracle to follow their trail.

That night, they again camped without fire, though the Indians finally broke their fast, digging several slices of jerked buffalo tongue out of their packs. It was a pitifully small amount of food to go around. Jemima expected them to feed themselves and let their captives go hungry, but to her surprise, they divided what they had equally. As hungry as she was, she found the taste of her tiny portion of meat, which was hard and unsalted, so foul she couldn't choke it down. She dutifully mouthed her portion until the Indians turned their backs and then spat it into the leaves.

The girls sat dejectedly in the darkness, listening to the rasping call of cicadas and the distant howling of wolves. Huddled together, they kept nodding off, then jerking suddenly awake. During one of Jemima's wakeful stretches, she lay on her side in the darkness and listened to the loud snores of one of the men and Fanny's soft weeping. Betsy's restless movements on their bed of leaves doubtless meant her arm was making it difficult for her to get comfortable.

Jemima watched the stars wheel overhead in the night sky. All the doubts she'd ever harbored about her place in her family rose to the surface to torment her. *Surely,* she thought, *if one of my brothers or sisters had been taken, Daddy would move heaven and earth to rescue them.* Perhaps he wasn't even searching for her—after all, she was the child folks said wasn't his. As the hours of their captivity lengthened into days, Jemima wondered if the reason they hadn't been rescued wasn't because their captors had successfully evaded pursuit but, rather, because in his heart of hearts, her father didn't care if she ever came home.

By their third day of captivity, Jemima sensed they must be drawing close to the Ohio River because with each hour that passed, their captors grew increasingly confident, shedding the tense watchfulness they'd worn throughout the previous days. As their spirits rose, Jemima's fell. For the first two days, she'd paid close attention to her surroundings, trying to memorize landmarks so she could retrace their steps if they somehow managed to escape. Now, she walked with her head down, convinced her inattention made no difference at all.

The clearest indication that the Indians no longer feared pursuit came toward midmorning when she heard the crack of a rifle. Shortly afterward one of the scouts appeared carrying a freshly butchered buffalo hump. His companions greeted him enthusiastically, and when they arrived on the banks of a small creek, Hanging Maw called a halt.

Jemima had a momentary flare of hope, seeing that the Indians hadn't taken the time to butcher the entire buffalo, as was their normal custom. Did it mean, perhaps, that they were still in a hurry to get across the river? Or did it simply mean that Indians, like whites, weren't too picky about rules when they were hungry enough?

The girls sat down on a fallen log, and as the Indians began to scrape out a fire pit, Jemima felt her last bit of hope dissolve. If their captors intended to cook on this side of the Ohio, they must feel sure they weren't being followed.

Even the prospect of her first real meal in three days couldn't lift Jemima's spirits. The Indians, however, were in a jovial mood; they spoke spiritedly to each other and burst occasionally into whoops of laughter. The stocky Indian used his flint to strike a fire, then carefully fed dry grass and twigs onto the slowly emerging flames. The tall Indian spitted the buffalo hump and sank waist-high poles into the ground to hold the meat over the coals. Once the fire was burning brightly, the stocky Indian looked up and motioned for Betsy to come tend the flames.

Betsy pulled her linen kerchief off her shoulders and wrapped it around her head to keep her hair out of the flames. She no longer looked anything like Colonel Callaway's elegant daughter. She looked like an Indian herself, with her long black hair hanging down her back and her gown chopped off near her knees. All their legs were indecently bare, their makeshift cloth leggings having shredded from such hard travel.

Jemima examined her own hands, which were filthy, and realized she must look as bedraggled as Betsy. Her inspection was cut short as Hanging Maw appeared and in one smooth movement sat cross-legged in the dirt at her feet.

"It itches here," he said cheerfully, pointing to a spot on his head. "I need you to check."

It took Jemima a moment to realize he was asking her to delouse his head. It was something they all did regularly, especially with the younger children in their families, but Fanny, who was sitting beside her, shuddered and scooted further down the log. Jemima dutifully parted Hanging Maw's hair with her fingers, searching for lice. She found one and crushed it between her thumb and forefinger, then continued to search.

Betsy, meanwhile, was using a slab of hickory bark to mound glowing coals beneath the spit. It wasn't long before the delicious smell of roasting meat filled the grove. The stocky Indian, who'd been standing to one side watching Betsy work, smiled his approval at her fire-tending skills. Playfully, he reached out and tugged a lock of her hair, saying something in Shawnee. Betsy spun about, eyes blazing, and dumped a scoop of coals on top of his moccasin. The man yelped, bent to brush them off with his hand, then screeched as he singed his fingers. The other Indians shouted with laughter as their companion danced about shaking coals off his foot and blowing on his hand.

"She has a fine spirit," Hanging Maw said, nodding toward Betsy, who'd thrown the bark scoop down in disgust and was striding back to the log. Seeing her furious face, Hanging Maw stood and grabbed a camp kettle, striding off toward the stream as if that had been his intention all along.

Betsy trembled with anger as she sat down on the log between Jemima and Fanny. "Nobody's coming for us," Betsy said in a choked voice. "They couldn't follow our trail. They must have given up."

Fanny laid her head in her big sister's lap and began to cry. Jemima felt tears in her own eyes but hurriedly wiped them away. *Be brave.*

The young Indian was gathering deadwood at the edge of the grove, while the stocky one had squatted by the fire to light his pipe.

Jemima raised bleary eyes to the ridge above, lit by the late afternoon sun, and felt her heart leap like a deer. Her father was crawling on his belly through the leaves near the top of the ridge, rifle in hand, inching his way down the slope in an effort to reach the cover of a clump of trees. She took a sobbing breath and fought the overwhelming impulse to jump off the log and run to him.

Partway down the slope, her father froze, as if sensing her eyes on him. Slowly he raised two fingers to his lips, warning her to stay silent.

She looked away, doing her best to hold still and keep her face impassive. An instant later, a rifle cracked, and the stocky Indian pitched to his knees. Rifle fire exploded off the ridge around them as the injured Indian struggled to his feet and began to run, blood spurting from his belly. Jemima saw the young Indian stagger as if he, too, had been hit, but he recovered his footing and dove into the brush. There was no sign of Hanging Maw.

From the ridge she heard her father yell: "Get down, girls!"

"That's Daddy," Jemima screamed. She slipped off the log and dragged Fanny down beside her, but Betsy sprang to her feet and ran. Jemima shut her eyes as one of the Indians ran after her, swinging his war club, his face contorted with rage.

Jemima expected to hear the sickening sound of wood meeting bone, and when she didn't, she knew his blow had missed. She opened her eyes, but her relief turned to horror when she saw one of their rescuers, mistaking Betsy for an Indian, was about to club her to the ground with his rifle butt.

"Stop!" her father's voice bellowed above the din, and the woodsman checked his swing at the last minute, missing Betsy by inches.

Jemima felt her knees go weak as several more riflemen emerged from the woods, and an instant later, she felt a hand on her shoulder. She looked up and saw her father standing over her, his gray eyes filled with tears. He opened his arms wide, and as she stepped into his embrace, the relief on his face told her clearer than words exactly what she meant to him.

"Daddy," she said, and for the first time in her life, she felt sure they both knew it was true.

24

Susannah

Susannah prayed constantly for her sister's return in the days after Jemima's kidnapping, vowing that if Jemima came home, she would never again take her for granted. Five days after the girls were taken, Susannah and her mother were husking corn when a shout went up from the river. They dropped the half-shucked ears and hurried out of the cabin just as the rescue party crested the riverbank with the girls in their midst. Her mother began to laugh and cry at the same time, her breath coming in short sobs. She gathered her skirts and began to run, her bare feet sending up puffs of dust that hung above the dry summer grass.

Susannah followed more slowly, cradling her firstborn, Elizabeth, watching as the girls and their rescuers were encircled by jubilant family and friends. Her father spotted Susannah and elbowed his way through the crowd to plant a gentle kiss on his granddaughter's forehead.

"We came close to losing them, Suzy," he said wearily.

Something in his tone made Susannah look closely at him. For the first time she noticed flecks of gray at his temples and a deepening of the lines around his mouth and eyes. Her father was forty-two, no longer a young man, but he'd accomplished what would have been impossible for most men half his age—tracking an elusive enemy over rough terrain while burdened with the knowledge that a single wrong turn could mean the difference between recovering the captives or losing them forever.

After her sister's return, Susannah made a point to spend more time with Jemima. It wasn't long before she realized how blind she'd been.

She'd never noticed that her quiet little sister possessed a wicked sense of humor and a talent for mimicry. One night, Susannah laughed till she cried as Jemima transformed herself into Colonel Callaway, arching an eyebrow and looking down her nose. "But of *course* I should be first in line," she said haughtily, "I'm a Callaway, don't you know."

Encouraged by Susannah's laughter, Jemima brought other neighbors to life as well. Soon half of Boonesborough paraded across the hearth, captured perfectly through a telling expression or choice turn of phrase.

"Wherever did you learn to do this?" Susannah asked, having laughed until her chest ached. It felt wonderful; laughter had been a rarity since Will had entered her life.

"I've always done it," Jemima said, ducking her head. "But Mama and James were the only ones who noticed."

Susannah felt a rush of shame at how unapproachable she'd been.

Jemima looked up and smiled, as if reading her sister's thoughts. "It's all right, Suzy," she said. "We've found each other now."

While Jemima's presence in Susannah's life had grown, her relationship with Dolly had been abruptly curtailed when Dolly's Virginia mistress, Elizabeth Callaway, arrived at Boonesborough. Though kindly, Mrs. Callaway was a proper gentlewoman who'd been served by slaves her entire life.

"My dear," she'd said, pulling Susannah aside just days after her arrival, "I realize you're young and unaccustomed to dealing with slaves, but you must always keep in mind that Dolly is not your equal. You simply can't allow her to speak to you so familiarly."

Susannah had opened her mouth to respond but swallowed her words as Dolly's eyes flashed a warning.

That night by the fire, she'd fumed quietly to her mother. "Why can't folks let us be? Our friendship doesn't hurt anyone."

"When you treat Dolly like an equal," her mother said, "it makes it harder for others to treat her like a slave."

Later that night, Dolly intercepted Susannah at dusk as she walked back to the hut in the sycamore hollow where she and Will still lived, awaiting a better cabin.

"Miz Hays?" Dolly's voice floated out of the shadows; it took Susannah a moment to see her standing near the spring, a bucket at her feet.

"Master Callaway sent me to get water, and he's expecting me back." She spoke hurriedly, as if the words burned her tongue. "Folks are saying I've forgotten my place, and Master Callaway is threatening to take me back to Virginia and sell me off. Miz Callaway's a Christian woman; I could do a lot worse than having her as my mistress. From now on, Miz Hays, I gotta pretend you ain't my friend no more."

Dolly paused, and as her words sank in, Susannah felt her heart crack open.

"If it wasn't for you, Dolly, Will might have killed me long ago," Susannah said, choking back a sob.

"You've got your family around you now, Miz Hays; you need to tell them 'bout how bad that man treats you."

Susannah went rigid at the thought.

"But I won't tell nobody if that's how you want it," Dolly added.

With a glance at the hut to be sure Will wasn't watching, Dolly stepped closer and hugged her. The rough woven cloth that covered Dolly's hair scratched against Susannah's cheek, and she caught the scent of bacon grease on the woman's shift. Then Dolly was gone, slipping through the trees with the wooden bucket bumping heavily against her leg.

After that night, though they saw each other daily and sometimes worked side by side, they might as well have been strangers. At best, they caught each other's eyes and risked a smile or exchanged a hurried word or two when no one was around, but there were no more long talks or leisurely laughter. Susannah did her best to be a true friend to Dolly by keeping her distance, while Dolly, in turn, kept quiet about Susannah's disastrous marriage. They understood each other; pride was one of the few things they could each still call their own.

Over the following months, Susannah watched Jemima do a far better job of navigating the rocky waters of courtship than she had. Even the men Jemima rejected seemed to respect her. Susannah cringed at the thought of how differently she'd behaved. Most of the men who journeyed to Boonesborough had passed through the Clinch settlements, and more than a few had clearly heard unsavory rumors about "Suzy Boone." If they chanced to find Susannah alone, some leaned in a bit too close or casually rested a hand on her shoulder. When she rebuffed them, some were embarrassed, but others grew angry. One would-be Romeo looked at her scornfully and uttered words that made her breath catch in her throat.

"Well, well," he said, "you're mighty picky for a prostitute."

Through the fall and winter of 1776, Jemima refused numerous marriage proposals. Susannah teased Jemima about her reluctance to choose a spouse, saying she'd taken the newly penned Declaration of Independence, a copy of which had arrived at Boonesborough in August, too much to heart.

"When in the course of human events," she intoned to Jemima, "it becomes necessary for a woman to choose a husband . . ."

Jemima grinned and swatted her.

After a while, it dawned on Susannah that Jemima, in her quiet way, was studying the settlement's bachelors.

"If they talk sweet to me," Jemima said, "but snap at a young'un or kick a dog, that tells me more about who they are than all their fancy words."

Even so, Susannah was caught totally off guard when Jemima agreed to wed Flanders Callaway, Betsy and Fanny's cousin.

"Why?" Susannah exclaimed, then realizing how dismissive that sounded, added, "He seems nice, but he's a Callaway, and I haven't seen him making eyes at you like the other men."

"That's one of the things I like about him, Suzy. Flanders and I got to be friends because I spent so much time with Betsy and Fanny, but he figured he didn't stand a chance, what with the other fellows milling around and the fact that his uncle and Daddy are always butting heads. I had to drop him some pretty broad hints."

Susannah pictured Flanders: early twenties, thinly built, with a face deeply pitted with smallpox scars. As far as she could see, there was nothing remarkable about him. Certainly, he lacked Will's dashing looks.

"Are you sure?" Susannah asked.

Jemima nodded.

"What makes you certain?"

"We can talk about anything."

Susannah managed to smile, but when Jemima turned away, she swallowed hard, well aware that, while her own husband was handsome and well educated, he had never, even in the earliest days of their court-ship, been her friend.

In the weeks leading up to Jemima's wedding, the entire settlement res-onated with an undercurrent of anticipation. The winter of '76–'77 had been long and dreary, but by March, the first faint stirrings of spring had arrived. Throughout the fort, the heavy wooden shutters that had stared like blank eyes all winter were flung open and dark rooms aired out. When Susannah took a deep breath, it was a relief to no longer smell the heavy odors of grease and smoke and unwashed bodies packed tightly together.

In the final days before the wedding, Susannah watched her mother sit up late by the fire, using all her sewing skills to conceal mended spots in the folds of Jemima's least-shabby gown. The settlement hadn't received a new supply of cloth goods since Henderson had first stocked the com-missary, but her mother had managed to save a few scraps of white linen and used them now to fashion a new kerchief and cap for the bridal outfit.

"These will have to do," her mother said with a sigh, holding the cloth up for Jemima's approval.

Jemima leaned over the back of her mother's chair and hugged her, resting her chin on her shoulder. "They're perfect."

On the day of the wedding, James Estill arrived for the ceremony accom-panied by his slave, Monk, who carried a worn fiddle under his arm. At Jemima's request, Monk played several hymns before the vows were exchanged, drawing himself up straight and laying his horsehair bow across the strings with a flourish.

When those first sweet notes floated across the gathering, Susannah's eyes filled with tears. Flanders had tears in his eyes, too, as he gazed at his bride. Jemima, in turn, looked at him with a quiet confidence that gladdened Susannah's heart to see.

After the vows were spoken and the crowd had dissolved into buzz-ing conversation, Monk rolled up his sleeves and launched into a series of reels and jigs, his eyes closed, head thrown back, his face gleaming with sweat.

The settlement's women, who still numbered less than a dozen, spent the rest of the afternoon dancing, being handed from one man to the next with barely a moment to rest. After an hour, Susannah managed to slip out of the crowd to sit on an empty bench under the eaves of one of the cabins. Her last partner had trampled her toes, and his breath on her cheek spoke of several visits to the whiskey keg. She fanned herself with her apron and looked around for Will. They'd danced the first two sets together, and he'd been in good spirits. His hands had been gentle on her back as he'd steered her through the steps, but the fact that the whiskey was flowing likely explained his disappearance, and she knew it would be best to avoid him until he was thoroughly drunk.

Susannah retied her kerchief around her shoulders, intent on rejoining the dancing after a quick visit to the necessary. The privies had been dug at the far end of the settlement, adjacent to the cattle pens, an arrangement that in the heat of the day made it the most malodorous—and therefore the most avoided—area at Boonesborough. When she walked around the edge of the log smithy, the sounds of celebration grew muffled, becoming a distant roar like the sound of a far-off stream. Even before the privy came into view, she began to breathe through her mouth, trying to block out the worst of the odors.

After a few moments in the necessary's dark confines, she was desperate for a breath of fresh air. Dropping her skirts, she pushed open the rickety door; it swung wide with a screech. She squinted at the sudden burst of sunlight and had taken only a few steps, head down and nearly blind, when she felt a hand on her shoulder. She looked up, but with the sun in her face, all she could see was a man's silhouette.

"You're in an almighty hurry," the shadow said.

"Will," she said, recognizing his voice.

"In a rush to get back to all those men who're asking about you?"

His tone made her think of a rattlesnake, tightly coiled and ready to strike. Her heart hammered, but she tried to keep her tone light. "There are so few women, even my younger sisters are dancing today. I guess the men are looking for anyone in a gown."

"Anyone in a gown," Will repeated, his words slurred, "or *out* of a gown."

She laid a hand on his sleeve. "Will—your mug's nearly empty. Let's refill it."

"I saw you slip off. You were meeting someone back here, weren't you?"

He raised his fist above his head and Susannah closed her eyes, but the blow never came. Instead, she heard a grunt, then the sound of scuffling on the hard-packed dirt in front of her. Cautiously, she opened her eyes.

Israel was gripping Will's arm, pinning it behind the drunken man's back. Her brother's hair flamed gold in the sun, making him look like an avenging angel as he leaned over Will's shoulder and spoke directly into his captive's ear.

"If I didn't know better, I'd think you were about to hit my sister." His voice was soft but laced with ice. Though he was shorter than Will, Israel's shoulders were broad like his father's. When Will didn't respond, Israel ratcheted his arm a few inches higher.

"For your sake, Will, I hope Suzy's gonna tell me this is the first time you've raised your hand to her." He twisted Will's arm yet another notch higher, and this time there was a popping sound. Will grimaced, and beads of sweat broke out on his forehead.

"If she tells me otherwise," Israel continued, "you'd better watch your back. I might mistake you for a deer when I'm out hunting. You hear what I'm saying?"

Will nodded, an almost imperceptible shake of his head that allowed him to keep the rest of his body stationary. Susannah could tell from his face that even the slightest movement was painful. She felt a ripple of satisfaction at seeing him on the receiving end for once.

"Glad we understand each other," Israel said. He let go of her husband's arm and gave him a shove that sent Will staggering against the privy's rough log wall. Will stood dumbly, facing the wall for a moment as if he couldn't remember how to make his legs work. Then he turned slowly, one hand touching the wall for support, and walked away with weaving steps. He didn't look back.

Israel looked directly at Susannah for the first time. "How much of that do you reckon he'll remember in the morning?"

"Most of it," she said, ducking her head, finding it hard to meet her brother's eyes. "I used to think he was out of his head when he was liquored up, but now I think the drink just makes him more of who he really is."

"And who is he?"

"A wife beater." The words hung in the air between them. It was the first time she'd uttered the truth aloud.

"Do Mama and Daddy know?"

"No," she said, "and you're not to tell them."

"But Suzy . . ."

"No! I'll not have my entire family pitying me. I couldn't bear it."

"Then you should leave him."

Susannah shook her head. "You know that's not possible. By law, everything a wife has belongs to her husband, including their children. I'd lose Elizabeth."

"But surely if the Court knew he was beating you . . ."

"It wouldn't matter. I overheard a woman at Fort Moore say the law allows a husband to beat his wife as long as he doesn't cripple her. The law didn't protect her, and it won't protect me."

Israel studied her for a moment, then said: "Promise me you'll tell me right away if he lays a hand on you again."

She nodded and felt her heart miss a beat, as if it had skipped for joy. Months of tension drifted from her like leaves swirling from a tree in a stiff wind. "Lucky for me you needed to use the necessary," she said, trying to lighten the mood.

"I didn't. Dolly said you needed me. She wouldn't tell me why—just sent me over here to find you."

Susannah smiled. "Then I guess I have two guardian angels."

When she crawled into bed that night, she slid carefully in beside Will, who was sprawled, dead drunk, across the bed tick. As she snuggled into the blankets, she said a silent prayer of thanksgiving for Dolly, who was still looking out for her as best she could, and for Israel, who wasn't afraid of Will and who loved her enough to do whatever it took to keep her safe.

25

Rebecca

Rebecca had never paid much attention to politics, so the fighting back east between the redcoats and General Washington's troops seemed distant and unreal; that is, until 1777, when the British turned their attention to the backcountry. *Fight alongside us,* the British told the Indians, *and when we prevail, the king will honor the Proclamation Line and force the settlers back across the mountains.* Rumors abounded that the British had offered payment for every white scalp delivered to their stronghold at Detroit. "I don't reckon I owe the king a God-damned thing," Rebecca heard one settler growl, "now that he's doing his best to get me scalped."

They began to see signs—moccasin prints at the edge of the fields and smoke from distant campfires—that told them small bands of Indians were frequently in the area. Daniel chose two young woodsmen, Thomas Brooks, and a newcomer, Simon Butler, to act as wide-ranging scouts. They stayed out for days at a time, roaming the countryside, trying to ensure the settlement would have plenty of warning if a large war party were moving their way.

Despite such precautions, most mornings Rebecca woke with a knot in her stomach. She missed Jemima's calming presence in their cabin now that the newlyweds had set up housekeeping in an empty cabin across the partially completed stockade. Though the couple had little in the way of household goods, it was clear to everyone they were glowingly happy.

"Some of the women warned me that the difference between courting and marriage was night and day," Jemima told her mother one afternoon as they sat on the bench in front of Rebecca's cabin, shelling freshly picked peas. "They said their husbands quit talking to them once they'd wed, but Flanders and I never run out of things to say."

Rebecca smiled. "I expect most of those men barely talked to begin with." She shook the discarded pods out of her apron, scattering them across the dirt in front of the bench; within seconds a half dozen hens scurried over, clucking loudly, to peck in the dust at their feet.

Rebecca stretched her arms over her head. "My shoulders stay tight all the time—I'm all tensed up, waiting for the Indians to show themselves."

Jemima's smile faded. "Daddy says we've angered the Shawnee by killing off the buffalo—they view it as a sacrilege, the same way white folks would if the Indians desecrated a church." She glanced around to be sure no one else was nearby, then added: "Part of me thinks we don't have any business being here at all. It's been Indian land forever."

"You can sympathize with the Indians after what they put you through?"

"They treated us girls as kindly as they could under the circumstances."

"And how did they treat James?"

Jemima was silent for a moment, then spoke slowly, measuring each word: "Big Jim was a cruel man. I'll never forgive him for what he did to James. But Hanging Maw was a good man. He was kind. I've thought about it a lot, Mama; the Indians are just like us—some good, some bad."

"That may well be," Rebecca said, "but if I had my way, all my loved ones would be safe on the other side of the mountains, and I'd never have to think about Indians again."

At long last, the men set to work building stockade walls, filling in the gaps between the cabins so that the entire fort was enclosed. Twenty-six cabins lined the walls of the enclosure that covered the better part of an acre, and while it was a relief to finally have solid walls around them, Rebecca was painfully aware that with powder and lead supplies dwindling and the edge of civilization more than a hundred and fifty miles distant, their newly completed walls could as easily be a death trap as a sanctuary.

Adding to their unease was the fact that Colonel Henderson's land purchase had been ruled an illegal usurpation of Virginia territory; they were no longer Transylvanians but Virginians. Disheartened, Henderson had washed his hands of Boonesborough and returned to Carolina, leaving all of them in limbo.

"Colonel Henderson promised you two thousand acres," Rebecca said to Daniel, "but Virginia hasn't promised you a thing. If we stay, we're risking our lives for land a Virginia judge could take away from us with the stroke of a pen."

"Everyone's land titles are in question, Becca," Daniel said, "but if we leave, we'll lose everything for sure."

"And if we stay, we could lose a lot more than land." She tilted her head to indicate the children. They were paying no attention to their parents' conversation and were gathered around the hearth, laughing as they played a spirited game of Put and Take, using hickory nuts in place of coins. Rebecca prayed they were just as oblivious to the danger that was closing in around them.

By late spring, the food they'd laid by the previous fall was nearly gone, but it was far too dangerous to work at any of the outlying homesteads; even working the fields closest to the fort was a risk, though it was necessary as the only way to stave off starvation.

Daniel divided the community in half so that folks took turns working the fields under a heavy guard. Even so, Rebecca had to steel herself to walk out of the fort with nothing but a hoe in her hand and spend the day on that exposed plain. They were easy targets for anyone watching from the sunken ground of the sycamore hollow or the heights of Hackberry Ridge, and on the days it was her family's turn to be in the fields, she'd wake with a knot in her chest that stayed there until they were all once again inside the fort's rough log walls.

She was churning butter inside the fort one afternoon when shots rang out in the cornfield. A sentry began frantically blowing his horn, and the folks who'd been working in the fields spilled through the gate, their faces contorted with fear. Everyone made it inside except a slave who'd been working at the farthest edge of the field, near the sycamore hollow.

"Dead before he hit the ground," one of the workers told Daniel breathlessly. "We didn't see a thing until they fired on us."

"It's surely just a scouting party," Daniel said. "Simon and Thomas reported back yesterday; if it was a large party, they'd have seen signs."

At dusk, Daniel and several other volunteers slipped out of the fort to retrieve the slave's body. Rebecca tried to hustle the children into their cabin before the men returned with the corpse, but the children glimpsed the man's mangled head as he was carried through the gate.

There was little conversation around the dinner table that evening, but when Rebecca bent over the trundle bed to tuck Jesse Bryan in, he looked up at her with worried eyes.

"Mama, will the Indians scalp us, too?"

She smoothed her hand across his forehead and smiled down at him. "How do you reckon the Indians can get to us with this sturdy fort all around us and your Daddy standing guard? Simon's watching over us, too."

Jesse's eyes brightened at the sound of Simon's name. He'd taken a shine to the young, broad-shouldered scout. At six foot four, Simon Butler bested all the other men in the fort by several inches and must have seemed like a giant to a boy of four. Jesse Bryan and Daniel Morgan loved to follow Simon around the fort, stretching their small legs, doing their best to match the scout's long strides.

Despite his imposing size, Simon possessed a kind heart. His gentle manner put Rebecca in mind of James, and once she'd made that association, the scout became a regular guest at their cabin. During one such evening, with the table set and their supper bubbling on the hearth, Simon haltingly told her a little about himself.

"I was apprenticed to a saddler, but I ran off when I was sixteen. I've been on my own ever since."

"Don't you have family, Simon?"

He shook his head and looked around the cabin, his eyes soaking in the bustling scene: the boys wrestling on the floor, Daniel trimming bullets by the hearth, the rise and fall of many voices, punctuated by the clang of pot lids. Jemima was dishing up plates of beans at the hearth, and Flanders was carrying them to the table, stealing a kiss from her between trips. The couple often took their evening meal with the rest of the family, saying their own cabin was too quiet with just the two of them at the table. When Simon looked back at Rebecca, his eyes were wistful. "I can't thank you enough, Miz Boone, for welcoming me into your home."

After that, she worried for Simon the way a mother would during the long days when he was out scouting, and whenever he returned to the fort, she made sure he got home-cooked meals, a warm place at their hearth, and the chance to bask in her boys' whole-hearted adoration.

There was a light fog hanging above the river on the morning in late April when Mister Goodman and another man drove the milk cows through the fort's gate and out to pasture, then set off to check the horses that had been turned out in a field several hundred yards distant.

The men had barely disappeared from sight when gunfire and war whoops erupted from the direction of the sycamore hollow. The guards at the fort gate bellowed warnings that sent everyone scurrying to their assigned posts. Clutching her rifle, Rebecca scrambled up the ladder that leaned against their cabin and slipped onto the roof, gaining a foothold on the wooden cleats tacked to the shingles. Lying flat on her belly, she peered cautiously over the crown of the roof.

In the distance she saw Goodman and his companion racing toward the fort with a dozen warriors in close pursuit. She watched helplessly as one of the Indians raised his gun and shot Goodman in the back. He tumbled into the dirt, legs flailing, and the Indians swarmed over him. She saw the flash of a tomahawk and shut her eyes, pressing her cheek against the rough-hewn shingles.

A bellow of rage, like the sound of an angry bull, echoed through the fort, and she opened her eyes in time to see Simon burst out of the gate, running straight toward the Indians, one of whom was holding Goodman's bloody scalp high and screaming in triumph.

"No, Simon!" she shouted.

For a moment she thought he'd heard her. He stopped abruptly in the dusty path that led from the fort, but only long enough to settle his rifle on his shoulder and take aim. The bullet spun the warrior around, and he fell heavily across Goodman's lifeless body.

By this time, Daniel and a dozen others had spilled out of the fort, running along the rutted road in Simon's footsteps, coming to his defense. Michael Stoner dropped one of the fleeing Indians but was hit by return fire. With a cry, Stoner fell to the ground, and Daniel turned to help him, then froze as dozens of Indians emerged from the hollow, flooding into the path between the men and the fort.

"Boys," Daniel yelled, "we're gone!"

Rebecca laid there, heart pounding, holding her fire in fear of hitting their own. With Daniel in the lead, the men began to fight their way back to the fort, taking turns shooting and reloading. Rebecca squinted, her heart in her throat, straining to see through the gun smoke that settled across the field. Every so often the haze would clear, and she'd catch glimpses of the action. Their men were still firing, but as the Indians closed in, both sides clubbed their guns and began swinging at their adversaries.

She gasped as she saw Daniel stagger, then slump to the ground. With a loud cry, a warrior, knife raised, grasped Daniel's hair, jerking his head backward.

She screamed just as Simon turned and shot the Indian at point-blank range. Simon clubbed his gun and crushed the skull of an oncoming warrior, then scooped Daniel up and slung him over his shoulder like a sack of grain.

Rebecca watched, barely breathing, as the path to the fort cleared momentarily, the Indians having taken cover behind trees and the rail fences that snaked along the cornfield. Simon ran toward the fort, bent nearly double beneath Daniel's weight, as bullets kicked up dust and gravel all around him. Behind Simon, Billy Bush was helping Stoner hobble along, while the other men, having fought off the initial wave of attackers, had formed a knot and were methodically firing and falling back.

Now that the Indians had scattered and their men had drawn closer, the fort's riflemen began laying down a covering fire. Spotting a warrior racing along the fencerow, intent on cutting off Simon's retreat, Rebecca steadied her rifle and took aim, bracing her feet to keep the kick of the gun from sending her sliding off the roof.

She peered through the smoke, certain she'd hit her mark, and felt a surge of hope. Simon was less than thirty yards from the fort, but as she watched, his strides began to slow, and he lost his grip on Daniel, who hung, blood soaked, across his back. Bullets rained around them; off to one side, Rebecca saw several braves running hard, gaining ground.

"Run, Simon!" she screamed, as she fumbled to reload. Her hands shook so hard she couldn't pull the plug from her powder horn. She froze as a solitary figure burst from the fort.

Jemima was running toward her father, bending low as bullets kicked up dust around her. She reached Simon and caught her father under an arm, helping support his weight. Daniel hung limply between them as she and the big man labored together toward the fort.

Rebecca slid down the roof, her skirt catching on the rough shingles. She yanked it free and dropped her empty gun over the edge, then scrambled down the ladder, taking two rungs at a time. As she raced down the row of cabins, dodging barking dogs and squawking chickens, she heard the heavy thump of bullets hitting the wooden logs alongside her; it was impossible not to imagine those lead balls tearing into the flesh of those outside the walls. She prayed every step of that dusty run, expecting to reach the gate and discover Daniel, Jemima, and Simon lying dead on the ground outside the fort.

26

Rebecca

Rebecca sprinted around the corner of the final cabin and saw Daniel lying motionless in the dirt just inside the gate. Jemima was bent over him, her shift and hands bloody. Simon sat alongside, breathing heavily, his fringed hunting shirt soaked with blood.

She slid to a halt in front of Daniel and knelt in the dust; he was still breathing, though shallowly.

"Where's he hit?"

"Leg, I think," Simon said shakily.

"Were either of you hit?" she asked, looking up to search their faces.

They shook their heads, and she turned back to Daniel, running her hands down both legs, searching for wounds. Blood was everywhere, so she couldn't pinpoint where the bullet had entered, but when she touched Daniel's left ankle, he moaned. She probed the area and felt a spurt of warm blood beneath her fingers.

"Simon, help me get him inside. Jemima, put some water on the fire, throw the oldest blanket over our tick, and gather all the clean rags you can lay your hands on."

Jemima sprinted off as Simon rose and picked Daniel up, cradling him like a baby. She walked alongside, keeping pressure on the wound, doing her best to slow the bleeding. Simon had to duck to pass through their doorway, edging in sideways, taking care not to bump Daniel's leg.

Suzy hurried in as Simon laid Daniel gently in the corner bedstead. She flashed Rebecca a look of silent concern before turning to her younger brothers and sisters who were huddled, wide-eyed, by the table. "Levina," she said, "you and Becky bring the little ones. We're going to my house." With a final anxious glance over her shoulder, she shooed the children through the door.

Cautiously, Rebecca lifted her hand from Daniel's ankle and was relieved to see the bleeding had slowed. She peeled the soft leather moccasin away from the wound, exposing shards of bone and ragged flesh. Even if Daniel lived, he might never walk again.

Simon stood helplessly at the foot of the bed, his big hands gripping the bedpost, leaving bloody marks on the wood. After a moment, summoned by calls for help, he hurried back outside.

Daniel was usually the one in the settlement who was called upon to tend gunshot wounds. She'd never done it herself. As her fingers probed deeper, searching for the ball, Daniel began to thrash about, his moans audible in the midst of the gunfire echoing around them.

"Should I go get Israel or Flanders to help hold him down?" Jemima asked.

It was clear the battle was still raging outside. Even now, the Indians might be scaling the walls, ready to drop in amongst them. "The men can't be spared," Rebecca said.

Rebecca used leather thongs to tie Daniel's arms to the bed frame, and Jemima climbed onto the tick and used her entire weight to keep him from rolling from side to side as Rebecca picked slivers of bone out of the wound and located the bullet. It had struck with such force that the lead ball had flattened itself against his ankle bone.

"We need to rig a sling," Rebecca said, pointing to the cross beam over the bed. "If we raise his leg it will help stop the bleeding."

After a morning of intense fighting, the sound of the guns grew more sporadic until by late afternoon, when Daniel regained consciousness, the Indians retreated, carrying their wounded and dead. Among the fort's defenders, Daniel and Michael Stoner had suffered the most serious wounds, but three others had been shot as well. Miraculously, Goodman had been the fort's only fatality.

"How'd I get here?" Daniel asked groggily.

"Simon and Jemima saved you," Rebecca said.

Daniel shifted his head on the pillow so that Jemima, who stood at his shoulder, was in his line of vision. He slowly raised his hand off the blanket, and she grasped it with both of her own.

"Thank you," he said, his voice raspy.

"Just returning the favor," Jemima said, her eyes moist.

Daniel tried to move his leg and grimaced as the sling rocked back and forth.

His eyes sought Rebecca. "How bad is it?"

She hesitated a moment too long.

"That bad, huh?"

"Your ankle's shattered. You'll be laid up quite a while."

"Hurts like hell."

"I'm brewing some willow bark, it should take the edge off the pain."

Daniel took a deep breath and closed his eyes. "Tell Simon I want to see him," he said.

Daniel hovered between feverish sleep and groggy wakefulness. Whenever his breathing deepened and it seemed as if he was finally asleep, his leg would twitch or he'd shift in the bed and awaken with a gasp.

"It feels like my foot's on fire," he said when Rebecca hurried to the bedside. Pain carved deep lines around his mouth, and when she took the opportunity to change his dressings, being as gentle as possible, he ground his teeth and his face went pale.

Rebecca finally sent Jemima home. "There's nothing more you can do here, and Suzy can surely use extra help with the children. I need you to keep the little ones at your place tonight. They don't need to hear this." She nodded toward Daniel, whose half-conscious moans filled the room.

Sometime after nightfall, Simon appeared in the doorway. "How is he?"

Hearing the big man's voice, Daniel opened his eyes and beckoned him inside.

"Becca tells me I wouldn't be here if it wasn't for you," Daniel said, as Simon stood at the bedside. "You have our deepest thanks." A ripple of amusement crossed Daniel's face. "I reckon I shouldn't speak for Becca. She might wish you'd left me out there."

Daniel dozed, unable to settle until around midnight, when he finally fell into a deep sleep, helped along by a liberal amount of whiskey. Simon offered to keep vigil with Rebecca, declaring the day had left him too agitated to sleep well anyway. The two of them sat at the table, drowsing as the night ticked slowly past. Every so often Rebecca peered toward the bed to check Daniel's breathing. In the dead of night, when she saw a dark spot on the bandage, she shifted to get a better look, unsure if it was the darkness of shadow or blood. *Just shadow.* Her chair scraped the floor, and Simon looked up, blinking sleepily.

"Is he all right?"

"For now," she said, keeping her voice low.

Simon stretched and stood, grasping the poker to stir up the fire. The room had grown chilly; the air filtering in through the chinking made Rebecca shiver.

Simon took a log off the stack beside the hearth and set it gently on the coals, doing his best to work quietly so as not to waken Daniel. The wood popped, sending up a shower of sparks, and as the flames licked upward, they chased the shadows to the far corners of the room. Satisfied, Simon sat down and looked at Rebecca across the table.

"You're worried he might not walk again, aren't you?" he said.

Rebecca glanced at the bed to be sure Daniel was asleep before she answered. "It will be a miracle if he does. Likely he'll need a crutch or a cane the rest of his life. I'm just praying I can save his foot."

She looked past Simon into the fire, wishing she could see the future in those dancing flames. What she saw instead was the past—a vivid image of one of her father's prized hounds who'd been mauled by a bear and had suffered a fractured hip. Forced to drag himself around, the hound's once proud tail had drooped, and his dark eyes had settled into deep pools of sadness. Whenever the other dogs swirled around her father, jumping and barking, ready for a day in the woods, there was human-like grief in that dog's eyes. Her father had finally put the hound down, and while she'd shed tears, in her heart she'd known it was a kindness.

What frightened her now was that she'd seen much the same look of despair wash across her husband's face when he'd awakened and realized the severity of his injury. Though Daniel was a passable gunsmith, having learned a good deal of the craft from his brother Squire, Rebecca knew he'd never be happy confined to the narrow boundaries of a workshop.

Simon's voice broke into her thoughts.

"Captain Boone may walk just fine. The way I see it, there's already been one miracle today—the fact that any of us got off that field alive."

Simon's back was to the fire. His face was shadowed, but something in his posture, a coiled tenseness, told Rebecca there was something else he wanted to say.

"Miz Boone," he began slowly, "when I was out there today, I felt sure I was a dead man, and I realized I didn't want to go to my grave without you knowing the truth about me."

He pressed his big hands against the table and took a deep breath. "My name's not Simon Butler—it's Kenton—Simon Kenton." He spoke the name haltingly, as if his tongue had forgotten how to shape the syllables. "I've hated lying to you. You've made me feel like part of your family. I really was apprenticed to a saddler, like I told you, and I ran away at sixteen, but it was because . . ."

He paused. She could almost see the words teetering on his tongue.

"I ran away," he said finally, "because I killed a man."

She stared at him, speechless, unable to picture this gentle young man as a murderer. As if reading her thoughts, Simon's eyes grew pleading.

"I was in the churchyard one Sunday, back in Virginia, and this fellow started goading me. I lost my temper and took a swing—caught him on the chin and laid him out flat. The next thing I remember, folks were hollering I'd killed him. I ran back to my master's workshop, gathered up some supplies, and lit out ahead of the law."

"What in the world did that man say to make you so angry?"

"I'd asked a girl to marry me, but her father wouldn't allow it because I was just an apprentice. He said a girl as pretty as she was could hold out for a rich man."

Simon swallowed hard and rubbed a hand across his face. "Everybody in the community knew how I felt about her. One day after church, this fellow made it a point to elbow his way through the crowd to tell me he'd gotten her father's blessing." His face grew pained at the memory. "I shouldn't have hit him, but he had this smirk on his face . . ."

"Maybe she'd have come away with you, Simon. Did you ask her?"

Simon shook his head. "I couldn't ask her to run off to the woods with a murderer. I'm gonna live the rest of my life not even using my real name." His voice sank to a whisper. "I reckon there's some things even the Lord can't forgive."

She reached across the table and gathered his big hands in both of hers. "A few years ago you accidentally took a life—today you saved one. Don't you reckon the Lord's smart enough to weigh those two things side by side and figure out what sort of man you are?"

She smiled as a flicker of hope stirred in the depths of the big man's eyes.

Daniel didn't even try to stand up until a month had passed. When he finally did, he leaned heavily on Israel's shoulder and shuffled only a few steps, barely putting weight on his injured foot. Israel fashioned him a crutch, padding the top with strips of material from one of Rebecca's old shifts, but even then, Daniel rarely ventured further than the bench beneath the eaves in front of their cabin. His leg was as stiff and awkward as a block of wood, and every move produced a muffled crunching like the slow cracking of a walnut beneath steady pressure. Rebecca began to think Daniel would spend the rest of his life hobbling out to that bench and doing nothing but staring into space. She told the girls that what their father needed was a distraction, something to take his mind off his infirmity.

The distraction they got was more than she'd bargained for.

27

Rebecca

One sweltering day in July, Rebecca had just stepped out of the cabin when Simon burst through the fort gate and staggered to a halt, leaning on his rifle as he struggled to catch his breath. Rebecca hurried to join the other folks who'd gathered around the scout.

"There's . . . there's at least . . . two hundred warriors," he gasped. "Less than a half day behind me."

There was a stunned silence, broken only by Simon's breathing and the thump of Daniel's crutch on the hard-packed ground as he came up behind Rebecca. "We've only got thirty riflemen and limited powder," she heard him say softly, as if to himself.

The crowd's silence gave way to a buzz of conversation as Daniel and Colonel Callaway stepped aside to confer. Since Henderson's departure, the two men had done their best to work together. Now, they organized the others, sending some out to round up as many cows and horses as could readily be found, knowing any left outside the stockade would be stolen or slaughtered. They set the women to work filling every bucket, barrel, and kettle in the fort with water from the spring outside the fort gates; the half-finished well within the fort was still producing only a slow trickle of muddy water that would be insufficient to sustain them.

All that afternoon, Daniel sat by the fire molding bullets, his leg propped up on a chair, while Israel and Will cleaned the family's rifles. Rebecca and the girls filled the powder horns, and the younger children helped cut a supply of bullet patches.

Rebecca's thoughts skittered around like a water bug on a pond. What if the Indians overran the walls? How long could they hold them off from inside the cabin? If the walls were breached, would it be best to drop the children over the stockade walls so they could make a run for it? Logan's Station, some thirty miles away, was the closest place they could hope to find refuge, but for all they knew, it would be under siege as well. The more the gravity of their situation sank in, the more helpless she felt. She was reduced to silently praying the same words over and over: *Dear Lord, don't let my babies die . . . don't let my babies die.*

One by one, the children fell into an exhausted sleep, snuggling against each other for comfort despite the summer heat, while Rebecca and Daniel sat at the table, waiting. Around midnight, Daniel stood and tucked his crutch under his arm.

"I think I'll check on the guards," he said.

She nodded and watched him step carefully over the door sill. After a moment she followed him outside and watched him stump across the yard in the moonlight. His movements were awkward, but there was a determined set to his shoulders.

The ladder leaning against their cabin beckoned her upward. From time to time, during the summer months, she'd sought a few moments of privacy and a breath of fresh air by climbing up to the roof. All day her imagination had filled the river bottom outside the fort with warriors spread as thick as berries in a cobbler. Now, she needed to see for herself what lay beyond the walls. She slipped onto the roof and lay flat, peering up at Hackberry Ridge, which stretched along the horizon like a shadowy backbone. When a whisper of wind rustled the leaves, she shivered, imagining it was the sound of moccasined feet slipping toward the wall. She stared into the dark, struggling to sift leaf shadow from human shadow, but all she could see was the moonlit outline of the fencerows and the towering silhouettes of oak and hickory trees at the edge of the fields. Rolling onto her back, she watched the stars wheel silently overhead. It felt as if heaven itself was holding its breath.

The following evening, she lay on her belly in that same spot, clutching her rifle as darkness fell and a barrage of flaming arrows arched into the sky, destined for the fort. For a moment it was like watching shooting stars, but the eerie beauty of the scene dissolved as the arrows rained down inside the stockade. She felt a rush of air as an arrow whistled past her head and buried itself in the shingles of their cabin. Using the tail of her apron to smother the flames before the wood could ignite, she slid cautiously to the edge of the roof but kept her eyes turned skyward.

When a second barrage of arrows arched into the sky, she slipped down the ladder and discovered Levina and Becky standing in the cabin doorway, their younger brothers peering wide-eyed from behind their skirts.

"Stay inside," she said sternly as she hurried past them, hugging the walls of the cabin to stay under the protection of the eaves. Ahead of her, several women were soaking blankets in a barrel of water. She glanced back to be sure the children had stayed put, then sprinted across the open space and pulled off her apron, thrusting it into the water as a flaming arrow whistled over her head and landed in the dirt nearby. She smothered the flames with her apron as the women scattered to beat back other fires erupting around the stockade.

The arrows rained down all night, starting and stopping with no warning, making it dangerous to move around the fort even with a sharp eye turned heavenward. The men stationed along the walls and inside the corner blockhouses grew increasingly frustrated, as Daniel had ordered them to hold their fire to conserve ammunition unless they had a clear shot at the enemy. Much of the time, the fort remained eerily quiet, except for the whir of approaching arrows.

Several times during the night, groups of warriors ran boldly out of the darkness, carrying torches up to the walls, intent on setting the fort ablaze. Each time a barrage of shots rang out and the figures scattered, dropping their torches, which flamed brightly in the dirt before guttering harmlessly out, one by one, like fallen stars.

As dawn broke, one of the sentries cried: "They're burning the corn."

Rebecca climbed up the ladder and peered over the fort's walls. The tall green stalks that stretched across the plain, heavily laden with still-growing ears, were already beginning to flame as the Indians moved along the rows with torches, too distant for the fort's rifles to reach them. The smoke rolled toward the stockade, and soon the entire plain was filled with a stinging haze that burned eyes and throats. *Months of work gone,* Rebecca thought, covering her mouth with her apron and breathing as shallowly as possible. *How will we keep the children fed this winter?*

Smoke hung heavy over the fort the rest of that day. Rebecca's limbs felt heavy and her vision blurry after being under siege for two days. Her face and shift were smeared with soot, her mouth was parched, and her apron was charred. She caught a glimpse of Daniel bracing himself against a rain barrel, his crutch in the dirt beside him, as he manned one of the loopholes. Her palms stung from smothering dozens of arrows. Behind her, she heard the terrified snorts of the horses each time fire fell from the sky.

Somehow the log walls held, and on the morning of the third day, the Indians departed, having tried their best to burn them out. In the welcome stillness of that third morning, Rebecca stumbled to the rain barrel to get a dipper of water and was startled by the sight of an arrow sticking out of the rim, like a skinny bird perched for a drink. A light tug pulled it free.

She held it up to the light and marveled at the way the turkey feathers at one end glowed in the sun. The birchwood shaft felt smooth on her palm. It was clear it had been crafted with care, but despite its beauty, the arrow brought nothing but death. Anger washed over her, and with it a torrent of memories: her son's murder, her daughter's kidnapping, the crippling of her husband, the long nights of terror they'd just endured. The Indians were gone, but she knew they'd be back, and she hated them for these past hardships and what she feared they'd inflict on her family in the future.

Even as these thoughts paraded through her mind, she could hear Jemima's voice saying, "But they're just like us, Mama. You'd be furious too if you watched your land being stolen, bit by bit."

It amazed her that Jemima, who'd undergone such a harrowing experience, carried less resentment toward the Indians than many folks who'd suffered much less. She knew in her bones that Jemima was right—that compassion and forgiveness were what the Lord would want—but forgiveness of any sort seemed far beyond what she could ever hope to feel.

Rebecca dropped the arrow in the dirt and leaned against the water barrel, clutching the rim. She stared into the water, and the ghostly face that looked back at her, wide-eyed and haggard, was a woman she no longer recognized.

28

Rebecca

"I've had enough," she told Daniel a few days after the siege was lifted. "The Indians have given up for now, but they'll be back. There's not a piece of land in this world worth putting our children through that again."

She'd asked him to walk to the river with her, away from the fort, so they could talk privately. As she waited for him to respond, she took a deep breath and shut her eyes, savoring the sound of the current spilling over the rocks.

"Becca, I understand how you feel," Daniel said, "but I can't abandon these folks."

She opened her eyes and stared at him.

"It's not about the land anymore," he said. "I don't even know if we have title to a single acre, what with Virginia seizing the land from Henderson. But I led these folks out here; I can't just leave them."

She squeezed his hand and turned back to the river, a thousand thoughts crowding her mind. She wasn't surprised. She felt torn about departing Boonesborough, too, but for very different reasons. There was a part of her that hated this place, yet she had to admit that here, for the first time in their married life, she and Daniel were spending long stretches of time together. For years he'd given the best of himself to the men he'd roamed the wilderness with; now, in this godforsaken place, he was finally giving the best of himself to his family.

During their time at Boonesborough, particularly during Daniel's long convalescence, all the things that had attracted her to him in the first place—his humor, his gentleness, his almost childish willingness to believe the best of his fellow human beings—had become apparent to her again. Despite their hardships, she felt closer to him now than she had since they were newlyweds.

"How's your ankle?" she asked, turning to look at him. He'd left his crutch behind this morning, which was a good sign.

"Stiff, but not hurting too badly." He flexed his foot, then grinned at her. "I had a good doctor."

She took a deep breath. "I won't ask you to abandon these folks right now—I know you believe they're your responsibility—but keeping our children safe is even more important. If things don't change for the better . . ."

"We've survived the worst the Indians can throw at us, Becca, and I think the British will forget about us if the fighting heats up back east. If we can hold out a bit longer, our children and grandchildren will have an easier life than we've had."

His eyes were shining, as if he saw a bright future shimmering above the water. She prayed he was right.

Any lingering hopes she had of convincing Daniel to leave Kentucky were dashed on the day a contingent of militia rode into the fort, sent to reinforce Virginia's tenuous hold on the backcountry. Men threw their hats in the air and women cried with relief as a hundred soldiers rode single file through the gate.

Rebecca was standing alongside Flanders and Jemima, watching the riders file past, when a lanky fellow wearing a wide grin pulled his gelding out of line and stopped in front of them.

"Cage," Flanders said, his voice full of wonder, "what are *you* doing here?"

"Hello, big brother. We heard the Indians were more than you could handle, so James and I thought we'd come out here and help set things right."

A second rider reined in alongside. "I'm guessing this pretty lady is our new sister-in-law that you wrote home about."

Flanders grinned and put his arm around Jemima's shoulders. "James, Micajah—my wife, Jemima."

In spite of her workday short gown and lack of shoes, Jemima must have passed muster because James said: "Damn, Flanders. Has she got a sister?"

Flanders laughed. "Maybe by the time you've whipped the Indians for us, Jemima's little sisters will have grown enough to give you a second look."

"They better grow fast," Cage said. "We aim to have the British *and* their Shawnee friends pushed back across the Ohio before the spring thaw."

Despite everyone's initial relief at the arrival of reinforcements, as fall faded into winter, the reality of a hundred extra mouths to feed became almost as daunting a challenge as the Shawnee themselves. The militia had packed in a supply of cornmeal, but those bulging bags were now empty. Rebecca, along with some of the other women, began following the cows in the morning when they went to pasture, watching to see what they ate and then cutting the wild greens to bring home and cook. After the first hard frost, even that source of sustenance was lost.

"With the cornfields burnt, the Indians know we didn't have a harvest," Daniel said. "It's likely they figure we'll be starved out by spring. Our only hope is to preserve enough game meat to get us through the winter, and to do that we've got to have salt."

After much discussion, it was agreed that thirty men would accompany Daniel to the salt springs at Blue Licks about fifty miles north to boil up a supply of salt. The Indians rarely undertook full-scale campaigns during the winter months, and the men would be well armed and ready to cope with small scouting parties.

When Daniel and Flanders rode north with the salt boilers, Jemima went about her chores with such a dejected expression that Susannah began to tease her.

"I hope Flanders is better at hiding his feelings than you are," Suzy said. "If he mopes around like this in front of the men, they'll torment him right out of camp."

"I *miss* him," Jemima said. "And you can't talk, your husband stayed here—how often have you had to be away from Will?"

"Not nearly enough," Suzy replied.

Something in her tone made Rebecca turn and search her daughter's face, but before she could question her, they were interrupted by excited voices just outside. Grabbing their cloaks, the women opened the cabin door to a blast of cold air; they stepped outside into ankle-deep snow.

Thomas Brooks, one of the salt boilers who'd been acting as a courier between the salt springs and the fort, sat his horse amidst a crowd, gesturing broadly. Even from a distance Rebecca could see that his mount was lathered with sweat despite the frigid February wind. She pulled the wool cloak around her neck as she and the girls hurried to see what the commotion was about.

"The camp was ransacked," Brooks was saying. "There were kettles and cordwood scattered all over the snow. Judging from the footprints, there were a hundred Indians at least."

Rebecca's pulse quickened.

"Any bodies?" called a voice from the rear of the crowd.

Brooks shook his head. "No one's left at all—alive or dead. It's the damnedest thing. There's no sign of a fight; they're just gone, like they packed up and headed north with the Indians."

The sounds around Rebecca grew muffled, as if her cloak had wrapped itself around her ears. She shook her head, trying to clear it.

Jemima stood rigidly beside her, and Susannah clasped her sister's hand. "No bodies, Jemima," she said. "So they're still alive, and Daddy will look out for Flanders."

But that wasn't what happened.

29

Susannah

Several days after Thomas Brooks brought news of the salt boilers' disappearance, the fort's dogs announced the arrival of a solitary figure who rode into the fort, shoulders slumped and reins hanging slackly as if instinct alone had carried him there.

Susannah was drawing water from the well while Jemima, having just filled her own bucket, waited alongside. When Jemima spotted the rider, she let out a muffled cry, and her bucket hit the ground, splattering water across the hard-packed snow. By the time Susannah realized the rider was Flanders, Jemima had already reached his side. He swung wearily down from his horse, and Jemima pressed her cheek into the curve of her husband's neck. Flanders rested his chin on top of Jemima's head and closed his eyes with a sigh, as if he'd arrived at the only destination that mattered.

A door creaked open behind Susannah, and she turned to see her mother, her cloak gathered around her against the bitter wind that swirled along the row of cabins.

"Bring Flanders inside," she called to Jemima.

Flanders was soon settled into a chair on her mother's hearth. Jemima's hands fluttered over him—touching his hair, his shoulder, his chest—as if her fingers were anxious butterflies unsure where to land. Ice clung to Flanders's snow-dampened hair, and his face was chapped red from the wind. Shortly after he sat down, he was overcome by a violent fit of shivering, which continued even after Jemima tucked warm blankets around him. Susannah helped her mother edge his chair closer to the fire, and soon the snow that was crusted up and down his woolen leggings dripped steadily onto the floor.

Flanders sat with his eyes closed during their ministrations, but after a while his lids fluttered open, and when he looked up, the despair in his eyes hit Susannah like a fist.

"They're all gone," he said, his voice raspy as a rusty hinge.

"We know," Susannah said hurriedly, wanting to spare him the retelling of news they'd already heard. "Thomas Brooks made it back to the fort and told us the company had been captured."

"We thought you'd been taken, too," Jemima said, her voice cracking.

"Captain Boone and I were out hunting. . . . We weren't in camp . . ."

Flanders's voice trailed off, and his eyes searched the faces around him. Susannah followed his gaze and saw that her mother's face had flamed with hope.

"Daniel?" she said.

Flanders shook his head, and her mother closed her eyes, trapping her pain before it could spill across the room.

"The first I knew something was wrong was when I found tracks in the snow where the Indians had ambushed Captain Boone while he was hunting. They chased him a ways—he didn't have a prayer of outrunning them with that ankle. . ."

The door banged open and Colonel Callaway strode in. "Flanders, what about Micajah and James?"

Susannah realized guiltily that Flanders's brothers were among the missing, and she hadn't given them a single thought.

"The Indians took them all north." Flanders's voice was hollow. "Their tracks were plain in the snow, but there was nothing I could do . . ."

The Colonel's eyes blazed. "The men were well armed, yet Brooks says there was no sign of a fight. Evidently Captain Boone lacked the backbone to resist."

"Colonel," her mother said sharply, "say another word against my husband and I'll remove you from this house myself."

There was a movement in the corner, and Susannah saw that Israel, who'd been silently observing the scene, had risen to his feet. The Colonel's eyes cut in his direction, then back to her mother.

"Your pardon, Miz Boone. It was thoughtless of me to speak ill of your husband under your roof." He turned to his nephew. "I'll need to draft a letter to your parents, Flanders. The commander of the militia will be sending an express rider to the Clinch settlements with the news. Come see me in the morning. Your parents will want to hear anything you can tell them about your brothers' disappearance."

Flanders's face turned ashen at the prospect.

Her mother said very little as the weeks slipped past and winter gave way to spring, but Susannah noticed she often stared northward across the Kentucky River.

"Your father will make his way home to us," she told the children.

Jemima nodded in agreement. "Daddy's probably waiting for the weather to warm before he makes his escape."

Susannah and Israel exchanged glances. Though their father no longer needed a crutch, his ankle still bothered him, and even if he had the opportunity to escape, it was doubtful he would elude his pursuers for long. Susannah recalled that when Jemima was kidnapped, her father had said it was critical to find the girls before the Indians crossed the Ohio. "White folks who cross that river rarely return," he'd said.

Now, those words echoed in her ears.

Of all the salt boilers, Andy Johnson was the last man Susannah would have expected to slip from the Indians' clutches and make his way home. Thin and undersized, from a distance he looked no more than twelve, an illusion that saved his life when he showed up at Harrod's fort in early May, clad in Indian garb. "We were hesitant to shoot an unarmed boy, even if he looked like an Indian," one of the sentries said. "Luckily we heard Andy hollering that he was a white man."

Word of Johnson's return swept through Boonesborough. Mrs. Callaway stuck her head in Susannah's door to tell them the news, her eyes bright with excitement.

"As soon as Mister Johnson has rested a bit, they say he's coming to Boonesborough. He's got word of our men—claims he saw some of them less than a week ago."

The moment Andy Johnson arrived, every soul in the fort swarmed around him, giving him barely enough room to dismount. Momentarily swallowed by the crush of people, the little man stepped onto an overturned cattle trough to address the crowd, reappearing like a swimmer bobbing to the surface. He was an odd sight, dressed in a hunting shirt and breeches like a white man, but with his hair in Shawnee fashion, plucked bare on either side of a bushy scalp lock.

When the jostling subsided, Johnson cleared his throat and began.

"After our capture, we were marched to a village called Chillicothe. Some of us were chosen for adoption into the tribe, but others were marched away to Detroit to be handed over to the British. Anyone labeled a troublemaker was sent north."

"So how'd they overlook you, Andy?" someone hollered.

There was a ripple of male laughter, which the women shushed immediately.

"I got adopted because I pretended to be a half-wit." Johnson glared at the crowd as if daring anyone to make a joke. "I once heard an Indian trader say the Shawnee honor such folks, and I figured anything was better than rotting in a British prison."

"William Hancock," cried a woman, unable to wait any longer. "Is there word of him?"

Immediately other voices were raised.

"What do you know of Bartlett Searcy?"

"Samuel Brooks," called another.

Colonel Callaway's voice rang out, rising above the others. "Mister Johnson assures me that to the best of his knowledge, all the men are still alive. He's agreed to speak privately with the families of the missing. But right now, what everyone needs to hear is why the men were captured in the first place."

The crowd subsided into scattered murmurs while the woman standing next to Susannah twisted the tail of her apron as though she might wring answers from it.

"We were captured because of Captain Boone," Johnson said, his high, thin voice carrying across the crowd. "He ordered us to surrender. He led the Indians to our camp, then told us to stack our arms or we'd be massacred."

The murmurs turned angry. Susannah looked around for her mother and was relieved to see Simon push his way through the crowd to stand alongside her. Someone grasped her arm, and she jerked backward, then realized it was Israel.

"Stay close," he whispered.

Johnson raised his voice and continued. "The British are offering twenty pounds for each prisoner. When they sorted out the men they intended to take to Detroit, Captain Boone was among them." Johnson paused and surveyed the crowd with stormy eyes. "Boone was the only one who returned. He rode back to the village on a horse given to him by Governor Hamilton himself."

There was a gasp from the crowd. Susannah heard several voices say, "Hamilton—the Hair Buyer." And then someone shouted, "Traitor!" The word rumbled through the crowd like a roll of thunder, passing from tongue to tongue. "Traitor!"

"That's a lie!" The crowd turned in unison to see her mother, eyes blazing. "Daniel would never betray the men in his command."

Johnson's thin face twisted with anger. "We were prepared to fight until Captain Boone ordered us not to."

"And if you'd fought, most likely you'd be dead!" Her mother's face was chalk white with anger. "My husband's not a traitor!"

But judging from the angry words swirling through the crowd, most of their neighbors disagreed.

For the rest of that afternoon, Mister Johnson went from cabin to cabin, offering families whatever scraps of information he possessed about their missing men. Susannah waited at her mother's with the rest of the family, but it was after dark when Simon finally escorted Johnson inside. The children had fallen asleep by this time, piled on her mother's corner bed like an exhausted litter of kittens.

Her mother stood and offered Johnson a chair, but he shook his head, stopping just inside the doorway and planting his feet on the puncheon floor as if he were astride the deck of a ship and expected foul weather.

"First of all, Mister Johnson," her mother said, "my family and I obviously disagree with your belief that Daniel betrayed you. We aren't Loyalists, despite rumors to the contrary. My husband has never taken sides."

"He damn sure took sides at the Licks," Johnson snapped.

Her mother's eyes flashed, but her voice remained low. "I understand you're angry, but I'm sure Daniel had his reasons. Right now, I'm asking you to put aside your feelings and tell me whatever you can about my husband."

Johnson hesitated as if he might refuse, then said grudgingly: "He was adopted by Chief Blackfish. He's settled into Indian life just fine—treats those savages like family. When the Shawnee adopt you, the women take you down to the creek and scrub you within an inch of your life. They believe they can wash the white blood out of you, and in Daniel's case, I think it worked." Johnson absently ran a hand over the stubble on his head. "Your husband ain't Daniel no more—they call him Sheltowee."

Her mother's face was pale. "Did Daniel ever speak to you about escaping?"

Johnson shook his head. "We didn't talk much—I was playing the village idiot, remember? But I'll tell you this—if he'd wanted to escape, he could have because Blackfish lets him go hunting alone. Seems he's taken an Indian wife, and . . ."

Her mother flinched as if Johnson had struck her.

Simon slammed his fist on the table and growled, "That's *enough*, sir!"

Johnson cast an anxious glance at the big man, then shrugged. "All I'm saying is—if I was you, I wouldn't hold my breath waiting for him to come back." He settled his hat on his head and turned to go, then paused at the door. "Truth is, given the way most of us feel about him, your husband's safer with the Indians."

Susannah wasn't surprised when her mother announced she was leaving Boonesborough and taking the younger children back to her parents' farm at the Forks. "There's a group of militiamen heading to the Gap in a few days," she said, surveying the solemn faces around the table: Susannah, Israel, Jemima, Flanders, Simon, and Will. "With me and the children gone, you'll have five fewer mouths to feed."

Jemima looked stricken. "Is it because of what Andy Johnson said about Daddy choosing to stay with the Indians?"

Her mother squared her shoulders. "Whatever the reason, your father's not here, and I'm no longer welcome. My presence makes it awkward for all of you. It's best I leave."

Even before her mother finished speaking, Susannah had made up her mind to go east, too. She wanted her little girl out of this place, away from the filth and the hunger and the endless gnawing fear that afflicted them all and that surely even a toddler could sense. Susannah rested a hand on her belly. Just days earlier, she'd felt the first faint stirrings of new life, but she hadn't yet told Will that a second child was on the way, uncertain how he'd take the news. Though Israel's vigilance had ended the worst of Will's abuse, she still moved warily around him, like a deer sniffing the wind to make sure the next step was safe to take.

Later that night, she screwed up her courage and told Will that another baby was on the way, and that she intended to leave Kentucky with her mother. She braced for his anger, maybe even his fists, but to her surprise, he agreed.

"I'll see you and Elizabeth safely to Carolina," Will said, "but I intend to return right away to bring supplies back to Boonesborough."

Hearing the resolve in his voice, she felt a grudging respect for her husband for the first time in a very long while, yet she had to admit that what pleased her most about his plan was the realization that soon there'd be a mountain range between them.

When Susannah begged Jemima to come with them, Jemima shook her head, her eyes sad. "I can't imagine being here without you and Mama, but Flanders will never leave Kentucky as long as his brothers are captives."

On the day of their departure, Susannah leaned down from her horse and whispered to Jemima, "If this baby's a girl, I'm naming her after you."

Jemima's eyes filled with tears, and she held tight to Susannah's hand as the column of horses started to move, walking alongside with her face turned upward as if memorizing her sister's features. With a final squeeze, Jemima let go as Susannah and her mount passed through the fort gate, following the column of riders that stretched across the meadow toward Hackberry Ridge.

When they reached the top of the ridge, Susannah pulled her horse to a halt for a final look at the fort below. It looked small and frighteningly vulnerable, perched alongside the river like a toy block dropped by a thoughtless giant. Jemima stood alone where she'd left her, a distant patch of blue against the log walls. As Susannah turned her mount away, she felt sure that Boonesborough was the place where she'd finally found her little sister—and would also be the place where she'd lose her forever.

30

Jemima

On a blistering day in late June, a little more than a month after Jemima had watched her mother and Suzy ride out of the fort, Fanny poked her head through Jemima's doorway, her eyes wide.

"Jemima! It's your father," she said. "He's here, and he looks like an Indian!"

Jemima hurried across the stockade to the Callaway cabin and pushed her way among the men who'd crowded around the open door and were peering inside. She had to stand on tiptoe to catch a glimpse of her father, and when she did, her breath caught in her throat.

He was standing with his back to her, but she saw that his thick hair had been plucked so that he was bald except for a narrow scalp lock. His back was bare and sunburned, and the scratches across his shoulders spoke of hard travel. When the crowd shifted, she saw that his buckskin moccasins were caked with mud.

"I'm telling you, there are more than four hundred warriors and some British advisors, ready to march," her father said. "We have to start preparing now."

"It's a trick," someone yelled. "He's up to something."

At the front of the room, Colonel Callaway banged on the table and the buzz of voices grew quiet.

"I distrust the messenger," Callaway said, "but we can't afford to disregard the message. Gather the rest of the men—we have decisions to make. One of you escort Captain Boone to his cabin and see that he stays there."

Jemima stepped back and waited for her father to cross the threshold. "Daddy!" she called as soon as he appeared in the doorway.

His eyes searched the crowd; when she raised her hand and he spotted her, his face lit up. He took a step toward her, but the guard grabbed his elbow. "Come along. You heard the Colonel."

Jemima spun on her heel and ran back to the cabin, determined to be there to greet him. When the guard pushed her father through the cabin door, Jemima fell into his embrace, crying and asking questions all at once.

"Are you all right? How did you escape? What about the other men?"

Her father kissed her on the head, but didn't answer. His eyes roamed the cabin's interior, and Jemima realized he was looking for her mother. The room must have looked empty to him without her mother's sewing basket by her chair and her kitchen plunder on the worktable. The last time her father had been here, the room had been filled with constant chatter and the scuffling sound of children in the loft above, but now the cabin was quiet.

"Your mother . . .?"

"She's gone. She took the children back to the Forks a couple months ago."

"She thought I was dead?"

"No," Jemima said, choosing her words carefully, "she thought you were happy."

Her father's brow furrowed.

"Andy Johnson said you were . . ." she fumbled for the right word. "He said you were *content* with the Indians. You've been gone five months, and . . ."

Before either of them could say more, Israel, Simon, Flanders, and Will crowded through the doorway, and her father turned to greet them, catching Israel in a hearty hug and clapping Will and Simon on the shoulder. Jemima wasn't surprised to see Flanders hang back, his face solemn.

"Listen, boys," her father said, "you've got to convince folks I'm telling the truth. The fort's in bad repair, and if the Shawnee show up now . . ."

Flanders interrupted him, his voice cold. "Two dozen men are missing because of you, including my brothers. Most folks believe you're working for the British. Why should we believe you?"

Jemima winced at the bluntness of her husband's words. Over the past months she'd done her best to convince Flanders that her father wouldn't have surrendered the men unless he had no other choice. Clearly she hadn't persuaded him.

Her father sank onto a bench and looked up at Flanders. "So you think I surrendered my men because I'm loyal to the Crown?"

Flanders stood stone-faced, letting the question hang in the air.

"The Indians were headed to Boonesborough when they captured me," her father said. "Surrendering the salt boilers was the only way I could keep the war party from continuing south and overrunning the fort right away. I was thinking of the women and children."

Flanders still didn't speak.

After a moment her father shifted on the bench and surveyed the room with a wistful expression. "I never thought Becca'd be gone . . ."

The Indians came, more than four hundred strong, just as her father had said they would. By the time they appeared on the grassy plain in front of the fort—a mass of color and feathers and bristling rifles—the walls had been repaired, and the men had made what preparations they could to face an enemy that vastly outnumbered them. From the beginning it was clear this was to be no stealthy attack, but rather a show of overwhelming force designed to intimidate the fort's inhabitants into surrender.

The Indians stood nearly motionless at the foot of the ridge, and the ominous silence weighed so heavily on Jemima's chest that she couldn't seem to draw a full breath. When she thought she couldn't bear it another moment, a lone voice, distant at first, floated across the plain.

"Sheltowee, my son, come speak with me."

Jemima saw a flash of sorrow cross her father's face, but when he turned to Colonel Callaway, his voice was matter-of-fact: "It's Chief Blackfish. If I go talk to him, we'll have a better idea what we're up against."

Colonel Callaway studied him a moment, then nodded. Clearly he didn't trust her father, but then again, none of the other men, including

Callaway, appeared interested in venturing outside the stockade to hear the Indians' terms.

Jemima climbed the ladder propped next to her parents' cabin and peered over the fort's walls, watching her father walk out of the gate alone and unarmed. Sixty yards from the walls, within range of the fort's rifles but also within rifle shot of that massed wall of Indians, her father met a delegation of his former captors, who greeted him warmly and motioned for him to sit down among them.

Her father and Chief Blackfish settled onto a blanket and began to talk, their heads inclined toward each other so they nearly touched. Even from a distance, Jemima was struck by the confident way the chief carried himself. He leaned forward to listen to her father's words, then sat back to contemplate them, calm and unhurried, before leaning forward again to offer his response.

"Boone's mighty friendly with them," a man standing near her said. A ripple of disgusted agreement passed among the men who stood along that section of wall, their rifles raised, ready to shoot at the least provocation. If the opportunity presented itself, she suspected more than one of them would happily draw a bead on her father.

After a thirty-minute council, her father returned to the fort and everyone gathered around him to hear the enemy's terms.

"If we surrender, Governor Hamilton guarantees us all safe passage to Detroit, where we'll be placed under British protection."

"Jailed, he means," a man shouted.

Her father ignored him and continued: "Soldiers who agree to fight for the British will be allowed to retain their current rank. However," he spoke more slowly, emphasizing each word, "if we choose to resist, the Shawnee say it will be to the death."

Everyone began talking at once. Jemima made out only a word here or there before Colonel Callaway's voice rang out over the din.

"I swear I'll shoot the first man who suggests we surrender."

That quieted the crowd.

"I sent a rider to the settlements for reinforcements as soon as Boone returned," Callaway continued. "If we can hold out long enough, there's a chance they'll come to our aid. So let's put it to a vote. All in favor of fighting, say aye."

"Aye," roared the men.

Her father stood silent.

"And you, Captain Boone?" Callaway said, eyeing him coldly.

"I guess I'll die with the rest."

The Indians had given them a day to consider their terms. Late that afternoon, her father drew Jemima aside.

"I told Blackfish you'd step outside the gate with me just before dusk."

"What?" she said, thinking she'd misheard him.

"I told Callaway the Shawnee are curious to see you because I bragged about you when I was a captive. That's true, but there's more to it."

"I don't understand."

"When I was first captured, one of the reasons Blackfish abandoned his plan to attack Boonesborough and took the salt boilers instead was that I promised to accompany him to the fort this summer and surrender it to him."

She looked at her father, eyes wide. This sounded like treason, even to her.

"At the time I was willing to say anything to keep the Indians away from the fort with all of you sitting here defenseless. When Blackfish arrived today, he expected me to honor my promise and turn the fort over to him." Her father's eyes held a sad, haunted look. "I lied to Blackfish last winter when he was an enemy—I had no idea he'd become like a father to me. When we met today, he had tears in his eyes. He told me I'm still his son."

Jemima put a hand on her father's shoulder. "You did what you had to do."

"But now—tomorrow or the next day—I'll be fighting against men who've treated me kindly to defend a group of people who believe I'm a traitor."

"Did you really plan to surrender the fort?"

Her father shook his head. "No—not when I first said it. But now, having lived at Chillicothe, I can tell you that life as an Indian is a heap better than dying in this place. This morning I told Blackfish that I'm no longer in charge of the fort, and that I doubted the new leaders would consider surrender. After he heard that, Blackfish asked to see you."

"I still don't understand."

"If the Indians overrun the fort—which is likely, given their numbers—Blackfish said he'd do his best to see that you're spared."

"But why? Why would he do that?"

"Because," her father said softly, "it's what a father would do for his son."

Jemima and her father slipped out of the gate, stopping just outside the fort's log walls as the sky dimmed to dusk. A cluster of warriors stood near the tree line, and one of them yelled to her father in Shawnee.

He turned to Jemima. "They want you to let down your hair."

She looked at him, confused, but when her father nodded, she pulled the pins from her hair and let it cascade over her shoulders and down past her waist.

The Indians hooted, speaking rapidly to each other. Finally one of them shouted in English: "Pretty daughter, Sheltowee."

Blackfish stood quietly to one side, staring intently at Jemima as if memorizing her face. When she acknowledged his presence with a bob of her head, he gave her a slow, courtly nod of his own. Even after she'd turned to follow her father into the fort, she could feel the chief's eyes on her back.

Once they were inside the stockade and the gate was shut behind them, Jemima pulled the pins from her pocket and put her hair back up.

Her father stood beside her, his face thoughtful, as she recoiled the long strands. "If the fort is overrun," he said, glancing around to be sure no one else was in earshot, "I believe Blackfish wants you to let your hair down as a sign you're the one to be spared. You need to do it, Jemima." His eyes were pleading. "Whatever happens to the rest of us, trust me, you can have a good life with the Shawnee—it will be different, but it can be good."

She had trouble falling asleep that night. She listened to the soft rise and fall of Flanders's breathing beside her and wished she could stop this moment and hold on to it forever. How could it be that by this time tomorrow he might be dead? How could she love someone this much, yet be helpless to save him? She tossed and turned for most of the night, and when she finally dropped off to sleep, she dreamt she was floating on her back in a river of blood, her hair streaming loose around her head.

* * *

The Indians swarmed out of the woods, carrying logs that they hammered against the front gate in an attempt to batter it down. The thuds echoed through the fort, and Jemima shivered with every blow. Fire from the fort's riflemen drove the attackers back, carrying their wounded and dead, but they returned again and again, each time filling the air with their defiant cries.

One of the fort's first casualties was a German man, David Bundrin, who was struck in the forehead by a ball as he peered through a loophole. Bundrin's wound was small and bled very little; he sat on a bench in front of his cabin, wordlessly rocking back and forth, holding his head in his hands. His wife sat beside him, and each time someone passed, she said: "It was Gott's blessing the ball didn't hit him in the eye." Despite her optimism, Bundrin was dead before nightfall.

Jemima worked alongside Mrs. Callaway, carrying buckets of water to the men stationed in the corner blockhouses and along the walls. She felt as if she were swimming through a sea of noise: screams, gunshots, children crying, the bellow of cattle, Indian war cries. It was so loud that her ears rang. When they came to the loophole manned by Fanny's husband, John Holder, he was swearing vehemently, firing and reloading as fast as he could.

Hearing her son-in-law's language, Mrs. Callaway pursed her lips. "You should be praying for deliverance, John, not cursing."

"I don't have time to pray, goddammit," he yelled, thrusting his gun through the loophole.

The Indians placed riflemen on the cliffs across the river, and from those heights they could see directly into the stockade. It made Jemima's hands sweat just to look up at the cliffs and know the enemy was staring down. The distance was so great that many of the bullets that reached the fort were nearly spent by the time they landed, though some still proved deadly. The horses and cattle penned in a corner of the stockade were easy targets; their terrified bellows filled the fort as every so often one of the herd fell, writhing in pain. Jemima watched, heartsick, as one of her favorite mares was struck; her legs buckled under her, and she thrashed in the dust for many long moments before lying still.

The men chopped openings between the cabins that lined the fort's walls, enabling them to move about under cover as much as possible, but venturing into the open couldn't be avoided entirely; Jemima's heart was in her throat each time she scurried across the stockade. She'd just delivered a new supply of lead balls to her father in one of the cabins and was standing inside the doorway, reloading one of his rifles, when she felt a hard blow from behind.

She yelped and dropped the gun.

Her father swung round, his face pale. "Are you hit?"

"Yes, but . . ." Jemima rubbed her hip and the ball fell out of the folds of her skirt and plopped into the dirt.

Her father smiled in relief. "Thank God. It didn't draw blood, but you'll have a hell of a bruise by morning."

Hour after hour of constant gunfire and dodging bullets from above so unnerved the fort's potter, a man named Tice Prock, that he sought refuge beneath the bellows in the smithy. Informed of his whereabouts, Mrs. Callaway chased him out with her broom, whereupon he jumped into the partially dug well in the center of the stockade. Colonel Callaway stomped up to the hole and threw a shovel in on top of him, bellowing: "If you mean to stay down there, you at least need to dig."

After several days of repelling continuous attacks, the men manning the walls above the riverbank noticed a curious plume of mud staining the water as it flowed downstream. Jemima watched as her father climbed up to take a look. When he scrambled down, his face was grim.

"They're tunneling," he said, "trying to dig their way beneath our walls. If they put gunpowder down there, they can blow up a section of the stockade and overrun us."

He set some of the men to work digging a counter tunnel in hopes of intercepting the Indians outside the walls. Jemima and several other women took up the task of hauling buckets of dirt away from the trench. For a while the men piled up the rocks they uncovered, but then someone got the idea of hauling the larger ones up to the walls and hurling them over. The men cheered as each rock crashed through the brush and rolled off the riverbank, bouncing toward the unseen mouth of the Indians' tunnel.

When a series of afternoon thunderstorms swept across the fort, the ditch became a quagmire of mud that coated Jemima's skirts and caked her moccasins. Every step became weighted. The mud-filled buckets got heavier and heavier, and each time gunfire echoed around her, she had to force herself not to throw down the bucket and run. She shut her eyes and tried to imagine herself back in Carolina, swimming in the creek with James by her side, his voice in her ear, telling her all would be well—*relax,* he'd say, *I've got you*—but it was no use. *We're like hogs in a pen,* she thought. *Hogs waiting for slaughter.*

Jemima thought the siege would never end, that they'd be trapped on that riverbank fighting for their lives forever. When a massive rainstorm struck on the tenth night of the siege, pummeling the fort with thunder and lightning, it felt like an assault from heaven itself. She sank down in the mud, her back against one of the walls, and covered her ears. *Stop,* she thought, *please stop.*

The rain pounded down all that night, but the next morning, the sun rose over the freshly washed fields, and the fort's defenders were greeted with a sweet silence. Jemima heard a hawk calling from the ridge above, a wild, free sound, reminding her that only a short distance from this battered patch of ground, life had gone on as usual.

While she welcomed the silence, it was also eerie after days of constant gunfire. At midday, several scouts ventured cautiously from the fort and soon hurried back with the news that the Indian tunnel had caved in thanks to the rain, and the Indian camp was empty.

At the news that the siege was finally over, Jemima rested her head against Flanders's chest and shut her eyes. He smelled of mud and gunpowder and sweat.

"Listen," she said.

He cocked his head. "I don't hear anything."

"I know. Isn't it lovely?"

Over the next weeks, Jemima heard folks say that God had a hand in their deliverance; that it was His will that they'd held out against the Indians; that He'd sent the rain; that He'd strengthened their walls. Jemima had her doubts. *If deliverance was on His mind, ten days sooner would have been nice,* she thought.

She noticed her father didn't join in such talk. Privately, he told her he believed there were enough saints and sinners on both sides—Indians and whites—to make it hard for a God of justice to choose one over the other.

31

Rebecca

The tall trees surrounding the Joppa meetinghouse offered a welcoming shade as Rebecca reined her horse to a halt in front of the building. She'd ridden there alone, but a mockingbird perched in a cedar tree broke the silence, trilling a long string of notes. Since her return to the Forks six months earlier, Rebecca had come to this place from time to time to savor the peacefulness, relishing the chance to escape the crowded cabin in the midst of the Bryan settlement where she and the children had found refuge.

Suzy had delivered her second child after their arrival at the Forks. Baby Jemima had been frighteningly thin due to the meager rations Suzy had subsisted on at Boonesborough for part of her pregnancy. Rebecca had spent many long nights walking her colicky granddaughter in the cool night air, hoping Suzy and the rest of the children could get some much-needed sleep. As for herself, she'd barely slept a full night since Daniel's capture and sometimes doubted she'd ever sleep soundly again.

Peace of any sort, whether in their own cabin or in the colonies as a whole, had become a rarity. The fever of war had infected the Forks, dividing the community, just as it had in Boonesborough, forcing families to choose between King or Congress. Armed ruffians roamed throughout Carolina, burning houses and tarring and feathering folks whose politics differed from theirs. But on this day in late fall as she sat her horse in the meetinghouse yard, such atrocities seemed scarcely believable, like bad dreams only half-remembered in the morning light.

The mockingbird ended its song, and the churchyard fell silent except for a whisper of wind through the trees. Rebecca swung down from her horse, tethering him near the meetinghouse door. She and Hannah had planned to ride here together, but when Rebecca had arrived at Hannah's cabin this morning, she'd found her indisposed.

"Go on without me," Hannah had said.

Rebecca was sorry not to have Hannah's company. Reconnecting with her sister-in-law had been one of the few bright spots about returning to the Forks. She'd been delighted to discover Hannah was no longer a heartbroken widow but the wife of Richard Pennington, a man she'd met after her return to the Forks.

"I grieved for John, for years," Hannah confided. "I never expected to marry again, but then I met Richard." Just speaking her new husband's name made Hannah's face brighten. "He has the kindest eyes, and he's taken the girls in as if they're his own."

Rebecca gave her mount a final pat before making her way around the side of the meetinghouse. The sun shone through the gold-tinged leaves above her, dappling her shoulders with shadows as she picked her way among the scattered stones, stopping finally alongside two markers that stood side by side. Moss softened the edges of the larger one, which marked her father-in-law's resting place. She sounded out the letters until they slowly formed into words: "Squire Boone departed this life . . . in thay year of our Lord 1765."

The smaller stone was her mother-in-law's. Rebecca knelt and ran her hand across the chiseled words—"Departed this life 1777 aged 77 years." The letters' rough edges pricked her fingers and her heart as well. She'd gotten word of Sarah's passing while she and the children were still at Boonesborough, but until Rebecca had stood beside her grave, she hadn't really accepted that Sarah was gone.

Rebecca brushed away the leaves and handfuls of hickory nuts that lay scattered across the graves. As she worked, she could almost hear the soothing rise and fall of Sarah's voice, laced with her gentle thees and thous.

A twig snapped behind her. She rose to her feet and turned to face the road, thinking her horse must have slipped his tether. Instead, Daniel appeared around the corner of the meetinghouse. For an instant she thought she'd conjured him, like a restless spirit risen from one of the graves. But as it dawned on her that he was real, she stood in stunned silence, watching him thread his way toward her through the stones. She'd gotten word that he'd reappeared at Boonesborough and that the fort had withstood another siege, but she'd had little news beyond that.

An arm's length away, he stopped and took off his hat as if greeting a stranger. The sudden sight of his shorn head, stubbly as a newly cut cornfield, was a startling and unwelcome reminder of his months with the Shawnee. In the past, after a lengthy separation, Daniel had often tried to lighten the mood between them by cracking a joke or playing a good-natured prank, but this time his face was solemn. As for herself, though they'd been apart for nearly a year, she wasn't about to jump unquestioningly into his arms.

"I got your letter," she said finally.

He nodded. "I sent it right after the siege was lifted. I would have come to the Forks right away, but Colonel Callaway—"

"Had you court-martialed for treason," she said, finishing the sentence for him.

Her father had read and reread Daniel's letter to her when it had first arrived, and then she'd carried it in her pocket, pulling it out at spare moments, running her hands over the words and sounding them out for herself. She'd spent weeks fingering that parchment, probing it the way a doctor would an open wound, trying to discern the extent of the injuries between them.

Daniel's anger toward Richard Callaway had leapt off the page, and he'd also made clear his determination to regain his good name. But while the letter contained assurances that he longed to be reunited with her and the children, it said nothing about the months of his captivity, and that missing stretch of time haunted her. She and Daniel had grown so close in the months just prior to his capture—closer than they'd been since the first days of their marriage. When she'd heard Andy Johnson's pronouncement that Daniel had chosen to stay with the Indians, it had fallen like an axe stroke, a searing pain that left her wondering if the intimacy between them during the previous months had been a lie.

"I left Kentucky as soon as the court-martial was settled," Daniel said. "I was cleared of all charges. They even promoted me; I'm Major Boone now." His smile was half-hearted and didn't reach his eyes. "Callaway still believes I betrayed the settlement, and there are plenty of folks who agree with him."

"Trust is hard to rebuild," she said.

"Hard," he agreed, "but hopefully not impossible."

They stared at each other, faced off like two bristling barn cats. She was in no mood to look for the best opening or dance around the truth. She came out swinging.

"Why did you stay with the Indians instead of coming home as soon as you had the chance?"

His jaw tensed. A breath of wind blew a swirl of bronzed hickory leaves off the limbs above them; one of them floated down and settled on Rebecca's shoulder. When Daniel leaned over to brush it away, she felt the touch of his fingertips through the material, and it was all she could do not to grasp his hand and cling to it. Her insides churned, but she managed to stand, unmoving, while she waited for him to answer.

"At first they watched me so closely escape wasn't possible." He spoke slowly, weighing each word. "After I'd won their trust, I didn't run because I felt responsible for the other men who were captives; it didn't feel right to leave them behind. When I finally did run, it was because Boonesborough was about to be attacked and I needed to warn them. To warn you." He paused and bit his lip, before adding: "But that's only part of the truth."

He dropped his eyes to the graves at their feet. The silence was so deep she could hear the soft rustling of a bird as it scratched through the leaves nearby. When Daniel looked up, his eyes were pleading.

"I know how you feel about Indians, Becca, so I know this will be hard for you to understand, but I hope you'll try. My adopted father, Blackfish, was one of the finest men I've ever met. I learned a lot from him—things that will make me a better woodsman, and, I hope, a better man. I truly believed that if we could build an understanding between us, it might help our people live in peace."

She felt the hair prickle on the back of her neck. "Peace? How can you forget what they did to James?"

"I haven't forgotten. But Blackfish and his people had nothing to do with our son's death."

"They're Indians," she hissed.

"And we're white," he snapped, "but we aren't responsible for every evil thing our kind does."

She opened her mouth to say something else about James, but what spilled out instead caught them both by surprise.

"Andy Johnson said you'd taken an Indian wife."

He blinked, eyes wide. For a moment he looked so much like an owl she fought the urge to laugh, only to realize that what was really welling up inside her was a sob. She swallowed hard.

When Daniel finally spoke, his voice was calm, but she could hear a thread of tension running through it, like a thin vein of quartz in an outcropping of rock.

"I'll tell you the truth about anything you want to know, Becca, but before you start asking questions, I need you to think back to Culpeper, to all the rumors about you and Ned."

"If you're saying I don't have a right to be angry because—"

He shushed her. "That's not what I'm saying. What I'm getting at is this—I never asked you to explain your feelings toward my brother, did I?"

"No," she admitted.

"It's not that I wasn't curious, but I felt sure that knowing the details about what you felt for Ned wasn't going to help us stay together, and that was what I wanted more than anything. So here's the main thing you need to know now: when I had to choose between you and the Indians, I chose you. If that doesn't satisfy you, then go ahead and ask me whatever you need to know."

She stood in silence, staring up at the swaying branches above them, looking back over the years of their marriage, weighing the good and the bad. Daniel stood with his hat in his hand, his eyes once again fixed on the graves. After a bit, he knelt and rested his hand on his mother's stone. It flitted through her mind that this was the first time he'd seen it. As she looked down on his hatless head, she thought, too, that it would be years before his hair grew long again.

They stayed that way, the birds singing above them and the wind sweeping the dry leaves around the stones, and somewhere in those long minutes she decided she didn't want to know the details of her husband's time with the Shawnee. Whatever had happened in that Indian village was in the past, just as surely as her years in Culpeper were.

When she was a young woman, she'd believed that when a couple said, "I do," it settled things between them forever and always. But as she stood in that sun-swept graveyard, it dawned on her that marriage was not about choosing one's partner just once, but over and over again.

She put a hand on Daniel's shoulder. "It's time to go home," she said.

In the months that followed, she discovered that it's one thing to make a choice and another thing entirely to live with the consequences. When she'd spoken of going home, she'd meant the Bryan settlement at the Forks. But to Daniel, "home" meant Kentucky.

She had no desire to return to Kentucky and told Daniel so repeatedly, but her protests grew progressively weaker as it became clear that nearly all her loved ones from the Forks, including her elderly parents, were eager to head west. There were many reasons behind this exodus; for some it was the lure of cheap land, for others the lack of safety to be found in Carolina due to the ongoing war, particularly for those who'd been branded as Tories, which included many of her Bryan relatives. Kentucky wasn't safe, but neither was Carolina.

Relatives of all sorts came and went constantly, consulting with Daniel about everything from land prices to how many bags of cornmeal or pounds of lead a family needed to pack into the wilderness to get them through the first year. She listened to their excited conversations and could summon nothing but a weary resignation. It appeared she was destined to be carried back across the mountains on a rising tide of Boones and Bryans.

One August morning in 1779, shortly after sunrise and a few weeks before their intended departure, Rebecca stepped onto the porch, her eyes still heavy with sleep and her hair tousled. The day promised to be hot; even at this early hour the air felt thick and heavy, as if a woolen blanket was draped across her shoulders. She dipped her hands into the washbasin and splashed water onto her face, letting the cool droplets run down her neck and under her shift. When she heard footsteps at the edge of the porch, she didn't bother to glance up, assuming it was Daniel.

"When you get a chance," she said, wiping water from her eyes, "I need help with the brindled cow—she's come up lame again."

"I'm not sure that's a good idea," a voice said, "given what happened the last time I helped you with a cow."

She spun about, water spattering the porch like rain. "I thought you were Daniel," she said, and to her dismay, felt herself blush.

It was uncanny how much Ned still looked like his brother. The passage of time had left identical marks on the two men—crow's feet around their eyes and a slight thickening of their torsos. Ned, however, still possessed the thick head of hair, sprinkled now with gray, that Daniel had lost to the Shawnee.

"Sorry to startle you," Ned said. "I figured early morning would be the best time to catch Daniel." He put his hat back on and studied her. "It's good to see you, Rebecca. You're looking well. Martha sends her greetings and said to tell you she can't wait to see you. Guess there'll be plenty of time for us to catch up on our way to Kentucky."

Her thoughts skittered back and forth like a chicken under a hawk's shadow. She hadn't seen Ned and Martha since her return to the Forks. It had been easy to avoid encountering them, since they'd moved further west, to the slopes of the Blue Ridge, but clearly Daniel had been in touch. She felt dazed at the thought of traveling to Kentucky with them.

She stood, barefoot and mute, acutely aware of her damp face, thin shift, and unbound hair. Ned was waiting for her to speak—expecting a word of greeting or perhaps an expression of pleasure at seeing each other after all these years—but her tongue felt as thick and useless as a block of wood. When she finally found her voice, all that came out was: "I expect Daniel's down at the barn."

Ned's eyes flickered—she saw both surprise and hurt in their depths—but he smiled and touched his hat brim before turning away. She stood rooted to the porch, watching him walk down the rutted path toward the barn, feeling many things at that moment: shock at his sudden appearance; regret for her rudeness; wistfulness at the memory of the camaraderie she'd once shared with this man; and most of all the realization that however deeply the past is buried, from time to time it will work its way to the surface, rising the way a swimmer does for a breath of air before plunging downward again to move, unseen, beneath life's currents.

32

Rebecca

There were many landmarks on the trail to Kentucky, names that rolled off travelers' tongues as a way to mark the miles through the wilderness: Martin's Station, the White Cliffs, Cumberland Gap, Cumberland Ford, the Hazel Patch. But for Rebecca, a simple pile of stones just off the trail in Powell Valley marked the most important piece of ground in the midst of all those long miles, the one place along the trace that she yearned toward, yet dreaded to reach.

By the time the trail sloped down to Wallen's Creek, leading to the low ground where James had spent his last night on earth, she could feel the shadows gathering in her heart. James's burial had been hasty, but on his first visit to the grave, Daniel had piled rocks on it to protect it from wolves. It had become their family's custom to add to the pile whenever any of them passed that way. Rebecca always found a special stone, no bigger than a hen's egg, and carried it along the trail to place at the head of the grave. She favored pieces of quartz because they glistened in the sunlight as if they were alive, something to keep James company in that lonely place where not a soul passed for days or weeks at a time.

Unlike their other, hurried journeys along the trace, this time their traveling party was composed mostly of family members who were willing to pause in remembrance. They encircled James's grave, Boones and Bryans together. Rebecca's heart was full as she looked around the circle at all those dear faces. She bit her lip as her father spoke of James's bright smile, deep love of learning, and gentle spirit. As she stood alongside

Daniel, their hands clasped, she felt at long last a sense of peace that had always eluded her in this place.

As the last prayer was spoken and the others turned away, she knelt and put a final stone, laced with gold flecks, at the head of the grave. She let her hand linger there for many long moments, sensing in her bones that this was the last time she'd pass this way.

"Godspeed, sweetheart," she whispered.

Boonesborough was even filthier than Rebecca remembered, having become by this time little more than a military outpost, a quagmire of mud and manure and vile odors. It was clear that many of the fort's inhabitants were decidedly unhappy to see them return. The fate of many of the salt boilers was still unknown, and Colonel Callaway continued to harbor a deep distrust of Daniel; his feelings were shared by most of the families whose loved ones remained unaccounted for.

Rebecca's parents and the rest of her Bryan relatives had chosen to bypass Boonesborough altogether, heading instead to a tract of land further north on Elkhorn Creek. "I'm proud of my allegiance to the Crown," her father had said to Daniel, "but since most of the folks at Boonesborough don't share my sentiments, it will go easier for you and Rebecca if we don't parade into the settlement with you."

For those who remained at Boonesborough, the plan was to stay at the fort just long enough for Daniel to get a hearing with the land commissioners and confirm his claim to a tract of land several miles northwest, a site he'd picked out years before. While they waited, they crowded into several vacant cabins and continued to live out of their packs as if they were still on the trail. *This is temporary,* Rebecca told herself several times each day.

What made the waiting more bearable were the hours she spent with Martha. At the beginning of their journey, they'd been awkwardly shy with each other, but after a week of painful politeness, Martha broke the silence one morning while the two of them were cooking breakfast. Rebecca was bent over the fire, stirring up the coals from the previous night, when she felt a hand on her arm.

"I've been looking for a moment with no one else around," Martha said. "I want to clear the air and be done with it." Her face was flushed, and her words came out in a rush. "Do you really think I'd have agreed to come west with you if I believed you'd slept with my husband? For a long time, Ned and I thought it was best for everyone, especially Jemima, if we kept our distance. We thought the talk would die down, but I guess we'll live with those rumors the rest of our lives. I don't want them to keep us apart any longer, Becca. Can we please get back to being sisters?"

As Martha spoke, Rebecca suddenly felt light enough to float up to the treetops. Stepping around the fire, she laid her hands on either side of Martha's face and bent so they were eye to eye.

"Sisters," she said.

Autumn faded into winter as they lingered at Boonesborough, their land titles still in limbo. The temperatures kept dropping until the Kentucky River was frozen to a depth of two feet. The river cane, which normally served as winter fodder for the deer and cattle, withered away, and the livestock grew gaunt and sickly. Daniel came back from hunting and told of deer lying dead from the cold, their muzzles iced over, their final breaths tethering them to the ground. He reported seeing flocks of wild turkeys sitting lifeless on tree branches, frozen to their roosts. No one could recall a winter as harsh as this.

The youngest children had to be held almost constantly to protect them from frostbite; Rebecca spent much of each day sitting next to the fire wrapped in a buffalo robe, cradling Suzy's daughter, Betsy, while Suzy nestled baby Jemima beneath a robe of her own. "This must be how a mother possum feels," Suzy said, "moving around with young'uns clinging like burrs."

Worst of all, fever had crept into the fort. One night, as they gathered around their fire, Rebecca said: "We've got to get out of here. Three other children down the way are on death's door with fever."

"If we go to the claim now," Daniel said, "we'll have to camp for weeks in this cold. It will take time to get even a couple cabins up and roofed."

The fire popped and silence hung heavily over the group. Finally Rebecca said: "Better to freeze to death out there than sit here and wait for the children to sicken."

They departed Boonesborough on Christmas Day 1799, walking north through calf-deep snow toward the piece of land Daniel had chosen.

Rebecca prayed it would be their final homeplace. As she and the rest of their party walked across the iced-over Kentucky River as if it were dry land, she couldn't help but think about Moses parting the waters to escape the Egyptians. She listened to the crunch of snow-dusted ice beneath her feet and prayed their story would have a different ending; that, unlike Moses, her family wasn't destined to wander in the wilderness for another forty years.

33

Jemima

Cozy was the word that came to Jemima's mind when she saw the piece of land her father had chosen for their new home. Everything was on a smaller scale than the settlement at Boonesborough. Instead of a broad, open plain, this land was gently rolling, and rather than the deep currents of the Kentucky River, Boone Station sat alongside a winding creek with a spring that her father claimed had the tastiest water in the world, though it was clogged with ice when they arrived and wouldn't flow free until the weather warmed.

Jemima helped gather wood from several deadfall trees while her mother dug out a fire pit. As the flames licked upward, Jemima bent over the fire and savored the rising heat. She couldn't remember ever being so cold; they'd all be in danger of freezing to death if they weren't under shelter by nightfall.

As the men lashed saplings together to form frames for several three-sided shelters, the women cut evergreen branches and ripped slabs of bark from a downed oak so they could quickly cover the frames. Commonly used by hunters, half-faced camps were poorly suited for families since fires had to burn day and night in front of the open sides; the children would have to be watched every second for fear they'd wander too close to the flames.

Jemima worked alongside her mother, banking thick mounds of snow over and around the bark and branches that covered the frames to serve as extra insulation. The snow dampened her woolen mittens and made her hands ache so badly she had to stop every so often and step close to the fire to warm them.

"I wish I could help," Susannah said, the first time Jemima took a break to warm up. Suzy was seated as close to the fire as possible, wrapped in a buffalo robe with the children buried deep within its folds. Her cheeks were red and chapped from the frigid air, and her breath hung above her, like mist rising off a creek.

"Just keep the children warm," Jemima said. "We'll have the first shelter ready soon."

Their father stepped up to the fire and added more logs, then clapped his gloved hands together to warm them.

Susannah looked up at him. "What's to keep the Indians from slipping in here and scalping us all?"

Jemima had been wondering the same thing.

Their father grinned. "Because, ladies, unlike us, Indians have better sense than to be out in weather like this."

For the remainder of the winter, they all worked feverishly to replace the half-faced shelters with a handful of sturdy cabins and then picket the ground around them. Each day the women walked to the spring, hatchets in hand, and chopped through thick layers of ice to reach the fresh water that bubbled up underneath. The cabins were roofed and the walls of the tiny stockade were nearly complete on the day in March when Jemima and her mother carried their buckets to the spring and heard, for the first time since their arrival, the melodious sound of free-flowing water.

Having survived the worst winter any of them could remember, Jemima promised herself she'd never again complain about being too warm. But as mild spring days gave way to steamy summer months, she found it hard to keep that vow. The hearth-centered chores that she'd looked forward to during the coldest months grew nearly intolerable as the sun beat relentlessly down, day after day, scorching the grass and curling the cedar shingles on the cabins clustered within the stockade's walls.

On a sweltering August morning, Jemima walked out of the station and down the hill to the creek, carrying a basket piled high with dirty laundry. The night before, the station's women had reluctantly agreed that despite the oppressive heat, washday couldn't be delayed any longer.

Looking down the slope, Jemima saw that her mother, Susannah, and Aunt Martha were already at work. Mounds of laundry dotted the grass along the creek bank, and someone had rolled the large wash pots out of their storage place in the hollow sycamore that overhung the water. Jemima set her basket down and began sorting, adding her family's clothes to the piles—whites for the first wash, colored clothes for the next, and the dirtiest items for the final wash of the day. Her shift was soaked with sweat before she'd even finished sorting.

The pots were steaming and the first load of linens had been dumped into the water when Jemima cleared her throat. "I have some news."

The chatter around the pots died down as the other women turned to look at her.

"Flanders and I are expecting."

Her mother beamed at her through the steam that rose above the iron wash pot. Suzy let out a whoop. "It's about time you gave my young'uns a cousin," she said.

Soon the air was filled with questions, observations, and advice.

"Ginger tea is the best thing for morning sickness," Aunt Martha said.

"Horehound worked better for me," Suzy noted.

"When do you think you're due?" someone asked.

Everyone paused to hear the answer.

"March or April."

Her mother was shaving pieces of soap off the homemade block, letting the pieces fall into the steaming water. "Me, too," she said, softly.

They all turned to stare at her.

"But it's been five years since William was born," Suzy said. "I figured you were . . ."

"Too old?" her mother said with a smile.

Aunt Martha turned to look at her sister, her face suddenly stern. "Seems like more than a coincidence that the minute you and Ned are back in the same vicinity, another baby's on the way."

Everyone froze. It was so quiet Jemima could hear the sound of the creek water riffling over the rocks. Her mother's face had gone ashen. For a long, tense moment, she and Aunt Martha stared at each other through the steam. Then Martha burst into laughter and her mother let out her breath.

"That's not funny, Martha," her mother said. "Do you want to start another round of gossip?" She shook her head in admonishment, though there was a ghost of a smile on her lips.

"We're all family here, Becca," Martha said cheerfully, "and it's long past time we laughed about it."

Martha smiled and reached over to take Jemima's hand in hers. One by one each of the women took the hand of the woman standing next to her until the circle was complete.

"Here's to new beginnings," Martha said.

It was easy for Jemima to believe in new beginnings as summer faded into fall and her belly swelled beneath her apron. The world seemed full of promise, as if their dark days were far behind them. She found it both wonderful and odd to be experiencing her first pregnancy while her mother faced her tenth.

"These babies will be like twins," Jemima said. "Flanders wants a boy, but I don't care which we have."

"Healthy is all that matters," her mother said. She straightened up from the hearth and pressed her hands into the small of her back. "I'm grateful for this cooler weather—carrying a baby in the summer heat was wearing me out."

The men greeted the crisp fall weather by ranging farther afield to hunt. Her father was eager to show Ned the countryside; together they scouted the waterways they'd revisit to set trap lines when the weather turned cold.

The maples and hickories were flames of red and yellow on the hillsides surrounding the station on the day Jemima spotted her father hurrying into the stockade, head down. He strode straight to Aunt Martha's door and knocked. Something about the set of his shoulders made Jemima uneasy.

She finished pouring ashes into the hopper, then rested the bucket on the rough wooden frame as the cabin door opened and her father disappeared inside. A minute later, an unearthly wail echoed through the station, so long and drawn out it sounded like the howl of a wolf.

Jemima dropped the bucket and began to run. By the time she'd reached her aunt's doorway, her mother was right behind her. Inside, they found Aunt Martha bent double, her hands pressed against her chest while her father held her by the arm, supporting most of her weight. Jemima's eyes flew to her father's face as her mother took hold of Martha's other arm and helped ease her onto a bench.

"Ned's dead," her father said softly.

The words made Martha moan. Jemima caught only a glimpse of her mother's stricken face as she leaned down to grasp her sister's shoulders, bending over her as if her own body might somehow shield Martha from the truth.

Her father watched the women a moment, his own face anguished, then motioned Jemima to follow him outside.

"Find Flanders and Israel and tell them I need help fetching Ned's body."

"What happened?"

Her father's eyes flattened with grief, as if the reality of his brother's death was only now sinking in. "They thought he was me."

"But the Shawnee like you."

"Not all of them. Some resented Chief Blackfish treating me like a son." His voice cracked. "If they hadn't mistaken Ned for me, they might just have taken him captive . . ."

Jemima put her hand on his sleeve, but he shook it off without looking up and said, "Go get the boys. We need to head out before dark."

After supper that night, Jemima slipped outside in the gathering dusk, seeking fresh air and a reprieve from the constant chatter of Suzy's children. When she looked across the stockade, she half expected to see the log walls of Aunt Martha's cabin bulging outward from the misery inside. A square of flickering light shone through the open door and into the dusty yard, but that was the only sign of life she saw anywhere in the station until she approached the lower end of the stockade and saw a shadowy figure pacing back and forth along the wall.

"Mama?" she said.

Her mother turned to her in the fading light, her face filled with such pain that Jemima stepped closer and gathered her into her arms. She held on tightly as her mother took deep, shuddering breaths, trying not to cry aloud. They stood that way a long time.

"Ned was such a good man," her mother said finally, her voice choked. She took a step back and wiped her eyes. "He kept me from losing hope at one of the worst times in my life. With the old hurts buried, the two of us were finding our way back to being friends again."

Her mother's mouth twisted at the thought, and Jemima reached out and grasped her hand, squeezing it tightly.

"For years I thought Martha was the lucky one," her mother said. "She married the brother who was content to stay home."

34

Susannah

Although Susannah mourned her Uncle Ned, in many ways, the first few years at Boone Station were the happiest of her married life. Their tiny community was made up mostly of family, which meant neither she nor her mother were dogged by the gossip that had made their lives miserable at Fort Moore and Boonesborough. The people who surrounded them were inclined to think the best of them, and to Susannah's surprise, this included Will.

Susannah felt sure Will was finally contented with her because at long last he was pleased with himself. Will and her father had established a successful surveying business; her father knew the woods and the rudiments of surveying, while Will handled the correspondence with clients and kept the paperwork in order. Her husband's dark eyes grew less stormy each time he tramped into the woods with the other men, a valued member of each expedition rather than the butt of their jokes.

"People are pouring into Kentucky, and all of them need surveys," Will told her. "Only a handful of our clients can pay cash, but if your father and I do surveys in exchange for acreage, we'll wind up rich in spite of ourselves."

Will still drank too much, but if Susannah was careful she was sometimes able to speak her mind without fearing his fists. It seemed to her that the early years of her marriage had been a bad dream, like paddling a canoe through rough water; it had been all she could do to keep from being smashed against the rocks. But at Boone Station, she'd reached calm water at last.

When she confided to Israel that it had been years since Will had struck her, he squeezed her hand and said: "Don't let your guard down, Suzy. Will's still a drunk—right now he's just a happy one."

On an August morning in 1782, Israel sat on Susannah's porch, bouncing her newest baby, Willie, on his knee. Israel had spent the previous week in bed with a fever that had left him too weak to go to the fields with the rest of the men. During his convalescence, Susannah had put him to work helping her with chores around the house—snapping beans, rolling skeins of yarn, telling her stories to help pass the time. This morning, when he'd declared himself fit enough to take up a hoe again, she'd plunked Willie on his lap and said he needed another day's rest.

Around noon, her father hurried in from the fields and stopped at the edge of the porch. "The militia's been called out," he said. "The Indians have Bryan's Station under siege. Get your rifle, son, and pack a few supplies."

"Israel's still not well," Susannah said.

"We need every rifle we can muster." Her father gave Israel a pointed look and hurried off to spread the word.

Israel stood and handed Willie back to her.

"I should go, Suzy." He touched a finger to her lips as she sputtered in protest. "Mama's folks are in trouble. Besides," he said, wrinkling his nose, "if you take a deep breath you'll realize somebody needs changing." He gave her a lopsided grin. "I believe I'd rather fight Indians."

All that day and the next, Susannah walked about with her nerves strung tight. Not only were her father and Israel in harm's way, but her mother's parents, brothers, and a bushel of cousins were as well. As usual when her mother was deeply worried, she retreated into silence, but Susannah noticed that she and Aunt Martha sought each other out even more than usual, as if their Bryan blood drew them together. They sat in the shade during the heat of the day to shuck corn and break beans, the youngest children playing in the grass at their feet. Besides Susannah's son Willie, there was Jemima's John and her mother's youngest, Nathan, filling the air with their chatter. But despite the children's noisy play, the women's faces were grim, and a heaviness of spirit filled the stockade.

On the day her father told her Israel had been killed at Blue Licks, Susannah ran. She spent the rest of the day and far into the night pacing back and forth across the stockade, stone-faced, cradling her disbelief to her chest as if it were a child, ignoring the procession of worried faces and gentle hands that urged her to come inside. She could see their mouths moving, but all she could hear was Israel's voice, saying over and over, "I won't leave you." He had said those words to her father during the battle, but they echoed in her head as if they were meant for her.

By the next morning, she'd made up her mind that Israel wasn't dead. He'd been wounded, she told herself, and was recovering in some distant cabin; soon he'd make his way home. She avoided her family's pitying eyes and clung to that thought; it was all that enabled her to put one foot in front of the other.

Several days after the battle, Susannah was hoeing the bean field when she looked up and saw Israel's horse cantering up the road toward the stockade, his thin figure silhouetted in the saddle.

"I told you," she shouted to Jemima, who was working a few rows over, "he's alive!"

Susannah dropped her hoe, lifted her skirts, and began to run, feeling the weight that had sat heavily on her shoulders lift and soar like a bird taking flight. When the rider spotted her running down the dusty row of beans, he reined the mare in and waited.

"Israel!" she cried.

Even in her excitement she had the presence of mind to slow as she drew near, knowing the mare was easily spooked. The horse stamped a foreleg as Susannah reached the road and rested her hand on the mare's velvety shoulder. Susannah looked up just as the rider took off his hat.

"Good morning, ma'am. I was told this mare belongs to someone from Boone Station. She's a fast one—saved my life at the Licks. I found her with her reins dragging and . . ."

Susannah screamed, then felt Jemima's hands gripping her shoulders from behind. She fought, desperate to escape, to run from the realization that her beloved brother was gone forever.

35

Rebecca

Rebecca shuddered inwardly each time someone mentioned Blue Licks. Her son had lost his life there, and the battle had cost her a daughter as well. Rebecca watched helplessly as Susannah withdrew into herself in the days after Israel's death; she moved silently through her chores, her eyes lifeless.

One morning, Suzy was churning butter alongside Rebecca, and the motion of the dasher caused her shift to slip off her shoulder. Rebecca gasped at the sight of horrible bruises across her daughter's upper back. Suzy let go of the dasher and jerked the fabric over her shoulders, then crossed her arms over her chest and refused to look up.

"I should have known," Rebecca said.

"There's nothing you could have done, Mama. In the beginning I even hid the truth from myself. But Israel . . ." Susannah stopped as though his name burned her tongue. After a moment she tried again, her voice choked: "Israel began looking after me, and Will stopped. There really wasn't anything to tell for the longest time, but now . . ."

She didn't have to go on. Israel was gone, and their family's surveying business, which Will had taken such pride in, was in shambles due to lawsuits over contested claims. Recently he'd begun drinking more than ever.

That night, when Rebecca told Daniel what she'd discovered, he went in tight-lipped search of his son-in-law. Will received no pity from anyone when he appeared the next day with an eye swollen shut and his jaw the color of rotten apples. In the months that followed, Rebecca made sure their entire family closed ranks to protect Suzy, but despite their vigilance and the love they showered on her, she remained just a ghost of herself. As weeks went by, Rebecca was forced to accept that her daughter had become a world-weary woman whose only interest in life was plodding through her days and shielding her children from their father's anger. Her bold, bright Susannah was gone.

Rebecca had always heard that losses came in threes. Not long after they'd lost Israel, and then Susannah, they lost Boone Station as well. In the rush to settle Kentucky, surveys had been done so hurriedly, and claims filed so haphazardly, that no one was certain where their own land ended and their neighbor's began. Folks spoke of Kentucky being "shingled over" because claims overlapped as badly as shingles on a roof.

She was hardly surprised when another claimant with enough money to hire a lawyer challenged her family's title to Boone Station and won. All over Kentucky, folks who'd risked their lives to settle in the wilderness were stripped of their property by men back east that sent their attorneys into the backcountry to secure contested tracts of land.

"Kentucky's plumb ruint," lamented one of their neighbors when it was clear he was going to lose his farm, just as they were. "This place used to be a paradise, but first came the preachers and then came the lawyers, and since then there ain't been a bit of peace for nobody."

It was during this dreary time that Simon Kenton, the big scout they'd last seen at Boonesborough, reappeared in their lives. He'd aged considerably in the intervening years, having been captured by the Shawnee and subjected to brutal treatment. But when Rebecca looked into Simon's eyes, to her surprise, the haunted expression he'd worn as a younger man was gone.

"I spent years believing I was a murderer," he explained. "Turns out the fellow I thought I killed didn't die after all. Now I can go by my real name and marry without living a lie."

Simon's presence was a comfort to Rebecca—one lost son who'd managed to return and begin life anew. Since his escape from the Indians, Simon had made his home on Kentucky's northernmost edge, not far from the Ohio River.

"Boat traffic on the Ohio is growing," he told them. "There's ways to make a living in those parts besides hunting or farming."

Daniel looked thoughtful. "Game's getting scarce. It might be time to think about a change."

Though Rebecca doubted he meant it, Daniel surprised her by scouting out a place along the Ohio River at a tiny outpost called Limestone.

"I'm nearly fifty, Becca," he said. "Reckon it's time to do something other than hunting. I figure we'll start up a tavern by the river."

"A tavern?" she said. "What do you know about running a tavern?"

He grinned. "Nothing. I'll leave that to you and the girls."

In the weeks leading up to their move from Boone Station, Rebecca did her best to savor each day, saying a silent goodbye to this place she'd come to love. The outside world had left them largely alone here. Surrounded by family, she and the girls had endured no gossip, never having to wonder what was said behind their backs. All that was likely to change now since Daniel's plans meant they'd be living in a small, but growing, community, operating a tavern whose lifeblood would depend on welcoming whoever walked through the door.

"We'll miss this water," Rebecca said as she and Martha knelt on the grass beside the spring and dipped their buckets into the cold, clear depths. "I doubt there's a spring as tasty as this where we're headed."

Martha didn't answer. When Rebecca looked up, she saw that her sister was biting her lip.

"So," Martha began, "there's a nice plot of ground for sale not too far from here."

Rebecca sank back on her heels. "You're not going to Limestone with us."

"The boys are trying so hard to fill Ned's shoes; they want to take care of me and the younger children. It will take all of us to get a farm going."

Rebecca nodded, unable to find her voice. *Another loss.* Not only would it mean the end of working side by side with her sister, but she could guess what Martha's future held: living first with one grown child, then another, never again the mistress of her own home. Such was the lot of widows and spinsters.

"I'm blessed tired of saying goodbye to folks I love," Rebecca said at last. She took hold of Martha's hand, thinking back across the years that she and Martha had been separated by the rumors that refused to die. Those lost years made it so much harder to say goodbye now. "You know you can always come live with us."

Martha nodded, her eyes damp.

"I need to warn you, though," Rebecca said, doing her best to smile, "you'll be stuck running a tavern."

36

Rebecca

In the quiet hours just after dawn, Rebecca stood on the banks of the Ohio, watching the river flow past. The rising sun lit the riffles, making them sparkle, and the swishing sound of the waves washing against the tangled tree roots at her feet was soothing. She came to the river almost every morning. She loved the way the water bent wide just below Limestone, breaking up the currents and making the whitecaps dance. She felt a kinship with the flowing water and the unseen shadows that moved beneath its surface, shadows that mirrored the ones in her heart. Something had broken within her when they'd departed Boone Station, as if all the years of losses had finally added up to a weight too heavy to carry.

Having lived so long on one isolated homestead after another, she found the task of running a tavern burdensome and unnatural. Folks came and went at all hours, and her ears felt assaulted by their constant chatter.

She and the girls offered meals and sold supplies to the steady stream of settlers who traveled the Ohio, their belongings piled onto rough-hewn flatboats. She prided herself on serving tasty food, though most folks fresh off the river would pay whatever price she asked for anything hot. Outwardly, she tried to be a good hostess, but what she really wanted to do was climb into her bed and pull the quilts over her head. A few stolen moments each morning were the only time she had to herself all day. At forty-six, she was as worn and ragged as the workday apron she hung on a peg behind the tavern's bar each night.

Most of the travelers they served arrived by floating down the Ohio because it was physically easier than taking the overland route through Cumberland Gap. But the river route bordered Shawnee territory, and more than once Rebecca had seen boats floating into Limestone with arrows bristling from every surface, the dead and dying sprawled across the decks like rag dolls flung down by an angry child. One image that haunted her was of a woman lying pale and cold with an unharmed infant latched to her breast, desperately trying to nurse. Despite such horrors, folks kept coming, all of them searching for something they hadn't found back east: riches, adventure, second chances.

Rebecca was bent over the fire, stirring a pot of stew, on the day a stranger in travel-worn clothes stepped through the tavern door and asked to speak to Daniel. The man reminded her of a heron, thin and long legged, his movements hesitant.

"It appears you've journeyed a long way, sir. The stew's nearly ready—that is, if you've a stomach for possum." She gave the pot a final stir and straightened up from the hearth, just in time to see his nose wrinkle in distaste. Well, possum was all she had, and if he wouldn't eat it, there'd be plenty of others who would. Soon the river men would drift up from the docks for their midday meal, and whatever they didn't eat would be finished by travelers tying up their flatboats for the evening.

A swirl of wind swept down the chimney and blew smoke into the room as the stranger continued to study her, his riding crop tapping a rhythm against a dusty leather boot. She knew well enough what he saw: a tall, dark-haired woman—a tavern keeper's wife—with a trace of gray in her hair and a grease-stained apron, scraping out a living in the back of beyond.

"My name's John Filson," the man said at last. "I'm told Colonel Boone has stories of Kentucky's earliest days; it's my intention to put them in a book."

Her heart began to pound. Print their stories? The whispers that had followed her like a stray dog skulking in the shadows had grown muted over the years, and she'd begun to hope they'd disappear for good. *What if it starts all over?*

Despite her deep misgivings, Filson boarded with them for several weeks, asking Daniel endless questions and making the rounds of the men who lived nearby, gathering stories wherever he could find them. Though she and the girls washed Filson's clothes and grained his horse and emptied his chamber pot, he never once asked to hear their side of the stories.

Each night, while Rebecca sat with her mending, she watched Filson's quill scratch across the paper's face in the candlelight and sensed, deep in her bones, the danger bound up in those little black marks. Those marching, ant-like rows held her family's stories. It made her palms sweat to think about it. *What's written down takes on the seeming-ness of truth,* she thought, *but truth is a slippery thing—one's lucky to catch a glimpse of it, like the silver flash of a brook trout just below the water's surface.*

A little more than a year after Filson had saddled his horse, stuffed his papers into his saddlebags, and headed back east, Daniel placed a copy of Filson's book, *The Adventures of Colonel Daniel Boone,* in her hands for the first time. It was a small book to carry such a load of pain and anger and gladness between its covers. It sat on the mantel, unopened, while she went about her chores that afternoon. She had the odd sensation that the book was crouching there, shoulder high and ready to pounce, like an angry housecat.

After supper, Daniel scooted his chair close to the fire, book in hand, and began to read aloud, the light catching the hints of gray threaded through his hair. Her chair was in its usual place, opposite Daniel's, close enough to the flames so she could see to do her mending. It didn't take more than an hour for Daniel to read Filson's story to her from beginning to end. Filson had written the book as if Daniel was telling his own story, but the words he'd put in her husband's mouth made him sound like a pompous, long-winded preacher. It surprised her that Daniel didn't seem to mind; every now and again, he looked up and said, "Filson got it right. He stretched it here or there, but there's not a real lie in it."

She sat tensely as Daniel read, waiting to hear her name. She'd made it into Filson's pages as "wife" a time or two, and even "beloved wife" once, but when she realized Filson had said almost nothing about her—that he hadn't even bothered to record her name—the tightness in her chest began to ease. She sat in silence, letting Filson have his say, until she saw Daniel was ready to close the book.

"Read that last part again," she said.

Daniel ran his finger down the final page. "I now live in peace and safety, enjoying the sweets of liberty and the bounties of Providence with my once fellow-sufferers in this . . ."

His voice faltered as she began to laugh. She laughed so hard her tears dampened the stocking she was darning. The absurdity of Filson's words, coupled with her own relief, made her shake with laughter. Daniel sat silent, the book open on his lap. After a few moments she saw his lips twitch and knew he was struggling to keep his face solemn.

When she finally caught her breath, she leaned forward so he could see her face in the firelight and said: "'I now live in peace and safety?' Did you really say that? You know full well we still aren't safe."

Daniel shrugged. "I told Filson we hadn't seen a Shawnee war party on this side of the Ohio in nearly a year; I expect that accounts for the 'peace and safety' part. As for the 'sweets of liberty'—everyone knows what a tangle my land titles are in—soon I won't have an acre to my name. I suppose that's liberty of a sort." Daniel was smiling now. "You can hardly blame the man, Rebecca. What kind of book ends with the hero propertyless, penniless, and legging it out of Eden just ahead of his creditors?"

"A truthful one," she said.

Susannah looked lost in her own thoughts as Daniel read Filson's book to the rest of the family. Rebecca thought her daughter was barely listening until Daniel began reading the section about cutting the trace.

"I undertook to mark out a road in the best passage from the settlement through the wilderness to Kentucky," Daniel intoned. "Soon I began this work, having collected a number of enterprising men, well armed."

"Not just men," Susannah said.

They all turned to stare at her, startled to hear her voice.

"Dolly and I were on that journey." There was a spark of life in Suzy's eyes that hadn't been there in years.

"Indeed you were, Suzy," Daniel said gently, laying the book in his lap. "You and Dolly were a big part of the success of that expedition. I'm certain I told Filson that; I don't know why he didn't mention it."

"We were there," Susannah said, "but no one will remember us."

And Rebecca watched the spark fade away.

* * *

In the months that followed, Rebecca's relief at having been ignored in Filson's book gave way to the realization that—now that Daniel was famous—all the old stories, even the ones Filson left out, had been resurrected. Everybody in the backwoods suddenly claimed to know their family and thought nothing of making up outlandish tales about them. As Daniel's fame spread, the whispers about her grew louder. Daniel was famous; she was infamous.

It wasn't long before the folks who journeyed down the Ohio River to Kentucky or up the rugged trace through Cumberland Gap traveled miles out of their way to catch a glimpse of the famous Boone. They expected to encounter a giant who was itching to kill every Indian who crossed his path. What they found instead was a quiet, fifty-something man of average height who was openly friendly to the occasional Indian courageous enough to venture into Limestone to trade their furs.

Toward the end of his book, Mister Filson had put some grand words in Daniel's mouth: "Many dark and sleepless nights have I been a companion for owls . . . an instrument ordained to settle the wilderness." To Rebecca, those words sounded churchlike and conjured up light streaming down from heaven and angels singing, but the truth was, their stories—the good and the bad—were fashioned from earthbound things: mud and blood and tears.

When the attention prompted by Filson's book became too wearisome, Daniel would disappear into the woods in search of some peace. Rebecca searched for peace, too, but instead of heading to the woods, she slipped down to the Ohio. If it was hot, she sat with her feet in the shallows, mulling over the questions that bedeviled her, thoughts that buzzed in her brain like flies around a butter dish. Why did Israel have to die so young? Was there a way to coax Suzy back to life? How could she keep her grandchildren safe from Will's fists? Why did God let her gentle James suffer so when his life was taken?

For a time she prayed for answers, but as months, and then years, rolled past and no enlightenment came, she found herself praying, instead, for acceptance, never suspecting an answer would appear on her doorstep in the shape of an Indian woman.

37

Rebecca

Her name was Nonhelema, and she arrived at their tavern as a prisoner.

"She's some sort of queen among the Shawnee," the militia captain told Daniel as his men hustled the woman into one of their storage rooms, locking her in before Rebecca had even caught a glimpse of her. "I'll post a guard—she shouldn't be much trouble. Just shove a little food through the door every now and then."

The thought of an Indian living in her house made Rebecca's skin crawl. Daniel reported that the woman spoke exceptionally good English, but that didn't lessen Rebecca's resolve to see her gone as soon as possible. Whenever she saw an Indian, all she could think of were the faces of her lost sons.

"You know I can't abide her kind," she said. "I want nothing to do with her."

It was Jemima who volunteered to carry bowls of stew into the back room each day and bring out the chamber pot as needed.

"She really seems like a queen, Mama," Jemima said, after her first visit to the storeroom. "It's like her spirit's still her own, even though she's a prisoner. And she's the tallest woman I've ever seen—you and I would look short standing next to her."

While that piqued her curiosity, Rebecca still did little more than glance at the closed door whenever she passed by—that is, until the day she heard the woman singing. The thick oaken door muffled her voice, but something in those low tones made Rebecca pause, then shut her eyes and lean her forehead against the doorframe to listen.

Jemima, who took every opportunity to learn Indian phrases, just like her father, might have understood the words, but they were gibberish to Rebecca. Now, to her surprise, she found herself wondering what that soft voice—part song, part chant—was saying.

The guard's chair stood empty. He'd taken to spending most of his time in the taproom with the other men, leaving the key hanging on a nearby peg so Jemima could come and go as she pleased. As the song continued to filter through the closed door, rising and falling like wind through the trees, Rebecca slipped the key off the peg and let herself in.

Nonhelema was sitting, gray haired and straight backed, on a pallet of blankets spread out on the floor, surrounded by barrels of ginseng that were ready to ship upriver. Her body swayed gently forward and back in rhythm with her chant, and she continued singing as Rebecca entered the room. When she finally raised her eyes, they were dark pools that seemed to see beyond the four walls that enclosed her. Rebecca willed herself not to be the first to look away.

As the woman finished her song, the final quavering note hovered in the air. Rebecca shifted uncomfortably and caught the scent of bear grease that wafted from the row of crocks on the shelf by her shoulder.

After studying Rebecca a moment, Nonhelema cocked her head to one side and laid her hands in her lap, palms up, as if in supplication. "So, white woman," she said, her voice soft yet commanding, "I see hatred in your eyes. Would you tell me why this is so?"

"I don't hate—" Rebecca began, but couldn't finish the sentence, knowing it was a lie. She closed her mouth and studied the Indian woman in return. She was dressed in a red calico shirt and matching skirt with a blue woven sash tied around her waist. Her legs were covered in brightly beaded leggings. Though her face was weathered and spoke of years of hard living, Jemima was right—there was something regal about her.

"My oldest son," Rebecca said finally, "my firstborn, was tortured to death in Powell Valley by Indians. A few years ago, another son was killed at Blue Licks."

"Ah," she said, bowing her head slightly, acknowledging the losses. When she looked back up, she said: "But I have never been in Powell

Valley, nor was I at Blue Licks the day our people battled; yet I see you find me guilty of both these things."

"Not just you—*all* of you—your people, I mean."

"Ah," she said again. She patted the pallet, inviting her visitor to sit, but Rebecca stiffened and shook her head, determined to keep her distance.

Nonhelema's dark eyes softened. "Your hatred will eat you from within."

Rebecca drew a sharp breath. "Have you ever lost a son?"

Nonhelema shook her head. "Not a son, but many kinsmen. My brother was a great chief among my people and a man of peace. The whites called him Cornstalk."

Rebecca pursed her lips, trying to recall where she'd heard that name; most likely in a snippet of conversation she'd overheard amid the bustle of the taproom.

Nonhelema's voice dropped to little more than a whisper. "My brother and his son went to Fort Randolph to treaty with the soldiers, hoping to end the killing, but the whites locked them in a room and hacked them to death. Not long ago, the day of my capture, I stood next to my husband, Chief Moluntha, as he greeted the soldiers who entered our village. My husband offered his hand in greeting, but one of your kind shouted, 'Blue Licks' and . . ." Her voice trailed off. After a moment she added: "He died that day. It would be easy to hate."

It was so quiet in the room that Rebecca could hear a fly buzzing around the jug of maple syrup that was stored on a nearby shelf.

After a moment, Nonhelema said: "My people never asked for this fight. Yours did, by choosing to come here."

"So how can you *not* hate us?"

"Because I've chosen not to."

Caught off guard by the woman's reply, Rebecca said the first thing that came to mind: "That song you were singing—what did it mean?"

For the first time, a faint smile played across Nonhelema's lips. "It was a prayer for all things."

"A prayer for your people?"

She shook her head. "All things."

* * *

Over the next week, Rebecca spent many hours in Nonhelema's company. Not only did she take over the duty of carrying the woman's meals into the storage room, she often brought her mending with her so they could sit and talk long after the meal was over. She marveled that the Indian woman could read and write, and in addition to speaking English and several Indian tongues, she was fluent in French as well. When Rebecca spoke admiringly of these accomplishments, Nonhelema said: "I learned the languages because I'd hoped to help people understand one another. I was peace chief for my people."

"A woman chief?"

The disbelief in Rebecca's voice made Nonhelema smile. "Shawnee women have always had a say in tribal decisions. I've often wondered why white women let their men rule over them."

"Why, indeed," Rebecca said drily, which made both women laugh.

As their laughter died away, Nonhelema's expression grew solemn. "When I was young, I fought alongside our warriors, but I came to see that fighting solved nothing. Since then, I've worked for peace between our peoples. I dreamed of Indians and whites living side by side in this land, but my dream is dead. Many of my people have already headed west, and I pray they'll find a new home where they can live in peace. As for me, I'm too old for such a journey."

She fixed her dark eyes on Rebecca. "It is very hard to live as a person between—a person not solely on one side or the other. Both sides grow wary of you, until one day you feel as if you no longer belong anywhere at all."

The words "a person between" circled round and round in Rebecca's mind that afternoon as she scrubbed the tavern's pewter tankards, then chopped up stew meat for the evening meal. The more she thought about it, the clearer it became to her—her husband had always been "a person between."

In the days that followed, Rebecca found herself peeling away layers of anger she'd carried for years. It wasn't just the fury she'd felt at the loss of James, Israel, and Ned, but also a deeper, long-buried anger directed at Daniel. She'd felt relegated to second place in his affections, unable to compete with his need to wander. Slowly she began to face, rather than bury, all the questions that had plagued her for so long: How could Daniel care deeply for his family, yet choose to live so much of his life removed from them? Why had her beautiful, bold Susannah faded to a shadow of herself, living now with her heart cold and shuttered? And how was it that her quiet, steady Jemima could walk through the challenges of her own life—her kidnapping and the loss of her favorite brother—and emerge largely unscathed?

Who could say why one soul sinks and another rises?

More than once, Rebecca contemplated leaving the storage room unlocked, offering Nonhelema the chance to slip away, back to her people on the other side of the Ohio. What stopped her was the damage it would do to Daniel's standing in the community. He was already rumored to be far too sympathetic to the Indians, and having been accused of traitorous behavior in the past, he could ill afford another incident. And yet, as her friendship with the woman grew, Rebecca was increasingly torn.

One day Nonhelema listened quietly as Rebecca expressed regret at harboring ill will toward the woman's kinsmen for so many years.

"You've forgiven me and my people, and that's a good beginning," Nonhelema told her.

"Beginning?"

"Now, you must forgive yourself."

The next morning, Rebecca went down to the river at dawn, slipped off her moccasins, and settled onto the bank with her feet ankle-deep in the cool water. A squirrel in a nearby sycamore scolded her, and a heron stalked along the bank on long legs, moving close enough that she could see the iridescent blue of his feathers.

You must forgive yourself. She could hear the words in her head but couldn't feel them in her heart. She was haunted by all the ways she'd fallen short. *If only I'd been a better mother—a wiser woman—I could have warned James not to return to Castlewoods; kept Susannah from marrying a drunkard; protected Jemima from the rumors; prevented Israel from marching off to Blue Licks.* As the litany of her failings unspooled in her mind, the weight of it felt unbearable.

For much of her life, in unsettled moments, she'd sought the comfort of flowing water and imagined there were voices speaking to her in the currents. Now, she closed her eyes and listened for what the river might say. The water lapped around her ankles, its touch cool and soothing. The leaves above her head rustled as a breeze swept along the riverbank, and she breathed in the fresh scent of damp earth. Beneath it all was the rumble of the river flowing steadily, relentlessly onward.

Forward, the current seemed to say. *One's life, like a river, can only flow forward.*

Rebecca opened her eyes and felt in the pocket of her gown for a handkerchief. She blew her nose, startling the heron so that it rose from the water, its powerful wings fanning the currents. As she watched the bird lift into the air, something shifted in her chest, a flicker of hope that forgiving herself might one day be possible.

Rebecca pulled her feet from the water, stood up, and brushed off the back of her gown. *Forward,* she thought, as she turned from the solace of the river to face the clamor of the tavern.

They had no warning on the day a half-dozen militiamen arrived at the tavern to take Nonhelema away.

"Leave her alone." Rebecca said, grabbing the arm of the soldier who'd stooped to shackle Nonhelema's legs. He shook her off and kept working, the iron chain clattering loudly against the wooden floor. "I'm just following orders, Miz Boone."

"Where are you taking her?"

The man shrugged, not meeting her eyes. "If you ask me, hanging's too good for the likes of her."

Rebecca stepped around him to grasp both of Nonhelema's hands in hers, ignoring the man's sputtering protest. The iron bands around the Indian woman's wrists were icy to the touch. When their eyes met, Nonhelema smiled, her face calm, as if she'd already accepted whatever fate might befall her.

The chains on her hands and feet clanked as the soldiers shuffled her out of the storeroom, across the empty taproom, and into the street. Rebecca hurried along behind, stopping to grab a pistol and shot bag from a shelf in the taproom. She could hear the soldiers' horses stamping restlessly in the dusty street; they hadn't departed yet.

She let herself out the side door and ran to the stable. Her hands shook as she saddled their fastest mare. When she led her mount into the stable yard, a shadow fell across her path. Daniel, rifle in hand, stood alongside, watching her with a quizzical expression.

"Rebecca?"

"I have to follow them," she said in a rush. "I need to know where they're taking Nonhelema."

He put a hand on her arm. "I'll go. I'm a colonel now, remember? I can pull rank and order them not to harm her. That should at least buy her some time. But Becca," he said, brow furrowed, "you've never cared a whit about an Indian before. What's changed?"

"Everything."

He looked puzzled but pulled his hat low and swung up on the mare.

When Daniel returned two days later, he reported that Nonhelema had been taken further south, away from the river, due to rumors that the Shawnee might try to rescue her.

"She's safe for now, Becca. She's under Colonel Patterson's care; he and I have a difference of opinion about what should be done with her, but if we play our cards right, there's a chance we can gain her freedom."

For weeks, Rebecca and Daniel worked to negotiate Nonhelema's release, arguing that an Indian queen could be traded for a large number of white captives held by the Shawnee. Daniel took the lead in brokering a deal, volunteering to ferry across the Ohio to talk with the tribal chiefs.

On the morning Daniel reported that Nonhelema had been returned to her people, Rebecca went down to the river and softly sang the prayer the Indian woman had taught her—half song, half chant—a prayer for all things.

38

Rebecca

The earthy smell of ginseng clung to Rebecca's hands. She'd spent the morning packing the lumpy roots into wooden barrels to be shipped upriver alongside a summer's worth of deerskins. She wiped her hands on the tail of her apron and sat down in the grass with a sigh, thankful to give her feet a rest. She watched Daniel and the other men roll the heavy barrels down the bank and hoist them onto the keelboat, carefully positioning the cargo so the boat rode evenly in the water. The keelboat was Daniel's pride and joy; he'd purchased it with an eye toward the burgeoning river traffic that ran from Limestone northward to Pittsburgh and beyond.

She and Daniel had turned the running of the tavern over to some of the children and had begun to spend weeks at a time traveling the Ohio; she'd come to know the river in new and intimate ways. She'd learned to gauge the currents and eddies along the watery highway, memorizing the landmarks that warned her when a swift-moving stream would soon enter the larger current, creating swirling eddies that could capsize even a good-sized boat if the crew wasn't vigilant. The river had become a living, breathing thing to her—calm and welcoming on some days, dark and brooding on others.

Today, the autumn sun felt warm on her face. She was grateful for time ashore after long days spent poling the boat upriver, stopping at backcountry landings to pick up cargo for the Pittsburgh markets. Folks called this place Point Pleasant, and it was surely one of the prettiest spots along the river, a peninsula where the Ohio and Kanawha Rivers met. Sitting here on the shoreline, she could watch the two rivers flow together, their differing currents creating whitecaps that glistened in the sunlight.

She heard footsteps approaching and looked up. Eleven-year-old Nathan, his face grimy with sweat from rolling the heavy barrels onto the boat, plopped down beside her with a sigh.

"Something bothering you?"

Nathan made a face. "I don't want to go to school." He turned pleading eyes her direction. "I want to stay on the river with you and Daddy."

Rebecca smiled. "I know. But you'll be among family in Lexington, Nathan. Simon has promised to keep an eye on you. He says he'll take you hunting whenever you want."

Nathan rubbed his eyes. "You don't need book learning to be a good hunter."

It was Rebecca's turn to sigh.

"The wilderness is disappearing, son." She nodded toward the boat. "Even your father's had to find new ways to make ends meet."

Nathan picked up a rock and threw it as hard as he could. It hit the water with a splash. "I'll go to Lexington," he said, "but don't be surprised if I don't stay."

Rebecca captured his hand and gave it a squeeze. "Honey—given that you're my tenth, there's not much you could do that would surprise me."

With Nathan settled at school, Rebecca and Daniel returned to the river. It felt strange at first to be alone together. Even as newlyweds there'd been children to care for, but now she had no towering mounds of laundry, no piles of dishes, no endless sewing to keep her hands occupied. When Daniel went hunting, she was free to accompany him, entering the shadowy world he'd inhabited for so many years without her. She relished witnessing Daniel's deep delight in all things wild—everything from a dew-covered spider's web to a sweeping vista of blue-green mountains. It was a balm to her heart to realize that his departures from her had never really been a running away but, rather, a running toward something that was as necessary to him as breathing.

Together, they explored along the Ohio and up its many tributaries; they dug ginseng in the fall and set trap lines each winter. Often, in damp weather, Daniel's ankle stiffened and ached with rheumatism, and on those days, she carried his rifle to lighten his load.

They discovered a salt spring along the Kanawha River, a tributary of the Ohio, where the game was still plentiful, and settled down for a time because Daniel had only to hobble a few hundred yards from their campsite and wait patiently for the game to gather at the lick to supply all their needs. They discovered a rough cabin, long abandoned, near the site, and set about cleaning it up, though the chimney drew so poorly that on most days Rebecca continued to cook outside, as if they were still on the trail.

"I wish we could have roamed together like this years ago," Daniel said one chilly fall evening as he stirred the embers of their campfire, sending a shower of sparks into the darkness.

Seeing Rebecca shiver, he sat down on the deerskin next to her and pulled her close. She rested her head on his shoulder, savoring his warmth, and said: "Back then, even if you'd asked me, I'd never have left the children."

"I know," he said. "Knowing you were with them made it possible for me to go. I guess I've never thanked you properly for that."

She smiled and straightened. The firelight danced across Daniel's face as she turned to look at him.

"By all means, go ahead," she said. "I'm listening."

Rebecca stamped her feet to warm them and watched her breath plume out in front of her in the frosty air. It was peaceful in this grove of maple trees alongside the Kanawha River. The silence that surrounded her was broken only by occasional birdsong or the splash of a fish leaping into the air and returning to the water with a smack that echoed among the trees.

She pulled off her gloves and broke a piece of frozen maple sap off the edge of the small wooden spile that she'd tapped into the tree's trunk days earlier. She popped the icy chip into her mouth and tasted a hint of the rich sweetness the tree would yield when its sap was boiled down into maple syrup.

She'd found this grove of stately maples shortly after she and Daniel had settled along the Kanawha and had noted its location in anticipation of sugaring time. Just this week, the approaching spring had brought daytime temperatures above freezing, prompting the sap to rise. Soon they'd have syrup for their johnnycakes and maple sugar for baking.

In the past, sugaring had been a family affair; she and the children had eagerly anticipated the sweetness of this season and reveled in the togetherness of working amid the maples in whatever locale they'd found themselves. Now, she worked alone, though at times she could almost hear the echo of her children's long-ago laughter among the trees.

Rebecca tapped a new spile into one of the maples and hung a tin cup underneath to catch the sap. She was intent on her work, moving from tree to tree, when she sensed a presence behind her and turned to see a man standing in the shadows on the far side of the clearing. It was rare to see anyone along this stretch of the Kanawha, and his sudden appearance made her heart beat faster; she'd left her rifle at the cabin this morning for the short walk to the river, having been burdened with kettles and cups.

When the man stepped out of the shadows, his face was expressionless. His shoulders were draped in a buff woolen trade blanket, and his head was shorn except for a scalp lock. His presence in this territory almost certainly meant he was Shawnee.

Rebecca cleared her throat. "Howasewipine," she said, using the Shawnee greeting Nonhelema had taught her.

The man's eyes flickered in surprise. "Howasewipine," he responded. He pointed to her bucket. "Skepiye malise."

Rebecca shook her head to show she didn't understand.

The man reached over and patted the trunk of one of the maples. "Seseqimese," he said. Then he pointed to the liquid that was dripping into the cup and pantomimed dipping a finger in and putting it to his mouth. "Skepiye malise."

Rebecca smiled. "Yes," she nodded. "Maple syrup."

He smiled in return, but then his face sobered and he looked at her questioningly. "Sheltowee?" he said.

Startled to hear Daniel's Shawnee name, Rebecca stood silent.

The man tried again. "Boone?" he said, then placed a hand over his heart. "Newekini."

As this last word registered, Rebecca heard, in her mind, Nonhelema's soft voice explaining its meaning to her years before.

"Newekini," Rebecca said aloud. "Friend."

When Rebecca walked into the cabin yard with the man following behind her, Daniel's face registered shock, then joy. The two men clasped each other's forearms and began speaking rapidly in Shawnee. Rebecca had no hope of keeping up as the words flew back and forth between them. When the men settled down near the fire, she busied herself mixing up corn mush to offer their guest. She punched up the coals, added some wood to the fire, and hung her worn copper kettle above the flames.

As she worked, she glanced at Daniel's face from time to time and watched his expression change from excited to sad to thoughtful. The men's conversation continued without pause until she walked around the fire and offered a steaming bowl of mush to their guest.

"Neyiwa," he said, and began to eat.

Daniel stood and stretched. "Red Wolf and I were friends when I lived with the Shawnee. He's journeyed here for the last time to see the places he knew as a child. And he's brought us a message from Daniel Morgan."

"Are all the children well?"

Daniel nodded. "But Daniel Morgan thinks we should come back to Kentucky, at least for a while. Most of the Shawnee have headed west, but a remnant are determined to fight."

"Then we should go," Rebecca said. She glanced across the fire where Red Wolf was scraping the last spoonful of mush from his bowl. "Ask him if he knows where Nonhelema is."

At the sound of Nonhelema's name, Red Wolf looked across the fire at Rebecca. He shook his head, then turned to Daniel and spoke slowly so that Daniel could translate his words.

"He says Nonhelema passed on shortly after she returned to her people, but he says you shouldn't be sad; she'll remain in her homeland, as she wished, and will never have to journey west."

That evening, toward twilight, Rebecca left the men sitting by the fire, still talking, and followed the worn path down to the river. The full moon was rising, casting a silvery light through the bare tree limbs. The night air made her shiver, a reminder that winter still held the land in its icy grip. She stopped on the riverbank and watched the Kanawha flow past, a shimmering ribbon in the moonlight.

A whip-poor-will called, a lonely sound from somewhere in the trees behind her. Though she was grateful for the time she'd spent with

Daniel along these waters, it now felt safe to admit to herself just how much she'd missed having the swirling presence of family around her. She knew she'd carry this place with her when she left, just as she had all the other creeks and rivers she'd lived beside and grown to love.

She carried people in her heart, too—those she was apart from, and all the dear ones who'd passed on. Once Nonhelema had told her: "My people believe that one day we'll be reunited with those we've lost, so we have no need for goodbye. Instead, when we part ways, we say, 'Silinoke kanola.' It means: 'Again, we'll see each other.'"

Of all their sons, Daniel Morgan looked the most like his father, and he'd inherited his father's restless spirit and friendly relations with the Shawnee, as well. Not long after Daniel and Rebecca arrived at his Kentucky cabin on Brushy Fork, Daniel Morgan began to talk about making an expedition westward to explore the far-off country where many of his Shawnee friends had already settled. Rebecca could tell Daniel chafed to go with his namesake but was realistic enough to know that he'd only slow his son down.

Rebecca reveled in the constant stream of family that visited them at Brushy Fork, giving her a chance to catch up with her children and marvel at how much the grandchildren had grown while she'd been away. Daniel bounced the babies on his knee and gave the youngsters jouncing piggyback rides that made them laugh and beg for more, but his eyes often held a distant look.

When Daniel Morgan returned to Kentucky after long months of exploration, he sang the praises of a well-watered wilderness, and the look on Daniel's face swept Rebecca back to their firelit cabin in Carolina on the night John Finley had first uttered the fateful word "Kentucky" in their midst. Now, she sensed their lives were about to change again.

When Daniel Morgan finally fell silent, the only sound in the cabin was the crackle of the fire on the hearth. After a moment, Daniel turned to her and said, "So, Becca—what would you say to starting over?"

Both men were watching her with undisguised eagerness.

"Is there a river we can settle beside?" she asked.

Daniel Morgan grinned. "A big one," he said. "They call it the Missouri."

In the months prior to their departure, Daniel and the boys spent many long days hollowing out a huge tulip poplar, fashioning a dugout nearly sixty feet long. Other boats, of varying sizes, would accompany them down the river since many of their children and grandchildren were heading west as well. Daniel Morgan had been chosen to pilot their dugout, which would carry Rebecca, Jemima, Susannah, assorted children, and much of their household plunder down the Ohio to the Mississippi and on to Missouri. Daniel, Flanders, and Will would follow overland, driving the livestock.

The morning they left Limestone, which had grown sufficiently by this time to be renamed Maysville, the sun was glinting off the river, marking the Ohio's every crest and swell. Their boat, heavily laden with supplies, rode deep in the water even before its human cargo was aboard. Friends and family who'd chosen to stay in Kentucky lined the bank ready to wave them off. There were ghosts hovering above the river that morning, too—James and Israel, Ned and Nonhelema. Rebecca could feel them watching from somewhere just beyond her sight.

Having said her goodbyes, she stood to one side, observing a steady stream of folks clap Daniel on the shoulder and wish him well. He was limping slightly, but his face was joyous. When her gaze shifted back to the boat, she saw that Jemima and Susannah were already seated and beckoning her to join them.

Suzy had done her best to rouse herself from her lethargy these past weeks and help with the packing. Rebecca prayed Missouri would be a new beginning for her. As for Jemima, Rebecca had no doubt that she would thrive because whatever life threw at her, she met it with the same resilient spirit that Daniel possessed. Truth be told, Jemima had grown to be her father's favorite because they were so much alike.

As for all the old rumors, Rebecca fully expected they'd follow her to Missouri, just as they'd trailed her from Carolina and up the trace through Cumberland Gap. Folks were free to believe whatever they chose about her and her family—she was done worrying about it. She intended to live her life looking forward, not back.

She remained at the water's edge, waiting for Daniel. When he finally broke free from his well-wishers, he scrambled down the bank and wrapped her in a final embrace.

"If the livestock don't give us too much trouble, we should get to Missouri about the same time you do," he said, stepping back, though still holding tight to her hand. She nodded, using his hand to steady herself as she lifted her skirts and stepped into the dugout, taking a seat between two bulging bags of cornmeal.

"See you in Missouri," she said as his hand slipped from hers.

Daniel, with help from a half-dozen men, pushed the dugout clear of the wooden pilings, and as the boat swung wide, Rebecca looked over her shoulder and searched the crowd for her husband's face. Daniel was waving at her, wearing a smile so broad she felt herself smiling in return.

The dugout rocked unsteadily for a moment, wallowing like a great beast unable to find its footing on the river bottom. But as the boys paddled away from the bank, the current caught the boat, and they began to move smoothly downstream. With a final glance back at Daniel, Rebecca turned her face toward the sparkling water, settled into the dugout, and let the river carry her.

Afterword

In 1799, many members of the Boone family left Kentucky to settle on the northern bank of the Missouri River.

Shortly after arriving in Missouri, Susannah Boone Hays died of "bilious fever" at the age of thirty-two. It was the family's opinion that years of abuse had weakened her.

Martha Bryan Boone never remarried. She lived with her children in Kentucky until her death in 1793.

Hannah Boone Stewart Pennington and her second husband, Richard Pennington, moved to Kentucky around 1797 and spent the rest of their days there. The couple named one of their sons John Stewart Pennington.

Jane Van Cleve Boone and Squire Boone were among the earliest settlers at the Falls of the Ohio, now the site of Louisville, Kentucky.

In Missouri, Daniel and Rebecca were often visited by the Shawnee tribesmen who'd moved west after the loss of their Ohio homeland.

In 1813, Rebecca fell ill while making maple sugar and was taken to Jemima's house near what is now Marthasville, Missouri. She died there, aged seventy-four, with Daniel at her side.

Daniel survived Rebecca by seven years. He died at his son Nathan's house, on September 26, 1820, a month shy of his eighty-sixth birthday. Jemima and Nathan were at his bedside. The house is now open to the public as the Nathan Boone State Historic Site near Ash Grove, Missouri.

Jemima dictated her memoirs to one of her sons, but the manuscript was lost when the family fled an Indian attack in Missouri and the canoe that carried the family's valuables capsized.

In 1815, one of Jemima's sons was killed in a skirmish with the Sac and Fox Indians. His name was James.

Jemima died in 1829 at the age of sixty-six, having outlived all of her siblings except Daniel Morgan and Nathan.

The Boone women were prolific. Rebecca had ten children, Susannah had eight, Jemima had ten, Martha had six, Jane had six, and Hannah had eight. Their descendants are scattered across the United States and abroad; many of them are members of the Boone Society, which is dedicated to preserving the history of this remarkable family.

Daniel and Rebecca's travels didn't end with their deaths. In 1845, their bodies were exhumed from the family graveyard in Missouri and shipped to Kentucky to be reinterred in a cemetery on a bluff overlooking the state capital of Frankfort.

Acknowledgments

When you've worked on a manuscript for nearly twenty-five years, a multitude of people have helped along the way. I'm deeply grateful to each and every one of them.

The Appalachian Writers' Workshop welcomed me as a fledgling writer in 1983 and has been a source of fellowship and inspiration ever since. I was incredibly fortunate to have two Appalachian literary giants, Harriette Arnow and Wilma Dykeman, as my first writing instructors.

Writing group friends, Sandy Ballard and Mary Hodges, offered valuable feedback on early drafts of this novel as well as decades of encouragement. George Ella Lyon, former Kentucky poet laureate, never quit believing in *Traces* even when its author was full of doubts. My dear friend Thea Yoder traipsed to Boone sites in Kentucky and Missouri with me and cheered me along with tea and front-porch pep talks.

Robert Morgan, novelist, poet, and Boone biographer, generously shared his thoughts on all things "Boone." Author Randell Jones graciously answered geographical questions regarding the Boone family's travels. I'm grateful to frontier scholar, Ted Franklin Belue, for his unparalleled knowledge of Kentucky's long hunters. Many thanks to Sam Compton, president of the Boone Society, and Carolyn Compton, a descendant of Hannah Boone, for their warm welcome.

Deep appreciation to Annette Saunooke Clapsaddle, enrolled member of the Eastern Band of Cherokee, and George Blanchard, enrolled member of the Absentee Shawnee, for their help with Cherokee and Shawnee languages and customs.

I was fortunate to interview and learn from a number of historical reenactors who specialize in frontier life, including Billy Heck, Nathan Harrison, David Cadle, Frank and Carol Jarbo, Alan Hawkins, and Randall Ross.

The Naslund-Mann Graduate School of Writing's low-residency MFA program at Spalding University allowed me to continue my work as a journalist while learning how to think like a novelist. I'm especially grateful to Eleanor Morse, who believed in this story and helped Rebecca and her girls find their way through the wilderness.

Numerous writing friends saw pieces of this work at various stages and offered valuable insights, including: Darnell Arnoult, Jenny Barton, Amy Belding Brown, Fiona Claire, Leslie Daniels, Stephanie Renee Dos Santos, Susan Dunekacke, Cynthia Ezell, Elizabeth Felicetti, Amy Greene, Rachel Harper, Lauren Harr, Willamaye Jones, Catherine Landis, Susan Lefler, Jody Lisberger, John Pipkin, Melanie Sakalla, Alice Schaaf, Pamela Schoenewaldt, Noelle Sciulli, and Lee Smith.

The staff at the University Press of Kentucky have been a pleasure to work with every step of way. Special thanks to Ashley Runyon, Patrick O'Dowd, Meredith Daugherty, David Cobb, freelance copy editor Iris Law, and cover designer Hayward Wilkirson.

Silas House, the fiction editor for Fireside Industries, provided crucial insights and a discerning eye that deepened this book in countless ways. Thank you, Silas, for making the editing process a journey of discovery.

I'm indebted to my agent, Deborah Schneider, whose belief in Rebecca and her girls at a critical juncture allowed them to find the best possible home.

And finally, my beloved family—Sam, Elizabeth, and Erin—if you secretly believed this manuscript would never be completed, you were kind enough not to say so.